AUSTRALIAN SCIENCE FICTION

Australian
Science Fiction

Edited and Introduced by
Van Ikin

Academy
Chicago
Publishers

© Copyright 1982 by University of Queensland Press

First American Publication 1984

Academy Chicago, Publishers
425 N. Michigan Avenue
Chicago, Illinois 60611

Printed and bound in the U.S.A.

208180

Library of Congress Cataloging in Publication Data
Main entry under title:

Australian science fiction.

Bibliography: p.

1. Science fiction, Australian.   I. Ikin, Van,
1951–

| PR9617.35.S33A9 | 1984 | 823'.0876'08 | 84-377 |

ISBN 0-89733-104-4
ISBN 0-89733-103-6 (pbk.)

Contents

Acknowledgments

I would like to offer by deepest thanks to Dr Elizabeth Webby for help in locating the earliest examples of Australian science fiction reprinted here; to Keith Curtis for valuable bibliographical advice; to Lucy Sussex for information on the authors of *The Germ Growers* and *Colymbia*; to Lee Harding, George Turner, Michael Wilding, and Dr Adrian Mitchell for their assistance; to Terry Dowling for inspiring my interest in science fiction; to Rosanne Fitzgibbons for meticulous editing; and to my wife, Marjory, for assistance and encouragement far beyond the call of duty.

Acknowledgments are due to the Mitchell Library, Sydney, and the Rare Book Library of the Fisher Library, University of Sydney, for their co-operation in providing copies of some of the material used. Thanks are also due to the Department of English, University of Western Australia, for making it possible for me to carry out research in these libraries.

For permission to reproduce material in this volume, acknowledgment is made to the following:

Damien Broderick for "A Passage in Earth" from *Rooms of Paradise*, ed. Lee Harding (Penguin, 1981); Frank Bryning for "Place of the Throwing-stick" from *New Worlds Science Fiction* 15, no. 45 (March 1956); The University of Queensland Press for "Report on the Shadow Industry" from *The Fat Man in History* (1974) by Peter Carey; A. Bertram Chandler for "Kelly Country" from *Void* no. 3 (1976); Curtis Brown (Aust.) Pty Ltd for extract from *Tomorrow and Tomorrow* by M. Barnard Eldershaw; Hyland House for extract from *Displaced Person* (1979) by Lee Harding; David J. Lake for "Re-deem the Time" from *Rooms of Paradise*, ed. Lee Harding (Quartet Books); Schwartz Publishing for "Inhabiting the Interspaces" by Philippa

C. Maddern from *Transmutations*, ed. R. Gerrand (Outback Press, 1979); Curtis Brown (Aust.) Pty Ltd for "The Gentle Basilisk" from *The Scholarly Mouse and Other Stories* by Dal Stivens (Angus & Robertson, 1957); George Turner for "In a Petrie Dish Upstairs" from *Rooms of Paradise*, ed. Lee Harding (Quartet Books); Cory and Collins for "One Way to Tomorrow" by Wynne N. Whiteford, first published in *Void*, issue 4; The University of Queensland Press for "The Words She Types" from *The West Midland Underground* (1975) by Michael Wilding; Void Publications for "One Clay Foot" by Jack Wodhams from *Alien Worlds* (1979) ed. Paul Collins.

Introduction:
The History of
Australian Science Fiction

Why write science fiction in Australia?

There is no single answer to that question. The answers are determined by individual choice and by historical imperative. For example, in *The Fiction Fields of Australia* (1856) Frederick Sinnet complained that

> No storied windows, richly dight, cast a dim, religious light over any Australian premises. There are no ruins for that rare old plant, the ivy green, to creep over and make his dainty meal of. No Australian author can hope to extricate his hero or heroine, however pressing the emergency may be, by means of a spring panel and a subterranean passage, or such like relics of feudal barons, and refuges of modern novelists, and the off-spring of their imagination. There may be plenty of dilapidated buildings, but not one, the dilapidation of which is sufficiently venerable by age, to tempt the wandering footsteps of the most arrant *parvenu* of a ghost that ever walked by night.[1]

Some early writers responded to this problem by turning to science fiction and filling the Australian emptiness with lost races and secret civilizations. As Australian society took on its own identity, writers turned to utopian speculation, or addressed themselves to specific issues such as racial fears, socialism, and working conditions. In recent years a newer set of concerns has arisen and science fiction writers are projecting their fears of technology, nuclear warfare, and genetic engineering, or writing about the alienation of the individual in an increasingly impersonal society.

Given the extent of these historical changes in the form and concerns of Australian science fiction, it would not have been advisable to compel every item selected for this volume to conform to one particular definition of science fiction.

There are two controversial issues which any definition of
sf must resolve. First, there is the relationship between
fantasy and science fiction. An "exclusive" approach defines
sf narrowly, implicitly denying any connection with fantasy:

> Science fiction is that class of prose narrative treating of a situa-
> tion that could not arise in the world we know, but which is hypo-
> thesized on the basis of some innovation in science or technology,
> or pseudo-technology, whether human or extraterrestrial in
> origin.[2]

The "inclusive" approach links sf with fantasy:

> Science fiction is a branch of fantasy identifiable by the fact that
> it eases the "willing suspension of disbelief" on the part of its
> readers by utilizing an atmosphere of scientific credibility for its
> imaginative speculations in physical sciences, space, time, social
> science and philosophy.[3]

The second controversy concerns the uses or "purpose" of
science fiction. Both the definitions quoted above support
the notion of sf as "a literature of ideas", the second going so
far as to imply that the proper study of sf is science, not
man. This is the "functionalist" approach,[4] and when taken
to extremes it results in the philistine utterances of its chief
apostle, Robert Heinlein:

> I claim one positive triumph for science fiction, totally beyond the
> scope of so-called main-stream fiction. It has prepared the youth
> of our time for the coming age of space. Interplanetary travel is no
> shock to youngsters, no matter how unsettling it may be to calci-
> fied adults. Our children have been playing at being space cadets
> and at controlling rocket ships for quite some time now. Where
> did they get this healthy orientation? From science fiction and
> nowhere else. Science fiction can perform similar service to the
> race in many other fields. For the survival and health of the
> human race, one crudely written science fiction story containing
> a single worthwhile new idea is more valuable than a bookcaseful
> of beautifully written non-science fiction.[5]

In opposition to this there stands the saner "literary"
approach, which asserts that "science fiction . . . is nothing
unless it justifies itself as itself, just as a cat is its own justification whether or not it catches vermin".[6] This literary
approach claims that science fiction is literature, and so must
stand or fall as literature, having neither more, less, nor a
different relevance to man and his life than any other form
of literature. Such an outlook is reflected in Angus Taylor's
definition:

> Science fiction is fantasy in its most typical (though not exclusive)

modern guise: it is that form of non-mimetic fiction uniquely characteristic of industrial and post-industrial societies, a form of fantasy that outfits itself with the garments of scientific/techno-logical paradigms *in order to explore age-old questions of man's relation to the universe-at-large* in terms suitable to the modern age. (My italics)[7]

Over the years, different Australian sf writers have pro-duced works which confirm or contradict each of the defini-tions cited above. Since my aim in compiling this volume has been, simply, to represent the field, it has seemed best to adopt a relaxed approach to definition and to cast my nets widely, thereby allowing individual readers (with their indivi-dual views on definition) to establish their own limits. Readers with a further interest in the matter of definition are referred to the clash between Terry Dowling and George Turner in the pages of *Science Fiction: A Review of Specula-tive Literature,*[8] this being the liveliest Australian manifesta-tion of the definition debate.

Predictably, many of the earliest works of Australian sf are romances, with hearty heroes and adventurous heroines, but often without the technological marvels of Jules Verne's *Mysterious Island* or *Twenty Thousand Leagues Under the Sea* (both of which appeared in 1870). Fergus Hume's *The Expedition of Captain Flick* (1896) begins with a negro servant bowing and chanting to Aphrodite. Why should a negro from an Indian Ocean island worship Aphrodite? The answer lies on the isle of Isk, where the natives are ruled by a white king and the priestesses run a shrine to Aphrodite. Around 300 BC a youth stole a statue sculpted by Praxiteles, ran off with a local priestess of Aphrodite, and was ship-wrecked on Isk, causing considerable alteration to the religious and political customs of the natives. Sixty-five year old Captain "Roaring Tom" Flick (who is "Falstaff for girth, Samuel Johnson for domineering, a very whale for unwieldi-ness") sets off with Harry Greenvile (sic) and his sister Bertha, hoping to restore the Praxiteles statue to civilization. In a series of predictable clichés, Bertha is kidnapped by the natives, the high priestess falls in love with Harry, and the island's dormant volcano erupts and destroys the whole works — but not before our heroes escape. (The statue, naturally, is lost forever.)

Though equally romantic in conception, G. Firth Scott's *The Last Lemurian* (1898) is far more imaginative and

colourful, and reflects the contemporary interest in speculation about the location of the "lost continent" of Lemuria.[9]
In 1902 another writer, Mrs Campbell Praed, reflecting upon
the uncanny "primeval" quality of the Australian bush, was
drawn to speculation about Atlantis and Lemuria:

> But before Atlantis was, old books say that the world had shaped
> itself into a great and different land, which was Lemuria. And of
> Lemuria the largest part that remains to this day is Australia.
> This is what certain records tell, but of the truth of them, who
> can speak with knowledge? Yet also, who can see the land in its
> hoariness, and the convulsions that have torn it, and upon no
> other land, and the gum trees of such weird conformation unlike
> all other trees that are − who can see these things and ponder over
> them, without pondering too and greatly wondering over the story
> of the lost Atlantis and of Lemuria that was before. . . .[10]

The plot of Firth Scott's *The Last Lemurian* resembles the
tale of Lasseter's lost reef: an old Aborigine tells a story of a
mountain in "the Westralian Never Never" where gold
nuggets lie underfoot and the people are yellow-skinned.
During an expedition to find this source of wealth, our two
heroes learn that the Australian desert was the location of
the lost civilization of Lemuria. According to the character
known as "the Yellow Hatter" (in reality a down-on-his-luck
English gentleman), the Lemurians were "a race which was
on a higher plane of civilization and culture than our own".
Discussing the ways in which plants and animals have
changed through the ages of history, and asserting that even
the shape of the continents has altered ("Once Australia was
divided into two parts by a sea which rolled where now
South Australia exists"), the Yellow Hatter asks: " . . . if
such changes have taken place in land, in animals, and in
plants, why not in man also during the time he has been on
earth? How do we know that he was not, in the past, more
highly civilized and cultured than we are today?" (p. 130)
Unfortunately Scott offers only one example of the
Lemurians' superiority: the water-powered artificial doorway
in the cliffs surrounding their kingdom is described as "one
of the grandest schemes of hydraulic energy ever dreamed
of by man". The rest of the story degenerates to standard
romantic adventure as the Yellow Hatter falls in love with
the last Lemurian, and a volcano (as usual) puts an end to the
hidden land. (One is prompted to claim that Australia excels
all other nations in its number of volcanoes per square mile
of hidden kingdom.)[11] In the extract reprinted here, the

heroes encounter the fearsome yellow giantess Tor Ymmothe, Queen of Lemuria, and they kill the legendary bunyip.

Both *The Expedition of Captain Flick* and *The Last Lemurian* offer little more than escapist entertainment. There are two further romances, however, which attempt to offer their readers "food for thought", and in both cases the matter for mental digestion is related to the role of women. As various critics of sf have noted, the genre has a poor reputation for its attitude to women. Sam Moskowitz observes that "stories in which female characters *appear at all* are in the minority in the magazines of prophetic literature", and Sam J. Lundwall concedes that "The sex roles [in sf] are as unyielding as the metal in a space ship's hull; emancipation is an unknown word".[12] Nevertheless, in 1889 it was possible for Sir Julius Vogel, KCMG[13] to write a novel peopled with female politicians and to observe that "statesman" is "a word . . . which includes both sexes" (p. 37). In his preface to *Anno Domini 2000; or, Woman's Destiny* (1889), Vogel states that in the writing of his book "three leading features have been kept in view". These are: (1) that "a recognized dominance of either sex is unnecessary"; (2) that "the materials are to hand for forming the dominions of Great Britain into a powerful and beneficent empire"; and (3) the question of "whether it is not possible to relieve the misery" of poverty and oppressive social conditions (pp. 328–29). Pursuing these concerns, Vogel describes a world in which a thirty-five year old woman is the president of the United States of America, and the British dominions have been consolidated into "the empire of United Britain" (with Australia as a separate empire, ruled from an imperial palace on the banks of the Yarra). Poverty and social injustice have indeed been minimized, and this has been done "without approaching communism": foreign labour has been outlawed, and high tariffs have been imposed against overseas (non-empire) goods. Even the educational system has been overhauled, with *thoroughness* being the keynote in 2000 AD: "The superficial apology for preferring quantity to quality [in education] was [that] 'Education does not so much mean imparting knowledge as training the faculties to acquire it'" (p. 75). (One result of this ideology is that the learning of languages in schools has been abandoned, and instead the pupils are taught engineering and science.)

Interesting though these speculations may be, Vogel does nothing more than tease his readers with possibilities. There is no social analysis, no attempt to show the *process* by which reform has been achieved. The battle to win a serious commitment to the eradication of poverty is glossed in a line: "it had long since been decided that every human being was entitled to share in the good things of the world". And similarly with the struggle for female equality: "It has, in fact, come to be accepted that the bodily power is greater in man, and the mental power larger in woman. So to speak, woman has become the guiding, man the executive, force of the world" (pp. 28–29). Fine; but *how* were those decisions and acceptances brought to pass?

Vogel ignores these crucial matters because he becomes embroiled in the inanities of romantic plotting. His heroine, Hilda Fitzherbert (a twenty-three year old New Zealand born member of parliament) is confronted with crises on two fronts. In the public sphere the issue of the day is that of the law of succession within the imperial family: should the parliament remove the last vestiges of sexual inequality by passing a law which allows the emperor to be a woman? The parliamentary opposition, including Lord Reginald Paramatta (sic), is opposed to the change, and the emperor vetoes the new law when it is passed. To make matters worse for Hilda, Lord Reginald wants her to marry him, and is prepared to go to extremes to achieve this. (At one point he lures her aboard a boat with a clergyman hidden in the cabin, ready to perform the marriage ceremony!) Predictably, all ends well: Hilda marries the emperor, the emperor relents, and Princess Victoria becomes the heir apparent.

An interesting but equally flawed combination of romance and feminism is *A Woman of Mars; or, Australia's Enfranchised Woman* (1901) by Mary Ann Moore-Bentley (the pseudonym of Mrs H. H. Ling). After a remarkably silly and soapy opening scene (in which an angel and the soul of a deceased Earthling look in on Mars on their way to heaven and, in a moment of embarrassing literalism, pause to listen to the music of the spheres) the Martian girl Vesta is despatched to Earth to see to "the emancipation of Woman and the regeneration of the [human] race". According to the passing angel, the Martians have achieved a state of "human perfection", and it is therefore highly significant that they should see the question of "the Woman's Right" as "the bedrock foundation upon which a statesman must seek to establish a happy, progressive, social State". Sir Julius Vogel says little about the restrictions placed upon women in his own time; he sees women chiefly as *resources,* and prefers to outline a future in which those resources are utilized. Moore-

Bentley shares this "resource mentality", for she too advocates emancipation for the good of the state (not for the sake of the otherwise unfulfilled individual), but she is forthright in her analysis of the present-day plight of women:

> "I thought how truly Mary Magdalene personified fallen womanhood upon this planet. What cruel fiend seduced her? What subtle influence made her first betray the divine trust, and prostitute the holiest of all things created, that highly wrought, finely constructed, beautifully designed masterpiece of all Nature's machinery, Woman?"
>
> "But you cannot mean to infer that every woman is a Magdalene in the general sense of the word," said Lady Little-Mind, looking much shocked.
>
> "What is its general sense?" calmly inquired Vesta.
>
> "Nothing less," said Lady Little-Mind, in an indignant, injured tone, "than the direct prostitution of woman's most sacred functions."
>
> "Let her who is guiltless among you cast the stone of condemnation," returned Vesta, in a firm voice, with that searching gaze, with which truth ever puts falsehood to confusion. (p. 76)

Despite the angels and souls-in-transit, *A Woman of Mars* can lay some claim to being science fiction. Vesta travels to Earth by means of a "machine" that is steered by remote control, and it is asserted that she will be able to cope with differences in gravity because "the Martians [were] masters of all such phenomena". Moreover, the novel examines man's social problems in terms of cause and effect, and offers an answer to the speculation, "What if the role of women were to alter?"[14]

Despite its sometimes radical feminist ideas, *A Woman of Mars* has strong leanings towards Christianity. (The "perfect" Martians, for example, observe the sabbath.) Christian ideas are more important in Robert Potter's novel, *The Germ Growers* (1892), but this is hardly surprising, for Potter was a canon of St Paul's Anglican Cathedral, Melbourne.[15] During exploration of the Kimberleys, two English youths stumble upon a plot to destroy humanity through the breeding of new forms of plague. At first the conspirators appear merely to be members of some secret society, but it is soon revealed that they are nothing less than devils from outer space (their leader being Signor Niccolo Davelli!). The heroes refuse to work for these disease-disseminating devils, and Good triumphs over Evil when they are rescued by an angel.

Potter's scientific knowledge is uneven. His plague germs are cultivated in agricultural gardens, and are big enough to be "sorted out and distributed" by hand. However, as Lucy Sussex has noted,[16] his account of a trip to the Moon shows a degree of accuracy, for his characters experience reduced gravity and a thinner atmosphere. Unlike most other Australian writers of his time, Potter shows genuine concern for scientific plausibility. He describes his "special effects" patiently and clearly — as in the scene in which his hero spies upon workmen who are painting air-cars to make them invisible:

> At each of these objects [the visible air-cars] a man stood, as it would seem, painting them, and he seemed to dip what I thought to be a brush in a bucket beside him. And at first I thought that he was painting the whole object, car and supporting framework, but presently I perceived that the brush which he was using and which showed a very irregular and jagged edge, never touched, or never at least was seen to touch anything at all, but that what it passed over disappeared. I watched the operation with breathless attention, and I saw the body of the car which had seemed to hang in the air gradually disappear as the brush passed over it, until nothing was left either above or below. I watched another which was complete in all parts until nearly the whole of the supporting framework disappeared beneath the brush. It looked for all the world as if some sort of invisible paint were being smeared over the conveyances. (p. 99)

Having thus described the effect, Potter goes on to offer a scientific rationale for the invisible paint, claiming that "there are some rays at either end of the spectrum which are not visible, and . . . it is possible to treat some substances so as to cause them to reflect these rays only, just as other substances reflect only the yellow or the red". The opening chapters of *The Germ Growers*, reprinted here, provide further examples of this patiently methodical approach (especially in the dialogue with which the passage concludes). Despite such earnest scientific sincerity, Potter wrote no further science fiction books. In fact, it appears that he was reduced to giving away copies of the novel as Christmas gifts to his Sunday School pupils.

Whilst *The Germ Growers* pointed to spiritual redemption, other Australian sf writers pursued a materialistic or utopian grail. In May 1832 the *Sydney Gazette* published a series of five articles by "Mephistopholes the Younger" titled "Australia Advanced; or Dialogues for the Year 2032".[17] Aside from discussing developments in the arts ("Scott, Campbell, Moore, are now little read", but "Shakespeare's fame ... lives in a thousand tongues"), these dialogues mention the construction of two suspension bridges across Sydney Harbour, the "extinction" of the indigenous timber and brush-wood of Australia (and its replacement with "the noble wood of the Old Country"), and the construction of "the *Lightning* locomotive engine, which runs (or flies rather) at 60 miles per hour". If sceptics wondered about the funding of such ventures, their questions were answered by the earliest item in this collection, "The Monster Mine" (1845), which celebrates the prosperity generated by the mining industry. Two years later, in "Oo-a-deen; or, The Mysteries of the Interior Unveiled" (1847), an unknown author not only pioneered the "lost civilization" motif in Australian sf, but also gave Australian readers their first taste of a utopia in the "moral" tradition of Sir Thomas Moore. (Materialism, however, is far from banished in "Oo-a-deen", for the narrator is more interested in gold and wild horses than in seeking out the lost civilization.)

According to my research, the earliest work of Australian science fiction published in book form[18] is Robert Ellis Dudgeon's *Colymbia* (1873).[19] This too is a work of utopian speculation, but the setting is a submarine colony linked with one of the Pacific islands — indicating that, even as early as 1873, the state of Australian society was such that it no longer seemed appropriate to site a utopia in Australia. Other writers shared this disenchantment, and thus the list of sub-sequent utopian speculations includes Christopher Spots-wood's *The Voyage of Will Rogers to the South Pole* (1888), G. McGiver's *Neuroomia: A New Continent* (1894), G. Read Murphy's *Beyond the Ice: Being a Story of the Newly Dis-covered Region Round the North Pole* (1894),[20] and Joseph Fraser's *Melbourne and Mars: My Mysterious Life on Two Planets* (1889). Ironically it is this last item, in which utopia is to be found on another *planet*, that is the first major work of utopian sf in Australia.

The only clue to Joseph Fraser's background comes from an advertisement in the back of his book:

> J. Fraser, Phrenologist and Physiognomist, of Lennox Street, Haw-thorn, Melbourne. Has no Superior as Delineator of Character and Talents.

In pursuit of these interests he published books on *Hydro-pathy in the Household, Physiognomy Made Easy, How to Read Men as Open Books,* and the title that was apparently his bestseller, *Husbands: How to Select Them, How to Manage Them, How to Keep Them.* Despite such colourful authorial interests, the early chapters of *Melbourne and Mars* record in close and realistic detail the family background of Adam Jacobs, born in 1818 to a family of Lancashire hand-loom weavers. After a political brawl in 1828, Jacobs' father is transported to Botany Bay for the crime of manslaughter; the mother and son travel south with him, and are soon embroiled in the injustices of the convict system.[21] The novel traces in detail Adam Jacobs' business career, from his humble beginnings as a ship chandler and outfitter to his move to the expanding city of Melbourne and his bankruptcy when the land boom of 1842 goes bust. Depressed but not defeated, Jacobs goes to Bathurst seeking gold, then (after a period of illness) follows in the footsteps of Richard Mahony and joins in the Ballarat gold rush "to supply provisions to the diggers".

At the age of forty-five he begins to have strange dreams of a second childhood, and it is gradually revealed that he is living a second life on the progressive and utopian planet Mars. In the extract from *Melbourne and Mars* published here, Jacobs speculates that he may be in his dotage and that old people become childish "because they are children else-where". This is revealed to be a false hypothesis when Jacobs' Martian self overhears a conversation between his Martian mother and a Martian doctor:

> "My studies in medical psychology have taught me that there are three kinds of earth-borns on our planet. First, those who have lived on earth and become fit for introduction to our higher life, which is to them a kind of heaven and reward for virtuous and religious living; second, those who, while still living on earth, put out a new life and live here also quite unconscious of the old life; third, those who live on both planets, and are conscious of the two lives. Your boy belongs to the second class at present, but can at any time begin to belong to the third. In his earth life he is con-scious of this life, but in this he is unconscious of the other." (p. 28)

Joseph Fraser's utopian speculations cover a range of topics, from flying machines and the thorough-but-painless education of the young, to economics and the mysteries of electricity:

> [The teacher] claimed for electricity something more than a first place amongst the forces of nature. Said he: — "We have not to regard wind as one force, water as another, heat and light as two more forces. We have rather to regard electricity as the one great force, and all the rest of the so-called forces of nature as various manifestations of and modifications of that one force.
> "The sun is the central dynamo of our system. All the positive forms of electricity come from him." (p. 37)

Fraser's utopia is presented in dignified detail; *The Coming Terror: A Romance of the Twentieth Century* (1894) by Sydney anarchist S. A. Rosa begins in a somewhat less reserved manner:

> Crash! Crash!! Crash!!! went the falling timbers of the Austral Bank, while a furious and ferocious mob, drunken with wine and victory, shrieked, fought, and swore in front of the burning edifice. The features of the men and women who composed this mob, rendered savage by want, suffering, and oppression, were distorted by hate, the desire for vengeance, and lust for destruction, while they were lit up by the huge fierce flames which issued from the rapidly perishing but once magnificent building. (p. 1)

The object of this rage, the Austral Bank, has for generations "reigned supreme over the financial institutions of Australia, and [has] gathered within its octopus-like grip half the great industries of the country". Thanks to Panmort, a gas developed by a French chemist who is a member of the "Brotherhood of the Poor" (an international alliance which has replaced trade unions), the revolutionary mob is able to quell all opposition, overrun Parliament House, and turn it into the headquarters of the Revolutionary Committee. Oliver Spence is elected leader of the people, and he proceeds to fix prices, remodel the criminal law, prescribe male wages for female workers, and set maximum daily work hours and a minimum weekly wage. The people are obviously pleased, so they appoint him Dictator: " . . . for centuries the people had been swindled, plundered, and oppressed by corrupt ruling gangs called Parliaments. They would now see what could be done by the rule of one good, wise, and capable man" (p. 10). Oliver marries his beloved Mary Lovelace, and under their conjoint rule Australia enters a golden age.

Unlike Sir Julius Vogel, Rosa is prepared to offer some insight into the *process* by which the revolutionary spirit gains acceptance. He sees the capitalist system destroying itself from within: paper money depreciates and finally becomes useless, thereby creating a "ruined middle class" which is ripe for conversion to the revolutionary cause. Discussing the use of violence to further these aims, Rosa argues: "War is a dreadful thing, but is sometimes as necessary to save and secure the lives and liberties of peoples, as on occasion a surgical operation may be, to preserve the life of an individual" (p. 17).

These ideas become the basis of utopian philosophy in G. Read Murphy's *Beyond the Ice: Being a Story of the*

Newly Discovered Region Round the North Pole (1894). Marooned in the arctic, Dr Frank Farleigh discovers a technologically advanced civilization, and is soon indoctrinated in its ways. "Marriage", he learns, "is the first law of God and nature, and the foundation of civilization". Men without a spouse are not permitted to vote, and neither are married women (for marital discord might arise if wives could vote, and besides, "the sensible married women . . . control their husband's vote"). At the time of Dr Farleigh's arrival social attitudes in the polar community are changing, and humane (if sexist) liberalism is giving way to ominously simplified "scientific" social thinking:

> In our community no thing or animal that is detrimental to the general welfare is allowed to increase its species. And yet the community maintains in its midst human beings who are ill-fed, ill-clothed, and oftentimes diseased. . . . We misinterpreted liberty to mean that a man who does no active wrong must be allowed to do all the passive wrong that suits him. (p. 61)

In the excerpt published here, the redefinition of "liberty" leads to the ruthless extermination of the savages (known as "Rodas") who live on the fringe of the polar community.

Australia's other utopian offerings are far less exotic. The characters in W. H. Galier's *A Visit to Blestland* (1896) are at sea in a strong wind when the ocean takes on the appearance of fire and gives off electrical sparks. Losing control of their boat they are whisked along through the air, shrouded in the "Cimmerian darkness" of a mysterious cloud. Once they arrive on the planet Blestland[22] the narrative dwindles to the level of most utopian works (talk, talk, and more talk, with the inspection of a few buildings and institutions). Galier's title has religious connotations, but these are largely ironic, for religion is seen as a hindrance to social justice:

> I have long been of opinion, and am still, that the earthly citadel of Monopoly will remain perfectly impregnable so long as the flower of Earth's people remain riven by sectarian hate; and despairing as I do of their ever becoming otherwise, I long since gave up all hope of the emancipation of the unhappy masses ever being reduced to an accomplished fact. (p. 148)

The following year saw William Little's *A Visit to Topos, And How the Science of Heredity is Practised There* (1897). This twenty-eight page booklet is little more than a treatise, yet it clings doggedly to the fiction that the author has visited "that land of Sabbath quiet" and that "the stupendous facts that came within my observation [there], are of such public interest that I must briefly sketch some sights I witnessed". He goes on to pontificate about various social issues (for example, prohibiting marriage and procreation between consumptives, for "Under the cloak of love, the selfish thousand makes the million die of broken hearts and loathsomeness"). Little's thought is often mystical — "How slow we are to learn, that Spirit-force may control all matter — that pain and pleasure are but mental states — that Man's own Spirit may say to its own body 'do this', 'be that', and like the Caliban of Prospero, it will obey its behests." (p. 21) — yet he is prepared to discuss the social application of these ideas, outlining a scheme of "thought-transference" whereby babes in the womb are prepared for their role in the work-force (producing, for example, "a pre-natally taught electrician").

Whilst William Little was devising a future in which Big Brother could feel right at home, other sf writers were worrying about who Big Brother might be — or, more specifically, about the colour of his skin.

Racial antipathies had been strong in Australia since the 1850s. The increasing number of Chinese on the Victorian goldfields had forced the Victorian government to impose a poll-tax on Chinese immigrants in 1885, and when Henry Parkes was confronted with similar anti-Chinese feeling in New South Wales in 1888, he spoke out against England's reluctance to accept Australian legislation aimed at restricting coloured immigration. In 1891 a Privy Council decision affirmed Australia's right to pass laws to exclude Chinese, but by the time of federation the racial hatred had intensified, and people had begun to fear that "the yellow peril" might threaten not only their jobs and livelihood, but their nation. As Deakin put it in 1901, the matter touched upon " . . . the profoundest instinct of individual or nation — the instinct of self-preservation — for it is nothing less than the national manhood, the national character, and the national future that are at stake."[23]

Motivated by fears of the Asian hordes, a number of writers turned to fiction. K. Mackay's *The Yellow Wave: A Romance of the Asiatic Invasion of Australia* (1895) was followed by *The Coloured Conquest* (1904) by "Rata" (a pseudonym for Thomas Roydhouse), and in 1909 a journalist named C. H. Kirmess eclipsed these two works with a blockbuster titled *The Australian Crisis*. Though some might argue that these are not works of science fiction, there are strong and convincing reasons for considering them as such.

Rata's novel is set in 1913, nine years in the future, and is narrated by "the last free Britisher" after Japan has taken over the world. The narrator, Danton, emphatically asserts that the coloured uprising is a logical consequence of the white man's overbearing behaviour, and that the success of that uprising is the consequence of the white nations' refusal to spend money on defence. In short, he presents his material as being an extrapolation from present tendencies — and that, certainly, is one of the characteristics of sf. Danton observes that "All the Whites claimed to be 'highly civilized', yet they robbed and murdered quite as much as the Blacks, and, for the most part, hid under a mask hypocrisy that the ordinary Coloured man was incapable of" (p. 30). Thus it is no wonder that "all Coloured peoples hate the Whites", and it is therefore scandalous that the national defences are so depleted that "Australia's total stock of ammunition could be shot away . . . in one engagement lasting twenty minutes". After the attack and occupation by Japanese forces, "The Mikado's Australian Government" reduces the white population to slaves and sets about developing the dead heart of the continent. The right to reproduce is denied to most whites, and though the "fairest" caucasians are allowed to inter-marry, they are then condemned to live in "Fair Lily Colonies" where they breed female beauties who will be "wives" for the Japanese conquerors. (Danton's beloved disappears forever into one such settlement.)

One of Rata's chief concerns is the weakness of the Australian navy. To stand against an Asian onslaught, Australia would need "an invincible Navy", but since invincible navies are none too easy to acquire, Rata argues in favour of naval ties with Britain. Kirmess condemns this attitude in *The Australian Crisis*, skilfully constructing a plot in which a dependence upon Britain proves to be Australia's undoing.

Published in 1909, *The Australian Crisis* purports to be "a retrospection from the year 1922 upon events supposed to have happened less than ten years earlier, viz., in 1912". Like *The Coloured Conquest* it presents itself as an extrapolation from current tendencies, but Kirmess is more perceptive (and perhaps more cynical) than Rata. "The central idea of the book", Kirmess writes, "[is] the possibility of a coloured invasion of Australian territory, organized on such lines that the Australians would be unable to persuade the heart of the [British] Empire that there was any invasion" (p. 5). According to this scenario, a Japanese colony has secretly been established in northern Australia, and by the time its existence is discovered the first generation of offspring has been born. This constitutes a cunning invasion by diplomatic stealth, for these Japanese babies are "natives of Australia — whom birthright would entitle to a share in the continent".

Australians are outraged by the presence of the colony, but the British with their liberal sentimentality are eager to Christianize the "poor yellow savages", and are sympathetic to the Japanese government's argument that the colonists are merely eking out a livelihood on land which Australia has chosen not to develop. Britain declares her support for the Japanese colony, the Australian stock market crashes as British investors withdraw their funds, and the governor general of the day precipitates a double dissolution of the houses of parliament by rejecting legislation contrary to Britain's pro-Japanese stance. The Australian crisis has begun. Soon Japanese prostitutes are burnt at the stake in Sydney race riots, while a gallant group of para-military vigilantes (called "The White Guard") is decimated by Asian dum-dum bullets in a futile attempt to win back the north. Western Australia attempts to secede from the federation, but this rebellion is put down after a brief civil war. Ultimately northern Australia is declared a British Protectorate, and the Royal Navy upon which Australia has so foolishly relied is ordered to blockade the Japanese colony and protect it against Australian attempts at reclamation. Thus perish all nations which compromise their independence.

Of all the Australian sf novels published before 1925, *The Australian Crisis* has the most complex and skilfully integrated plot. Unfortunately, it features some of the worst writing as well. Kirmess is at his best when he maintains an ironic reserve (describing Japanese plans for the colony as "An Unadvertised Immigration Policy"). When that reserve is abandoned, Kirmess is appalling, as in the opening to the chapter titled "Pereat! (The Flaming Elections)": "Decks clear for action! What matter if a world outside cries horror over thee, Australia? Better be Devil than King Log, croaked over by Frogs" (p. 125). Because of these defects in style and because of the ponderously discursive nature of Kirmess's narrative, the racial invasion motif in Australian sf is represented here by Rata's dramatic account of the Japanese occupation of Sydney in *The Coloured Conquest.*

The Australian Crisis was the last major novel about the "Yellow Peril" until A. J. Pullar's *Celestalia: A Fantasy A.D.*

1975 (1933), Erle Cox's *Fool's Harvest* (1939), in which a bush resistance movement is forced to resort to sabotage to repel the oriental invaders, and John Hay's *The Invasion* (1968), in which Australia is overrun by the "Armada of the South East Asian Republic". In 1925, however, there appeared a novel which combined lurking racial fears with super-human science and the prospect of a fearsome "utopia". That novel was Erle Cox's *Out of the Silence,* and it has since come to be regarded as the first classic of Australian science fiction.

Digging on his rural property, Alan Dundas uncovers a portion of a huge impervious metal dome. Fighting the interruptions imposed by his girlfriend, Marian Seymour, he unearths a doorway into the dome and finds a massive structure that goes deep into the earth. Eluding many vicious booby-traps, Dundas explores the building's five galleries, realizing that he has uncovered the remains of an eons-old, highly advanced civilization. The sixth gallery contains the body of a beautiful woman in suspended animation, and Dundas calls upon his friend Dr Richard Barry to help revive her. Named Earani, the woman is one of three people chosen to go into suspended animation when her race was destroyed by a shift of the Earth's axis twenty-seven million years ago. After showing Dundas some of the marvels of her civilization (and after falling in love with him), Earani reveals her plans to rule the human race along the lines in which her own civilization had developed. This includes the annihilation of all coloured races, and the control of human breeding. She intends to do these things with the help of Andax, a male of her race buried beneath the Himalayas.

Out of the Silence is noteworthy for its fast-paced plotting and for its scientific detail. The five underground "galleries" represent exhibits devoted to Art, Biology, Science, Engineering, and Religion, offering Cox ample opportunity to discuss such marvels as "light without heat", "lozenges" that are "a meal in tabloid form", and a light-weight air-cruiser propelled by the neutralization of gravity. More importantly, Cox is prepared to *explore* his theme. The author himself seems appalled by Earani's ideas and philosophy, and towards the end of the novel he makes her admit that her race had lost its soul or "spirit force". But Cox allows Dundas to be *attracted* by the prospect of Earani's utopia, and this gives rise to an admirable dialectic tension throughout the latter half of the novel. The excerpt published here is an illustration of this: the reader is invited to be

disgusted by Earani's bland account of cold-blooded geno-
cide, but is then compelled to agree with some of the points
she makes in the debate which follows.

An earlier novel, Harold Johnston's *The Electric Gun*
(1911), had also displayed a more mature and searching
approach to theme. In the excerpt published here, set in
1926, the journalist Edward Bruce (whose book, *Liberty*,
helped to establish socialism in Australia) finds his dream
turning sour. Twenty-four years later, in 1950, his son takes
up the struggle against socialist oppression, and the Henson
Street Bakery in Balmain becomes the focal point for resistance. Thanks to the accidental acquisition of one of the
electric guns used by the police, the freedom fighters eventually prevail. The novel ends five years after this "Great
Revolt" with the narrator claiming that "We have greatly
extended local government, and the people manage practically all their own affairs. In fact, the duty of an Australian
Parliament today may be described as one of our members
recently put it: 'To leave the people alone'" (p. 256).

Johnston's case against socialism is cogent. He has
sympathy for the working class (as can be seen from *Australian White Slaves*, his book on industrial conditions in
Australia) but, as Edward Bruce's experience shows, he
believes that socialism merely has the effect of turning
"officialdom" into "a hereditary caste", creating a situation
in which "The life and liberty of every man and the honour
of every woman of the working class were at the mercy of
the officials". Johnston is fair and objective, conceding that
"although Socialism had brought about much that was evil, it
had, at least, placed the sexes upon an equal footing". But
his final judgement is that socialism ignores human nature.

In 1931 Australian sf ventured into outer space. Born in
Geelong in 1897, James Morgan Walsh had published over
one hundred books (mostly mysteries) before he wrote the
stylish space-thriller *Vandals of the Void* (1931).[24] The fore-
runner of modern films such as *Star Wars*, this book established the now classic theme of an interplanetary alliance
(consisting of different planetary governments and strange
races, trading, intriguing, and existing in uneasy equilibrium),
and it revealed Walsh as a writer to be ranked with E. E.
"Doc" Smith and John W. Campbell, Jr.

The success of *Vandals of the Void* rests upon Walsh's
skill in interweaving a suspenseful plot with authentic

sounding accounts of conditions in outer space, and his
ability to offer plausibly "scientific" explanations of a
breathtaking array of technological marvels. The latter
include a "Crystal Eye" which provides superior long-range
X-ray images, the ultimate weapon — an atomic disintegrator
— and even one of the earliest robots in Australian sf:

> . . . I was wondering how we would set about removing [our
> luggage] when a robot — or, to give him his Martian name, a Toro,
> appeared. Much of the menial labour on [Mars] is done by these
> mechanical men, though to give them their due the average
> Martian is not backward in putting his shoulder to the wheel when
> necessity arises.
>
> Dirka spoke into the televox apparatus situated in the Toro's
> metal diaphragm, giving orders that were picked up by an
> extremely sensitive selenium cell which in some very ingenious
> fashion operated the mechanism.
>
> The Toro picked up as much of the baggage as he could con-
> veniently carry in his metal hands, and unerringly led the way
> through the exit doors of the building to the duralmac road out-
> side. (pp. 184–85)

The story opens in the space ship *Cosmos*, first of a new
generation of craft designed to reach the outer planets of our
solar system. The space ship's passengers come from the
three major planets — Earth, Mars, and Venus — and include
a mysterious humanoid giant from the unexplored planet
Mercury. Disturbing events are taking place in space, for an
unknown race of beings is causing havoc with the schedules
of space-traffic. The efficient and respected Interplanetary
Guard is investigating the case (and has a Guardsman aboard
the *Cosmos*), but the crisis escalates as the Guard's own ships
are attacked and destroyed, and it is soon apparent that
Earth, Mars, and Venus are threatened. The plot reaches its
climax in an epic battle.

Walsh delineates his alien races very clearly. The mysterious Mercurians, with their deep purple eyes and a ridge of
horn on their heads, are rendered physically and psychologi-
cally distinct from the "Venerians" (Venusians), "those
quaint, not unlovable people who somehow remind one
almost equally of a bird and a butterfly". Particular care is
taken to characterize the Martian race, with attention being
paid to their elliptical thought-processes, their customary say-
ings ("It is carven in stone" is the Martian phrase signifying
agreement), and their elaborate social rituals: "I had never
quite accustomed myself to the long string of phrases,
flowery and complimentary, which with these Martians take

the place of our more direct 'Mr.' or 'Miss'" (p. 35). (On a lighter note, there is even some humorous by-play about the Martian reaction to H. G. Wells' *The War of the Worlds* – a book which "is ever a sore point with your Martian".)

To the modern reader Walsh's most interesting achievement is his creation of an interplanetary "James Bond" figure more than twenty years before Ian Fleming published *Casino Royale* (1953). Walsh's hero, Mr Sanders, is number 723 in the elite Interplanetary Guard, and bears the rank of Space Captain. Like James Bond he is cool, aloof, and astutely intelligent. Though not a womanizer (Sanders *marries* his Martian girlfriend), he is – like Bond – closely identified with the masculine realm of gadgets and weaponry:

> I opened one hold-all and delved down to the bottom of it, and sighed with relief as I felt my hand touch the cold metal of the box I had planted there. It was sealed and locked, but I broke the one and undid the other, and drew out the ray tube from its nest of cotton wool. It was a queer little weapon, six inches long, and no thicker than a lead pencil, but it could do deadly work up to fifty yards. I slipped the full magazine of twelve charges, things no bigger than match-heads, into the hollow butt and slid the catch over. (p. 18)

One year after *Vandals of the Void,* another notable (but less original) thriller appeared. In *The Hidden Kingdom* (1932) M. Lynn Hamilton (Hamilton Lewis) provides a crisp updating of the "hidden world" motif of the earlier romances. In order to create a sense of authenticity,[25] the novel is presented as the "manuscript" of Dr Louis Zaring, who has been held captive for five weeks in "an unknown natural fortress" in the north west of Australia.[26] (There is even a full-page "Declaration" by "Wm. Halston, Supt. of Police" asserting that the details of Zaring's disappearance and recovery are true.) Ruled by a Colonel Ord, the hidden kingdom is a thriving concern, recalling the materialistic utopia of "The Monster Mine": the land is cultivated, cattle are grazed, and the suburban areas are landscaped with parks and lakes. Ord has been systematically luring aside the world's thinkers, and the fruits of this "brain drain" have included "smokeless fuel" and the exploitation of natural gas. The book is weakened, as usual, by the exigencies of "love interest".

Other works of the 1930s are disappointing. *The Temple of Sähr* (1932) by William Pengreep (W. T. Pearson) deals with an unscrupulous scientist in north west Australia. Attempting to find a new form of medical anaesthetic, the scientist has devised a ray capable of producing unconscious-

ness, and has used this to enslave the survivors of an ancient
race. Helen Simpson's *The Woman on the Beast* (1933) is a
laboured and jejune elucidation of a worthwhile theme. As
she says in her foreword:

> This book tries to interpret a contradiction, that the most hateful
> actions are, as often as not, performed for the best of reasons. . . .
> Men are driven to persecute and betray, not by malice or folly, but
> by the good they passionately wish their fellow men.

Only the third section of the novel, set in Australia in 1999,
is science fiction. The evangelist Emma Jordon Sopwith has
converted the civilized world to religion, with only Australia
resisting the New Gospel. Books and newspapers have been
banned since 1982, and harassment by the New Gospellers
has caused the Australian population to abandon the cities
and adopt a nomadic existence, moving about the continent
"in swarms, like locusts, a thousand or so persons at a time".
These nomads are divided into hostile factions which meet
peacefully once a year (at opposite ends of the rusting
Sydney Harbour bridge) to celebrate their mutual love of
horse-racing and sea-bathing. Australia's fate is sealed when
the Gospellers kill the Sydney population in a gas attack,
but then the Last Trump sounds (literally) and redemption is
at hand. Helen Simpson shows no imaginative interest in
science or technology (the people of 1999 still fly in conventional aeroplanes), and her only contribution to Australian sf
lies in her use of what could be called the ultimate *deus ex
machina*.[27] Technology plays a part in Dale Collins' *Race the
Sun* (1936), but this story of "the first lower stratosphere
flight to Australia" by Britain's ace airman, Sir Rex Masters,
merely uses technology as the basis for a conventional
adventure.

   The impact of the second world war is evident in George
Spaull's children's adventure, *Where the Stars are Born*
(1942). This simple-minded account of an undersea utopia
offers the childish thought that war can be eliminated if
children are Obedient and Reject Money as the Root of all
Evil. The general dreariness of Australian sf in the 1940s was
broken dramatically by *Tomorrow and Tomorrow* (1947) by
M. Barnard Eldershaw (Marjorie Barnard and Flora Eldershaw). This is the first Australian novel which can be
regarded unequivocally as "good literature"; it is a "thinking
man's novel". The opening pages, published here, show the
authors' skill with words and images, and their ability to
create mood and atmosphere. The extract also reflects the

intelligent sensitivity that underlies the novel. There is compassion for the white settlers, despite their stupid pride and
eternal grumbling, yet there is also a firm conviction that
their values and lifestyle are sterile:

> The Australians [white settlers] coming after the First people
> [Aborigines], disinheriting rather than inheriting from them, had
> laid a different pattern on the earth, a free pattern, asymmetrical,
> never completed, because their life was so disrupted, complex, and
> unreasoning. (p. 11)

A sentence such as this places Barnard and Eldershaw in the
long tradition of Australian writers (including Katharine
Susannah Prichard, Xavier Herbert, and David Ireland) who
have advocated a more "natural" lifestyle. By actively "dis-
inheriting" rather than "inheriting", the settlers have refused
to weave themselves organically into the patterns of history
and nature.

Tomorrow and Tomorrow offers two separate glimpses of
Australia's future. It is set in the twenty-fourth century, but
the central character, Knarf, has written a novel about life in
the twentieth century (covering the period from 1920 to the
1940s — M. Barnard Eldershaw's "present" — but then extending into a retrospectively viewed "future" which envisages
global pestilence and world war III by 1950). The novel
divides its space between Knarf's account of working class
life during the Depression (the issues being employment,
housing, sexual morality, working conditions, and the peace
movement)[28] and an account of growing social dissatisfaction
in Knarf's own time. Working within the system, twenty-
fourth century dissidents are hoping to bring about social reform by means of a referendum conducted by "votometer":

> "At four o'clock the motion will be read from the Library steps
> and everyone will be asked to keep silent for two minutes and
> record his vote. Think it, you know? . . . No one has to do any-
> thing but stand still and just make a mental affirmation or denial,
> no possible interference. . . . Democracy always fell through
> before because it wasn't scientific. The votometer records the
> unadulterated will of the people."
> "How?" asked Knarf.
> " . . . It depends on the recording of thought waves. Wireless
> telegraphy was the first crude exploitation of wave records in
> ether. Later it was possible by a refinement of the apparatus to
> record the thoughts of the individual. Scientific justice. [The voto-
> meter] can record mass thinking. . . . Thinking isn't, well, just
> gelatinous, it's words, and when you think words it's a physical as
> well as mental process. You say it in an inaudible truncated sort of
> way, your larynx contracts infinitesimally. . . . " (p. 28)

(Hardly a sophisticated account of the thought process, even
for the 1940s.) The reformist motion is lost, just as the twentieth century struggle for peace and justice is lost, but the
parallel structuring and dual time-scheme point to the fact
that the quest for individual freedom will continue.

The early 1950s saw a spate of local sf magazines — *Thrills
Incorporated* (1950–52), *Future Science Fiction* and *Popular
Science Fiction* (1953–55) and *Scientific Thriller* (1948–52)
— all of which helped to perpetuate the dreary pulp hack-
work of writers who signed themselves Ace Carter, Bella
Luigi, Wolfe Herscholt, and Otto Kensch. Graham Stone
remarks that "None of these [magazines] was successful, and
no wonder. They present an overall picture of wasted opportunities and misdirected effort".[29] The most prolific writer
of the time was Vol Molesworth,[30] who produced a dozen
pulp novels with titles such as *Monster at Large* (1950),
Blinded They Fly (1951), and *Let There Be Monsters* (1952).

The decade of the fifties also unfolded the career of the
redoubtable children's hero, Simon Black. Created by the
award-winning children's author, Ivan Southall, Simon Black
— with his partner, Alan Grant, and Rex the Alsation — made
his debut in 1950 (*Meet Simon Black*) and continued adven-
turing until 1961 (*Simon Black at Sea*). There was always a
touch of science fiction in the series, for in addition to being
an ace airman (like his ex-RAAF creator), Simon Black was
also an aeronautical genius and had invented a supersonic
wonder aircraft called the *Firefly*. Southall's reverence for
technology is evident in the following description of the
space-going *Firefly 3*, first seen in *Simon Black in Space*
(1952):

> In front of them, emerging from the assembly shop, towed by a
> crawler tractor, was *Firefly 3*.
>   No paint marked its surface. It was silvery, polished to a blind-
> ing, mirror-like finish. It flashed and sparkled in the brilliant lights.
>   Abruptly, the scene was silent. The tractor driver cut his
> engine. The hush was almost magical. It was a long, long moment.
>   There stood *Firefly 3*. A machine seventy feet long from its
> needle-like bows to its sweetly curved stern. A rocket-shaped fuse-
> lage perfectly, invisibly moulded into a near-circular knife-edged
> wing section, sixty feet from tip to tip, fifty feet from leading
> edge to trailing edge, a dream, a poem in alloys and steel. (p. 38)

Though Simon Black was to have adventures on Mars (*Simon
Black in Space*), chase flying saucers to Venus (*Simon Black*

and the Spacemen [1955]), and confront little green aliens in his parents' home town of Sunshine Valley (*Simon Black Takes Over* [1959]), the series is memorable for the derring-do of its hero and for the marvels of the *Firefly* programme, rather than for its vision of other planets and other races.

Frank Bryning was the most important writer to emerge in the fifties. The two significant areas of Bryning's work are his "Commonwealth Satellite Space Station" stories, which reveal him to be Australia's most scientific sf writer (though that title would later have to be shared with George Turner), and his "Aboriginal" stories, which reveal him to be the first Australian sf writer to take an on-going interest in the Aborigines. The ten "CSSS" stories form a cycle linked by the female central character, Dr Vivien Gale, and are set in the mid twenty-first century.[31] The scientific content of the tales is impeccable, and Bryning weaves suspenseful plots around the scientific problems of astronautics (how to administer a spinal anaesthetic under conditions of weightlessness, how to rescue an astronaut who has come adrift during extra-vehicular activity).

The "Aboriginal" stories are completely different, and represent an important development in Australian sf. Our earliest writers showed contempt or indifference toward the Aborigines. When the heroes of *The Last Lemurian* are ambushed by Aborigines, they have no qualms about laying a trap and cold-bloodedly killing every one of their attackers. *The Coloured Conquest* makes no reference to the Aborigines at all (even though it would be extremely interesting to know of their fate under Japanese rule), and *The Australian Crisis* dismissively states that "the native aboriginals . . . were not credited with sufficient intelligence to be dangerous" (p. 90). Earani, in *Out of the Silence,* describes the Aborigines as "useless", and the novel's least racist character, Dr Richard Barry, defends the extermination of the Aborigines as a case of "survival of the fittest". By 1947 a change in attitude has occurred, and the opening pages of *Tomorrow and Tomorrow* (reprinted here) provide a strong defence of the Aboriginal way of life, arguing that it is a more natural (and thus saner and more fulfilling) lifestyle than that of the white man. Frank Bryning writes in this tradition, for his stories celebrate Aboriginal culture and mythology by bringing it into ironically triumphant contact with supposed-ly "superior" white technology. "Mechman of the Dreaming" (1978, brings the Aboriginal legend of Woolgooroo (a "mechanical" man made of saplings, stones, and kangaroo-gut) into conflict with a multi-purpose research robot used by the Department of Aboriginal Affairs, and in "Place of the Throwing-stick" (1956) (published here) there is a more direct confrontation between Aboriginal myth and western technology. Thirty-five years after the publication of his first sf story, Frank Bryning is still an important voice in Australian sf.

The 1960s brought an upsurge in Australian science fiction writing. Whilst writers such as Frank Bryning, Wynne Whiteford, and A. Bertram Chandler went on to consolidate their achievements of the fifties, new writers joined the ranks. John Baxter, Damien Broderick, Lee Harding, and Jack Wodhams each achieved publication in overseas magazines, and managed to move Australian sf away from its dependence on American models. Their work showed a greater concern for style and for the need for each writer to speak with a distinct individual "voice". The work of this decade is well represented in John Baxter's two anthologies, the First and Second *Pacific Books of Australian Science Fiction* (1968 and 1971).

Despite the brightening prospect of the sixties, it was not until 1975 that the current "renaissance" in Australian sf began. This was the year of "AussieCon", the year in which the 33rd Annual World SF Convention (usually an American affair) was held in Melbourne, with Ursula Le Guin as guest of honour. Since this event led to the burgeoning of contemporary Australian sf, it is important to note the vital role of the Literature Board of the Australia Council in funding both the convention and subsequent book-publishing activities. It would not be too extreme to claim that without Literature Board support Australian science fiction would not have had a future. AussieCon had two chief effects. First, it led to a number of significant publishing ventures, including the founding of two small independent sf publishing houses (Bruce Gillespie and Carey Handfield's Norstrilia Press, and Paul Collins' Void Publications), the appearance of Lee Harding's anthology, *Beyond Tomorrow* (1976), in which stories by "big name" overseas sf writers were set beside the work of Australians, and the launching of two small sf magazines, Neville J. Angove's *The Epsilon Eridani Express* (1977−) and Van Ikin's *Science Fiction: A Review of Speculative Literature* (1977−). (Australia's foremost sf magazine, Bruce Gillespie's *SF Commentary*, had been in publication since 1969, filling the gap left by the demise of John Bangsund's *Australian Science Fiction Review* [1966−

69].) Secondly, AussieCon gave rise to a writers' workshop (conducted by Le Guin) from which there emerged a new generation of talented writers (the chief of them being Philippa C. Maddern).[32]

The current lordly figures of Australian sf are Captain A. Bertram Chandler and George Turner, but there are contenders a-plenty, and they are gaining ground. Chandler's achievement is a vast *oeuvre* of swashbuckling outer space adventure, most of it involving Commander Grimes and the "Rim Worlds" sector of space. Chandler's nautical background is evident in these works, and so too is a genial sense of humour. The short story "Kelly Country", included here, demonstrates his versatility and his strong sense of being Australian. The only "alternative history" of Australia yet attempted, it considers what might have happened if Ned Kelly had *won* the siege at Glenrowan.

George Turner, by contrast, began his writing career as a "mainstream" novelist (*The Cupboard Under the Stairs* shared the 1962 Miles Franklin Award) and then became known as a tough and often controversial reviewer and critic of sf. He claims that his "thirty year apprenticeship" to the novelist's craft has given him the critical confidence "to stand in awe of no-one but Shakespeare and Tolstoy".[33] His first sf novel, *Beloved Son* (1978), belongs to the "sound-science-and-social-commentary" tradition of Huxley's *Brave New World*, but Turner's plotting is more intricate than that of Huxley, his characters are less one-dimensional, and his vision of society is more shrewd and complex. Set in the reconstructed post-holocaust world of 2032, *Beloved Son* is ostensibly an attack on cloning and a warning about the dangers of genetic engineering, but Turner's deeper concern is with the uses of power. The story included here, "In a Petri Dish Upstairs", is set in the world of *Beloved Son* and displays similar thematic concerns.

The "contenders" are the newer breed of Australian sf writers. They can be divided into two camps, the first consisting of writers who have already established their reputations: Damien Broderick, Lee Harding, and David J. Lake. Becoming addicted to science fiction whilst receiving a Jesuit education in Bowral, New South Wales, Damien Broderick went on to spend time as editor of *Man* magazine and to name and edit the Monash University student newspaper, *Lot's Wife*. His first important novel, *The Dreaming Dragons* (1980), is a quick-witted intellectual teaser which uses the notion of intelligent feathered dinosaurs to pose an alternate view of the prehistory of the human race. Such witty, allusive playfulness is a recurring feature of Broderick's work, but his distinctive authorial "voice" is chiefly heard through his rich (though sometimes florid) diction. Both qualities are present in "A Passage in Earth", the story by which Broderick is represented here.

The verbal characteristics of Lee Harding's writing are less individualized than those of Broderick, for Harding cultivates a less ostentatious "natural" prose style. Harding is perhaps the leading exponent of characterization in contemporary Australian sf (though none of his works has yet rivalled the depth of characterization achieved in Sumner Locke Elliott's 1975 novel, *Going*), and his novels and short stories reveal a gift for creating situations in which reality trails off into teasing uncertainties. *A World of Shadows* (1975) explored the psychological and ontological plight of an astronaut whose personality becomes infused in the body of another man, and *The Weeping Sky* (1977) showed an ostensibly medieval society confronted by the terrifyingly beautiful phenomenon of an immense weeping "wound" in the sky. In *Displaced Person* (1979), his most accomplished work to date,[34] Harding presents a fable of alienation as teenager Graeme Drury finds himself slipping away from the reality of suburban Melbourne (seen in terms of parents, girlfriend, and the local McDonald's fast food outlet) and entering a strange "grey world" or limbo.

The work of David J. Lake, by contrast, places greater emphasis upon ideas, exotica, and escapist entertainment. *The Gods of Xuma, or, Barsoom Revisited* (1978) presents a skilful reconstruction of the planet Mars as portrayed in Edgar Rice Burroughs' "John Carter" adventures. The impulse behind *The Gods of Xuma* is playful, but the literary mimicry is more sober in *The Man Who Loved Morlocks* (1981), which reflects Lake's scholarly interest in the works of H. G. Wells.[35] Purporting to be "A Sequel to *The Time Machine* as Narrated by the Time Traveller", *The Man Who Loved Morlocks* seeks to "correct" the socio-political pessimism of Wells' narrative. This feat is achieved by allowing the Time Traveller to tell his *own* story (whereas in the original his tale was filtered through the recollections of another narrator), and by asserting that *The Time Machine* told only part of the story, and was incomplete. Wells had portrayed a future void of hope, with mankind splitting into two distinct races: the physically beautiful Eloi (who appear human, but are effete and intellectually inert) and the grotesquely repulsive Morlocks (who are no longer human, yet preserve mankind's genius for achievement and progress). In the Wellsian view, such a separation of human qualities leads inevitably to the extinction of mankind; but in Lake's scenario the separation is a prelude to a healthier *coalescence*, and this guarantees the survival of the race. With the exception of *The Man Who Loved Morlocks*, Lake's short stories are generally more ambitious than his novels,[36] and so his work is represented here by the punningly titled story "Redeem the Time", which is a darkly humorous satire on man, society, and science fiction itself.

The second camp of "contenders" consists of the latest generation of younger sf writers, many of whom came to the forefront as a result of the Le Guin writers' workshop or its successors. They are represented here by Philippa C. Maddern, but this category could also have included Leanne Frahm, David Grigg, and Petrina Smith (on the basis of the small body of work they have so far produced), or John J. Alderson and Bruce Gillespie (on the basis of individual works: Alderson's flawed but lively political satire, "The Sentient Ship", and Gillespie's memorably original excursion into alien movie-making, "A Laughing Stock".)[37]

Maddern has been included for the quality of her work, but her story "Inhabiting the Interspaces" also represents a new approach to the female characters in science fiction. As already mentioned in this survey, science fiction has a poor reputation for its treatment of women, and Australian sf offers few exceptions to this rule. Even in the seemingly progressive "feminist" romances, women are viewed at best as untapped "resources" and are generally woven into the plot by means of their involvement with male characters. The fearsome Earani succumbs to the ockerish Alan Dundas, and whilst it is true that she is a dynamic and free-thinking individual, these very qualities are aspects of her villainy. Frank Bryning's female astronaut, Dr Vivien Gale, is the first woman to break free of the sexist mould: she has chosen a career in astronautics and medicine, and in many of the Satellite Space Station stories she uses her brains (*not* her "feminine intuition") to solve problems which have baffled the males. Lee Harding's female characters are often independent and assertive, but they too are drawn into the narrative only through their involvement with the central (male) characters. There is no such problem with the presentation of Alethea Hunt, the central character in David Ireland's *A*

Woman of the Future (1979), but the girl's obsessive pre-occupation with sex raises the possibility that she is to some extent a projection of male fantasy. Maddern's story suffers from no such drawbacks. It deals with a girl who lives in the spaces left vacant by the pattern of man's use of office blocks and building spaces. Like a mouse inhabiting the inter-spaces of a home, she finds nooks and niches where it is good to sleep, raids the many office refrigerators, and establishes a comfortable (if lonely) pattern of nocturnal existence. Aside from dramatizing the inefficient wastefulness of the office-block syndrome, the story presents a paradigm of the plight of woman in a male-oriented society, seeing woman as the mouse forced to struggle for existence.

Finally, in a third camp, there are the "Non-contenders": the mavericks who have frequently written science fiction, but have never regarded themselves as "committed" sf writers and have never seen themselves as part of the Australian sf "scene". Dal Stivens has frequently used the "props" of science fiction (such as space warps and rockets) to enhance his fables and tall stories, and there are elements of scientific speculation in D. M. Foster and D. K. Lyall's novel, *The Empathy Experiment* (1977). Though he is neither a frequent nor a "committed" science fiction writer, Michael Wilding has produced some of the very best Australian sf stories. "The Man of Slow Feeling" and "See You Later"[38] present grimly original concepts, and both stories achieve moments of great lyrical beauty. "The Words She Types" (included here) is a more austere piece, and is more correctly labelled "fantasy" rather than science fiction. However, if "The Words She Types" is compared with Dal Stivens' "The Gentle Basilisk" (or with the works of Patricia Wrightson) it can be seen to represent what we might call "uneasy fantasy": fantasy which has its roots in the "real" and the "normal" (rather than dealing with basilisks or creatures from Aboriginal mythology), and fantasy which is achieved by an unsettling blurring of reality. This collection closes with a story by Peter Carey in which "uneasy fantasy" and science fiction are brought together. In tone and stance, "Report on the Shadow Industry" is clipped, matter-of-fact, and detached: in a word, scientific. Moreover, the account of the actual shadow-making industry shows that the shadows are produced by a scientific technological process (for there are factories and chimneys which billow smoke). Yet there is no blow-by-blow account of shadow-manufacture, no attempt to explain why such an industry has come into existence (and acceptance), and the story's ending seems to curl inward toward fantasy.

According to orthodox critical views, Australian fiction is essentially earnest and realist in orientation. Michael Wilding has already observed that "there has always been much more variety than critical orthodoxy allows",[39] and this volume provides a sampling of that variety. Never afraid to tackle the topical and controversial (though sometimes unable to deal with such material effectively), Australian sf has mirrored the nation's apprehensive fascination with its own unexplored emptiness, and its fear of forfeiting its never-too-clear racial identity. If the nation's early sf reveals Australians to have been racist, sexist, and materialistic, it also reveals their more altruistic utopian aspirations, and the more recent offerings of Australian sf show that ignoble attitudes are receding.

Except in the case of a few individual works, no great claims can yet be made for Australian science fiction. But that is a judgement which rests upon works that have already appeared, and when dealing with literature about the future it is incongruous not to look forward as well. The prospect for future Australian sf is exciting: the Great Australian SF Novel is yet to be written.

NOTES

1. Frederick Sinnett, *The Fiction Fields of Australia,* ed. Cecil Hadgraft (1856: St Lucia: University of Queensland Press, 1966), p. 23.

2. Kingsley Amis, *New Maps of Hell* (London: New English Library, 1969), p. 14.

3. Sam Moskowitz, *Strange Horizons: The Spectrum of Science Fiction* (New York: Scribners, 1976), p. 1.

4. For a more detailed account of the shortcomings of the "functionalist" approach, see my editorial in *Science Fiction: A Review of Speculative Literature* no. 2, vol. 1, no. 2 (June 1978): 4–10.

5. Robert A. Heinlein, "Science Fiction: Its Nature, Faults and Virtues", in *The Science Fiction Novel: Imagination and Social Criticism,* ed. Basil Davenport, Robert A. Heinlein, C. M. Kornblath, Alfred Bester, Robert Bloch (Chicago: Advent Press, 1969), p. 46.

6. Brian Aldiss, "On Being a Literary Pariah", *Extrapolation* 17, no. 2 (May 1976): 169.

7. Angus Taylor, *Philip K. Dick and the Umbrella of Light* (Baltimore: T–K Graphics, 1975), p. 7.

8. See Terry Dowling, "What is Science Fiction?", *Science Fiction: A Review of Speculative Literature* no. 4, vol. 2, no. 1 (May 1979): 4–19; George Turner, "Who Needs a Definition of Science Fiction? And Why?" and Terry Dowling, " . . . A Much Richer Phenomenon . . . ", both in ibid., no. 5, vol. 2, no. 2 (December 1979): 161–74 and 174–83; and George Turner's letter in ibid., no. 7, vol. 3, no. 1 (January 1981): 47–48.

9. For a full account of this phenomenon, see J.J. Healy, "The Lemurian Nineties", *Australian Literary Studies* 8, no. 3 (May 1978): 307–16. Healy observes that such Lemurian speculations "opened up Australia as a continent *in* space and time, as a continent *of* space and time" (p. 311), so that instead of being "a land where nothing, from the European point of view, had happened", Australia became "a land where everything – the cradle of man, the rise and fall of a primal civilization, cataclysms – had happened" (p. 316). (Interestingly, a similar effect is achieved – without reference to Lemuria – in the 1847 story "Oo-a-deen", reprinted here.)

10. Mrs Campbell Praed, *My Australian Girlhood* (London: T. Fisher Unwin, 1902), pp. 10–11.

11. The vogue for volcanoes may be explained by the spectacular eruption of Krakatoa in August 1883.

12. Sam Moskowitz, *Strange Horizons: The Spectrum of Science Fiction* (New York: Scribners, 1976), p. 70; and Sam J. Lundwall, *Science Fiction: What It's All About* (New York: Ace Books, 1971), p. 145.

13. Sir Julius Vogel is one of the few early sf writers about whom biographical details are known. In 1847 he published a volume on *The Pathological Anatomy of the Human Body*, and in 1865 he wrote a pamphlet on *Great Britain and Her Colonies*. His love for New Zealand was reflected in his editorship (in 1875) of *The Official Handbook of New Zealand*, by a paper on "New Zealand and the South Sea Islands, and their Relations to the Empire" (which he read to the Royal Colonial Institute in 1878), and by various references in *Anno Domini 2000*.

14. Science fiction is of course "based mainly on the question *What would happen if. . .?*" (Lundwall, p. 125).

15. Potter's interests lay chiefly in writing on religious subjects, for he published *The Relations of Ethics to Religion* (London: Macmillan, 1888) and articles on "The Credibility of Miracles" and "Miracles and the Law" in the *Melbourne Review*. Born in County Mayo, Ireland, in 1831, Potter came to Australia in the late 1850s and died sometime before 1912.

16. Lucy Sussex, "*The Germ Growers*: An Early Australian SF Novel", *Science Fiction: A Review of Speculative Literature* no. 6, vol. 2, no. 3 (August 1980): 229–33.

17. See the *Sydney Gazette* 30 (1832): no. 2129 (Thursday May 17),

p. 3; no. 2130 (Saturday May 19), p. 3; no. 2131 (Tuesday May 22), p. 3; no. 2134 (Tuesday May 29), p. 3; no. 2135 (Thursday May 31), p. 3. The author's pseudonym has been misspelled in the first article.

18. In "The Trek of Burke and Wills: or, The Triumphant March of Australian Science Fiction" (published in the *AussieCon Fifth Anniversary Memorial Fanzine* 2 (January 1981), pp. 5-8., John J. Alderson mentions *"The Atmotic Ship"* (sic), published in 1855 by "Dr Bland (1789-1868)". Having been unable to find this item, I am tempted to conclude that it may have been published as a magazine serial rather than in book form.

19. S. L. Larnach's *Material Towards a Checklist of Australian Fan-. tasy to 1938* (1950) inexplicably gives the author as "Clotilda".

20. No date of publication is given in the book itself, but in a letter to *SF Commentary*, no. 58 (February 1980): 10-11, Sam Moskowitz offers the year 1894.

21. Fraser acknowledges the "harrowing" accounts of convict life provided by Marcus Clarke (p. 14). He pays particular attention to the method used to flout the law which declared that no man was allowed to inflict punishment upon his own assigned convict servant, but must instead deliver him up to a magistrate or to the stockade. According to Fraser, the squatters circumvented this ruling by having themselves sworn in as justices of the peace, so that they could carry out punishments for each other.

22. Perceptive readers are left wondering how the characters managed to survive a space-trip in an open boat, but in the end it is revealed that It Was All a Dream.

23. Quoted in Manning Clark, *A Short History of Australia* (New York: Mentor Books, 1969), p. 185.

24. Some of Walsh's earlier works were written under the pseudonym "H. Haverstock Hill".

25. In their article on "The Novel" in *The Literature of Western Australia*, ed. Bruce Bennett (Perth: University of Western Australia Press, 1979), Veronica Brady and Peter Cowan remark that "the story might well have been seen as fact by some readers" (p. 82).

26. The device of presenting the work as a character's "manuscript" had been used in *Melbourne and Mars, Beyond the Ice, The Expedition of Captain Flick,* and other early works.

27. A more sympathetic account is given in H. M. Green's *A History of Australian Literature*, vol. 2 (Sydney: Angus & Robertson, 1962), pp. 1142-43.

28. These sections, representing "Knarf's novel", resemble the "social realist" fiction of the period. The account of the peace movement has affinities with works such as Katharine Susannah Prichard's *Subtle Flame* (1967).

29. Graham Stone, *Australian Science Fiction Index 1925-1967* (Canberra: Australian SF Association, n.d.), p. 156. The most reputable professional sf magazine in Australia (excluding maga-

zines of sf criticism and commentary) was *Vision of Tomorrow* (1969–1970).

30. This was his real name, Vol being short for Voltaire.

31. Bryning discusses these stories – and his life and work in general – in "The Science in Science Fiction: An Interview with Frank Bryning" (interviewer: Van Ikin), *Science Fiction: A Review of Speculative Literature* no. 4, vol. 2, no. 1 (May 1979): 21–39.

32. Lee Harding's anthology, *The Altered I* (1976), provides a unique record of this workshop.

33. "George Turner: The Man, the Writer, the Critic – an Interview" (interviewer: Van Ikin), *Science Fiction: A Review of Speculative Literature* no. 3, vol. 1, no. 3 (December 1978): 120.

34. For further discussion of Lee Harding's work, see Van Ikin, "The Novels of Lee Harding: A Survey", *Science Fiction: A Review of Speculative Literature* no. 2, vol. 1, no. 2 (June 1978): 28–44, and my interview with Harding on pp. 46–56 of the same issue.

35. A Reader in English at the University of Queensland, Lake made a study trip to the USA in 1978 to examine the original manuscript of *The Time Machine*, and has since published material on Wells' many drafts of the story.

36. David J. Lake provides an interesting personal appraisal of his novels in a letter to *SF Commentary*, no. 58 (February 1980): 11–12.

37. These stories first appeared in anthologies edited by Paul Collins: *Envisaged Worlds* (1978) and *Alien Worlds* (1979) respectively.

38. Both stories appear in Michael Wilding's collection, *The West Midland Underground* (1975). "See You Later" has also been published under the less ironic title, "Illumination".

39. Michael Wilding, Introduction to *The Portable Marcus Clarke* (St Lucia: University of Queensland Press, 1976), p. xxvi.

A Note on the Text

Many of the items in this collection are excerpted, and this has been clearly indicated in the notes introducing each section. Wherever possible, the title given to each excerpt has been taken from the title of the excerpted chapter. Except for the material taken from *Melbourne and Mars* (1889) and *The Coloured Conquest* (1904), none of the items in this collection has been abridged. (Details of the abridgement of the two abovementioned items are given in the notes introducing the sections in which they occur.)

Some minor errors and spelling mistakes have been silently corrected. There have been slight changes in punctuation and spelling to standardize the text to UQP house style.

Part I
The Past

1845–1872

These earliest examples of Australian sf writing foreshadow the varied forms and concerns of the genre. Published in 1845, but purportedly written in *1945*, "The Monster Mine" is identifiably a work of fiction, and emphatically proclaims the materialistic benefits of industrial and technological progress. By contrast, " 'Oo-a-deen': or, The Mysteries of the Interior Unveiled" (1847) is accompanied by a declaration that it is "founded throughout on Fact". This item, too, has utopian leanings, but its chief function is to project colonial apprehensions about the unknown heart of the Australian continent. Marcus Clarke's "Human Repetends" (1872) combines semi-autobiographical background details with an account of occult events, thereby offering yet another combination of fact and fiction. The story's claim to being science fiction lies in the mathematical analogy drawn in the final paragraphs.

"The Monster Mine", by PGM, first appeared in *The South Australian Odd Fellows' Magazine*, vol. 103, no. 5 (August 1845). " 'Oo-a-deen': or, The Mysteries of the Interior Unveiled", by an unknown author, appeared in three instalments in the *Corio Chronicle and Western Districts Advertiser* (Geelong), 2, 6, and 9 October 1847 (vol. 1, nos 8, 9, and 10), p. 59, pp. 67–68, and p. 75. "Human Repetends", by Marcus Clarke, appeared in the *Australasian* (Melbourne), 14 September 1872, p. 326.

The Monster Mine

PGM

(1845)

Hope Lodge
Hayloft Hotel
August 16th, 1945 *

This day is memorable in the annals of the principality as the centenary of the purchase by a Company of the Great Copper Mine on the Burra, and will be celebrated by a grand festival.

One hundred years ago a few individuals of limited means subscribed together, with much difficulty, the (at that time large) sum of £20,000. With this they purchased, of the Local Government of that period, twenty thousand acres of mineral land; and the spot fixed on is that immense tract of country now occupied by the seven great and flourishing cities — Featherstonhaugh, Stockton-on-Burra, Aston, Buncely, Grahamstown, Bagota, and Snobsgain.

At that time the district was approached with great difficulty, the roads over hill and dale being infested with wild dogs (*wolves*) and natives (*ourang-outangs*), and almost impassable to other than travellers on horseback, the few wheeled vehicles which existed being clumsy conveyances called drays, and drawn by bullocks; for so great was the demand for, and scarcity of, horses at that time, that bullocks, goats, and even dogs were employed in drawing the valuable ore to the port of shipment, which was the now inconsiderable port of Adelaide. The splendid harbour of Boston Bay was then either unknown or treated with a

* Editor's note: The date signifies that the author is writing one hundred years in the future.

neglect almost inconceivable to those who now know it as the most important resort for shipping in the known world. Atmospheric railways and aerial machines were, it is true, talked of, but the matter-of-fact men of the day considered them theoretical, visionary, and impracticable; and when we consider that the vessels of the period occupied a space of four months in transferring the ore (for no means for smelting were then established) to England, then the *only market* for it, we shall cease to wonder that, for a length of time, it was doubtful whether the scheme would prove successful or otherwise.

To those who are acquainted with the immense wealth of the proprietors of this property — the Princes of the soil; to those who look at their palaces, their castles, and their villas, it is almost incredible that, so short a time back as one century, their ancestors were at immense trouble to raise the paltry amount referred to, which each of the one thousand proprietors could now readily pay ten times over; that, in fact, two great political parties, called the Nobs and Snobs, (supposed to be the same as the Whig and Tory of a still earlier period), actually coalesced to attain this object, notwithstanding the almost frantic opposition offered by two gentlemen of the name of Manager, who apparently held very influential positions in the principality, or rather, as it was called at that time, the colony.

The City of Adelaide, then, as now, the seat of Government, boasted few of the splendid buildings which now embellish it. The ancient monument in the midst of Light-square was scarcely completed. A monument erected by the Odd Fellows, to the memory of a deceased brother, was only then in the course of erection.

A few of the oldest Churches and Chapels that are dotted over our vast city were certainly in existence, and one Catholic Bishop had lately arrived in the place.

No splendid Cathedral, either Protestant or Catholic, reared its proud head in this our embryo city. The Prince's palace, the palaces of the Archbishops and Bishops, were not thought of. The great man of the place, who, from his advanced years, was known by the soubriquet of the Grey Governor, resided in a portion of the Prince's palace, which those curious in antiquarian researches may still find occupied as apartments and offices by the Lord Steward's clerks; and one unpretending Chapel, in the Monastery of St Murphy, is still pointed out by the venerable father O'Recollect as the nucleus of that great building.

No Colleges actually existed, except in the legends of the oldest inhabitants, who spoke (without, however, anything like confidence) of a College which had existed in air (*Quere* in Eyre?) in earlier days.

The great-grandfather of our present beloved Prince was then but an infant in the cradle; and the land was governed by nominees of our great ally, England, with whom *friendly relations have been maintained* from that time to the present; indeed, as our readers must be aware, this ancestor of our beloved Prince was afterwards the renowned Albert Edward the First of England.

Records have, however, been handed down of a visit to this clime paid by King John, who died eight hundred years ago; after which a long blank of seven hundred years occurs in the documents in the hands of the Lord Keeper of Records.

We are afraid we are occupying too much space in the oldest established journal of the principality, but cannot resist one more circumstance, which is amusing to those who consider the rude state in which our ancestors carried on their commercial arrangements. It is a well-recorded fact that the great monetary medium was a simple paper document, signed chiefly by one of the Mr Managers before alluded to, which was taken currently as cash, the knowledge of electricity being so confined at that time that our present excellent monetary system was unthought of, and he who had proposed such a scheme would have been looked upon as a madman.

One fact more. It is said that wheat-seed was sown *months* before it was reaped, and the fructification was left entirely to nature. Much doubt has arisen in the minds of many scientific men as to the possibility of growing wheat without electricity; and we have the satisfaction of informing our readers that a series of experiments are now being carried on by Professor Oldenough to ascertain the fact.

But the ringing of bells and the firing of the great steam cannon at Fort Boston announce the fact that the festivities of the day have now commenced, and as our Lodge takes a prominent part in them, I must resign my seat in the electro-phonotypographical chair to some one more worthy to fill it.

"Oo-a-deen": or, the Mysteries of the Interior Unveiled*

Anonymous

(1847)

When I first came to this colony, I had a station the other side of the country, between the Peel and Gwydir Rivers — It was, I may say, on the very outskirts of location — the last link between the known and the unknown Land — I had a great fancy just then, for breeding horses, paying more attention to them, and going to more expense in the purchase of a herd of brood mares, than in my outlay to Sheep or cattle. At first I thought the run very well suited to the purpose, the horses never straying for want of grass, water, or shelter, but, at length I found out, that they were drawing off their beat, in a very unaccountable way; and, it was not until after tailing them for several days that I discovered that one of my Entires had picked up an acquaintance with some wild mares in the bush, and was seducing the whole ruck of tame ones, to follow him in his wanderings.

The wild breeders I tried ineffectually to drive in to my own stock yards. In the attempt, I lost not only my labour, but also the whole of my herd; for the wild horses not liking, seemingly, to be perpetually cheveyed, took to their heels for safety, and in company with the tame ones, went off into a country, that cost me many a day's hard ride, before I could recover them.

On one occasion when I was out after them, I was "tracking a stringy bark range" that bothered me to get out again — the fact is, I had missed the sun which was clouded

---

* This curious narrative nouvelette ... is worth the reader's attention, for which we pledge ourselves, that it is founded throughout on Fact.

Editor's note: The original text uses hyphens in the title, presumably as a guide to pronunciation.

over; the morning was fine enough when I started; but about eleven o'clock, it came on one of those nasty drizzling days, with mist and cold, that would spoil the search of the best bushman in the country. Whilst I was looking about for some means of regaining the way, I lit all at once upon a patch of cultivation; it might have been an acre of land cleared and fenced in. As I rode up, I saw it was a garden planted with potatoes and cabbages, and a strip of barley. "Where there's smoke there's fire," thinks I, "so that where there's a garden there's pretty sure to be a hut." I stood up in the stirrups and looked about, for what I expected to find, but as I could see nothing, I coo-ed and cracked the whip. I was answered, sure enough, and by a man, but where the fellow sprang from, I could not for the life of me tell.

"Who's place is this?" said I.

"Mine," said he.

"Where's your hut then, I've been looking for it this half hour, and couldn't make it out."

The stranger laughed, and directing me around the fence to a gate, said he would show me; the sliding rails of the panel were fixed at one end of a tree, and this tree I found, when I went through the fences, hid the hut or rather cave, for it was half dug out of the bank of the hill, that just there backed the garden paling. Tying the horse up, I went in, and found every thing very neat and comfortable; there was a table made from a sheet of bark flattened out, and looking very stiff and even, a couple of log ends, sawn smooth at the top and bottom, answered for stools; another sheet of bark made the bed-place, which was furnished with opossum and cat furs, while the skin of an emu turned inside out so as to be stuffed with its own feathers, made a fine pillow; the ground was clean swept, and being compounded out of clay and wood ashes looked like a chunam floor; on the shelves were a tin plate or two, as many horn cups and other odds and ends for eating and drinking out of; there was a double barrelled piece, which had a rifle bore for ball, and the other for shot — to judge by the quantity of lyre pheasants' tails, emu tufts, and other trophies of game, I should have expected that he could have used it to some purpose.

All this was well enough, but when I saw a furnace with a bag of charcoal and a crucible, some mining tools and a small box of chemical tests, I was rather surprised.

"Have you a run here?" I began.

"No more than a kangaroo run," said he.

"What do you keep then?" I enquired.

"Nothing, but a dog," he answered.

"But how do you live?" I asked, getting a little puzzled.

"By my garden and my gun, sometimes I use a fishing rod and a trap."

"You have some object still, I suppose," I said, "beyond just the mere maintenance of life."

"I have," said he.

"Is it gathering curiosities for museums, and bird fanciers?" I asked, looking round at the skins of birds, water moles, porcupines, and even snakes, that garnished the sides of the hut.

"No," was his monosyllabic reply.

Well, I thought, I shall never get it out of you this way, so I just said in a straightforward manner: "What the devil are you then?"

"A gold seeker!"

"Oh!" said I, "you understand mining, I suppose?"

"I know something about it," he answered.

"You're the agent perhaps, of some Mining Company speculation, in Sydney, and you've come here to see whether it's worth while to open a mine in these ranges."

"I seek it, for myself alone."

"What! have you no partners in this scheme?" I enquired.

"None."

"Are you not in communication with anyone on the subject?"

"With no one."

"What is your ultimate object?" I continued enquiring. "Is it to get a reward from government for discovering a mine?"

"No," replied he, "but it is my habit of life. My father was a gold seeker before me, I am one myself, and my son, if I ever have one, will be another after me."

"Where do you come from?" said I, getting interested in the strangeness of the man and his occupation.

"I am an American, of the United States. My father brought up three brothers of us in the Alleghany Mountains — there he lived a gold seeker to the day of his death — he sent one of us to the Mountains of South America, another to the backwoods of Canada and one to search the rocks of Australia. He took good care to send us where we could get our living with a rifle. Here I can never starve or want food or shelter; and I might find a diamond that the wealth of England's crown could not purchase."

"Have you met with any success yet?" I enquired.

"Yes - pretty fairish," he replied. "I have taken valuable specimens of ore into Sydney once or twice, but the situations I got them from, would be inaccessible to the miner without more cost than it was worth, to dig the metal."

"Then," I said, "you search mostly for stones now?"

"Yes," he answered, "and although I have had no luck yet, I am very contented, and shall go on searching until I am turned fifty."

"Why to that particular age?"

"Because a wise woman once told my father that one of the family would gain the worth of a kingdom on the day he turned fifty."

This observation at once satisified me, that he was ignorant enough to be absurdly superstitious; indeed I afterwards learned that his education had been of the scantiest description, that he was the living type of a species of idiosyncrasy, which is to be found, I believe, in all countries where the precious metals and stones abound — and that, in this instance, the monomania was an hereditary, or family disease.

"Have you been long here?" I went on to ask.

"About three years."

"Do you ever go down to the stations on the river?"

"No — and unless I can help it I never even sight a man's track."

"Do persons ever fall across you, in the way that I have done?"

"You're the first I've seen since I fashioned this hut and garden — except it may be," he added after a pause, "the creature, that's about here, is, as I take it, a wild man —"

"A Wild Man!" I repeated in astonishment.

"Ay," he said, "and not a native either — his skin's as white as ours, that I am certain of, but when I first saw him, I was scared by his wildness. I caught a glimpse of him running, and leaping over rocks, but his long hair, and his skin dress, made me doubtful what it could be. I have seen him two or three times since, and tried to follow him; but the wild horses down there in the lime-stone gully are not more shy, or more swift."

"Wild horses too," I said eagerly. "Are there many, and of what sort are they — for I've lost a heard of tame ones, which by this time, I dare say, are wild enough."

"Not at all," he answered, "the animal must be born so, to be ever truly wild — but if you've lost any, there they are, I'll be bound, for the herd that belongs to these parts went away about six months since and returned the other day, with somewhere nigh fifty strangers. I could see at a glance, that many of them had been handled."

"You'll greatly oblige me," I followed up, "by showing me this run where the horses are, as I make no doubt, mine are amongst them."

"I'll take you where you can put your hands upon them, in an hour," he replied, and offered me refreshments. He lit his forge, which was his only fire place, and roasting a couple of bandicoot rats, set them before me, with barley scones.

As soon as we had had a feed and a smoke, I set off with the gold seeker to hunt up the horses. After about an hour's walking we came upon a place in the range, where a valley abruptly intervened. It was in general shape of a deep basin, the descent to which was gradually broken by regular steps in the hills, that seemed to wind down to the bottom, like the turnings of a screw. Ferns, cedars, mimosas, and all the handsomest trees of the Austral forest added to the beauty of their grass clad sides, which together with an under ground of vines, and flowering creepers, made the spot really like one of enchantment. At the bottom were grazing my roguish animals, abandoned to all the luxury and untamed freedom of their aboriginal friends.

"Now, we must just go quietly down upon them," said the gold seeker, "and if we can manage to drive them into a pass, which I will show you, we may contrive to separate them from the wild ones, for that you must do, if you want to get your own animals home."

As we worked downwards the gold seeker led my horse, and gave me his piece to carry. I had just taken it in my hand, and was looking to see that the locks were secured at half cock, when a creature that had been lurking under a rock, exactly on our path, sprung up with a wild cry, and dashed across our road. I was so startled myself, that I had not presence of mind enough to discern the creature's figure, before I unconsciously fired: with a shriek and a bound, it leapt down the side of the nearest hill, and it was not until it had reached the bottom, that I recognized in his nearly naked form, tangled elf locks, swift foot and general outline, the "Wild Man" described by the gold seeker! When it struck me that I had just committed an act of the most cruel barbarity on a human being, I gazed intensely and sorrowfully after the flying figure. It did not, however, maintain its pace long, but after two or three convulsive springs, fell, as if dead.

"You've hit him hard at any rate," coolly remarked my companion.

"Pray God, I haven't killed him," I answered; "let us go down and see."

"Be wary, be wary," interposed the guide, "may-be it's the cunning of the creature to feign death, and when you go near him he might get up and strangle you."

This made me nervous, but as I could not bear the idea of a fellow creature bleeding before my eyes, from a wound unfairly given by myself, I went down towards the fallen man, although a little cautiously at first; there was however no danger, for as I approached he raised himself with a feeble effort on his elbow, and pointing to the bullet hole in his side, from which the blood was slowly trickling, gave me a look so full of melancholy reproach, that my heart was sore with pain for him: I stopped and laying my hand upon his, in token of friendship, I enquired who he was?

His eyes gleamed with the sudden and fitful fire of insanity, as he answered, speaking rapidly and wildly: "I am Salathiel the Hebrew of the living judment, I am the Lost Chieftain, the Banished Lord, the Wandering Monarch of the Wold and Wood! For this, for this, you shall be launched down the stream, of the dark river Madideeroo, never more to dwell in the savannahs of Ooadeen, – down, down its whirling stream, under the caverns of central earth, until tossed up again on the land of this bleak wilderness." (Here he paused for a moment, and drew his fingers across his eyes, as if struggling with the pain of his emotions.) "Aye, there, there we went," he continued, "expelled like the guilty pair from Paradise, never, never to return." He stopped again. "Better," he added presently, as if more composed, "better to have sent the lead to my heart at once, than have left me to linger over the thought that now I can no more look for the lost valleys of Ooadeen, never again behold the godlike beauty of her daughters, nor listen to the weird wisdom of her ancient Seers – the reality of the vision was given to my experience alone – none can discover that unknown land but I, and to me even the traces of the road are fainting fast, see, the envious wind sweeps away the tracks, and – and – I sink under dizziness and darkness."

Exhausted by the rapidity and vehemence of his utterance, he fell back in a swoon.

The being that laid there before me was, I think, the most

beautiful model of a man I have ever seen. In stature, he was several inches over six feet, his limbs were muscular yet finely formed, his hands and feet were small, as was his head in proportion to his body; his features in repose were a little effeminate, but when lit with emotion, the scorn and wrath they could express was fearful; his eyes were black and most brilliant, and his hair of the same colour, fell in thick curls on his shoulders, the skin of his body, which then was nearly naked, had a reddish tinge probably from exposure, but his face at that moment had paled to a deadly white, and was beaded over with the sweat of pain and faintness.

Raising his head on my knees, I poured some water and spirits out of my flask, into his mouth, and calling the gold seeker to my assistance, bid him support the man whilst I looked at his wound. The bullet, I saw, had made a very clean passage for itself, just under the last rib — a dangerous place, but as, at its entrance, the ball did not seem to have gone deep in, towards the intestines, I had great hopes that the danger was not very serious. Making a probe out of a straight twig, I bound it over with a strip of linen, torn from my shirt. I passed it carefully in, and discovered in a few seconds that the bullet was nearly through on the other side, and had gone but little under the skin — in fact, I opened the lancet in my knife, and cut it out with a single gash. It appeared, however, to have divided some artery, for he immediately bled profusely, and could sit up only with evident and acute pain. After some hours of unremitting toil, I succeeded in getting him conveyed to the hut of the gold seeker, to whom I promised any remuneration in my power, for the trouble occasioned.

"The man," I said, "is certainly insane, but I feel assured of his gentleness, and it would gratify me beyond measure to be the means of restoring his health and his mind together."

Close to my own station lived a neighbour who was a surgeon by profession. I naturally went to him for assistance, and with our joint care he recovered in a few weeks. During the early parts of his illness he suffered much from a delirious fever, in the paroxysms of which he raved perpetually about a country, which he had before designated as Ooadeen; the language, however, that he used to describe its beauties, and the people who inhabited it, was singularly thrilling and poetical. As he got better, I questioned him about this Unknown Land, when he startled me by declaring that it was hidden in the centre of Australia. I gathered from him in his more rational mood, that he had travelled far inland and had become acquainted with a race of men who inhabited a country there of advanced civilization. Still thinking that all this was owing to the heat of a distempered fancy, I did not of course give it any credence, but proceeded to take steps for his removal to Sydney, and finally to England, where I learned, afterwards, that his friends placed him in a private lunatic establishment, of a high character for combining gentleness and skill.

Before we parted, he gave me a MS which he had written, he said, to satisfy me about the existence of Ooadeen, the Unknown Land, but which he did not expect anyone would rediscover but himself, and if he lived to regain his health, he would resume, he declared, his search for its position.

THE "MS"

For many years of my youth, I was an object of envy to my compeers. The best gifts of fortune had raised me to independence and consideration and, what I coveted far more, to influence. I lived in luxury and power, the advantages of wealth, and, I may add, of talent, gave me a mastery over the actions and minds of others, that had been from childhood the whole purpose of my aspirations. I cared not for love, or even esteem, so long as the former did not gratify my passions and the latter fired not my vanity. I thirsted for praise, and worked only to secure the admiration of others. To be looked at and wondered at, as a successful author, an eloquent speaker, and a shrewd politician, was the chief aim of my existence. I made my hospitality subservient to my self love; to be flattered at my table for the display of my conversational powers, my polished manners, my taste in dress, and the elegant consistency of my *ménage* was the intoxication I ravined for. Mere animal graftications I despised. For me, the wine cup had no attraction, my food consisted of the simplest viands, and from common sexual indulgence, I shrunk as from contamination. Woman was to me only another means of gratifying my pride; the vice of illicit amours I acknowledged when beauty, or rank, or talent, could be paraded as humbling itself to my genius. Thus whilst the sunshine of prosperity lasted, everything conduced to satisfy my craving after distinction, and I became intolerably selfish and headstrong, but I was not to run my career without experiencing that "pride cometh before a fall". In one hour I became the dupe of an artful *intriguante*, the victim of a roué, was ruined by the failure of a bank, was worsted by my bitterest political opponent, made a quarrel that shut me out of the circle of society, engaged in a duel that nearly cost me my life, and awoke to the sense of my miserable and degraded condition, chastised by shame, sickness, and poverty. Then I grew reckless of conduct, manners, and person; my fine sense of propriety in outward behaviour was lost, I was careless as to my associates, I abandoned my former literary pursuits, was no longer abstemious, but gave myself up to the deepest inebriation, and found even a pleasure in the lowest haunts of lust. Neither by night nor by day could I escape, however, from the sting of mortified and disappointed ambition. I resorted to drinking, gambling, and drugging to stimulate the jaded appetite, and afford relief to the wearing reflections that followed me like the relentless fly, in the pursuit of Io.

Naturally of a delicate constitution, I was soon taught that such a course of life must shortly bring me to my grave, but I continued in the same destructive habits until a fever seized and prostrated me. For months I was unconscious of existence, reason tottered on her seat, and the life blood ebbed to its lowest wave. Happily to me it was a period of mental obliviousness, so that when I recovered I almost regretted the feeling of helplessness that obliged others to attend to my wants, and took from me care and thought alike.

A year had gone, and I was flying from the old world and its reminiscences, to the untainted scenes of a new, I had resolved upon travel, and made my choice of the then scarcely settled group of the Australian Islands. It was in traversing the wilds of New Holland that I was first restored to tranquillity, if not to happiness. Its fine climate renewed my physical strength and its untrodden lands supplied me with an abundance of entrancing recreation and pursuit. Everything was fresh and new, the very geological construction of the continent was primitive and rare; the animal and vegetable kingdoms were classed into uncommon tribes and specimens, human physiology in the natives of soil was very curious, and even the mineralogical economy of the mountain ranges which I transversed in solitary enthusiasm, furnished me with resources of the most pleasing occupation. Far, far towards the wild and unknown interior, I tracked my lonely way, passing from tribe to tribe of the wandering aborigines, with a speed and safety that was insured to me by my perfect knowledge of their manners, customs, and principal dialect of intercommunication.

From my earliest acquaintance with the aborigines, in the districts nearest the sea coast, I had met with traditions concerning the existence of a superior race in the country, either at that or at some previous period. So shadowy was the rumour conveyed by the blacks who visited Sydney, that their report was assigned to their having fallen in with some runaway convicts; and in the direction of Port Phillip (the plains of which I had traversed before the arrival of Governor Collins with the first expedition) I attributed it to the visits of the early navigators on the coast. The further, however, that I penetrated inland, the more consistent became the traditional records of the tribes concerning a light coloured people who had inhabited the land before, and it was with a degree of thrilling surprise that I at length came upon indubitable traces of anterior civilization.

Buried in the recesses of a forest that looked as if never human eye had penetrated into its recesses — so awful was the quiet — so profound the stillness, I discovered the indications, as it were, of human possession. These consisted of caverns of various sizes, that had been shaped and enlarged with the materials and instruments of art, many of which were adorned with curious paintings and hieroglyphics. I also found one or two piles of stones or rather rocks, to which with little trouble I could give the finished outlines of pyramidical monuments.

Stimulated by this accident, I extended my researches on every side, and on mentioning the circumstances to Moorwattin, an intelligent native who had sometimes been the companion of my expeditions, he guided me still further towards the interior by several days' journey to the banks of a river, where he introduced me to a tribe that lived upon its banks, and who resided, I found, in a tract of country abounding with similar remains. Spurred by enthusiasm, my diligence in exploring was now almost ceaseless, and I traced that river for nearly three hundred miles towards its source, led onward by the repetition of these singular relics of a race that had died and left no sign. I found that its springs were seated in a lofty range of mountains, whose bare summits were caped with perennial snow; towards their bases, however, the grass and timber were plentiful, and they discharged as it were from almost every valley head a stream of water, the sources as I afterwards learned of many rivers. Starting impetuously from their mountain homes, they hurry foaming and sparkling forth in columns of great strength and size, but, their rapid descent soon bringing them to the level territory, they gradually become sluggish, and break into chains of lagoons or expand into marshes. The mountains themselves bend into almost a crescent, and send their waters downwards towards the south, until (somewhere about three hundred miles north of the river Murray) they open out into, and lodge on a space of country some thousand miles square, forming a body of water which in some seasons must present the appearance of a sea; this tract of land is of a very irregular shape, and unless avoided at once by the traveller, would mislead by the apparently dry passages, which are to be seen in some parts, and confuse by the tortuous windings of its outlines.

Induced by the natural phenomena of these noble mountains, one of whose vast peaks has a cone no less high and beautiful than the Peak of Teneriffe, I wandered for months through their frowning passes, climbing steep after steep and surmounting ridge after ridge, in a vain endeavour to obtain a sight of the land on the other side, and if possible to descend and pursue my way into the very heart of this mysterious country. God of Heaven! how my soul exulted when first I gazed down from the loftiest summit of that chain, on the object of my search. For weeks I had been toiling up the steep sides of that lofty cone, which rose like a monarch amongst the surrounding masses of rock, and lifted its grand head far apart, in the air, veiling in purple clouds its diadem of beam-darting crystals. Suddenly through a cleft that had been riven by the force of volcanic convulsions, I looked and beheld a country fair as the "land of promise" seen by the Hebrew Lawgiver from the top of Mount Pisgah. The sun from its meridian height was pouring down a volume of light which burnished with its searching spendour every hill and valley that was rolled out before me. By gradual declivities the mountains descended to the plain below, and these were crested by majestic cedars with threw out for a hundred feet their lateral branches on every side. Lower down the pendulous leaves of the thorn acacia, with its fragrant white blossoms, and mimosas of the most beautiful growth, rich in their perfumed golden flowers, relieved the sombreness of the darker forest. On the level campaign green and gay savannahs opened out in space, that looked as if steeped in the spirit of picturesque repose, while afar the sheen of some distant river or line of water glittered like molten silver on the horizon. My heart leaping with delight, I took myself down a spur of the mountain that led me, by easy stages, to the object of my journey. Here my food (which had consisted chiefly of the flesh of the animals which I shot, and the roots that I had learned from the natives to find) was diversified by the grape, nectarine, water melon, and green fig, which grew everywhere in profusion. Following the windings of a stream that led me down to the valley and plain below, I at length became sensible of the existence of civilization, for I caught glimpses at intervals of figures and animals that seemed to be tended in herds. On the third day of my journey I had reached the base of the mountain when, overcome by fatigue and noon day heat, I flung myself down by the side of some springs of water, pellucid and gurgling, that seemed to invite repose. Scarcely had I yielded to the slumber that was provoked by the soft winnowing air, the perfume of blossoming trees, the music of waters, and the grateful coolness of umbrageous shadows, when I was startled by the sound of voices; looking from behind the leafy covert which I had chosen, I observed a number of women holding their way towards me, but of course unconscious of my presence. Such a constellation of beauty I shall never see again; all were beaming with the sweetest marks of loveliness while their dress and manners were as strange as their softly yet merrily chiming tongues. They were all riding too, not horses but animals of various kinds: one was seated gracefully on the back of a white antelope, on whose neck she leaned with one arm while the other guided the reins, which were fastened to rings of silver pierced through the nostrils; another stood in an attitude exquisitely graceful and free, upon the back of a zebra, guided in the same way; another rode a creature like a small finely shaped brahminee bull, and others in postures of elegance and ease were carried by animals which were like delicately formed deer, of different species. The apparel of these radiant women was equally novel and attractive — their dresses were tunics of a glossy silk-like hue and fabric, sandals were on their feet, ornaments of precious stones glittered on wrist, arms, and bosom, while gorgeously hued feathers and flowers adorned their profusely flowing hair.

Arriving at the banks of the springs, they fearlessly turned loose the animals they had ridden, and, disrobing themselves with many a pleasant laugh and playful jest, flung themselves into the water that gleamed and sparkled round them. Only one retired from her companions, guided as it were by a tender and shrinking sensitiveness and sought apart the embrace of a cool and silent spring that was swept by the leaves of the very covert where I lay.

Oh! how shall I find words to describe the unveiled beauties of Yarranee, while the wind that played in her hair, the sun light and shadow that glanced upon every dimpled limb, seemed entranced by the odorous spirit of her charms. But, I who dwelt afterwards in her presence, and drank from her eyes and her lips the most fervid sensations of love, was then as overpowered by the sudden emotions caused by her appearance, as I am now unable to do justice to her loveliness. I had been in Ooadeen, the country of the Mahanacumans, about twelve months, when I was seated one day in the presence of the august Hululua, the Priest and Law Giver of the people, and father to the bewitching Yarranee. It was for the purpose of instructing me generally, with regard to all that I yearned to know respecting the origin and history of the Mahanacumans, that the venerable Seer had granted me the interview. During the time that had elapsed since my first reception amongst these strange people, I had diligently studied their language, that I might obtain at length the knowledge that I wished. With the aid of Yarranee, who became my Instructess, I had advanced sufficiently to be able, I hoped, to peruse the ancient records preserved by their rolls of hieroglyphic MSS. Meanwhile, Hululua had undertaken to satisfy in part my curiosity, and on the day I allude to, commenced a series of lectures, by which I learned that I shall linger on my narrative briefly to relate.

In the dark time of Eld, a gigantic and powerful race dwelt in central Earth, whose name it was to cluster together in one vast city, leaving the country to be cultivated by the bondmen, who were allowed to reside there on condition of their supplying the necessities of their masters in flesh, bread, fruit, wines, and succulent roots. In this city, the name of which was Naksheewan, the kings always dwelt in a palace whose most conspicuous portion was a tower of immense height, yet to the altitude of which every successive Monarch added a storey, until it soared as far into the heavens as the snow crowned peak of Tutuna, the mountain from which I first obtained my view of Ooadeen. This act was a solemn obligation imposed upon them through the authority of their Seers, by whom it was foretold that the dispersion of their race and the end of that dynasty of kings, would take place when it was found impossible to continue raising the wondrous structure upwards. In the reign of Ninivelus, the Fire of

Heaven smote the summit of the tower and cast down several of the storeys. The haughty king, however, refused to acknowledge the omen, and commenced rebuilding the damaged portions, thinking that it might be restored as before. But the Chief Priests, Havakana and Eber Eber, refused to dwell longer in Maksheewan, and, quitting the city with their families, relations, dependants, and allies, went down to the borders of the great sea Boideonasa and built a house to float on its waves. Into that they entered with a large stock of everything that could be required in a new country such as they had determined to seek, whether of animals to breed, or seeds and roots to raise. In this manner the floating house reached an inhabited land many days travel towards the rising sun, which they settled and called Hindooin. Having lived there many hundreds of years, a Priest named Boobooda (who was descended from the leaders of their forefathers) made another migration, and settled another country still further towards the rising sun, which was thereafter called Ken Chin. Thence, after the lapse of as many more hundred years, a third Priest, named Malaya, made a third mission to the southward, and, coming to a vast archipelago, caused them to be settled by the various families who accompanied him. The one that went the farthest towards the south was Mahana, who discovered and settled a great country. It was called Ooadeen, which means the Place of Perfect Rest, and after him the inhabitants were called Mahanacuman, or the Children of Mahana. By diligent attention to all that could be recollected, it does not appear that this last migration could have taken place further back from our era than about one thousand years.

It appears that Mahana was a person of deep wisdom and peculiar principles. Directing his followers to eschew all their former habits, he weaned them back to customs of primitive simplicity. They lived almost in the open air, or in buildings erected of the frailest materials, so that the movements of a pastoral life were easy to them. Caverns and mountain tops were their temples; of war they were ignorant, as they lived in harmony amongst themselves, and their isolation from the rest of the world was their safeguard from the attacks of others. Their government was Patriarchal, and their social ties and relations all of the simplest kind.

At first they spread their tribes over a large space of country, but were often frustrated in their views of settlement by the natural sterility of the land and the badness of the climate. Some parts that were afflicted by droughts were frequently depopulated, until at length the separate bodies, reuniting, congregated in that part of the country which is now solely occupied by their descendants. There the Mahanacumans found at length a soil and climate suited to their purposes, and there they have continued to reside probably for the term of the last five hundred years.

Such is the sum of the narrative given me by Hululua, regarding the history of Ooadeen — and in order to satisfy those few, to whom only it is my intention to reveal my knowledge of it, I will add here some information upon the appearance and size of the Unknown Land, of the customs of its inhabitants, and the natural history of the country. The tract of territory inhabited by them lies, as far as my calculation now enables me to judge, in the very heart of Australia, and the space (which measures about one hundred miles each way) is enclosed on one side — that to the south — by the lofty tier of mountains I have described, and to the north by impenetrable morasses and jungles. Within that space the soil teems with fertility, the climate, although tropical, is healthy and enlivening, the population is comparatively thin, nor does it increase, but at a very slow rate of progression. What may be the actual number of its inhabitants I cannot say, as on this and many other subjects I was kept in studious ignorance — the reason of this behaviour with regard to myself I will explain. Hululua, the Patriarch, when I first introduced myself to the people, ordered me to be treated with the utmost respect, and even distinction, but as he said there was a prophecy extant, that his race was destined to be extinguished by the avarice and oppression of a strange people, who, in the course of time, were to visit the continent in which lay the possession of Mahanacumans, he informed me from the first that my liberty would be circumscribed and that I must reconcile myself to detention for life in their kingdom. This I would readily have borne with, for nature and society alike conspired to render it the most delightful region under the sway of human civilization, but when he also announced to me that the restraint on my actions extended to prohibition from marriage with any woman of the Mahanacumans, my delight passed away from me, for I had seen, conversed, and lived, on terms of peculiar intimacy with Yarranee, and my whole existence was absorbed in the vows of love we had secretly interchanged.

The government of this people remains as established by their ancestor in the patriarchal form, their chief being at once their father, priest, and Law Giver – but the restraint of laws is hardly needed, for their simplicity of life keeps them virtuous, and the whole are regulated as one great family. They cultivate the ground for the production of corn, wine, and oil, vegetables, and fruits, grown almost without care, and their meat is supplied from the flocks of Alpaca, sheep, and herds of Brahminee cattle, or animals most nearly approaching to the natural properties and characters of those creatures.

They ride, as I intimated before, various kinds of animals, and their peculiar fashion of standing or reclining in various postures has all the artistical and wonderful grace displayed by the professed equestrian performers of England: amongst the animals thus subjected, but which is so rare as to be reserved for religious processions, is one that has the shape and limbs of a small fine and delicately bred horse, but being distinguished by a horn that shoots out from the centre of the forehead, is, I believe, the living type of a long lost Unicorn. Many are the curious specimens exhibited by the animal kingdom: the land is inhabited by lizards far exceeding the iguana in size, but perfectly harmless; the water (but only the vast marshes are spoken of, as forming the northern boundary of Ooadeen) by creatures more huge than the hippopotamus; and the air is peopled by animals that have the body and wings of a bat, with the beak of an adjutant bird, and these prey mostly on gigantic dragon flies that hover about the lakes and rivers. There are no serpents indigenous to the country, but there is one species which, it is said, was brought there by their ancestors and is domesticated for a peculiar purpose. It is of immense size and resplendent beauty, being covered with scales of a bright green and golden colour; it is not poisonous; and has the attribute singular to itself of travelling with its head erect instead of crawling its length in the dust, as was said to have been the case with all the serpent tribe before Satan entered into the body of one, to effect the ruin of the first pair. It is kept in the temples of the people, where it guards the sacred fire.

The religion of the Mahanacumans is the worship of one supreme being, to whom they sacrifice with fire; the holy element has for this offering been hourly perpetuated since their first arrival and settlement in Ooadeen. These temples are caves curiously adorned with paintings and hieroglyphs, and they have besides sacred monuments which assume two shapes, the one pyramidal and the other after the construction of the celebrated tower of Naksheewan.

Their dress consists of fabrics woven out of the fibres of various kinds of stones and trees and is worn in the style of the most elegant oriental drapery; their ornaments are flowers, feathers of birds, and the beautiful stones which abound in the mountains, set prettily in gold and silver; in person they are remarkably fine, the stature of both men and women generally exceeding our own, but in the males the skin is slightly tinged with a reddish hue, and in the females with that very soft yellow which is seen in some kind of ivory. From their abstemious habits and healthy pursuits, they are extremely long lived and are full of sprightliness of manner, affectionate feelings, and virtuous thoughts.

In brief, if the state of being which was enjoyed by our first parents in Eden has ever been attained by their mortal descendants, it is experienced by the inhabitants of the Unknown Land.

Yarranee, the beautiful, the tender Yarranee, was mine — my own. Unconsciously love stole upon her gentle soul, and she surrendered herself, mind, heart, and person, to its influence. I had imbibed the passion when first, unknown to her, I saw her standing graceful as a goddess by the wells of Kiambeth; she learned from me to love, at the same time that I learned from her the sweet language of Ooadeen, rendered as it was exquisitely musical by her silvery voice. Ah, those moments, those moments were too entrancing to retain their full and overflowing measure of bliss; yet, how could we pause amidst our delicious reveries to consider or anticipate the dark shadow of fate, that was destined to thrust its impenetrable veil between us. Let me pause here, to recall the picture of her whose every lineament is engraven on my soul. Cast was her figure in the form of Nature's fairest mould — with graceful ease she moved, as if her feet kept time to song — yet glowed there in her steps such pride as may become a maiden's spirit. Gentle her motion as boughs of palm or cypress, undulating to the wind that stirs and dips them to the water's face, over which they grow; in loose luxuriance flowed her glossy hair around the yielding parian of her neck, like the rich flowers of trailing hyacinth, or dark hued ivory, with its tendrils twining about some polished plinth. Her cheeks beamed with the colours that wears the grape or peach, when laughs the ripened fruit with summer's mellowest glow. From her blue eyes, deep, and dark with the intensity of their own light, flashed beams of joy and pleasure, "as through the skies when darkened by no storm, the vivid lightning throbs". Beneath her loosened gown did gently heave the billows of her lustrous breast, and her voice, whose music might have drawn from realms of light immortals down, such Orphean melody dwelt in every tone, did fall on the captivated sense, impregnate with the spirit of its sweet eloquence.

In the familiar intercourse which our daily tasks encouraged, we drew towards each other, hour by hour, until our beings were united too deeply, too intimately for recovery; and thus it was we loved and lived in love, every moment was devoted to her, every thought of mine, sleeping and waking, was Yarranee's, while her father engaged in his patriarchal duties furnished us with continual opportunity for strengthening our mutual preference.

The love I bore for Yarranee, however, was not the selfish feeling with which, amongst the associates of my early youth, I indulged in diversions for the gratification of my vanity, nor was it tarnished by a particle of the grosser impetus of passion.

My abstemious habits, my healthy pursuits, and the contentment of heart and mind which I now felt, had subdued those evil affections and left me free to woo Yarranee with all the fine fervour, the tender desire that should animate the spirit of one, whose soul acknowledges the influence of Nature's reality and romance, her poetry and religion.   The character of Yarranee, which had ever been governed by the original simplicity and purity of her birth and nurture, taught me

Not to love hotly, madly, furiously,
Such is the spirit of tigers; not to love
With tearful eyes, and strange fantastic passion,
That's full of contradiction, wills and wants,
Ungrounded hopes, and unprovoked fears,
Such is the love of boys and silly girls.
But to love like a man, as one who will
Into the delicate soul of her he loves,
Pour his whole being, thence receive his form,
There seek his second shape; for he who loves
Cannot remain the same, but must re-cast
His very nature.

It came at length, that paralyzing pang that taught me I was forbid to marry a Mahanacuman maiden. Choking with emotion, I flew at once to Yarranee and told her of the dread sentence of separation. Together we wondered, wept, and

then like creatures under the influence of madness, determined to brave everything rather than be parted. She consented to follow me if it were to the world's end, and I made
preparations to quit the blooming land of her birth, and seek
again the abhorred society of man, trusting that the sunshine
of her presence would illumine my future path through the
social haunts I detested.   But alas, our intercourse had
impressed a sign upon Yarranee, which, while it might have
added to our gladness, was rapidly approaching a point that
threatened to betray us to despair. Beneath her bosom and
around her heart, were strange pulsations that told her of
another life that was to spring from her life, a being of her
being, and soon the experienced eyes of matrons discovered
to her father that she was about to become a mother.

The strength and storm that arose in the old man's breast,
was fearful. It was not that he held himself aloof from such
an alliance for his daughter on any account, save, and except,
that I was a stranger with whose fortune was linked a destiny
that might cause the destruction of his race, and the omen
and the prophecy that placed a bar between me and the
Mahanacumans was too awful to yield, even to paternal ties.
Not the love he bore his daughter, not the strong feeling of
affection and esteem which he acknowledged to entertain
for me, could move the high and inscrutable resolve of the
Patriarch and the Seer.   I was doomed to die, tears of
anguish, passionate entreaties, profound submissions alike,
failed to soften or alter my sentence, and I was led forth to
an end equally horrible and new. There was a river — the
Madideroo — in Ooadeen, that after rising amidst the
mountain peaks of Tutuna, and pursuing a short course down
its sides and across the plain, suddenly sunk underground;
its raging and turbid waters penetrated the earth by means of
a cavern whose depths were too dreadful even to be looked
into — and down that gulf of terror and woe I was to be
lauched into eternity! I was led out amongst a throng of
men, whose eyes — moist with pity — looked upon me from
faces pale with suppressed horror and compassion. Placing
me on a raft which floated on the stream scarce a hundred
yards from the yawning cavern into which the roaring waters
of the river were engulphed, I was abandoned to its powers.
For days before my reason had been wrung to madness, and
at the moment of execution I was almost stupefied from contemplating the terrible judgment which tore me from
Yarranee and from life.

The raft left the bank; in a moment it was in motion, as

caught by the current of the Madideroo, swift, fierce, and ruthless, it was hurled amid the bewildering flash and stunning roar of its waves, down, down the midnight cavity of its exit from air and light and life. Memory carries me clearly to the moment I was plunged into the terrific deep, but beyond that all is the agonizing wrestling of horrible dreams.

When my consciousness returned, I was lying on a bank to which the raft had borne me, free from harm and in full possession of my faculties. I rose and looked around me, but found no object that I could recognize. I paced, as I recovered, the side of that mysterious stream, and discovered ere long the manner of my extraordinary deliverance. A short distance from where the raft had lodged, I saw that the river burst forth from the bowels of the earth through a rocky arch that formed for it a natural tunnel, and I was thus taught that I must have been carried along its subterranean course until it emerged again to upper air.

Since that day, still wedded in thought and memory to Ooadeen, and to Yarranee, I have never ceased my exertions to rediscover the Unknown Land, and those exertions shall and can only cease with life, or be thwarted by imbecility.

(End of MS)

When I first came to Port Phillip, I rode up to the high parts of the Plenty River, expecting that a run might be found there. One day when crossing Mount Disappointment, I again fell in with a piece of solitary cultivation in the most jungled parts of the range, and there I again found my friend the gold seeker, who this time, however, had narrowed the limits of his domicile to the trunk of a hollow tree. He had come overland in company with one of the earliest stock expeditions from Sydney to Port Phillip. In Melbourne — then a settlement of a few huts — he became acquainted with Buckley, the man who (having deserted from the establishment of Lieutenant Governor Collins, when in 1804 that officer first attempted to establish a colony here) had since lived with the aboriginal natives for upwards of thirty years, and had been restored to civilization on the ultimate formation of Melbourne under the adventurers from Van Diemen's Land in 1836.

Discovering something congenial, I suppose, in the habits of the gold seeker, Buckley departed from his usual reserve and taciturnity, and communicated to the other the existence of gold dust in a stream at Mount Disappointment. There the man had consequently gone, and there he was diligently engaged in washing the sand for gold dust when I so curiously met him for the second time. After much conversation, he told me that he had projected a visit to the Unknown Land of Ooadeen, which had been discovered by Mr Grantley (for that indeed was the name of the erstwhile Wild Man). Upon my asking him how he got his information from that gentleman, he admitted — but with great reluctance — that Grantley was in the Province, having escaped from the custody of his friends in England, and with incurable lunacy was resolved on setting forth again to seek his shadowy paradise. At some distant date, perhaps, the bones of these two monomaniacs may be found, bleaching in the wilderness, by the inland navigator who succeeds in penetrating through the interior.

I think meantime I can furnish a clue to this mystery. I learned in a letter from his sister (who wrote to thank me for my attention to Grantley) that previous to his coming to Australia he had visited Mexico, and penetrated into many of those parts where it is known by the accounts of other travellers that the remains of cities are to be found, the former possessions of a civilized but extinct race. At that period his mind was evidently going, and it was the perpetual object of his wanderings to find, as in his poetical language he described it, a "Land of Perfect Rest". He flattered himself that amongst some of the tribes of the aboriginal Mexicans he should meet a people advanced in civilization, yet free from the contaminations of society, and his whole account of Ooadeen is probably to be traced to some adventures in that quarter, although in his craziness he had confounded its locality with that of Australia. Such, at least, is the only rational solution I am able to give of Grantley's Problem of Ooadeen.

Human Repetends

Marcus Clarke

(1872)

"Come!" cried Marston, "the story of your embodied ghost! Speak, thou gloomy Pythagorean!"

"Most men," began Pontifex, "however roughly the world has used them, can recall a period in their lives when they were absolutely happy, when each night closed with the recollection of new pleasures tasted, when the progress of each day was cheered by the experience of unlooked-for novelties, and when the awakening to another dawn was a pure physical delight unmarred by those cankering anxieties for the fortune of the hour which are the burden of the poor, the ambitious, and the intriguing. To most men, also, this golden time comes, when the cares of a mother, or the coquettish attention of sisters, aid to shield the young and eager soul from the blighting influences of wordly debaucheries. Thrice fortunate is he among us who can look back on a youth spent on the innocent enjoyments of the country, or who possesses a mind moulded in its adolescence by the cool fingers of well-mannered and pious women.

"My first initiation into the business of living took place under different auspices. The only son of a rich widower, who lived but for the gratification of a literary and political ambition, I was thrown when still a boy into the society of men thrice my age, and was tolerated as a clever impertinent in all those witty and wicked circles in which virtuous women are conspicuous by their absence. My father lived indifferently in Paris or London, and, patronized by the dandies, artists, and scribblers who form, in both cities, the male world of fashionable idleness, I was suffered at sixteen to ape the vices of sixty. Indeed, so long as I was reported to be moving only in that set to which my father chose to ally himself, he never cared to inquire how I spent the extravagant allowance which his indifference rather than his generosity permitted me to waste. You can guess the result of such a training. The admirer of men whose success in love and play were the theme of common talk — for six months; the worshipper of artists whose genius was to revolutionize Europe — only they died of late hours and tobacco; the pet of women whose daring beauty made their names famous — for three years; I discovered at twenty years of age that the pleasurable path I had trodden so gaily led to a hospital or a debtors' prison, that love meant money, friendship an endorsement on a bill, and that the rigid exercise of a profound and calculating selfishness alone rendered tolerable a life at once so deceitful and so barren. In this view of the world I was supported by those middle-aged Mephistopheles (survivors of the storms which had wrecked so many argosies), those cynical well-bred worshippers of Self who realize in the nineteenth century that notion of the devil which was invented by the early Christians. With these good gentlemen I lived, emulating their cynicism, rivalling their sarcasms, and neutralizing the superiority which their experience gave them, by the exercise of that potentiality for present enjoyment which is the privilege of youth.

"In this society I was progressing rapidly to destruction, when an event occurred which rudely saved me. My father died suddenly, in London, and, to the astonishment of the world, left — nothing. His expenditure had been large, but as he left no debts, his income must have been proportioned to his expenses. The source of this income, however, was impossible to discover. An examination of his banker's book showed only that large sums (always in notes or gold) had been lodged and drawn upon, but no record of speculations or of investments could be found among his papers. My relatives stared, shook their heads, and insulted me with their pity. The sale of furniture, books, plate, and horses, brought enough money to pay the necessary expenses of the funeral, and leave me heir to some £800. My friends of the smoking-room and the supper-table philosophized on Monday, cashed my IOU's on Tuesday, were satirical on Wednesday, and 'cut' me on Thursday. My relatives said that 'something must be done', and invited me to stay at their houses until that vague substantiality should be realized. One suggested a clerkship in the War-office, another a stool in a banking-house, while a third generously offered to use his interest at head-quarters to procure for me a commission in a marching regiment. Their offers were generously made, but *then*, stunned by the rude shock of sudden poverty, and with a mind debauched by a life of extravagance and selfishness, I was incapable of manly action. To all proposals I replied with sullen disdain, and desirous only of avoiding those who had known me in my prosperity, I avowed my resolution of claiming my inheritance and vanishing to Australia.

"A young man with money and a taste for *bric-a-brac* soon gathers about him a strange collection of curiosities, and at the sale of my possessions I was astonished to find how largely I had been preyed upon by ews, print-sellers, picture-dealers, and vendors of spurious antiques. The 'valuable paintings', the curious 'relics', the inlaid and be-jewelled 'arms', and the rare 'impressions' of old prints were purchased by the 'trade' for a third of the price which I had paid for them, doubtless to be resold to another man of taste as artless and as extravagant as myself. Of the numberless articles which had littered my bachelor-house, I retained but some three or four of the most portable, which might serve as remembrances of a luxury I never hoped to again enjoy. Among these was a copperplate engraving, said to be one of the first specimens of that art. The print bore the noted name of Tommaso Finiguerra, and was dated 1469. It was apparently a copy of a 'half-length' portrait of a woman dressed in the fashion of that age, and holding in her hand a spray of rue. The name of this *grande dame* was not given — indeed, as I need hardly say, the absence of aught but the engraver's signature constituted the chief value of the print.

"I felt constrained to preserve this purchase for many reasons. Not only had I, one idle day, 'discovered' it, as I imagined, on the back shelves of a print-shop, and regarded it as the prize of my artistic taste; not only had it occupied the place of honour over my mantel-shelf, and been a silent witness of many scenes which yet lingered fondly in my memory; not only had I seemed to hold communion with it when, on some lonely evening, I was left to reflect upon the barrenness of my existence, but the face possessed a charm of expression which, acknowledged by all, had become for me a positive fascination. The original must have been a woman of strange thoughts and (I fancied) of a strange history. The *pose* of the head was defiant, the compressed lips wore a shadowy smile of disdain, and the eyes — large, full, and shaded by heavy lashes — seemed to look through you and away from you with a glance that was at once proud and timid, as though they contemplated and dared some vague terror, of whose superior power they were conscious. We have all, I presume, seen portraits which by accident or design, bear upon them a startling expression, rarely seen upon the face of the original, but which is felt to be a more truthful interpreter of character than is the enforced composure which self-control has rendered habitual. So with the portrait of which I speak. The unknown woman − or girl, for she did not seem to be more than three-and-twenty − revealed in the wonderful glance with which she had so long looked down upon me, a story of pride, of love, of shame, perhaps of sin. One could imagine that in another instant the horror would fade from those lovely eyes, the smile return to that disdainful lip, and the delicate bosom, which now swelled with that terror which catches the breath and quickens the pulse, would sink into its wonted peacefulness, to rise and fall with accustomed equanimity beneath its concealing laces. But that instant never came. The work of the artist was unchangeable, and the soul which looked out of the windows of that lovely body still shuddered with a foreknowledge of the horror which it had expected four hundred years ago.

"I tried in vain to discover the name and history of this strange portrait. The artists or men of taste to whom I applied had neither seen another copy of the print, nor heard of the original painting. It seemed that the fascinating face had belonged to some nameless one, who had carried with her to the grave the knowledge of whatever mystery had burdened her life on earth. At least, hopeless of discovering the truth, I amused myself by speculating on what might, perchance, have been the history of this unknown beauty. I compared her features with the descriptions left to us of women famous for their sorrows. I invented a thousand wild tales which might account for the look of doom upon her fair face, and at last my excited imagination half induced me to believe that the mysterious print was a forged antique, and represented, in truth, some living woman to whom I had often spoken, and with whom my fortues were indissolubly connected.

"A wickeder lie was never uttered than that favourite statement of colonial politicans − more ignorant or more impudent than others of their class − that in Australia no man need starve who is willing to work. I have been willing to work, and I have absolutely starved for days

together. The humiliation through which I was passed must,
I fancy, be familiar to many. During the first six months
of my arrival I was a honorary member of the Melbourne
Club, the guest of those officials to whom I brought letters
of introduction, the temporary lion of South Yarra tea
parties, and the butt of the local *Punch* on account of the
modish cut of my pantaloons. I met men who "knew my
people", and was surprised to find that the mention of a
titled friend secured for me considerable attention among
the leaders of such secondhand fashion as is boasted by the
colony. In this genial atmosphere I recovered my independence. Indeed, had my social derelictions been worse than
those incurred by poverty, I was assured that society could
find it in its colonial heart to forgive them all. I was
Hugh Pontifex, who had supped with the Marquis of Carabas,
and brought letters of introduction from Lord Crabs. Had
Judas Iscariot arrived armed with such credentials South
Yarra would have auburnized his red hair, and had him to
dinner. To my surprise, instead of being cast among new
faces, and compelled to win for myself an independent
reputation, I found that I was among old friends whom I had
long thought dead or in jail. To walk down Collins-street
was like pulling up the Styx. On either side I saw men who
had vanished from the Upper World sooner than I. Tomkins
was there to explain that queer story of the concealed ace.
Jenkins talked to me for an hour concerning the Derby
which ruined him. Hopkins had another wife in addition to
the one whom he left at Florence, while Wilkins assured me
on his honour that he had married the lady with whom he
had eloped, and introduced me to her during a dinner-party
at a trading magnate's. The game was made in the same old
fashion, only the stakes were not so high. The porcelain was
of the same pattern, only a little cracked.

"For six months life was vastly pleasant. Then my term
of honorary membership finally expired, and I left the Club
to live at Scott's. By and by my money ran short. I drew a
bill on England, and the letter which informed me of its pay-
ment contained a stern command to draw no more. I went
on to visit the 'station' of an acquaintance, and on returning
to town found that my hotel bill was presented weekly. I
retired into cheaper lodgings, and became affiliated to a less
aristocratic club. Forced to associate with men of another
'set', I felt that my first friends remembered to forget me.
My lampooned trowsers began to wear out, and I wondered
how I could have been once so reckless in the purchase of

boots. I applied to Wilkins for a loan, then to Tomkins and
to Hopkins. I found that I could not repay them and so
avoided those streets where they were to be met. I discarded
gloves, and smoked a short pipe publicly at noonday. I
removed to a public-house, and talking with my creditor-
land-lord at night, not unfrequently drank much brandy. I
discovered that it is possible to be drunk before dinner. I
applied for a clerkship, a messengership, a 'billet' in the
Civil Service; I went on the stage as a 'super', I went up the
country as a schoolmaster, I scribbled for the newspapers,
I wrote verses for the Full and Plenty eating-house. I
starved in 'genteel' poverty until fortune luckily put me in
the way of prosperity by suggesting Coachdriving and
Billiard-marking. Thanks to an education at a public
school, a licensed youth, a taste for pleasure, and the society
of the 'best men about London', I found myself at three-
and-twenty master of two professions, driving and billiard-
playing. You will understand now that my digression
concerning pictures was necessary to convince you that all
this time I never sold the mysterious print.

"One Sunday evening, towards the end of August, when
the windy winter had not yet begun to melt into sudden and
dusty spring, I was walking up Bourke-street. You, Falx,
who have made a study of Melbourne city, know what a
curious appearance the town presents on Sunday evening.
The deserted road, barren of all vehicles save a passing cab,
serves as a promenade for hundreds of servant-maids, shop-
-boys, and idlers, while the pavement is crowded with young
men and women of the lower middle class, who under
pretence of 'going to church', or of 'smoking a cigar',
contrive to indulge their mutual propensities for social
enjoyment. Those sewing-girls, who, at 6 o'clock in the
evening, are to be nightly seen debouching from Flinders-lane
or Little Collins-street, frequent these Sunday evening
promenades, and, in all the pride of clean petticoats and kid
gloves, form fitting companions for the holiday-making
barbers, or soft-goods clerks, who – daring rakes! – seek a
weekly intrigue at the Peacock, on the unsavoury strength of
a 'Sunday' cigar. Examining these groups as I walked, I found
myself abreast of Nissen's Cafe, impeding the egress of a
lady. I turned with an apology, but the words melted on my
lips, when, beneath the black bonnet of the stranger, *I found
the counterpart of the unknown print.*

"For an instant surprise rendered me incapable of action,
and then, with beating heart and bewildered brain, I followed

the fleeting figure. She went down Bourke-street, and turned to the left into Swanston-street. When she reached the corner where the Town-hall now stands, a man suddenly crossed the moon-lit street, and joined her. This man was wrapped in one of those Inverness cloaks which the slowly-travelling fashion of the day had then made imperative to the well-being of Melbourne dandies. A slouch hat of the operatic brigand type shaded his face, but in the brief glance that I caught of him I fancied that I recognized those heavy brows, that blunt nose, and that thin and treacherous mouth. The two met, evidently by appointment, and went onwards together. It was useless to follow. I turned and went home.

"I passed the next day in a condition of mind which it is impossible to describe. So strange a coincidence as this had surely never happened to man before. A woman has her portrait engraved the year 1469; I purchase the engraving, try in vain to discover the name of the original, and meet her face to face in the prosaic Melbourne of 1863. I longed for the night to come that I might wander through the streets in search of her. I felt a terrible yearning tug at my heart strings. I burned to meet her wild sad eyes again. I shuddered when I thought that in my wildest dreams I had never sunk that pictured face so deep beneath the social waters as this incarnation of it seemed to have been plunged. For two nights I roamed the streets in vain. On the morning of the third day a paragraph in the *Herald* explained why my search had been fruitless. The body of a woman had been 'found in the Yarra'. Society — and especially unmarried society — has, as a matter of course, its average of female suicides, and as a rule respectable folks don't hear much about them. The case of this unfortunate girl, however, was different. She was presumed to have been murdered, and the police made investigations. The case was sufficiently celebrated in the annals of Melbourne crime to excuse a re-petition of details. Suffice it to say, that against the many persons who were presumed to have been inculpated in the destruction of the poor girl no proof was forthcoming. The journals aired Edgar Poe and the Mystery of Marie Roget for a day or so, but no one was sent for trial, and an open verdict left the detectives at liberty to exercise their ingenuity without prejudice. There was some rumor of a foreigner who was implicated in the deed, but as the friends of the poor outcast knew of no such person, and as my evidence as to seeing a man of such appearance join the deceased was in reality of little value (for I was compelled to admit that I had never seen the woman before in my life, and that my glimpse of her companion was but momentary), the supposition was treated with contempt and the 'case' dismissed from the memory of the public.

"It did not fade so easily from my mind. To speak truth, indeed, I was haunted by the hideous thing which I had been sent to 'view' upon the coarse table of that wretched dead-house which then disgraced our city. The obscene and cruel fate of the unhappy woman whose portrait had so long looked down upon me filled me not only with horror, but with apprehension. It seemed to me as if I myself was implicated in her fate, and bound to avenge her murder. The fact of my having speculated so long upon her fortunes, and then having found her but to lose her before a word could pass between us, appeared to give me the right to seek to know more of her. The proud queen of many a fantastic dream-revel; the sad Chatelaine of many an air-built castle; had this portrait leapt to life beneath my glances as bounded to earth the nymph from beneath the chisel of Pygmalion? Had the lost one who passed me like a ghost in the gloaming come out of the grave in which they had placed her four hundred years ago? What meant this resurrection of buried beauty? What was the mysterious portent of this living presentment of a dead and forgotten sin? I saw the poor creature buried. I wept — no unmanly tears, I trust — over her nameless grave. And then I learned her history. 'Twas no romance, unless the old story of a broken home and the cold comfort of the stony-hearted streets may be called romantic. She was presumed to have been well-born — she had been a wife, her husband had left her, she was beautiful and poor — for the rest ask Mother Carey, who deals in chickens. She can tell you entertaining histories of fifty such.

"At the inquest I met Warrend — you know old Tom, Marston? — and he sought me out, and took me home with him. We had been schoolfellows; but though my taste for prints and pictures had now and then brought me into his company, I had seen but little of him. He was — as we know him — kindly, tender, and generous. He offered me his help. He was in good practice, and could afford to give me shelter beneath his bachelor roof. He wrote for *The Argus*, knew the editor, would try to procure work for me. That meeting, Noah, laid the foundation of such independence as I now claim. Shaken in health by my recent privations, and troubled in mind by the horrible and inexplicable mystery upon which I seemed to have stumbled, I was for some weeks seriously ill. Warrend saw that something preyed upon my spirits, and pressed me to unbosom myself. I told him the story, and produced the print.

"I must beg your grace for what I am about to tell you. You may regard the story as unworthy of credit, or sneer at it as the result of a 'coincidence'. It is simply true, for all that.

"Warrend became grave.

" 'I have a copy of that print,' said he, in a tone altogether without the pride usual in a collector. 'I think a unique copy. It is the portrait of a woman round whose life a mystery spun itself. See here.'

"He opened the portfolio, and took out the engraving. It was an exact copy of mine, but was a proof after letters, and bore in the quaint characters of the time the name, *JEHANNE LA GAILLARDE*.

"I fell back upon the sofa as if I had been struck in the face. The name of the poor girl whom I had buried was Jenny Gay! 'Warrend,' said I, 'there is something unholy about this. I met a week ago the living original of that portrait, and now you, a man whose name re-echoes that of the Italian artist who engraved it, tell me that you know the mystery of her life. What is it, then? − for before you speak I know I figure in the scene!'

"Warrend, or Finiguerra, took from the book-shelf a little volume published by Vander Berghen, of Brussels, in 1775, and handed it to me. It was called *Le Coeur de Jehanne la Gaillarde*, and appeared to be a collection of letters. In the advertisement was a brief memoir of the woman whose face had so long puzzled me. I glanced at it, and turned sick with nameless terror. Jehanne la Gaillarde was a woman whose romantic amours had electrified the Paris of Louis XI. She was murdered by being thrown into the Seine. 'All attempts to discover the murderer were vain, but at length a young man named Hugue Grandprête, who, though he had never seen the celebrated beauty, had fallen in love with her picture, persuaded himself that the murderer was none other than the Sieur de la Forêt (the husband of the beautiful Jehanne), who, a man of an ill-life, had been compelled to fly from Paris. Grandprête communicated his suspicions to none but his intimate friends, followed De la Forêt to Padua, and killed him.' As I read this romance of a man who bore a name which reflected my own, I shuddered, for a sudden thrill of recollection lighted up the darkness of the drama as a flash of lightning illumes the darkness of a thunder cloud.

The face of the man in the cloak was recalled to me as that of a certain gambling lieutenant who was cashiered by a court-martial so notorious that the sun of India and the snows of the Crimea have scarce burned out or covered the memory of his regiment's nickname.

"As Jehanne la Gaillarde was the double of Jenny Gay; as Hugue Grandprête lived again in Hugh Pontifex; as the Italian artist was recalled to life in the person of the man at my side, so Bernhard de la Forêt worked once more his wicked will on earth in the person of the cashiered gambler, Bernard Forrester. If this was a 'coincidence', it was terribly complete."

"But 'twas a mere coincidence, after all," said Marston, gently. "You do not think that men's souls return to earth and enact again the crimes which stained them?"

"I know not. But there are in decimal arithmetic repeated 'coincidences' called *repetends*. Continue the generation of numbers through all time, you have these repetends forever recurring. Can you explain this mystery of numbers? No. Neither can I explain the mystery of my life. Good night. I have wearied you."

"Stay," cried I, rashly, "the parallel is not yet complete. You have not met Forrester!"

"No," cried Pontifex, his large eyes blazing with no healthy fire, "I have prayed that I might not meet him. I live here in Melbourne at the scene of his crime, because it seems the least likely place to again behold him. If, by accident, in the streets I catch sight of one who resembles him I hurry away. But I *shall* meet him one day, and then my doom will be upon me, and I shall kill him as I killed him in Padua four hundred years ago!"

1889-1898

Though published later than all but the last item in this section, Barcroft Boake's poem "A Vision Out West" (1897) provides a useful introduction to the earnest sincerity of most of the Australian science fiction of this period. Joseph Fraser's *Melbourne and Mars: My Mysterious Life on Two Planets* (1889) virtually abandons plot in order to allow a methodical survey of the utopian social conditions on planet Mars. Robert Potter's *The Germ Growers* (1892) builds on Fraser's achievement by expressing his ideas through dramatic plotting, and by offering a more satisfactory "scientific" justification for the marvels he presents. Both Fraser and Potter are liberal in outlook, showing a reverence for human life, but the excerpt from G. Read Murphy's *Beyond the Ice* (1894) demonstrates the ruthless self-righteousness of armed utopians. Finally, in G. Firth Scott's *The Last Lemurian* (1898), melodramatic plotting is brought to the forefront and the reader is offered sensationalism in place of vision.

The material from Joseph Fraser's *Melbourne and Mars* (Melbourne: Pater and Knapton, 1889) consists of three excerpts drawn from: Chapter IV – "Strange Dreams" (pp. 18-19), Chapter V – "School Days" (pp. 23-25), and Chapter VI – "Gaston's Class" (pp. 32-33). From Robert Potter's *The Germ Growers* (Melbourne: Melville, Mullens, 1892) I have excerpted Chapter I – "Disappearances" and Chapter II – "The Red Sickness" (pp. 6-25); from G. Read Murphy's *Beyond the Ice* (London: Sampson Low, Marston and Co., [1894]) I have taken Chapter XXIV – "War" (pp. 222-30); and the material from G. Firth Scott's *The Last Lemurian* (London: James Bowden, 1898) comprises Chapter V –

"A Pool of Mystery" and the opening pages of Chapter VI — "The Bunyip Dies" (pp. 38-60). Barcroft Boake's "A Vision Out West" was published in *Where the Dead Men Lie and Other Verses* (*The Bulletin*, Sydney, 1897).

A Vision Out West

Barcroft Boake

(1897)

Far-reaching downs, a solid sea sunk everlastingly to rest,
And yet whose billows seem to be for ever heaving toward
    the west:
The tiny field-mice make their nests, the summer insects
    buzz and hum
Among the hollows and the crests of this wide ocean stricken
    dumb,
Whose rollers move for ever on, though sullenly, with fettered
    wills,
To break in voiceless wrath upon the crumbled bases of far
    hills,
Where rugged outposts meet the shock, stand fast, and hurl
    them back again,
An avalanche of earth and rock, in tumbled fragments on the
    plain;
But, never heeding the rebuff, to right and left they kiss the
    feet
Of hanging cliff and bouldered bluff till on the farther side
    they meet,
And once again resume their march to where the afternoon
    sun dips
Toward the west, and Heaven's arch salutes the Earth with
    ruddy lips.

Such is the scene that greets the eye: wide sweep of plain to
    left and right:
In front low hills that seem to lie wrapped in a veil of yellow
    light –
Low peaks that through the summer haze frown from their
    fancied altitude,

As some small potentate might gaze upon a ragged multitude.
Thus does the battlemented pile of high-built crags, all
weather-scarred,
Where grass land stretches mile on mile, keep scornful solitary
guard;
Where the sweet spell is not yet broke, while from her wind-
swept, sun-kissed dream
Man's cruel touch has not yet woke this Land where silence
reigns supreme:
Not the grim silence of a cave, some vaulted stalactited room,
Where feeble candle-shadows wave fantastically through the
gloom —
But restful silence, calm repose: the spirit of these sky-bound
plains
Tempers the restless blood that flows too fiery through the
swelling veins;
Breathes a faint message in the ear, bringing the weary
traveller peace;
Whispers, "Take heart and never fear, for soon the pilgrimage
will cease!

Beat not thy wings against the cage! Seek not to burst the
padlocked door
That leads to depths thou canst not gauge! Life is all thine:
why seek for more?
Read in the slow sun's drooping disc an answer to the
thoughts that vex:
Ponder it well, and never risk the substance for its dim
reflex."

Such is the silent sermon told to those who care to read this
page
Where once a mighty ocean rolled in some dim, long-for-
gotten age.
Here, where the Mitchell grass waves green, the never-weary
ebb and flow
Of glassy surges once was seen a thousand thousand years
ago:
To such a sum those dead years mount that Time has grown
too weary for
The keeping of an endless count, and long ago forgot their
score.

But now — when, hustled by the wind, fast-flying, fleecy
cloud-banks drift

Across the sky where, silver-skinned, the pale moon shines
    whene'er they lift,
And throws broad patches in strange shapes of light and
    shade, that seem to meet
In dusky coastline where sharp capes jut far into a winding-
    sheet
Of ghostly, glimmering, silver rays that struggle 'neath an
    inky edge
Of driving cloud, and fill deep bays rent in the shadow's
    ragged edge —
Sprung from the gloomy depths of Time, faint shapes patrol
    the spectral sea,
Primeval phantom-forms that climb the lifeless billows
    silently,
Trailing along their slimy length in thirst for one another's
    blood,
Writhing in ponderous trials of strength, as once they did
    before the flood.

They sink, as, driven from the North by straining oar and
    favouring gale,
A misty barge repels the froth which hides her with a spark-
    ling veil:
High-curled the sharpened beak doth stand, slicing the waters
    in the lead;
The low hull follows, thickly manned by dim, dead men of
    Asian breed:
Swift is her passage, short the view the wan moon's restless
    rays reveal
Of dusky, fierce-eyed warrior crew, of fluttering cloth and
    flashing steel;
Of forms that mouldered ages past, ere from recesses of the
    sea,
With earthquake throes this land was cast in Nature's writh-
    ing agony.
As the warm airs of Spring-time chase reluctant snows from
    off the range,
And plant fresh verdure in their place, so the dim-visioned
    shadows change;
And glimpses of what yet shall be bid the past fly beyond all
    ken,
While rising from futurity appear vast colonies of men
Who from the sea-coast hills have brought far-quarried spoils
    to build proud homes

Of high-piled palaces, all wrought in sloping roofs and arching
    domes,
Smooth-pillared hall, or cool arcade, and slenderest sky-
    piercing spire,
Where the late-sinking moon has laid her tender tints of
    mellow fire,
And golden paves the spacious ways where, o'er the smoothen
    granite flags,
The lightning-driven car conveys its freight with force that
    never lags.

A goodly city! where no stain of engine-smoke or factory
    grime
Blemishes walls that will retain their pristine pureness for all
    time:
Lying as one might take a gem and set it in some strange
    device
Of precious metal, and might hem it round with stones of
    lesser price –
So from encircling fields doth spring this city where, in
    emerald sheen,
Man hath taught Nature how to bring a mantle of perennial
    green –
Hewing canals whose banks are fringed by willows bending
    deeply down
To waters flowing yellow-tinged beneath the moon toward
    the town –
Filling from mighty reservoirs, sunk in the hollows of the
    plain,
That flood the fields without a pause though Summer should
    withhold her rain.
Labour is but an empty name to those who dwell within this
    land,
For they have boldly learnt to tame the lightning's flash with
    iron hand:
That Force, the dartings from whose eyes not even gods
    might brave and live,
The blasting essence of the skies, proud Jupiter's preroga-
    tive ——
His flashing pinions closely clipt, pent in a cunning-fashioned
    cage,
Of all his flaming glory stript – these men direct his tempered
    rage:
A bondman, at their idlest breath with silent energy he
    speeds,

From dawn of life to hour of death, to execute their slightest
    needs.

Slow to her couch the moon doth creep, but, going, melts in
    sparkling tears
Of dew, because we may not keep this vision of the future
    years:
Swiftly, before the sunrise gleam, I watch it melting in the
    morn –
The snowy city of my dream, the home of nations yet un-
    born!

Utopian Dreams

from

Melbourne and Mars: My Mysterious Life on Two Planets

Joseph Fraser

(1889)

Life has not been easy for Adam Jacobs. Born in England, but forced to come to Australia when his father was trans- ported to Botany Bay for a minor political crime, Jacobs has been one of the many victims of the Victorian land boom of 1842. In an attempt to recover from his bankruptcy, Jacobs has spent time digging for gold at Bathurst, then – when ill- ness and a lack of luck have intervened – he returns south to Ballarat and plans to set up business selling supplies to the diggers.

His life has not been easy, but it has at least been normal. Now his diary-records show that this, too, is about to change, for in a series of graphic dreams Jacobs embarks upon a second life on the planet Mars. He experiences the struggle and trauma of birth, and commences to live through the early life of an infant on Mars. And yet, paradoxically, his established existence is preserved: he is simultaneously a middle-aged Earthling and an infant Martian.

(See also Introduction, pp. xvii–xviii).

Writing in the year 1863, his forty-fifth year, Jacobs tells of a few months of illness and of a low nervous condition into which he drops as a result of that illness. He never entirely recovers. He is often absent-minded, and he needs much more sleep than he used to require. His hard life has evidently told upon him, and the grand climacteric had come early.

He writes: – "I had a strange dream last night, a series of strange sensations mostly painful. and terribly real. I was struggling in the dark towards some end, and great forces were pushing behind and around me, and I, ever trying to escape, worked in the same direction, until at last I emerged into a blaze of light and a cold air that made me pant and gasp for a long time until I got relief, and cried out loudly for help. No sooner had I called than strong and gentle hands grasped me, and using soothing appliances made me comfortable, and then in my dream I went to sleep".

This experience is never repeated, but for several months he dreams that he is a little child, and all the time his surroundings are the same. He is frequently listening to sounds that he only understands in part and to music which he tries to imitate. No sooner is he asleep than he is on the knees of a gentle giantess, whom he learns to call mother. Sometimes he appears to pass hours lying on soft, white substances, and playing with any little object that he can grasp. A few months after the first of his strange dreams we find the record of his idea.

"I am at length forced to the conclusion that I have been born somewhere else, and am living the life of a happy, healthy baby in a most comfortable and cheerful home. Everything is built to that scale. The people about me are giants in relation to me because of my own littleness. I know several people, and am talked to and played with by first one then another. I am never tossed about, no one ever frightens me. I am learning to talk, and begin to understand much of what is said to me. I can get about in a tumbling sort of way, and might walk if I did not get tripped up by so many things. There is a bright warm fire, but I can never reach it. I am even puzzled to know where I am. There are certainly many things about me that would not be about me if I were a baby in Melbourne, or in any country that I know. Were I to tell anyone that I am at once a man of middle age and a baby in the arms, I should be regarded as qualified for a lunatic asylum. Am I in what is called dotage? Do old people who become childish do so because they are children elsewhere?"

The diaries now contain scarcely anything but a record of what he no longer regards as a dream. He says little of business, and not much of domestic life. He only works a few hours daily, and is frequently absent-minded. He attends spiritualistic meetings, and reads the literature of people who try to pierce the clouds surrounding birth, life and death. He analyses his memories and feelings, and comes to the conclusion that he is living a dual life, but is only half conscious of its duality, inasmuch as he can remember here what occurs in the new life, but cannot in the new life remember anything that happens in the old one.

* * *

Evidently our diarist has got into some Utopia. Reformers have tried to alter our written language and to make education easier for children, but in no part of the world have these results been so fully accomplished as in this land. The children are not quite angels even here, for in Hildreth's class punishment has to be inflicted. He writes:— "One day, when I had learned to make several kinds of buildings out of my box of various-shaped blocks, I took a fancy to erect a larger building, and for this purpose I took several of my neighbour's blocks when his attention was turned away. Hildreth was not long in seeing my trick and coming to the rescue. I knew I had done wrong, and felt very guilty, but cannot recollect being afraid. So far I had never wittingly done wrong, and had never seen anyone suffer punishment. I began to put back the blocks I had borrowed. When I took them I had no intention of keeping them, so that my crime was borrowing without leave, not actual theft.

"Hildreth did not ask me if I had taken any blocks; she simply told me to put those I had taken into a certain separate heap. This done, she called the whole class and pointed out what I had done. I felt very much ashamed, and began to cry, so did Frank, my victim, and several others.

"The class-mother — for that was what we called her — then asked us to tell her the kind of fault I was guilty of. My peers were not accustomed to crimes, and could come to no definite conclusion. Hildreth helped them to come to the conclusion that I had been guilty of selfishness, and that I had acted in a greedy manner by taking the blocks without asking for them. She did not call my action a crime; that in itself would have been too great a punishment. I was already more an object of pity than of anger.

"My fault had to be punished, and the class had to devise my punishment. Not one suggested the infliction of any kind of physical pain. Indeed, I had never heard of pain at this time as inflicted by one person upon another. One said 'take his blocks from him'. Another, a sharp-eyed little girl, the least in the class, said 'No; let us give him plenty of blocks; he can have all mine'. 'And mine', 'and mine', ran round the class. Hildreth consented, and in another minute I had more than twenty boxes of blocks. The class work went on another hour, and I felt very miserable. My sudden accession of wealth was a most painful experience. I did not want to play with blocks, my architectural ambitions were entirely scattered. For the first time my recess would not hold my possessions. I was the richest boy in the class, and each day I had to carry out the blocks and build, those who had no blocks looking on. I never opened any of the added boxes, and only built up a few forms listlessly out of my own, and was glad to carry them all back again.

"At the end of four days I was allowed to return to each of my class mates his own box, and to put mine in its proper place. I learned then once for all never to covet useless wealth, and to rest content with my own share. The punishment was in the line of my fault, and made me heartily ashamed of selfishness and greed.

"I told my mother all about the proceedings of each day. She did not make much comment. Evidently she knew I was in good hands. When it was all over she took me into her oval chamber and explained my fault. What she told me seemed quite correct then and there, but hardly harmonises with my waking experience.

"'The blocks and the other articles you use in the class are not yours; they are only there for your use so long as you need them. In a little while you will go to another class and find other toys, tools, and books, and will leave those you now have to your successor. It is so with everything; nobody has any private property in anything except personal belongings, such as clothes. If your father was wanted at some other place, and was willing to go — he would not have to go otherwise — we should leave this home, and all in it, and have another equally good to go to. But nothing here is absolutely ours; we could take nothing with us except what I tell you.'

"'Could we take father's new picture?' said I, looking at a new artistic production that seemed to be a living and conscious presentation of father.

"'Yes, that is our own.'

"'And your new travelling robe, is that yours?'

"'As long as I want it; yes, it is mine. But if I had no further need for it, and it was still good and nice, I would take it to the depot, so that another woman if she required it could wear it. We do this so that unused articles may not rot and go to waste.'

"'Our flying fish?'

"'That, too, is ours while we use it. It cost a great amount of labour to produce it, and is on that account very valuable.

If your father were not a highly skilled workman he would not have so valuable an article for his sole use; in that case we should travel by the public air-fishes. There, now, ask no more questions. I will tell you more by-and-bye; you are only a little boy yet. You will remember not to be selfish any more. Give me a kiss and go help Emma with her pretty picture puzzles.' " .

Our diarist has evidently got into a land where a number of ideas have got worked into practical shape. Real estate is only held by those who use it. There is no property except in personal belongings, and even these must not be heaped up and kept to rot. Several things tend to arouse his curiosity, but he is bound to wait. If he could make himself equally conscious in both spheres he might ask for information, but hitherto he can remember nothing of his old life in the new one, although he can remember all that happens in the new life while in the waking one. Indeed, the dreamland memories haunt his waking hours, and make him absent-minded and odd in manner.

One evening he writes:— "I have been all day bothering my head about the flying fishes I mentioned the other day. They are always going about in the air. I can never look up without seeing some. They are so common that no one appears to notice them. It is not long since we got one of our own. Sister Emma and I were in the garden, where we grow a great number of highly-coloured flowers, when we heard a familiar voice overhead. We looked up, and there was father on a flying fish descending in a spiral curve almost upon us. The fish came lightly to the ground with all its fins folded, and father got out. He and mother carried it into a long, narrow house, built on purpose for it.

"Next day we all went flying. Inside the fish was almost like a boat. Father sat at one end, mother at the other, Emma and I were in between. We were told to keep still, and then father pulled out some little knobs and the fish began to rise spirally, as if climbing an immense screw, until it got a certain height, and then its fins came out to the full length and made great sweeping strokes, and we went forward fast, very fast. I could not breathe when looking in the direction we were going. We could see through the floor, and looking down everything seemed to be in rapid motion running away behind us. There were other fishes, too, that kept crossing above and below us in all directions.

"When we had been flying some time we dropped in the same spiral way, and spent the afternoon with some friends.

When we came back it was night, and our fish had its eyes made into a pair of great lamps. I have no idea of how we got home or when. Emma and I were wrapped in a soft, warm rug, and must have gone to sleep. What is this fish? It has feathery-looking fans about the tail, and these move up and down and from right to left as we steer, and we have two pairs of wing-like fins at the sides. There is no smoke and no noise."

* * *

"Our home life seems easy and happy as compared with that of my earlier childhood. Lights and fires give no work. Mother has only one meal to cook. There are no dusty streets, smoke, dirt, and dust are almost unknown things. Labour-saving appliances of all kinds are freely used in household work, so that taken altogether the wife and mother has no need to work much longer than the husband and father. The winter evenings we spent very pleasantly. Sometimes we had visitors, at others we visited our friends. We had merry games — games of chance and skill, reading, impersonations, dramatic and musical performances, dancing, callisthenics. All the people had plenty of time and opportunity for self improvement, and most of them took care to excel in some accomplishment. First-class teachers of all the arts gave lessons to those who wished without any charge upon their labour. That is, all tuition of every kind is absolutely free.

"All other things are free to all appearance in some sense. At the depots we get all we want for asking. Only there is this difference: an account is kept with each responsible person or each head of a family, and his production balanced with his consumption. All consumed by an individual or family is practically paid for by the labour or production of the individual or family, and generally the account is much in favour of the worker, for there are no profits. The state is the only middleman, and the costs of carriage and storage and distribution are the only additions made to prime cost. The difference between lessons and personal necessaries is this, the former are not entered against his account, the latter are.

"Teachers, lecturers, doctors, writers, actors, musicians, preachers — in short, all who work for the amusement, instruction, and healing of humanity are provided for by the State, and when past labour are still surrounded by such comforts and luxuries as they have been accustomed to.

In all this world such a thing as poverty is unknown. Nor can anyone become rich. No matter how much a man or woman may spare the State account, he or she can hoard nothing, nor even draw upon the depot for articles that must run to waste. Nor can anyone own a foot of land. No one can make a will. At death, or prior to that even, purely personal belongings may be promised or given to various members of a family, but there can be no bickering over the distribution of wealth. The State is the heir of each generation, and as the lives of all our men and women are honourable and profitable, as we have no criminals and no paupers, and as all work who are permitted to do so, the State gains much by each generation, and can easily afford to sustain teachers and the like, maintain schools and places of amusement in each centre of population, and provide for the wants of worn out workers.

"And our workers do not wear out soon. The conditions of life are easy, and they are free from worry and almost free from temptation. Our day is twenty-five hours, and they only work five at a trade. The majority work a little in the afternoons in their fruit and flower gardens, or for their own amusement; but there is no such thing as bustle, strain, anxiety as to money or any other worrying matter. The general happiness and the zest manifested by comparatively aged people doubtless has its source in the conditions of life.

"Our intercourse with one another is very easy. We are not expected to provide foods and drinks for our afternoon or evening guests. Those who wish to eat together go to the caravansary, where wholesome and varied meats are supplied early in the afternoon to all comers, the only formality being that each name is sent to the depot for the district. You pay for your friend's dinner if you wish by repeating your own name. This, however, is rarely allowed, for your friend is your equal, and stands as well in the register as you do."

208180

The Red Sickness
from
The Germ Growers
Robert Potter
(1892)

In The Germ Growers *two young Englishmen, Robert Easterley and John Wilbraham, encounter a horrendous plot to
destroy the human race. This is how the adventure begins . . .*

Before I begin my story I must give you some account of
certain passages in my early life, which seem to have some
connection with the extraordinary facts that I am about to
put on record.

To speak more precisely, of the connection of one of
them with those facts there can be no doubt at all, and of
the connection of the other with them I at least have none.

When I was quite a boy, scarce yet fifteen years old, I
happened to be living in a parish on the Welsh coast, which
I will here call Penruddock. There were some bold hills
inland and some very wild and rugged cliffs along the coast.
But there was also a well-sheltered beach and a little pier
where some small fishing vessels often lay. Penruddock was
not yet reached by rail, but forty miles of a splendid road,
through very fine scenery, took you to a railway station.
And this journey was made by a well-appointed coach on five
days of every week.

The people of Penruddock were very full of a queer kind
of gossip, and were very superstitious. And I took the
greatest interest in their stories. I cannot say that I really
believed them, or that they affected me with any real fear.
But I was not without that mingled thrill of doubt and
wonder which helps one to enjoy such things. I had a double
advantage in this way, for I could understand the Welsh

language, although I spoke it but little and with difficulty, and I often found a startling family likeness between the stories which I heard in the cottages of the peasantry three or four miles out of town and those which circulated among the English-speaking people in whose village I lived.

There was one such story which was constantly reproduced under various forms. Sometimes it was said to have happened in the last generation; sometimes as far back as the civil wars, of which, strange to say, a lively traditional recollection still remained in the neighbourhood; and sometimes it seemed to have been handed down from prehistoric times, and was associated with tales of enchantment and fairyland. In such stories the central event was always the unaccountable disappearance of some person, and the character of the person disappearing always presented certain unvarying features. He was always bold and fascinating, and yet in some way or other very repulsive. And when you tried to find out why, some sort of inhumanity was always indicated, some unconscious lack of sympathy which was revolting in a high degree or even monstrous. The stories had one other feature in common, of which I will tell you presently.

I seldom had any companions of my own age, and I was in consequence more given to dreaming than was good for me. And I used to marshal the heroes of these queer stories in my day-dreams and trace their likeness one to another. They were often so very unlike in other points, and yet so strangely like in that one point. I remember very well the first day that I thought I detected in a living man a resemblance to those dreadful heroes of my Welsh friend's folklore. There was a young fellow whom I knew, about five or six years my senior, and so just growing into manhood. His name, let us say, was James Redpath. He was well built, of middle height, and, as I thought, at first at least, quite beautiful to look upon. And, indeed, why I did not continue to think so is more than I can exactly say. For he possessed very fine and striking features, and although not very tall his presence was imposing. But nobody liked him. The girls especially, although he was so good-looking, almost uniformly shrank from him. But I must confess that he did not seem to care much for their society.

I went about with him a good deal at one time on fishing and shooting excursions and made myself useful to him, and except that he was rather cruel to dogs and cats, and had a nasty habit of frightening children, I do not know that I

noticed anything particular about him. Not, at least, until
one day of which I am going to tell you. James Redpath and
I were coming back together to Penruddock, and we called at
a cottage about two miles from the village. Here we found a
little boy of about four years old, who had been visiting at
the cottage and whom they wanted to send home. They
asked us to take charge of him and we did so. On the way
home the little boy's shoe was found to have a nail or a peg
in it that hurt his foot, and we were quite unable to get it
out. It was nothing, however, to James Redpath to carry
him, and so he took him in his arms. The little boy shrank
and whimpered as he did so. James had under his arm some
parts of a fishing-rod and one of these came in contact with
the little boy's leg and scratched it rather severely so as to
make him cry. I took it away and we went on. I was walking
a little behind Redpath, and as I walked I saw him deliberately take another joint of the rod, put it in the same place
and then watch the little boy's face as it came in contact
with the wire, and as the child cried out I saw quite a malignant expression of pleasure pass over James's face. The thing
was done in a moment and it was over in a moment; but I
felt as if I should like to have killed him if I dared. I always
dreaded and shunned him, more or less, afterwards, and I
began from that date to associate him with the inhuman
heroes of my Welsh stories.

I don't think that I should ever have got over the dislike
of him which I then conceived, but I saw the last of him, at
least Penruddock saw the last of him, about three months
later. I had been sitting looking over the sea between the pier
and the cliffs and trying to catch a glimpse of the Wicklow
Mountains which were sometimes to be seen from that point.
Just then James Redpath came up from the beach beyond
the pier, and passing me with a brief "good morning", went
away inland, leaving the cliffs behind him. I don't know how
long I lay there, it might be two hours or more, and I think
I slept a little. But I suddenly started up to find it high day
and past noon, and I began to think of looking for some
shelter. There was not a cloud visible, but nevertheless two
shadows like, or something like, the shadows of clouds lay
near me on the ground. What they were the shadows of I
could not tell, and I was about to get up to see, for there was
nothing to cast such a shadow within the range of my sight
as I lay. Just then one of the shadows came down over me
and seemed to stand for a moment between me and the sun.
It had a well-defined shape, much too well defined for a

cloud. I thought as I looked that it was just such a shadow as might be cast by a yawl-built boat lying on the body of a large wheelbarrow. Then the two shadows seemed to move together and to move very quickly. I had just noticed that they were exactly like one another when the next moment they passed out of my sight.

I started to my feet with a bound, my heart beating furiously. But there was nothing more to alarm the weakest. It was broad day. Houses and gardens were to be seen close at hand and in every direction but one, and in that direction there were three or four fishermen drawing their nets. But as I looked away to the part of the sky where the strange cloud-like shadows had just vanished, I remembered with a shudder that other feature in common of the strange stories of which I told you just now. It was a feature that forcibly reminded me of what I had just witnessed. Sometimes in the later stories you would be told of a cloud coming and going in an otherwise cloudless sky. And sometimes in the elder stories you would be told of an invisible car, invisible but not shadowless. I used always to identify the shadow of the invisible car in the elder stories with the cloud in the later stories, the cloud that unaccountably came and went.

As I thought it all over and tried to persuade myself that I had been dreaming I suddenly remembered that James Redpath had passed by a few hours before, and as suddenly I came to the conclusion that I should never see him again. And certainly he never was again seen, dead or alive, any-where in Wales or England. His father, and his uncle, and their families, continued to live about Penruddock, but Pen-ruddock never knew James Redpath any more. Whether I myself saw him again or not is more than I can say with absolute certainty. You shall know as much as I know about it if you hear my story to the end.

Of course James Redpath's disappearance attracted much attention, and was the talk not only of the village, but of the whole country-side. It was the general opinion that he must have been drowned by falling over the cliffs, and that his body had been washed out to sea. I proved, however, to have been the very last person to see him, and my testimony, as far as it went, was against that opinion. For I certainly had seen him walking straight inland. Of course he might have returned to the coast afterwards, but at least nobody had seen him return. I gave a full account of place and time as far as I could fix them, and I mentioned the queer-looking clouds and even described their shape. This, I remember, was considered to have some value as fixing my memory of the matter, but no further notice was taken of it. And I myself did not venture to suggest any connection between it and Redpath's disappearance, because I did not see how I could reasonably do so. I had, nevertheless, a firm conviction that there was such a connection, but I knew very well that to declare it would only bring a storm of ridicule upon me.

But a public calamity just then befell Penruddock which made men forget James Redpath's disappearance. A pestilence broke out in the place of which nobody knew either the nature or the source. It seemed to spring up in the place. At least, all efforts to trace it were unsuccessful. The first two or three cases were attributed to some inflammatory cold, but it soon became clear that there were specific features about it, that they were quite familiar, that the disease was extremely dangerous to life and highly infectious.

Then a panic set in, and I believe that the disease would soon have been propagated all over England and farther, if it had not been for the zeal and ability of two young physicians who happened very fortunately to be living in the village just then. Their names were Leopold and Furniss. I forget if I ever knew their Christian names. We used to call them Doctor Leopold and Doctor Furniss. They had finished their studies for some little time, but they found it advisable on the score of health to take a longish holiday before commencing practice, and they were spending part of their holiday at Penruddock. They were just about to leave us when the disease I am telling you of broke out.

The first case occurred in a valley about two miles from the village. In this valley there were several cottages inhabited mostly by farm labourers and artisans. These cottages lay one after another in the direction of the rising ground which separated the valley from Penruddock. Then there were no houses for a considerable space. Then, just over the hill, there was another and yet another. The disease had made its way gradually up the hill from one cottage to another, day after day a fresh case appearing. Then there had been no new cases for four days, but on the fifth day a new case appeared in the cottage just over the brow of the hill. And when this became known, also that every case (there had now been eleven) had hitherto been fatal, serious alarm arose. Then, too, the disease became known as the "red sickness". This name was due to a discoloration which set in on the shoulders, neck, and forehead very shortly after seizure.

How the two doctors, as we called them, became armed with the needful powers I do not know. They certainly contrived to obtain some sort of legal authority, but I think that they acted in great measure on their responsibility.

By the time they commenced operations there were three or four more cases in the valley, and one more in the second cottage on the Penruddock side. There was a large stone house, partly ruinous, in the valley, near the sea, and hither they brought every one of the sick. Plenty of help was given them in the way of beds, bedding, and all sorts of material, but such was the height which the panic had now attained that no one from the village would go near any of the sick folk, nor even enter the valley. The physicians themselves and their two men servants, who seemed to be as fearless and as brave as they, did all the work. Fortunately, the two infected cottages on the Penruddock side were each tenanted only by the person who had fallen ill, and the tenant in each case was a labourer whose work lay in the valley. The physicians burnt down these cottages and everything that was in them. Then they established a strict quarantine between the village and the valley. There was a light fence running from the sea for about a mile inland, along the brow of the rising ground on the Penruddock side. This they never passed nor suffered any one to pass, during the prevalence of the sickness. Butchers and bakers and other tradesmen left their wares at a given point at a given time, and the people from the valley came and fetched them.

The excitement and terror in Penruddock were very great. All but the most necessary business was suspended, and of social intercourse during the panic there was next to none. Ten cases in all were treated by the physicians, and four of these recovered. The last two cases were three or four days apart, but they were no less malignant in character: the very last case was one of the fatal ones. I learned nothing of the treatment; but the means used to prevent the disease spreading, besides the strict quarantine, were chiefly fire and lime. Everything about the sick was passed through the fire, and of these everything that the fire would destroy was destroyed. Lime, which abounded in the valley, was largely used.

A month after the last case the two physicians declared the quarantine at an end, and a month later all fear of the disease had ceased. And then the people of the village began to think of consoling themselves for the dull and uncomfortable time they had had, and of doing some honour to the two visitors who had served the village so well. With this double purpose in view a picnic on a large scale was organized, and there was plenty of eating and drinking and speech-making and dancing, all of which I pass over. But at that picnic I heard a conversation which made a very powerful impression on me then, and which often has seemed to provide a bond which binds together all the strange things of which I had experience at the time and afterwards.

In the heat of the afternoon I had happened to be with Mr Leopold and Mr Furniss helping them in some arrangements which they were making for the amusement of the children who took part in the picnic. After these were finished they two strolled' away together to the side of a brook which ran through the park where we were gathered. I followed them, attracted mainly by Mr Furniss's dog, but encouraged also by an occasional word from the young men. At the brook Mr Furniss sat upon a log, and leaned his back against a rustic fence. The dog sat by him; a very beautiful dog he was, black and white, with great intelligent eyes, and an uncommonly large and well-shaped head. He would sometimes stretch himself at length, and then again he would put his paw upon his master's shoulder and watch Mr Leopold and me.

Mr Leopold stood with his back to an oak-tree, and I leant against the fence beside him listening to him. He was a tall, dark man, with a keen, thoughtful, and benevolent expression. He was quite strong and healthy-looking, and there was a squareness about his features that I think one does not often see in dark people. Mr Furniss was of lighter complexion and hardly as tall; there was quite as much intelligence and benevolence in his face, but not so much of what I have called thoughtfulness as distinguished from intelligence, and there was a humorous glint in his eye which the other lacked. They began to talk about the disease which had been so successfully dealt with, and this was what they said: —

Leopold Well, Furniss, an enemy hath done this.

Furniss Done what? The picnic or the red sickness?

Leopold The red sickness, of course. Can't you see what I mean?

Furniss No, I can't. You're too much of a mystic for me, Leopold; but I'll tell you what, England owes a debt to you and me, my boy, for it was near enough to being a new edition of the black death or the plague.

Leopold Only the black death and the plague were imported, and this was indigenous. It sprang up under our noses in a healthy place. It came from nowhere, and, thank God, it is gone nowhither.

Furniss But surely the black death and the plague must have begun somewhere, and they too seem to have gone nowhither.

Leopold You're right this far that they *all* must have had the same sort of beginning. Only it is given to very few to see the beginning, as you and I have seen it, or so near the beginning.

Furniss Now, Leopold, I hardly see what you are driving at. I am not much on religion, as they say in America, but I believe there is a Power above all. Call that Power God, and let us say that God does as He pleases, and on the whole that it is best that He should. I don't see that you can get much further than that.

Leopold I don't believe that God ever made the plague, or the black death, or the red sickness.

Furniss Oh, don't you? Then you are, I suppose, what the churchmen call a Manichee — you believe in the two powers of light and darkness, good and evil. Well, it is not a bad solution of the question as far as it goes, but I can hardly accept it.

Leopold No, I don't believe in any gods but the One. But let me explain. That is a nice dog of yours, Furniss. You told me one day something about his breeding, and you promised to tell me more.

Furniss Yes, it is quite a problem in natural history. Do you know, Tommy's ancestors have been in our family for four or five generations of men, and, I suppose, that is twenty generations of dogs.

Leopold You told me something of it. You improved the breed greatly, I believe?

Furniss Yes, but I have some distant cousins, and they have the same breed and yet not the same, for they have cultivated it in quite another direction.

Leopold What are the differences?

Furniss Our dogs are all more or less like Tommy here, gentle and faithful, very intelligent, and by no means deficient in pluck. My cousin's dogs are fierce and quarrelsome, so much so that they have not been suffered for generations to associate with children. And so they have lost intelligence and are become ill-conditioned and low-lived brutes.

Leopold But I think I understand you to say that the change in the breed did not come about in the ordinary course of nature.

Furniss I believe not. I heard my grandfather say that his father had told him that when he was a young man he had set about improving the breed. He had marked out the most intelligent and best tempered pups, and he had bred from them only and had given away or destroyed the others.

Leopold And about your cousin's dogs?

Furniss Just let me finish. It seems that while one brother began to cultivate the breed upward, so to speak, another brother was living in a part of the country where thieves were numerous and daring, and there were smugglers and gipsies, and what not, about. And so he began to improve the breed in quite another direction. He selected the fierce and snappish pups and bred exclusively from them.

Leopold And so from one ancestral pair of, say, a hundred and fifty years ago, you have Tommy there, with his wonderful mixture of gentleness and pluck, and his intelligence all but human, and your cousin has a kennel of unintelligent and bloodthirsty brutes, that have to be caged and chained as if they were wild beasts.

Furniss Just so, but I don't quite see what you are driving at.

Leopold Wait a minute. Do you suppose the germs of cow-pox and small-pox to be of the same breed?

Furniss Well, yes; you know that I hold them to be specifically identical. I see what you are at now.

Leopold But one of them fulfils some obscure function in the physique of the cow, some function certainly harmless and probably beneficient, and the other is the malignant small-pox of the London hospitals.

Furniss So you mean to infer that in the latter case the germ has been cultivated downwards by intelligent purpose?

Leopold What if I do?

Furniss You think, then, that there is a secret guild of malignant men of medicine sworn to wage war against their fellow-men, that they are spread over all the world and have existed since before the dawn of history. I don't believe that there are any men as bad as that, and if there were, I should call them devils and hunt them down like mad dogs.

Leopold I don't wish to use misleading words, but I will say that I believe there are intelligences, not human, who have access to realms of nature that we are but just beginning to explore; and I believe that some of them are enemies to humanity, and that they use their knowledge to breed such things as malignant small-pox or the red sickness out of germs which were originally of a harmless or even of a beneficient nature.

Furniss Just as my cousins have bred those wild beasts of theirs out of such harmless creatures as poor Tommy's ancestors.

Leopold Just so.

Furniss And you think that we can contend successfully against such enemies?

Leopold Why not? They can only have nature to work upon. And very likely their only advantage over us is that they know more of nature than we do. They cannot go beyond the limits of nature to do less or more. As long as we sought after spells and enchantments and that sort of nonsense we were very much at their mercy. But we are now learning to fight them with their own weapons, which consist of the knowledge of nature. Witness vaccination, and witness also our little victory over the red sickness.

Furniss You're a queer mixture, Leopold, but we must get back to the picnic people.

And so they got up and went back together to the dancers, nodding to me as they went. I sat there for awhile, going over and over the conversation in my mind and putting together my own thoughts and Mr Leopold's.

Then I joined the company and was merry as the merriest for the remainder of the day. But that night I dreamt of strange-looking clouds and of the shadows of invisible cars, and of demons riding in the cars and sowing the seeds of pestilence on the earth and catching away such evil specimens of humanity as James Redpath to reinforce the ranks of their own malignant order.

Years later, in Australia, whilst exploring the Kimberleys, the narrator and his friend again encounter the shadows of invisible air-cars. Discovering the mountain enclave of what they take to be a secret society, the youths witness the process by which the air-cars are painted to make them invisible (see the passage quoted on p. xvi).

It is soon revealed that they have stumbled upon beings who are more than mere conspirators. They are, indeed, creatures from outer space: inhabitants of the ether, and devils. They plan to destroy the human race by selectively breeding new strains of plague, and to aid them in their endeavours they roam the world recruiting men such as James Redpath.

Signor Niccolo Davelli, the head of the Daly River germ-growing enclave, attempts to persuade the youths to join the forces of evil, and goes so far as to send Easterley to the Moon in order to impress him with the feats of demonic technology. Naturally, the two heroes resist, and they are finally rescued by an angel named Lëafer. The Daly River enclave has been defeated – but the struggle against evil continues eternally.

War

from
Beyond the Ice
G. Read Murphy
(1894)

*The sole survivor of an arctic expedition, Dr Frank Farleigh
finds himself marooned near the North Pole, and is saved by
members of a socially and technologically advanced civilization. He soon learns that the area around the North Pole
(known as Fregida by its inhabitants) is divided into autono-
mous city-states: Zara, "the most perfect and powerful"
region; Ura, "a community like that which [we] call the
United States of America"; and Gurla. In addition, there is
a race of primitive native Fregidans – the Rodas – which
lives in the outer reaches of Fregida and periodically makes
raids upon the city-states.*

*Farleigh arrives at a politically crucial time for Fregida.
The people and rulers of Ura have decided that their liberal
and humane social code has been a disaster, for, in the words
of Vernon Dreman, President of Ura: "Charity has been
extended till now the wise and thrifty maintain the worth-
less, so that their numbers are increasing faster than are the
numbers of the provident, and chaos approaches." Consequently, the people of Ura have decided to repeal their own
laws and live instead under the more stringent and less liberal
code of Zara – a code which is best summarized by the
Zaran belief that "[when] Christ says, Give to the poor,
[this] does not mean support the unworthy".*

*To bring this political merger into effect, the two city-
states plan to unite and call themselves parts of the Commonwealth of Undara, with the Undaran parliament meeting
alternately in each city. This new alliance is soon put to the
test, for the Rodas (together with some Gurla factions)
launch a series of major attacks on remote Undaran outposts.*

Being trained in both medicine and surgery, and having

become integrated with Undaran society through marriage to a Fregidan, Dr Farleigh is ordered to one of the front-line areas.

(See also pp. xix–xx).

It was past midnight. Sleep had driven most of the excited multitude to bed. Cula came to me, and said, –

"Frank, I want an extra doctor at once, to go to the fort at the summit of Mount Boro. They are ready for a siege. I sent at ten o'clock ten nurses and an extra doctor. Nominate a man."

"I will have a doctor ready," I replied, "and with your permission will go with him to see that all is in order in my department."

"Go," he replied, "but if possible, return with the boat, though it will only allow you six hours to superintend."

And so it was arranged.

At two o'clock the doctor and I were in the launch with the grey-clad soldier nurses. Carefully they had stacked their rifles and baggage, and, after a short chat, went to bed, for they recognized the wisdom of taking care of themselves, so that they might the better perform their duties. At nine we all met at breakfast. The soldier nurses were merry, as if they were going to attend a marriage feast, instead of journeying to prepare for the dead and the dying. Youth and health cannot long be sad, even when approaching a chamber of horrors.

In the distance we saw three captive balloons, and on approaching Pentona, found that they were attached to stations that formed a triangle round the city, which was crowded with soldiers.

On the wharf we found Darcy Brenda, in the grey-green uniform of a general, waiting to receive us.

"All our prisoners are soldiers on parole," he told me, "and regard the coming campaign as an excellent holiday."

Martial law, we found, had been proclaimed, and every prisoner who desired – which included them all – was allowed to come out as a soldier, knowing that any disobedience of orders or breaches of discipline would be met by death.

Going to the central station, I found that a report was received from each of the balloons of all that took place within view of their powerful telescopes.

"They can see," said Brenda, "the enemy when they are over a day's march away."

After a brief stay at Pentona, we re-embarked and proceeded on our way. At fourteen o'clock we came to the end of the waterway, and were met by a troop of soldiers on double electric tricycles. These machines had sufficient power to progress slowly, so that it required but little exertion to travel on them at a speed of about fifteen miles an hour.

Mount Boro rose gently from the plain for some twelve hundred feet, when the ascent began to be both steep and rugged. Dismounting from our cycles, we guided them in front of us, and so commenced our ascent to the fort, through the cool shade of the great pines. Presently, on stopping to rest, we looked downwards and saw the road we had come pass beneath us several times, as corkscrew-like it wound its way to the lower part of the mountain. Nearing the summit, on which the fort was established, we entered the open mouth of a tunnel through which we could pass upright, two abreast. Hardly had we proceeded a few yards by the dim light of a few toches, when the tunnel became brilliantly illuminated, and we found that we were confronted by a series of cross bars, which were in the form of an isosceles triangle, three inches at the base, six on the longer sides, and a similar distance apart. On approaching them, we found they were slid down from the roof into a solid base, and were firm as the Rock of Cashel. They rose automatically as we approached, and we saw, some thirty yards behind them, an array of quick-firing machine guns which sank into a pit, from which they rose when required to send their deadly contents through the network of bars, and again sink to be reloaded.

Our journey had been performed with a stern, silent speed that was rather depressing, and which seemed to us to be quite unnecessary. Coming towards us, we now perceived a dark, grey-bearded man, rather above the middle height. Like every one else, since the declaration of war, he was dressed in the grey uniform of the soldiers. His eyes were almost black, and very piercing. His features were broad and swarthy, and wholly characteristic of the unmixed blood of the Rodas. Saluting me in military style, he held out his hand, —

"Your visit, Dr Farleigh, is very welcome, though unexpected. I have heard of you from General Cula Dero. I am Kit Troca, the Governor of the Fortress Borna. And your arrival is opportune. We will be attacked by the Rodas, probably at dawn."

On expressing my admiration for the defence of the tunnel, he replied, —

"You have not seen our best defence."

We passed on as we talked.

"Yonder fans," he said, pointing to some machinery, "will fill the tunnel with a gas that will kill every man or animal in it; and as they are round a turn, no weapon of the invading force can reach them."

"Would it not," I asked, "take a very considerable time to fill the tunnel with sufficient gas to be effective?"

"No," he replied, stolidly. "Even supposing it were full of as many men as it could hold, in less than a minute after the fans were set going every man would be insensible, and most of them would be dead."

At the end of the tunnel we came to a perpendicular flight of ladder steps and a double lift, on the latter of which we sent up the cycles and our party, after which Troca and I ascended, leaving the garrison below. The lift was hydraulic, and brought us up a distance of over eight hundred feet. On reaching the top we found that the fortress consisted of a large observatory, and sufficient accommodation for a considerable number of soldiers. A spring of water and a large stock of provisions made it able to stand a protracted siege, even if all communication with the outer world were cut off, which was very unlikely to happen.

The chief importance of the place was as an observatory and vantage ground, from which the movements of approaching troops could be seen. Communication was held with Pentona by means of a secret buried cable. In case, however, this should be discovered by the enemy, a number of carrier gulls were kept caged and sent to Pentona, when a number were received in exchange; and so communication could always be kept up.

Kit Troca took me to the telescopes, which were very powerful, and enabled any body of men to be seen from an immense distance.

"The Rodas," he said, "have scattered, and so approached in small parties of two or three, each carrying a young pine. There are now about a thousand of them encamped in the thick pine-grove on the mountain slope to the right."

"If they attack you bravely," I queried, in consternation, "surely they will carry the fort by sheer force of numbers? How many fighters have you?"

"Every member of the garrison", said Troca, "over ten years of age is a fighter. I have ninety-seven soldiers. The ten soldier nurses that came with you, twenty-one women and children, and ourselves. If, as I think, the Rodas attack us just before daybreak, over two thousand strong, and fight as they usually do, with fearless enthusiasm, we will slay at least four out of every five of them in a few hours."

The man smiled calmly, amused at my evident surprise.

"It seems an awful slaughter."

"What matter?" he asked with scorn. "They are murderous savages, who are too lazy and selfish to accept civilization. Your wife and General Dero have always advocated their subjugation, and, had their wishes been carried out, the Gurlas would never have been able to attack us as they soon will."

As I looked at the high walls surrounding the fort, I shuddered at the thought of the awful slaughter that must take place, if it were attacked by a brave foe. On three sides the walls were almost perpendicular, on the fourth they were approached by a very steep slope. The Rodas were expected to try and rush this slope and the tunnel; all the other approaches being impassable. No column of smoke, or other sign, indicated the encampment of the Rodas in the pines.

As we scanned the country far and wide, through the powerful telescopes, we could see in the distance the towns seemingly asleep, and the war balloons motionless, high up above them. The quiet, to my mind, seemed like that which in tropical regions comes before great storms, on a sudden to change, as the air becomes filled with the rumble and roar of the thunder, the vivid flashes of the lightning, and the downpouring rain torrents. I felt horror-stricken as I thought of the hissing shower of death-dealing bullets from the compressed air guns; the even more deadly current of poisonous gas in the tunnels, and the wounded falling back to be crushed as they rolled, or fell, down the steep approaches to the fort.

A carrier-gull was released, with a full report of the situation, written on two thin sheets of vellum paper, and wrapped round two stipped feathers, in the underpart of its tail.

With a shrill cry, it rose in the air, and rapidly winged its way to Pentona.

"The gull seemed certain of its direction," I said to Troca.

"Yes," he replied, "it has been the journey many times

before, and the rapid and direct start it makes, relieves it of nearly all danger from the enemy's bullets."

"Have you sent for assistance?"

"No. I have only given the full details of the situation, and suggested that, if possible, a force be sent to attack the Rodas when they retreat from the fort. This they will do, tired and utterly disheartened, shortly after daybreak, when, if they are assailed by a surprise force, who occupy their camp in the pines, they will be killed almost to a man."

Early in the evening, half the garrison were sent to lie down in their clothes.

I reclined in an easy chair in an unavailing effort to slumber. My thoughts kept me awake. Sentries were stationed, and everything was in readiness, I knew, but the thought of the coming slaughter drove away sleep.

At the first hour of the morning, the sentries and watchers were relieved, and lay down to rest. Everything was dark. I must have gone to sleep. Suddenly I was awoke by a roar of voices, and instantly started up alert.

The fort was bright as day with the electric light. Silently and quickly, without any sign of hurry, the freshly woke garrison took their places. Going to the edge of the battlements, I saw a crowd, a swarm of men, rushing into the tunnel. Another lot were rushing up the slope to the fort, firing the obsolete powder rifles, and shouting as they came.

All in the fort was silent, motionless. Just as the foremost of the storming party had almost reached the turret walls, the gas guns opened fire, and the crowd were swept back to block the way of their still advancing comrades, or fall down the steep mountain sides and disappear amongst the gloomy pines in the dark depths beneath. Suddenly a flame shot out of the tunnel, and with it a crowd of human bodies that appeared like dead flies. The gas in the tunnel had been ignited by the powder guns and an explosion had been caused. The savages, ignorant of the armaments of Undara, were amazed, but undaunted.

With a fearless bravery again they swarmed into the tunnel. The slope was again and again covered, only to be swept of its human freight by the silent hail of bullets. Suddenly an arm caught me by the shoulder and pulled me back.

"Come quickly, Doctor Frank."

It was one of the nurses who spoke.

"The Rodas are scaling the further wall."

Without a word I followed the nurse. Up the seemingly

inaccessible wall, a Roda had climbed with a silked cord in his teeth. Reaching the top, he leaped over, crouched under its shade, and hauled up the cord, to the free end of which, his comrade had tied a wire ladder. One of the nurses happened to see the man, and called the attention of the others.

By this time the ladder was put up, and fixed on the wall top. A nurse challenged the man, who replied, "All right!" Being still suspicious, she approached him and he drove his sword through her heart. In an instant another nurse had shot the man dead, and the Rodas coming up the ladder one after the other, leaped the battlements, to be received by the bullets of the soldier nurses. At the moment I arrived, a Roda, missed by the bullets, fired his revolver and shot a nurse, and in less time than I take to write this sentence, three Rodas were over the battlements. We, with our backs to the walls, were in the shade. The Rodas stood head and shoulders in bold relief against the sky. Faster than we could shoot them they appeared over the battlements, and the fort seemed lost. We had retired into the hospital building, and seven Rodas were over the battlements. Their powder guns had attracted the attention of the men. The next Roda, as he put his hands on the top of the wall to leap over, sank on his face, and lay still and quiet. Two of the seven who had scaled the walls, grasped their comrade, and quietly sank in a heap on his body. Several men appeared. I went to the motionless Rodas.

"Be careful, Frank." said Kit, "if you touch those corpses you will be killed. A current of electricity runs all round the bar on the top of the wall."

He placed a board on the battlement and said, "Now lean on that, and look over."

I did so. All along the wire ladder hung dead Rodas, grasping a rung with their dead hands. The metal had acted as a conductor, and killed every man on the ladder, their muscles being forced by the electricity to close their hands with a grasp impossible to free.

"Shut off the current," called Kit.

In an instant the dead men loosed their holds, and the corpses fell back into the black depths beneath.

We took in the dead soldier nurse, and the two who had been wounded.

The Rodas fought and were fighting like fiends.

The rosy dawn commenced to melt the darkness, and the Rodas gathered near the tunnel which was choked with their dead, and were evidently in conference. The base of the fort was bare of all covering. On a sudden, from the pines below, came a leaden shower, killing and scattering the Rodas. For a moment they hesitated panic-stricken under the fatal shower of lead. Then, with a shout, they rushed and rolled pell-mell fiercely down on the soldiers of Undara, who slaughtered them from their hiding-places in the pines beneath. Spellbound I gazed, and in a few minutes, which passed as a dream, realized that but a handful of our assailants remained alive, and that even they were prisoners. The carrier gull had duly reached Pentona, and a force been despatched to steal on the Rodas, while they were busy with the assault, and attack them at break of day.

A party were told off to dig a great trench, into which the dead savages were put. Another gang rolled the dead men down the side of the mountain and brought in the wounded. At the end of the day all that remained of our brave assailants, who were estimated at about 2500, was 27 prisoners, 193 wounded, a pile of arms and clothing, and 25 great mounds where the dead Rodas were taking their long last rest.

In all my hospital and dissecting experience, I had seen nothing so dreadful as this awful carnage, and the stripping of the mangled dead corpses, and huddling them on the top of teach other in the one grave.

When evening came, the three fort doctors, the seven soldier nurses and myself, were still busy setting limbs and dressing wounds. Next morning, at daybreak, the soldiers with the prisoners, and such of the wounded who could travel, returned to Pentona, leaving only such of their number as were necessary to enable us to care for the wounded. When we were left alone, arrangements were made to construct temporary shelter in the forest beneath the fort for the use of the wounded, so that in case of another attack, we would be free from possible traitors in our midst.

The second morning after the soldiers had left, as a soldier nurse and I went our rounds, in the bed of a wounded Gurla who was feigning sleep, we found a tiny six months old baby. The nurse stopped, and warningly held up one hand, as with the other she slightly lifted the bed clothes and showed the tiny mite of humanity, happily sleeping in the man's arms. Something — a movement of the man's arm, a dream fancy, or what not — woke the infant, who commenced to cry. From the shelter of a neighbouring bed there glided a woman, her long black hair streaming down her back, her big dark eyes wide open with terror. Crouching by the bed, she put one arm round the man's neck, the other round the crying babe, and turned a frightened imploring face to the nurse and me. The man, too weak to move, glared at us agonized, fierce, but without a trace of fear. Putting my hand on the poor woman's head I strove with voice and gesture to reassure her. For a moment she looked at me, and then, going on her knees, sobbingly placed my hand on her forehead. A voice from a neighbouring bed spoke, "She and her husband can only speak Roda". We turned and saw that we were observed by every man who was strong enough to lift his head.

"She has brought their baby and come to die with him," continued the man who had before spoken, and with whose aid we now satisfied the poor creature of our good intentions, and left her happy by the bedside of those she loved.

On returning to the fort, Kit Troca told us that many Rodas were concealed in the pines, but even if their fighting men were amongst them, which he doubted, they would abstain from making any attack on the nurses, or the fort, for fear we might retaliate on the wounded. Presently a messenger came from the hospital camp, and told us that Winda Garr, the woman who had come with her babe, had gone out to the pines, and reported to other women like herself who had come to search for their husbands or lovers, the kind treatment she had received, which had caused many of them to come timorously among the wounded.

On receipt of this news, I returned to the hospital, and found a scene even more heartrending than the profusion of open-eyed corpses that strewed the mountain side after the fight. In front of the hospital sheds were a group of women kneeling in a circle, their heads pointing centrewards. Sobbing and moaning, they leant forward on their hands, placing their foreheads on the ground, the while with their right hand from time to time putting earth on their heads. Their long black hair was loose, and at the mercy of a gentle wind that swayed it here and there, till the heads seemed to be joined, and they appeared like a fantastic representation of grief. As we passed, the women moaned and sobbed, unheeding our presence. Just inside the shed door, two babies of some two or three years of age played in the corner with the ribbon streamers of the spear ends, while in the shed itself, several infants, their hunger satisfied, slept content and happy. Beside several of the beds knelt women, their long black hair hanging down their backs, indicating grief and death, according to the custom of the Rodas. As we passed along, they came out to me, and kneeling, took my hand, and placed it on their foreheads, uttering the while a long moaning groan. Oh, the pity of it! The husband and father dead or wounded; the mother stricken with grief to the full, and – oh, wise and merciful nature! – the little children playing or asleep. The troubles of the men would end with death or recovery, the women's tears be dried, and their sorrows, diluted with the waters of Lethe, become memories to make the eye humid and heart soft; while the little children, grown to maturity, would, in the future, regard the incidents that agonized their parents, as only facts for a story.

Winda Garr's tears had been dried, her hair combed, and she now sat by her husband's bedside. Him we might have tortured and killed, but fierce to the last, he would have struggled and defied us. No force could subdue him. His wounds had been dressed, his wife received with kindness, and their helpless babe put to sleep on his arm. As I passed his bed, he held out his hand, and, with his dark eyes now beaming gentleness, signified his desire for my approach. On giving him my hand, he placed it on his forehead as the women had done, and murmured words of submission. The mighty power of kindness had subdued him, and on his recovery he would assist us to civilize his countrymen. Of the other women, those whose husbands were alive, did up their hair and were comforted. Those whose husbands had disappeared, grouped together in witch-like circles, weeping and sorrowing with dishevelled locks.

In the evening, the women still continued with their sorrowing. For five days they gathered at dawn, and, as the sun rose, commenced their wailing, which, fasting, they continued till it sank, when they rose, took food, and, wearied out, lay down to sleep. Exhaustion hushed their woe, and in the stillness of the forest, the music moved the feelings of the wounded and their watchers.

With hardly an exception, the men, though sorrowing for defeat, were reconciled, or anxious to join the people who comforted them in their weaknesses. Of the exceptions, all but one restrained their rage till future wars gave them a chance to slay their enemies or die for their country. This one man brooded on his fate, till his violent treachery brought on him retaliation and death. Towards the end of the first row of beds, on the right hand side of the entry, lay a restless Roda chief. His wiry, muscular form indicated physical strength, far superior of its kind to the mental ability shown in the sloping forehead, thick lips, and massive chin and neck. All his life, his brutal strength had enabled him to gratify his greed and lust, and remorselessly crush those who opposed him. Slave of his desires, he now lay fevered and savage, regarding every fresh kindness as an additional reason for revenge. Unhappy man. Strong against outside enemies, he was a victim to his own selfish, uncontrolled passions. As the music, softly rising and falling, soothed the feelings of the conquered Rodas, this human brute lay nursing feelings of revenge, and glaring on his more happy countrymen who surrounded him.

The Roda women had saved the fort nurses so much work, that they had time to soothe and comfort those sufferers who were fevered and restless. In her womanly ministrations, one fair-haired soldier nurse, going from bed to bed, came to the side of this foolish Roda. When she had beaten up his pillow, and smoothed his bed, she sprayed his forehead with scent and water preparatory to cooling it with a fan. Gently he took her hand, and placing it on his forehead, drew her down, muttering feebly some words of thanks. His other hand had gently slid into the bed, then — as a flash of lightning shows in an instant the nature of the dark surrounding — his face changed, his hand appeared grasping a dinner knife, which, momentarily uplifted, descended with all his strength on the nurse's shoulder. Horror stricken, patients and attendants watched the knife descend on its mission of death. With a shriek, the nurse recognized the situation. The descending blade, glancing from a knapsack strap she wore, pierced the bed clothes, and the nurse escaped. With a blow from a stick the Roda was disarmed, and as he cringed down, expecting death, his bed was smoothed, and he was left and forgiven — that is, by all those who lived under the wise laws of Undara. In the morning he was found cold and dead, with a Roda spear through his heart. Thus the savages, tamed by kindness, had avenged the treachery of their countryman in the way they thought just. They knew no better.

The Bunyip Dies
from
The Last Lemurian
G. Firth Scott
(1898)

According to the stories of an old Aborigine, there is a region in "the Westralian Never Never" where huge gold nuggets lie underfoot, guarded only by a race of shrivelled pygmies who are ruled by a yellow-skinned giantess. Determined to have this gold for themselves, Dick Halwood and the Yellow Hatter (a penniless English baronet) gather camels and set out to explore the desert.

After surviving attacks by treacherous Aborigines, the two men reach a verdant oasis which seems to be close to the mountain of gold.

The place where we found ourselves was at once romantic and weird.

Behind us, as far as we could see, there was only a weary stretch of dry, dead sand, gleaming and shimmering in the fierce, unbroken sunlight. Before us, beyond the luxuriant verdure of our haven, rose the range of barren, rocky mountains, free from all vegetation, and as arid as the desert, in all save the face of rock immediately in front of us. From a point nearby at the summit a stream of water bubbled, as if it were coming through an outlet pipe of some enormous cistern, and trickled over the rough surface of the rock in a thousand mimic cascades, tinkling and splashing as it fell until the air was full of the melody. At the base of the rock the water gathered into a deep pool so clear that one could see the pebbles lying at the bottom. Round the entire margin there was a luxuriant growth of vegetation, fine broad-leaved trees, of a kind I had never seen before, spreading far their branches, and shielding from the burning rays of the sun the velvety grass that grew right up to the stems. Towards the desert it stopped as suddenly as the edge of a well-kept lawn. There was no outlet that we could find for the water of the pool, and we could only surmise that it flowed away somewhere underground; for there were no signs of the pool ever having overflowed, and yet a considerable body of water was running into it every hour.

"Like all our Australian rivers, the biggest stream is underground, I suppose," the Hatter remarked. "I've seen the Murray almost in flood at one part, while a hundred miles or so away there was not enough water to float a wool barge."

I was looking at the stream as it came bubbling down the rock.

"It's strange the water has not cut a deeper scar in the rock," I said. "These trees look a pretty good age, judging by their size, and that stream must have been running a long time; but still there is hardly any of the stone worn away."

"It's a quaint place altogether," the Hatter said. "Look how the grass stops growing when it meets the sand, just as if it were trimmed every morning. Why, there are no birds about the place, nor flies, nor anything else that I can see with life, except the trees and the grass."

It was quite correct. We hunted through the trees for a sign of some token of animal life, but beyond our camels and ourselves there was none. In our search we came up to the rock down which the water tumbled. We understood then why it had worn away so little, for not even with the aid of a chilled steel drill and a heavy hammer could we make more than the faintest impression upon it.

"If this is our golden range and we have to mine in stuff like this, I'm afraid it will be a long time before we get our camels loaded," I said, as we rested from our fruitless efforts.

"We could have driven a hole a foot deep in the toughest rock I ever met with by this time, and there is hardly a dent in this, and the point flattened off the drill into the bargain."

"It *is* a quaint place, and I should not be surprised even if we met the Yellow Lady of twenty feet stature, and her hordes of shrivelled-up mummies," the Hatter answered, looking at the rock with a puzzled expression on his face.

"I wonder what dynamite would do," I suggested.

"Not worth wasting it. We may need all we have before we get to the end of our journey," he answered.

"I don't feel altogether comfortable," I said, as I rose

from the boulder I had been sitting upon. There was a strange oppressiveness in the air now that the first effects of the charm were wearing away. "I'm inclined to overhaul our rifles and sort out the ammunition. We may want them before long."

The Hatter looked at me with a smile lurking away down in the depths of his eyes.

"Getting nervous?" he asked.

"Not exactly, but — what's that?"

If ever I felt my heart in my mouth it was at that moment. The Hatter jumped to his feet with the blaze in his eyes that always came when he was suddenly startled, and I felt braver when I saw that he too had felt the shock.

We had been resting with our backs to the pool, and a heavy plunge and its accompanying splash, that sounded terribly loud in the quiet place, had been the cause of our alarm.

A few bubbles still floating on the surface and the race of ripples travelling from the centre to the sides were all we could discern.

The Hatter stood watching the pool, calm and unconcerned again, while I looked anywhere and everywhere for some explanation of the mystery.

"It is too absurd," I heard the Hatter say, and then he laughed, and I turned towards him.

"But we'll get our rifles all the same," he went on, looking round at me.

"Why, what do you make of it?" I asked, as we hastened to the spot where we had piled the packs when we lifted them off the backs of our tired camels.

"Bunyip," he answered. "Look at the camels."

The creatures that we had left browsing peacefully in the shade of the trees when we went to test the quality of the rock were now standing out in the sunlight on the desert, their necks swaying from side to side and their big blabby lips shaking, while their eyes rolled and glared in every direction.

"Here, let's get out of this," I cried, a horrible tremor of fear running over me.

The Hatter did not answer, but walked to the packs and drew out the rifles. Then he opened the box of ammunition and handed me a packet of cartridges.

"Load up the magazine, and put the rest in your pocket," he said, as he proceeded to set me the example.

When we had finished filling the Winchesters, the Hatter

produced two revolvers, which were also in the armoury of our treasure-trove camel train. We took one each, carefully loading all the chambers and keeping some spare cartridges in our pockets.

"Now we can look to the camels," the Hatter said.

We went to them and tried to soothe the terror they evidently felt. They came to meet us, and followed us as far as the beginning of the grass, but nothing we could do would induce them to come off the sand.

"It's no use wasting time over them. Let's go back and wait," the Hatter said.

"But what have we got to wait for?" I asked.

"The bunyip," he answered laconically.

"Oh! go slow!" I exclaimed. "You don't believe that silly yarn, do you?"

"My lad, I'm ready to believe anything about this place after the rock and that splash. The old man swore the pool he and his fellow niggers drank out of was the bunyip's lair, and that was why they all went to sleep. If this isn't the place and the range he talked about, then it's another equally peculiar. I've always thought there must be something in the bunyip yarn."

I laughed. "You're as bad as a new chum," I exclaimed.

"Wait-awhile," he replied. "You've heard the yarn the same as I have, and I suppose every other white man has who ever saw or spoke to an aboriginal. Only, perhaps, I have heard it more often, because I have had more to do with blackfellows, and that in every part of the continent, from York Peninsula to Wilson's Promontory, and from the Swan river to Moreton Bay."

"That's a pretty stiff bit of country," I interrupted.

"It includes what I say — every part of the continent," he continued quietly. "Now just add this up, and see what it comes to. From every blackfellow who has told me the yarn — and there have been a few hundreds of them — the description has always been the same. You can't talk about collusion between men and tribes who never saw or heard of one another. Firstly, they're all scared out of their lives of it. 'Baal th'at pfeller bunyip; 'im no good, 'im debbil-debbil,' they tell you, if they talk what they call English. If they don't they tell you the same in their own tongue. They've never seen it, but — and this is the second point — they tell you it lives in deep waterholes and lagoons, and for that reason they will never go into strange water nor camp near it, and sometimes will go for days without a drink rather than visit a pool where the bunyip is said to be."

"No one has ever seen one since the white man came here, at all events," I answered.

"Well?"

"And they've looked often enough. Why, scares are always getting up about the bunyip being heard or seen in some lagoon or other, and all the country side turns out and hunts, and hunts, and hunts, but nary a bunyip can be found."

"Well?" he repeated.

"Well, isn't that enough? If it isn't, how do you get over the fact that these scares get up at places hundreds, and sometimes thousands, of miles apart? Does the bunyip fly, or are there more than one, and if there are, why hasn't —"

"There is only one," he interrupted.

"Then how does he travel from one place to another?" I said.

"Look here, my lad, the water from that pool goes somewhere, doesn't it?"

"I suppose so," I replied.

"And so does the water of hundreds of other pools and rivers in Australia — but it does not flow on the surface. Why should there not be underground channels leading from one to the other, and perhaps ending or centring here, for example, as an ideal bunyip's lair?"

"That's too stiff for me!" I exclaimed.

"All right; we'll wait and see," he answered.

We dropped the discussion, and turned to consider our plan of campaign. I could not accept the bunyip theory, but at the same time there was no questioning the fact that something very mysterious had occurred when we heard that splash, or why should the camels be so terrified?

"I fancy the trees," I exclaimed, looking up into the leafy canopy of one. "If we get up above the lower branches the leaves will screen us from below, while we can see all that goes on, and have a grand command over any enemy underneath us."

"It's a stiff climb," the Hatter answered, looking at the trunk, which rose a good thirty feet without a twig to mar its smoothness.

"I think I can do it," I answered, for I was always a great hand at climbing, and rather plumed myself upon my prowess.

"But I doubt if I can," the Hatter said.

"Why, there's that rope ladder in the tool kit that we were nearly throwing away," I exclaimed, suddenly remembering the article which had caused us some wonder as to the reason of its inclusion in a miner's swag when we first found it.

"Our luck again," he answered, as we overhauled the packs until we came to the one we wanted. Taking a coil of light lanyard with me, and leaving my rifle at the foot of the tree (I did not care to go up without my revolver, in case I should meet anything unexpected), I started to swarm up the tree. It was, as the Hatter had remarked, a stiff climb, but I did it, although when I reached the lower branches I was pretty well blown. I threw one leg over a bough, and, holding on to the truck of the tree, I examined the situation.

The leaves grew thick almost to the stem, and about six feet above me another set of branches shot out from the trunk. The bough upon which I rested forked out into two prongs, as it were, some three feet from the trunk of the tree, and each of these again forked a foot farther on. Growing laterally, the twigs and minor branches formed a perfect network of stems, with the leaves so thick that it was difficult to see through, and impossible for any one to fall through them to the ground. The branches which stood out all round were equally dense, and I called out to the Hatter that I found a place where we could almost stow the camels.

Climbing on to the boughs I lowered my line, which he made fast to one end of the ladder, and I soon had it up. The other end lay on the ground in a coil, so I clambered up to the second tier of branches and made my end fast there. Then I called out to the Hatter to come up.

He came up and inspected.

"We'll fix our camp up here," he said, "and I reckon all the bunyips in the world won't reach us."

The sun was getting down towards the horizon, so that we had not much time. We made the most of it, however, and when it went down, we had all our ammunition and blankets up in our nest, besides food and water, to last us for a day or so. While we still had light we bent some of the boughs so as to enable us to have a clear view of the ground and the pool below us.

The moon was at the full, and as the sun went out of sight it rose. Out on the desert we could see our camels grouped together and crouched down as if asleep. The pool, lit up into a silver sheen, rested unruffled below us, and between the dense foliage of the trees the moonlight streamed upon an open patch of closely growing grass immediately in front of our look-out holes. Everywhere else the shadow was impenetrable.

We had taken a hasty meal, and now lay prone upon our blankets, with rifles ready, waiting and watching for anything which might eventuate.

The subdued tinkle of the falling water was the only sound to be heard, and the weird stillness of the scene was beginning to affect me more than I appreciated, when suddenly we heard a heavy grating noise from somewhere in the darkness beyond the trees.

The Hatter touched me, and I turned my face towards him.

"There's something in the air I can't make out," he whispered.

"Where?" I asked in the same tone, and looking quickly round.

"Nothing to see," he answered. "I feel it. Oh, look there!"

I peered through my loophole, and felt the blood run cold in my veins.

Beyond the glare of the moonlight upon the open patch I have spoken of, and through the black shadow on the far side of it, there came a faint greenish phosphorescence which increased slowly and spread as if the source of it were coming nearer. It lit up the trees and made even the grass distinct in its horrible ghostly flicker. Then in the centre of it there appeared a form which I shall never forget as long as I live.

Luminous with the greenish phosphorescence, and striding along with a majestic carriage that would alone have been awe-inspiring, was the form of a woman. Even from the place where we lay we could see that she was of enormous proportions, and the utter absence of drapery of any kind, together with the sombre depths of the shadow beyond her, made her appear really taller than she was. Her skin showed through the unearthly light like polished brass, and her eyes, which were wide open and gazing straight in front of her, gleamed like those of a cat.

I shuddered as I looked, and felt my flesh creep and the very marrow of my bones turned cold. The Hatter gripped me tight by the arm.

"The Yellow Woman!" he whispered hoarsely.

Across the open space she walked, the luminous sheen fading as she came into the full light of the moon, but the fire in her eyes burning more brightly and more horribly than it had done in the dark.

At the edge of the pool she stopped, and, raising her arms above her head, she shook down a mass of hair that was twisted and curled round her in a red wreathing cloak extending below her knees, and, to my mind, making her still more unearthly and fearful.

Silent she stood, as if waiting for something, while we, too startled to move, lay and gazed down upon her.

Presently she turned and uttered a cry in a voice that pierced the air like a shrill shrieking steam whistle. A sound more hideously, horribly fiendish, it would be difficult to imagine.

Again we heard the harsh grating sound and directly afterwards a peculiar pattering on the ground. A moment later and a swarm of figures ran from the shadows into the moonlight and surrounded the woman. At first they seemed to be small monkeys which scarcely reached to her knees, but as we watched them more closely we saw that they were men, small, wizened, shrivelled-up men, and involuntarily the expression of the Hatter's blackfellow came to my mind. They were moving and living copies of sun-dried mummies!

She waved her arms, and the swarm scattered round the pool until they stood, a ring of withered gnomes, at the edge of the water.

She clapped her hands, and the figures, stooping down as if impelled by one instinct, began to beat the surface of the water with both hands, so fast that it was soon a white foaming cauldron.

Again she clapped her hands, and the beating ceased, every little figure standing still and silent, so still that we could hear the bubbles bursting in a soft hissing sound.

The woman stood gazing intently upon the pool until the last of the foam had vanished. Then again she clapped her hands, and again the throng of figures beat the water till it frothed, and again she waited till the foam had disappeared. Three times was the performance repeated before she uttered a sound. Then as the last bubble burst she spoke.

I do not know what she said, but with the first word the Hatter exclaimed, "Ah."

I suppose it was due to the strain upon my nerves, and the intentness with which I had been watching the scene, but the sound of the Hatter's voice startled me so suddenly that I clutched my hands in sheer fright. I was holding my rifle with a finger on the trigger, and the result was a shot.

It rang out upon the night, the flash of the powder gleamed in the dark, and the bullet plunged into the middle of the pool. I heard the Hatter make a startled exclamation, and the rest was a wild nightmare.

The woman, turning her frightful eyes towards our hiding-place, raised her arms to their full length over her head with her fingers extended, and uttered a long, low wail, that horrified me and terrified me nearly to a stupor. The swarm of pigmies scattered from the pool, and ran hither and thither through the trees, making inarticulate sounds that were as though an army were gurgling in the last agonies of convulsions.

I felt the Hatter's hand grip my wrist, and in my ear I heard him whisper —

"Fool, sleep."

Then darkness fell upon me.

It seemed an age by the time that I recovered my senses, although the Hatter told me it was only a few minutes.

I heard his voice in my ear —

"Lie still, and fear nothing."

"All right," I whispered back, and at once I felt cool and collected.

Below me the woman still stood wailing, and round and round the pool the pigmy figures were pattering.

"Listen," the Hatter whispered again. "I think I know her language, and I'm going to play a bold stroke."

"All right," I answered. They were the only words I seemed to know.

For the account of the following scene, so far as the dialogue is concerned, I am entirely indebted to my companion, the language in which it was conducted being to me merely an aimless babble of sounds, without accent, rhythm, or anything else that distinguishes the chatter of apes from human speech. The Hatter told me afterwards that it was the tongue of a tribe he had come across somewhere in the Pitchorie district, a tract of country in North Australia, hundreds of miles from anywhere save desert, where the blacks find their much-valued narcotic, the pitchorie plant.

Leaning over his loophole the Hatter called out in a loud voice:

"Who seeks the King of Night?"

The effect upon the woman was dramatic. Her wail stopped at the instant, and, with her horrible gleaming eye lifted up towards us, she sank forward upon her knees, stretching out her arms towards us. The pigmies arrested their movements and fell down upon their faces, and the night was calm and quiet as it had been before they came.

"Who seeks the King of Night?" the Hatter cried out again.

"Nay, awful lord, I came but to seek him of the silent pool," the woman answered, her eyes still gleaming towards us.

"You lie," the Hatter cried angrily.

"Nay, nay, most mighty one. It is the time when the moon is full, and I come to greet him who shares with me the burden of the ages."

"If you speak truth, speak on and paint to me the image of whom you speak."

"He, monarch of all pools and waters, last of the race that sprang from the union of the ruler of all men and the chosen of the reptiles. He, who lives and has his realm in the streams that flow beneath the earth; his body clothed in the scales of his mother's kind; half fashioned like a man and half like a lizard of the pool. He who comes but once in the lifetime of a moon to view the world, where once his father ruled, till the end shall come, and I shall find the love for whom I languish, and he the way to ceaseless sleep."

"How name you him?"

"O mighty one, why ask? Was it not spoken from the clouds when he came forth in life, a word of terror to all men, to live while he lived, to last while our people lasted, and then to be a mockery in the mouths of those who shall come to jeer our fallen power and wrest the ruined fragments from our hold?"

"Name him."

The wail broke out again as the woman bowed herself to the ground and writhed in an agony.

"Need I speak again?" the Hatter cried.

She raised herself on her knees, pressing her hands to her head and swaying to and fro.

"O King of Night, forget not what it means. His name from me portends his doom and I shall be alone."

"Speak it or die."

With a shriek that made every pigmy form quiver, and cut my ears like a sting, she leaped to her feet and rolled on the ground again as she cried. "Oh, no, not that, not that."

"Then speak," the Hatter yelled.

She stood up again, her eyes flashing in a fresh horror.

"I name him. Bunyip!"

The pigmies seemed to shrink into yet smaller and more

repulsive forms at the mention of the word, and she who
uttered it crouched down upon the ground till her wealth
of hair spread over her and hid the glaring yellow skin from
our eyes, while sobs shook her frame and added still more to
the weird, unearthly spectacle below us.

"Go back from whence you came. Rest hidden till the
moon comes up again. Then come here once more."

She pushed back the hair from her face as she looked up.

"My destiny, O king," she said.

"Learn it then."

With a cry she sprang to her feet, and the pigmies, galvani-
zed, as it were, into life by her voice, jumped up and rushed
away into the shadows from whence they first appeared. She
waited till they had gone, and then, turning towards our
hiding place, she bowed seven times to the ground before she
followed her army into the darkness.

Again we heard the grating sound, and then the night was
silent.

"Thank heaven, that's over?" I exclaimed.

"But it isn't yet, my lad," the Hatter said. "The blacks are
right; there *is* a bunyip, and I reckon we're going to finish
him."

I was going to say something sceptical, when the Hatter
interrupted me. "Look at the pool," he said.

Its calmness had gone, and the surface was eddying and
bubbling, as if a fire had been lit beneath it and the water
was just coming to the boil.

"Keep your nerves steady, and be ready to shoot," the
Hatter said quickly.

As he spoke there was a splash and a swirl in the pool, and
a monster rose to the surface, almost more horrible than the
Yellow Woman. The head was that of a man, with huge
shining teeth showing through its mouth, and the eyes green
and phosphorescent, like those of our recent visitor. The
arms were long, and the hands were shaped like the fore feet
of a kangaroo, with long claws at the end of each finger.
Below the waist the limbs were formed like those of a crocodile, and there was an immense tail, frilled along the top with
a double row of jagged plates, shaped and standing up like
the teeth of a huge cross-cut saw. From the neck downwards
the creature was covered with scales that glittered in the
moonlight.

It swam to the edge of the pool, and dragged itself out

upon the grassy patch where the Yellow Woman had stood, and, opening its mouth, it gave vent to a laugh which seemed to contain all the blood-curdling elements of a thousand maniacal fiends.

"Aim at its eyes, and fire," the Hatter said, his voice expressing the horror that he felt.

Our rifles spoke together, and the huge beast rolled over and over on the grass, uttering cries and sounds that were even more horrible than its laugh.

"Fire till he stops!" the Hatter cried, and we went at it as hard as our rifles would work, till the form lay still where the moonlight streamed over it.

"Awful! Horrible!" I heard the Hatter say.

"Another night like this and I'm a lunatic, or dead," I answered.

"Bear up, my lad, we're as good as millionaires now; but that beast *is* hideous. Just what the blacks always described it."

"We are safe from interruptions till the morning, so I think we might have a camp," he answered.

"Sleep! What, with that thing down there?" I exclaimed. "I might as well try to fly."

The Hatter laughed.

"All right, my lad," he said. "Then we'll try the bushman's solace, and have a pipe. We can discuss the situation."

So we sat and smoked and yarned till the dawn, arranging our course of action in the meantime.

This "course of action" is a simple one: the two men press on and enter the kingdom of the Yellow Woman. There they learn that she is Tor Ymmothe, Queen of Lemuria (or all that remains of it), and eventually they trick her into allowing them to take tons of gold back to Perth.

Dick Halwood subsequently returns to England, and it seems that the adventure is over. But the Yellow Hatter has fallen in love with Tor Ymmothe, and asks for Halwood's help in planning a new expedition to lost Lemuria. . .

(See also pp. xi–xiii).

1901-1911

In the period before world war I Australian science fiction addressed itself to socio-political ideas of a more practical nature than those canvassed by the utopian writers. The problem for the writers of this period, however, was to *dramatize* their ideas, rather than merely using their novels as a soap-box from which to preach.

A Woman of Mars (1901) offers social commentary without debate, and at the expense of dramatic narrative. This imbalance is reversed in *The Coloured Conquest* (1904), where the emphasis upon the drama of invasion precludes any assessment of the attitudes and reactions of the beleaguered white population. (In the final paragraph of the excerpt, for example, the author refuses to offer his own view on whether or not one is better dead than enslaved.) *The Electric Gun* achieves a better mixture of action and commentary, but still relies heavily upon intrusive authorial moralizing.

Thus it is left to the writers of the post-war period to achieve complete unity of theme and action.

The excerpt from Mary Anne Moore-Bentley's *A Woman of Mars* (Sydney: Edwards, Dunlop and Co., 1901) is taken from Chapter V (pp. 29-33). The material from *The Coloured Conquest* (Sydney: NSW Bookstall Co., 1904) by Rata (Thomas Roydhouse) comprises Chapter XII — "Bennett Burleigh's Story — Sydney Burned and Pillaged by its Own People", and most of Chapter XIII — "The Japanese Land in Sydney — Treatment of the Citizens" (pp. 90-106). I have omitted seven sentences from p. 99, since these develop a sub-plot not otherwise mentioned in the excerpt. From Harold Johnston's *The Electric Gun* (Sydney: Websdale, Shoosmith Ltd, 1911), I have excerpted Chapter I — "The Shadow Falls" (pp. 1-13).

A Woman of Earth

from

A Woman of Mars

Mary Ann Moore-Bentley

(1901)

Whilst en route to Heaven with the soul of the dead Earth-ling, Marguerite, an angel makes a stop-over on Mars. This gives the Martian people a chance to learn about conditions of life, work, and motherhood on Earth — and they are scandalized by what they hear.

The Martian girl Vesta is chosen to go to Earth to set the Earthlings on the right path, and in the short excerpt which follows she recounts the story of Marguerite's sufferings in order to justify her interplanetary crusade.

Vesta began to relate Marguerite's story.

"Marguerite was the daughter of an astronomer living in the Australian continent. She was the only child of her parents. Her mother being a woman of the world — that is, I understand," said Vesta, "a woman who seeks her own individual welfare at the pain and expense of others — thought to benefit her child by compelling her to enter upon an early marriage with a wealthy man, a great many years her senior.

"Wealthy man," explained Vesta, by the way, "has somewhat the same meaning as wordly woman. It is one who accumulates wealth by condemning his fellow creatures to a life of brutalizing toil, whilst appropriating the productions of their labours in himself.

"You must not interrupt, Castor, or it will take an age to tell," said Vesta, smiling, as a burst of indignation from the former interrupted the tale.

"Marguerite's husband profusely lavished his wealth on his young wife, thus condemning her to a life of idleness and voluptuousness, which we would consider gross immorality.

"This Marguerite accepted and bore meekly, quite ignorant of the deteriorating effect it would have upon her offspring. At first she tried to respect, if she could not love, the husband of her mother's choice, but she found it utterly impossible and she had not lived with him long before she despised and loathed him as she despised and loathed herself, for she felt her position to be most degrading and bestial." And Vesta explained to Castor (for false modesty upon questions which so vitally affected the human race was utterly foreign to the Martian youth and maiden) how that woman upon Earth, by the force of ignorance and by the most diabolical customs and habits, allowed the sacred laws of propagation and maternity entrusted to them, to be outraged and degraded, man having debased the highest and holiest powers given unto him to the mere gratification of a low animal sense. "Upon Earth," continued Vesta, "custom carries its barbarous laws still further, compelling poor Marguerite to hand over her child the moment it was born to be nursed by a woman of the lower classes, thus utterly depriving her of her sole opportunity of moulding its mind, then plastic to receive impressions for good or evil.

"Marguerite existed under these trying and unnatural circumstances for ten years, during which time she bore her husband four children. When suddenly her fortunes changed, and by some means, which I do not understand, she and her husband were divested of all their wealth. The consequence was that they were immediately precipitated from the highest to the lowest rank in social position. Hence Marguerite and her husband were compelled to make their abode in the low ill-conditioned dwellings of the unfortunate victims of poverty and toil.

"To minutely narrate every detail of Marguerite's history, after the change in her fortune, is beyond my power, for I cannot comprehend, much less explain, all the social conditions surrounding it. These you will see, by the brief sketch I have given, are most perplexing and complicated, but by what I understand, they can all be summed up thus — that ignorance is ruled by avarice. The mass of human beings upon Earth seem darkly ignorant of the great social truths which should govern existence. Hence they are the helpless victims of a very small minority who, by their avarice, cunning, and brutality take advantage of their fellows' ignorance and superstition, nourishing their own unholy lusts at their brothers' expense. And, notwithstanding that their natural condition is greater than ours, still it is only by hardest toil, under the most trying conditions, that the majority are able to procure food enough to maintain a miserable existence. And even toil is denied them in capricious moments, when thousands are swept away by starvation and pestilence daily.

"Henceforward, Marguerite had to undergo all the trials and privations of the poor, and as she had been carefully sheltered from these evils all her previous life, she felt it extremely.

"Marguerite together with her husband and family wandered from place to place in their search for employment which everywhere was denied them. They were in a constant state of semi-starvation, Marguerite watching the children grow paler and thinner daily, until at length she grew impatient to seek employment herself, which would help towards their sustenance. However, she was compelled to wait until her youngest child was old enough to be trusted to the care of her eldest, who was but an infant herself. But to Marguerite's distress she discovered that she was to be a mother of a fifth child, which, under the circumstances, was most unwelcome." And Vesta explained how woman upon Earth was not consulted whether she desired motherhood. "Some time," she continued, "in the remote past of man's history, during his development, man has usurped thus her basic right, degrading it to be but the mere auxiliary to animal passion.

"It appears to me," said Vesta, "that woman in some remote period of human development has evolved intelligence sufficient to degrade a natural instinct, thereby deteriorating her species, and bringing about numerous and complex states of human existence, from which man has evolved to his present state of moral culture, which, compared with ours, is very low indeed. Meanwhile, man, during his moral and intellectual development, availed himself of many barbarous methods for coping with over-population. Infanticide, abortion, and other diabolical practices, were thus resorted to. Wonderfully rapid has been the nerve development of the human species upon Earth, and with it they have evolved abnormal propensities of grossest animalism.

"Marguerite tells me," said Vesta, "that already the regenerating law of love is at work, sympathy and self-sacrifice are not altogether strangers on Earth, but its future saviour must be woman, if it is ever to be raised to the high state of social happiness and moral beauty that we ourselves have reached.

"Marguerite gave birth to a son, and the sex of this unwelcome infant somewhat atoned for his hapless intrusion, as the previous children were girls, and the parents had craved for a boy. This child, however, did not live long to gladden the home of his parents, for, like thousands of his fellow victims, he early succumbed to privation and insanitary surroundings.

"Poor Marguerite did not long survive her child, the evils socially and morally of womanly existence upon Earth proving more than nature could endure."

"I perceive," said Castor, as Vesta finished Marguerite's story, "that sociology upon Earth is merely in its homogeneous stage of evolutionary progress, like the rhizopod germ of life, its organization of parts, with fixed functions of distribution, and uniformity of action, being very indefinite. A man's moral development may have been retarded by some violation of a natural law, as you say."

Vesta also told Castor of the present state of Earth's inhabitants, of the rivalry of Nations, and race competition, and of the problem of war, also of the slowly evolving sympathy in that direction with the growing desire for peace.

"But is it not impossible for the spirit of enmity to cease until Nations have solved the problems of race-multiplication and race-limitation?"

"The problem of race-multiplication must be fully met and coped with before wars and like modes of extermination may be dispensed with," said Vesta, "and it seems to me that this must be the next evolutionary grade of Man's social development."

"It is astonishing," said Castor, "that man is so low in the line of intellectual development, that he should adhere to the means which only the lowest forms of life rely upon to aid them in the competition of race survival."

"Yes," rejoined Vesta, "and yet he has evolved an astonishing degree of intelligence concerning other matters of social science, and the time must soon be, when he will understand that quality must survive quantity, and that that Nation which solves the problem of how to limit its numbers, at the same time preserving in them a healthy nerve development, must be the nation that will eventually survive all others."

"Sympathy is the basic law of moral evolution, and with

its mighty lever Self-Sacrifice, man may be raised to a high platform of moral culture," said Castor.

Vesta departs on her mission and spends a number of years crusading for women's rights in most of the major countries on Earth. "Of all places upon the Earth," she finds, "France was the lowest in moral and social degradation, considering the length of her experience of civilization". America is not much better: a land of "privations and misery". But Australia takes Vesta's message seriously, and social conditions in Australia are improved considerably.

At the end of ten years, as Vesta prepares to return to Mars, the forces of reaction gain strength on Earth and many feminist reforms are threatened. Vesta, however, remains confident: reaction is to be expected, but conservative small-mindedness can never stand for long in the path of genuine progress.

(See also pp. xiv–xv).

Led by the Japanese, the Coloured Races are taking over the world.

The Whites, of course, should have known that this would happen. As the narrator, Danton, puts it: "all Coloured peoples hate the Whites, for the reason that the Whites have looked down upon and scorned them for so long". If the Whites had been wise, they would have "shovelled all the gold they could spare into the building of an invincible Navy".

Now it is too late. Aided by the Japanese, the Chinese have built warships and are taking over their part of the world, and in America the Negroes have assumed control. Australia is next, and it has just been confirmed (by the war correspondent, Bennet Burleigh) that the Japanese fleet has defeated the British Navy and is now steaming toward Sydney.

Sydney was in a ferment. The excitement was added to by the arrival of Bennet Burleigh in the *Fulcrum*. He dashed into the harbour about midday, and interviews with him appeared in the evening papers.

He reported that the Japanese were not yet on the coast, but nevertheless might be expected to put in an appearance at any moment.

"The great battle!" he repeated, when asked about the smashing of the British fleet. "It was not much of a battle, it was just a slaughter. The Japanese had it all their own way from the jump. In the first place, their superiority in ships and armament was overwhelming, and the way in which they used their submarines made the thing a dead easy snap for them, though the British fought desperately."

"How did they get the submarines there?" asked the interviewer.

"They had them there for some months at an island of no importance, and not visited by traders. This island was within easy distance of the scene of battle."

"But how did the British come to fight a battle there?"

"It was a put-up job, as I learned from the Japanese. It was arranged by the Japanese Admiralty that a supposed Japanese traitor should sell the British certain information. The effect of that information was a concentration of various British squadrons at a certain point. I mentioned only two in my cable, but I am told there were four. It was simply a trap, one of the things that the ingenious Oriental mind rejoices in, and the British fell into it."

"And it meant the death-blow to the British nation?"

"Yes, no doubt; but the Japanese could have done the work without that trap had they so minded. It would have been easy for them to have met the squadrons singly on their own respective stations and beaten them by sheer weight — and a surprise, of course. No information was allowed to be sent from any Japanese or Chinese port for some weeks, and no one in the outer world knew where Japanese or Japo-Chinese squadrons and transports were going. The cable stations were seized, though the cable companies actually did not know it, for trained Japanese and Chinese cable operators were substituted, and carried on the services as though nothing had happened. The cable companies were sold, and the outside world was deluded until the blow fell."

"But you got information?"

"I did," said the famous war correspondent, with a smile. "I have good friends in the East even now. But they are unable to act openly, and I must take my gruel with the other Whites." He smiled somewhat dolefully. "But about the information. I got it and sent it off on a steamer to be wired from the nearest point outside Eastern control. It had to go a good way, you may guess. When they received it in England it was too late to do any good — even supposing the people there had believed it."

"And you had to do a bolt?"

"Rather! And I went for the scene of battle — the trap battle I may call it. The submarines did most of the mischief there. Versatile marine devils they proved themselves. It was done this way." The war correspondent was warming up.

"The battleships fired smoke shells across the track of the submarines as they approached their prey, and also kept in touch with them by submarine gong signalling. Every device they were up to, and really they 'enjoyed themselves thoroughly', as one of the officers I picked up said. The submarines were all round the British ships like a pack of dogs, and it was soon all over — all over."

A grey look came into his face, and he was so preoccupied that the next question had to be repeated before he heard it.

"Why weren't Japan and China stopped from building up a huge world-beating navy? That's an old question. The answer's old, too. Everybody's business was nobody's business. You remember when Russia entered into an undertaking with the Powers to quit Manchuria in October, 1903, and didn't do it? Did any or all of the Powers try to make her? No! Japan had to do it, off her own bat, although the European Powers and America had agreed — inferentially, at any rate — to step in. Interference meant fighting Russia. In this later business it meant fighting Japan and China."

"There might, at any rate, have been a European alliance to meet the Eastern invasion."

"The thought is reasonable, but the Powers were not. Their jealousies were at work. Each would cheerfully have seen the other throttled. The Continental Powers were willing that England should lose India. Very willing. And so it was all along the line."

"But they must at length have recognized a common peril and seen the necessity for common action?"

"You know as much about all this as I do. You know that there has not been united action, and now it is too late."

"And what shall you do, Mr Burleigh?" asked the reporter in conclusion.

"Do?" inquired Burleigh, nipping off the end of a cigar. "Why, sit tight and see the game out, of course. What the devil else is there to do? Come and have a drink."

The night Bennett Burleigh arrived there were other mass meetings in Sydney, but I did not attend any. I decided to go over to the North Shore with Mabel, at her request, and have a talk with her father about the position of affairs in the city.

We intended to tram it to the Quay, but after waiting at the corner of King and Pitt Streets for some time, and seeing no tram moving on either line, we inquired and learned the reason. A tram conductor standing on the footpath gave it:

"Why should the bloomin' tram men go on working?" he asked. "They can't get paid, can they? And why should they work for nothing? The Japs may get here at any time, and they won't pay us — not likely!"

"Are all the trams left in the streets?" I asked.

"Rather! We've done enough for nothing, ain't we? There's four days' pay owing us now. And wot's it matter, anyhow? The trams no more nor anything else here won't belong to us after the Japs arrive."

There was no answering that.

Mabel and I started to walk to the Quay. We had not taken many steps when the gas lights went out.

Soon the electric lights followed.

Excited remarks overheard from other pedestrians supplied information as to this development. The gas and the electric light men had heard of the action of the tram men, and thought it sound common sense. They dropped work on the instant.

A cabman shouted to an acquaintance that all the railway men had ceased work. There were no trains to the suburbs or anywhere else, he said.

We reached the Quay in due course, only to find that it was impossible to get across to the Shore. The steam ferries had ceased running, and there was not a waterman to be had. The watermen had gone up town to hear the news.

We waited for a considerable time, and eventually walked up Pitt Street again. The city was in darkness save for a few dim lights here and there given forth by candles. There were very few of these available, and no stores were open to sell.

In some parts of the city pandemonium reigned. Shouts and curses of men, with the shrieks of women intermingling, were frequently heard, but what was transpiring could only be guessed at.

Mabel shivered, and held tight to my arm. I reassured her as a man may under such circumstances, but I felt terribly depressed. The very atmosphere seemed laden with the microbes of dread, and the darkness of the night was that of the future.

A man passed talking to himself excitedly. He had gone mad. There were many such cases that night. I knew personally of several women who became demented owing to horrible apprehension.

"The mad people about the streets should be taken to one of the asylums," I said to an inspector of police, an old acquaintance of mine whom I met.

He laughed cynically.

"Who will take them?" he asked. "The police have all gone off duty — and so, for that matter, have the lunatic asylum staffs. I just heard, too, that all the warders have cleared out of Darlinghurst Gaol, and the prisoners also."

I paid a cabman two pounds to drive me to my residence in the Bayswater Road, Darlinghurst, and there handed Mabel over to the care of my mother, who, like all the people in the fair city of Sydney that night, was pale with fear.

I could not stay indoors. Taking my brother with me I walked down William Street to the city. At St Mary's a service was proceeding, and the cathedral was crowded. At Queen's Square the lamps were being re-lighted. We learned that the Premier and Lord Mayor had persuaded the gas and electric light employees, on humanitarian grounds, to resume duty. It was pointed out that the respectable citizens of Sydney were at the mercy of Sydney's criminals.

The light men did not care much about that.

"It's a time when everybody has to take his chance," said they.

"But think of the women," said the Lord Mayor.

That settled it. The gas and the electric workers were men, and they resumed their labours in order to help protect the women folk against the depraved of their own race.

The police, too, were induced on the same grounds to take on their duty again.

Other than these, the only people working were the newspaper men. No offer of reward was required by them. Loyalty and enterprise determined them to get out the news — "before the other fellow", if possible — until they were forcibly prevented.

But, stay; the telegraph operators also stuck to duty. The faithful fellows kept Sydney in touch with the other states without question of pay or reward, and thus maintained the tradition of a service that merits more public approval than it gets.

The Town Hall was lit up, and a meeting of city gentlemen sat there continuously waiting for news, and considering the situation.

At St Andrew's cathedral a stream of worshippers were coming and going, saying nothing.

About midnight the scum of the city made its presence felt more markedly. Offences against the person had already been very numerous. "Burn the banks and stores!" was a cry that was carried through the city by "pushes" of criminals who had already taken possession of and pillaged a number of hotels. Jewellers' shops were forcibly entered and the valuable contents carried off, some to be spilled on the road. The great general stores were also attacked, and goods of all kinds were soon scattered about the streets.

Processions of men carrying bottles of liquor streamed along the footpaths, screaming ribald songs, and constantly nipping until they fell cursing into the gutter.

The banks were broken into, but the strong-rooms defied the wreckers, and many were burned to death while working at the safes. For the cry of "Burn!" had been acted upon, and soon Sydney was aflame, blazing in a hundred places.

"Give the Japs a Moscow to come to," shouted a loud-mouthed politician. And the sentiment appeared to be greatly appreciated.

"Sydney won't be any good to us any more, let it be no good to the blanky Japs," said another. And so they yelled and cursed.

The flames spread with lightning rapidity, and soon all the business portion of Sydney was one huge furnace. Thousands of lives were lost, and even as I write I can hear again the screams of frenzied people caught in some fire-boundaried *cul-de-sac.*

The flames could not cross Hyde Park, and my people were safe. Before daylight I had them on the road to the Blue Mountains. I could not hire a vehicle, but took two horses and a sociable from a livery stable nearby, the owner and his men having fled with the other horses and carriages some hours before.

There would be nothing gained by dwelling on the details of what followed. Several books could be written about them; there is no dearth of material; but I only undertook to lightly sketch the main incidents of the upheaval that led to the whole world coming under Coloured rule, with the Japanese as the supreme nation.

The Japanese came to Sydney in due course.

They came to all Australia, and soon their occupancy was complete.

I was in Sydney for the invasion, having left my people at Springwood on the Blue Mountains. They were proceeding thence to Bathurst with a party of friends. . . . I wanted to ascertain what was likely to happen as a result of Japanese occupancy, so that I might be able to warn my people early.

Thousands of men, women and children were congregated at South Head the day the Japanese arrived.

Some torpedo boat destroyers first raced into view, followed by a line of beautiful cruisers, and another of stately battleships. A steamer containing the Japanese Acting-Consul-General, the Lord Mayor of Sydney, and the Premier, among others, was waiting outside the Heads. The Japanese Admiral was communicated with, and assured that Sydney would make no defence. The forts were, in fact, deserted; and Sydney, the once beautiful, lay in black ruins.

There was one man however, who determined that the Japanese should not have it all their own way. This was a member of the Submarine Miners' Corps, and he lived at Chowder Bay. He had quietly (it afterwards came out) laid a number of mines between the Heads and in the main harbour channels, and he watched the Japanese vessels with his finger on the key of the instrument of communication.

Thus it was that the people on South Head suddenly saw several explosions in the water between the Heads, and witnessed the blowing to pieces of one of the finest battleships of the fleet. Two cruisers and a torpedo boat-destroyer were similarly disposed of as they proceeded up the harbour.

The Japanese Admiral at once gave orders that the Premier and the Lord Mayor should be hanged. The Acting-Consul-General, however, managed to convince him that these gentlemen were innocent, and their lives were spared, though the Admiral declared he would have a full inquiry in Sydney, and then determine to whom punishment should be meted out. Some one would have to suffer for it.

Ten thousand troops were landed the first day, and took possession of the whole of the Metropolis. Placards printed in English were posted everywhere, warning all persons possessed of firearms of any sort that they must at once deliver them up.

If any cannon, gun, rifle, or pistol, or any other firearm, is found in the possession of any person after two days have passed the penalty will be death.

Thus ran the notice.

It was found necessary to carry out the penalty in only a few cases. Three persons were hanged in George Street, Sydney, one at Parramatta, one at Hornsby, and one at Penrith. Later on there were some cases in the country, but the promptness with which the Japanese executed any person found with a firearm had its effect.

"Thorough" was the Japanese motto. There were no excuses, no arguments — just death.

The morning papers came out as usual after the landing of the Japanese. They told of similar landings in Melbourne, Adelaide, Brisbane, Fremantle and elsewhere. The cables were in full work, and the story that came over them — from Japanese senders in London — was that India and Africa were now under Coloured rule. Europe was being invaded by a Yellow and Brown army that was just eating it up, like a plague of locusts, and the Japanese flag was flying over the British Isles.

America and Canada were as yet untouched, but there could be no question as to their fate. The eight million Negroes included in the population of the United States were already holding camp meetings and singing songs welcoming the approach of the new era, when the long-despised Coloured man would rule. Criminal assaults upon White women had increased enormously in the United States during the past month or two, and Japanese agents had warned the Negroes that they would be punished for such excesses a little later if they persisted in them.

So ran the cablegrams.

The Japanese Admiral received numerous official messages, and sent them to the morning papers with instructions to publish. It appeared from these that the Japanese plan was a very simple one. The British fleets being destroyed, the Brown men could land anywhere on British soil — sometimes with a fight, sometimes secretly. District or sectional disarmament quickly extended, and the cutting off of food supplies arriving from overseas were effective in every instance.

The army of occupation in the British Isles was not large,

but swift crushing of those who were even suspected of contemplating some overt act against it increased its power. Every force that endeavoured to check its progress into the country was pushed back with great slaughter by the superior guns worked by the world's best gunners. Japanese guns outranged those of the British, and the latter were smashed by shell fire before they could get near enough to hit back.

A cruel feature of the investment – an interesting one, the Japanese cable described it – was that the Japanese brought a large number of Indian troops with them, all in their British uniforms.

There were two or more Indian regiments in all the great cities of Britain, and they lorded it over the White people as (so they said) the Whites had lorded it over them in India.

A Japanese manager who could talk English was put in charge of every place of business in Sydney. All White people employed therein were given a ration consisting mainly of rice, and told that they would get two suits a year, one of woollen material and the other of cotton.

"But what of my family?" asked the department manager of a large store.

"Your family will not trouble you," replied the Japanese. "The Mikado's Australian Government is providing for all the people. Your wife will be employed, probably, in a factory; those of your children over seven will go to work of some kind or other."

"Why, they haven't left school!" gasped the unfortunate manager. His brain, like that of many another citizen in that terrible hour of stress, had become affected, so that he failed to realize the situation.

"Schools are abolished," returned the Japanese, in whose face there was as much expression as in a stone. "The Mikado's Australian Government," he went on, "will not educate any White children. In two or three generations the White people will become accustomed to their position, and will not, what you call, buck up; but if the children learn to read, and are allowed to read, they will never feel comfortable. You understand?"

The White man understood. Even his confused mind grasped the fact that the Brown rulers were taking the surest step to crush nationality. The Whites alive fifty years hence would know nothing of the grand past of the nation to which they belonged. To those who had been told it would all seem but a dream.

"My wife! Have you taken my wife!" demanded the manager.

"I cannot say; but you will not see her again. You will live here."

"In the store?"

"In the store — for the present. The Director-General of Supplies Distribution may make other arrangements later on."

"My wife! Where is she?"

"I cannot furnish any more information. The Government tell us to be courteous as ever to the White people, though firm. You will now proceed to your work."

"But — "

The Japanese officer — all officials, civil as well as military, were uniformed and carried arms — silenced him with a gesture towards his sword.

This scene was repeated all over Sydney, and later in the country towns. Sometimes it was accompanied with violence; but only those present knew of that. There was no Press record of such disturbances; if there was the Whites knew nothing of it. Only Japanese papers were now published. The English papers were suppressed the day after the landing. It was but natural that the comments of some, though conciliatory, had given offence to the pride-swollen conquerors.

A few of these were very arrogant. One of the cruel scenes of those early days of Japanese rule that linger in my mind — and is at this moment a vivid brain picture — was associated with the Press. The proprietors, editors, managers and staffs of the various newspapers were required to parade outside their respective offices, and there at the order of the Japanese officers shout —

"Banzai, Japan!" (Long live Japan.)

The grey-headed chief of one of the principal newspapers — a man whom all esteemed — could not be induced to utter the words. He was roughly dragged in front of his own men, and ordered to shout by himself.

Still his tongue was silent.

The staff looked on, their finger-nails eating into the palms of clenched hands; their faces distorted with rage.

There would have been death for some of the group —

including the swaggering Japanese tormentor – had not a
superior officer come along and rebuked him for satisfying
his personal antipathy at the expense of the dignity of the
Mikado's Australian Government.

All the newspaper staffs were ordered to the Northern
rivers, there to assist in preparing the country for agriculture.

The Premier and his ministers, together with the parliament, received precisely similar treatment.

One member openly and vigorously reviled the Japanese,
expressing the bitterness that was kept locked in the bosoms
of the Whites generally, and was shot.

There were many of his colleagues who said afterwards
that he was better off than they, and regretted that they had
not for that occasion permitted impulse to overleap caution.

*The easy conquest of Sydney and surrounding areas is merely
a foretaste of things to come. The Mikado's Australian
Government soon controls the nation, and the days of White
Australia are gone forever.*

*Contrary to popular illusion, there is no last-minute
rescue. At the same time that they were allowing their racist
attitudes to goad the Coloured Races into an attempt at
conquest, the Whites were foolishly neglecting to build up
their defences. Now the Japanese are in Australia to stay.*

(See also pp. xxi–xxii).

The Shadow Falls
from
The Electric Gun
Harold Johnston
(1911)

Subtitled "A Tale of Love and Socialism", The Electric Gun
*tells the story of the "great change" whereby Australian
society abandoned Socialism. In this, the novel's opening
chapter, Edward Bruce – the instigator of Socialist government in Australia – finds that he has become a victim of the
system he advocated.*

"A thousand years scarce serve to form a State;
An hour may lay it in the dust."

– Byron.

At the time of the great change, Edward Bruce was a journalist on the staff of one of the Sydney daily papers. The
attitude of the press towards what the Socialists called the
"Great Reform" was a curious mixture of friendliness and
fear, but Bruce himself was an ardent "reformer", and his
book, *Liberty*, published early in 1924, had greatly influenced the elections, which brought about the downfall of
individualism. The tide of popular opinion overwhelmed
both parliament and press, and the new system came into
force at the beginning of the following year.

Bruce was appointed sub-editor of the *State Daily News*,
but his innate love of justice brought him ere long into
conflict with the horde of place hunters who swarmed like
flies round the government offices.

Edward Bruce had always strongly advocated equal remuneration for all workers, as he recognized that any other
arrangement would lead to infinite trouble when the commission to regulate employment should be appointed. In a

community where all were supposed to have equal rights, he contended that it was absurd to say that the services of one man were of more value to the state than those of his neighbour. He quite failed to perceive, however, that while the amount of money actually paid might be the same in all cases, yet the position of the officials who regulated and controlled production must be very much better than that of the labourers on the farm or in the factory. This must be so, even if all men were industrious and virtuous, and in Bruce's calculations he entirely overlooked the important factor of human nature.

No sooner did the bureaucracy find itself firmly seated than it promptly kicked away the ladder by means of which it had climbed to power.

At this time Bruce was thirty-five years of age, married, with one infant son.

One morning he was politely informed that, as his services were no longer required on the staff of the paper, he would be expected to report himself for duty within three days to the superintendent of the wheat farm at Temora. He went round at once to the Labor Department, and, after some difficulty, succeeded in obtaining an interview with the Director. But it was quite in vain that he pointed out that his services would be of more value to the state in his present position.

"You may think so," said the Director, with a sneer, "but then your opinion is not wanted on the subject. Don't you, or can't you, see that if choice of occupation were permitted in your case, we should be morally bound to allow everyone to select his own work? Everyone might decide to become a lawyer or a policeman. The only fair, the only possible, way of allotting tasks is by rote. The farm superintendent at Temora has sent in a requisition for two hundred additional men. Your name happened to be drawn amongst the number. I can do nothing for you; good-day."

This was bad enough, but worse was to follow. When he reached his home, an hour later, he found that his wife had just been served with a notice, instructing her to proceed by the following Monday morning's train to Jervis Bay, to begin work there in the new jute factory.

"Good heavens!" exclaimed Bruce, when he had glanced at the notice: "there must be some dreadful mistake. I am being sent to Temora. They cannot intend to separate us!"

The young wife threw herself into her husband's arms. "I will not leave you, I cannot leave you, Ted," she sobbed.

"I'll die before I let them take me away."

Bruce soothed her as well as his own emotions would permit.

"Don't cry, Ellen, dear," he said. "I feel sure that it is only the result of a clerical error. I shall go back to town at once, and see the Director again. Don't worry! It will be all right."

Bruce was far from feeling the confidence which his words to his weeping wife indicated. He had already seen enough of departmental tyranny to realize that many of the officials were capable of anything, especially when it meant a demonstration of their own authority. They could always shield themselves behind the state. "The interests of the State demanded it."

Bruce found, upon his return to the office, that the Director had "just gone out for a few minutes". The great man did not return for an hour and a half, and, when he did come in, Bruce mentally diagnosed the case as "pretty full".

"What's the matter?" asked the Director, as he lurched into his chair. "Oh! it's you, Bruce, is it? What-ye-want? Out with it; can't ye see I'm busy?"

"I wish, sir, to put my case before you again," began Bruce. The Director interrupted him angrily.

"Your case! your case! Confound you and your case! One would think, to hear you talk, that nothing in the world is of any importance but your paltry affairs."

"But, Sir, you stated this morning that I must go to Temora."

"Well, what about it?"

"Only this, that since I saw you this morning, my wife has received instructions to proceed to Jervis Bay," replied the unhappy man.

"Look here!" exclaimed the Minister, thumping the table with his fist, "you understand this. The rights of the State are paramount — paramount. The individual is nothing — less than nothing. If your wife's name is drawn for Jervis Bay, or for Bourke, or for Tim-Timbuctoo, she must go; that's all about it. D'you think, do you really think, that a department such as this can be administered if I am to be constantly pestered by fellows such as you? Gerout the office!"

"But my wife's health —— "

"Oh! d——n your wife's health! What I care about y'r wife's health? She'll be orright. Plenty men at Jervis Bay. Soon console herself loss o' you. Plen'y women Temora; you get ri' side the superin'endent, he'll fix y' up. Gerout! I got lot o' work. Gerout!"

How Bruce reached his home on that dreadful day he did not know.

"What can I say to Ellen?" he groaned. He and his wife, though married for more than five years, were still lovers. Through all the struggles of the past few years he had been supported by the thought that he was working for Ellen. "For Ellen – and now!"

His cheeks burned as he recalled the insulting words of the brute, who, by virtue of his office, had power to inflict such injustice upon unoffending people. And then there was his little boy, whom he had temporarily forgotten. Heavens! Would that poor helpless child be torn from his mother's arms – taken away, to be handed over to the tender mercies of the nurses at the State Creche? And he – fool! idiot! madman! that he had been. He had been partly instrumental in bringing into existence this iniquitous, this devilish system!

Bruce found his wife at the door, waiting for him. He tried to smile, but it was a very feeble attempt. The little boy uttered a gurgle of delight, and tried to gouge out his father's eye with his own chubby fist.

"Come in, Ted," cried his wife. "I have been looking out for you for the last hour. How did you get on? Tell me quick – quick. You have good news, haven't you?"

"Ellen, my poor girl," he said, as he took her in his arms, "I have failed – utterly failed. The Director – he insulted me in the grossest manner – he will do nothing. No alteration in the arrangement is possible."

The poor wife bowed her head upon his shoulder, while he stroked the beautiful, chestnut hair tenderly. Presently she looked up, and exclaimed, in heart-broken tones: "But, surely, such a thing cannot be allowed. Isn't there anyone to whom we can appeal? You know all the members of the government so well; why not see some of the others?"

"My dear girl," he replied. "I am afraid that it is useless to apply to any of the members. I have already made myself obnoxious to most of them by constituting myself the champion of the workers. I feel sure that this is the reason why I am being sent out of the city. Little did I dream that my own case would so soon become even worse than that of those poor creatures for whom my heart has bled during the past six months."

"And this is what you call love!" cried Ellen, drawing herself away from his embrace. "We are to be separated –

perhaps for ever — and yet you can talk about the sufferings of others. What do I care for other people's troubles? My own, and those of my unfortunate child, are quite enough for me."

"Ellen! My God! Ellen!" he groaned. "What are you saying? Do you think that my remorse at having assisted in bringing about such a condition of things, at having handed over thousands of innocent men and women to those devils incarnate — do you think *that* is not enough without your reproaches?"

"Oh! Oh! Oh!" she sobbed. "Forgive me, Teddy dear, forgive me! To think that I could say *such* an unkind thing to my own dear boy! Kiss me, Teddy, dear. I'm *so* sorry."

Under the influence of her caresses, Bruce, who was naturally optimistic, rapidly regained his spirits. He would "look up Henson" (one of the members of the government) in the morning. Henson was always very friendly. Henson would be able to fix matters up. Even if they *were* separated, he felt sure that it would be for a very short time, as he would petition the government for an exchange to Jervis Bay. They would soon be together again.

Ellen dried her tears, and became comparatively cheerful as she listened to his words.

Next morning Bruce called at Henson's office, but was disappointed to learn that that gentleman was out of town. "How long would he be?" The clerk didn't know. "Mr Henson had gone to Bourke, in connection with the scheme for locking the Darling River. Any message?"

Conquering his pride, Bruce determined to see the Director of Labor once more, but the clerk, to whom he handed his card, returned in a few minutes, and informed him, with a grin, that "Mr Lewis requests Mr Bruce to go to the devil".

The unfortunate man returned home, and began his preparations for leaving the city. Before he left he drew up a statement of his case, and forwarded this to Henson's town address.

Bruce and his wife parted at the Central Railway Station, where he, blinded by his tears, staggered to the train set apart for the Temora farm labourers, after seeing his wife borne, half conscious, into that just on the point of starting for the South Coast.

They never met again.

Almost from the day of her arrival at Jervis Bay, Ellen Bruce, owing to her unusual beauty of face and form, attracted the unwelcome attentions of the factory manager. A virtuous, refined woman, she repelled the fellow's advances with scorn, with the result that she was subjected to all kinds of petty humiliations. Her only solace during this unhappy time was her little son. Jack was a bright little fellow, and just beginning to talk, when, instigated probably by his master, the devil, the manager had the child removed from his mother's room (during her absence at work), and transferred to the State Nursery at Kiama.

When she discovered her loss Ellen Bruce was, for a time, a mad woman, and while in that condition would have dashed herself from the window of her room to the court-yard below, if she had not been restrained, forcibly, by the other workwomen. After a couple of hours she became quiet, however, and when "lights out" was signalled at nine o'clock by the factory bell, the bereaved woman was in bed, and apparently asleep.

The next morning Ellen Bruce did not respond to her name at roll call, and the girl who was despatched in search of her reported that the room was empty. A hurried search was made, but the missing woman could nowhere be found.

Some days later the workmen employed on the wharf noticed an object floating in the bay, and a boat being sent out to investigate, the body of Ellen Bruce was recovered from the water.

"Poor girl!" said one of the boatmen, with a sigh.

"Poor girl!" repeated the other in a tone of scorn. "Happy girl, you mean, to get away from this God-forsaken country. If what the parsons used to tell us was true, this girl is now in Heaven, while we are still in hell — hell, do you understand? — and serve us right, too, for we walked into hell with our eyes open, while poor girls like this were dragged in. I wish to God I had courage enough to follow her example."

Immediately upon his arrival at Temora, Bruce, a man with but one idea for the time being, sought an interview with the superintendent of the farm. Some ten or twelve other workers were present — on similar errands. The officer listened to the tales of woe with but languid interest, but eventually informed Bruce and the others that he would communicate with headquarters and let them know the result.

A week later Bruce, in accordance with the regulations,

had his name "put down" for another interview with the superintendent, at the same time stating, in the prescribed form, the matter he wished to discuss. Before going out to work next morning he was curtly informed by one of the foremen that the superintendent did not consider an interview necessary, as "the matter was under consideration".

He next asked to be supplied with writing materials, in order that he might forward a petition to the government. The official to whom he applied directed his attention to "Regulation 41". He learned from this that "Workers are permitted to write letters, not exceeding three in number, on the first Sunday in every month, provided that no black marks are standing against their names", and with this he had to be content.

On "Letter Day" he first wrote a long and affectionate letter to his wife, and then proceeded to state his case to the head of the government. He took infinite pains over this statement, but might have saved himself the trouble, as the correspondence was all submitted to the superintendent before being sent out, and that gentleman promptly threw Bruce's petition into the waste-paper basket. A few days later he was informed that nothing could be done in his case — for the present.

Bruce was not alone in his misfortune. Quite one-third of the married men on the farm had been separated from their wives and families. It must not be supposed that the whole of these men submitted, without protest, to the arbitrary acts of the officials, but their attempts to obtain justice met with no success. The less scrupulous among the newly-appointed officials naturally forced themselves into the highest positions, and they were aware that they held these positions only so long as they could compel others to acknowledge their authority.

Shortly after Bruce's arrival at the farm there was a mutiny amongst the workers, led by one of the married men, who persuaded the others that, provided they stood firm, the authorities must give way, as they had always done in the old days. The revolt lasted only a few hours. The leader was led out into the yard and there shot dead, while twenty others were put on reduced rations for a fortnight. At the same time the superintendent announced that the government intended establishing a factory near the farm, and that diligent workers would be allowed to rejoin their wives, who would be brought from the other factories, while workers guilty of any insubordination would be deprived of this privilege. Of course the government did not intend doing anything of the kind, but the poor workers did not know this, and the combined threat and promise had the desired effect of keeping them quiet.

For the next six months Bruce worked strenuously, hoping to find, in the severe manual toil, an outlet for the suppressed forces within him. At the end of that time he was handed an official document, wherein he read that some individual, with an indecipherable name, had the honour to inform him that "Female worker Ellen Bruce, employed at the jute factory, Jervis Bay, died on the 10th day of November, 1926".

Nothing else! No word of explanation! No cause of death assigned! No expression of regret! The State was indeed paramount; the individual nothing.

During the four years which followed the death of his wife the only communication which Bruce received from the outside world were the half-yearly notices stating that his son, John Bruce, was alive and in good health. Then these ceased.

When the usual form failed to arrive Bruce concluded that his child was dead, and he thanked God for his kindness in removing the poor child to a better world. But he discovered later, from a remark by one of his fellow-workmen, that no one at the farm had received any notice, and one of the foremen condescended to inform them that the central authority had decided, in order to save unnecessary expense, that, in future, parents would know that their children were alive unless they received notice to the contrary, but that, in case of death, the parent or parents would be notified in due course.

This statement was received with apathy. Why should they — dumb, driven creatures — be a cause of unnecessary expense to the paternal State?

They slouched away to their daily tasks, and from that day until just before he was removed to the Home for Aged Workers at Callan Park, twenty years later, Edward Bruce, the one-time journalist, author and philanthropist, held no communication with any person other than his fellow workers and the farm gangers.

There was a tolerably good library at the farm lodging house, and here, among the books, Bruce spent most of his leisure. The great majority of the workers, however, seemed to think of nothing beyond devising schemes for obtaining more food and doing less work.

Fear of punishment was the only incentive to exertion, and lying the only weapon of defence against the tyranny of officialdom. The virtues which had been created by a thousand years of struggling against oppression vanished at the first touch of the slavery of Socialism.

Honesty, diligence, and truthfulness had disappeared. The system had destroyed virtue.

Edward Bruce has been destroyed by the system — but his son has not. The child has survived, and twenty-four years later he takes up the struggle against Socialism.

Using a bakery in Balmain as headquarters, Jack Bruce establishes a select anti-Socialist enclave. Members are chosen on the basis of their usefulness to the cause, and are given jobs at the bakery as a way of keeping in contact.

As Australian Socialism grows more and more oppressive, revolt begins. In the course of trying to help the rebels, Bruce and his supporters steal a government aircraft, and in it they find a fully operational electric gun of the kind issued to the police. With such a formidabie weapon at their command, the anti-Socialist forces finally prevail.

(See also p. xxv).

1925–1947

The three items in this section represent the maturing of Australian science fiction. Erle Cox's *Out of the Silence* (1925) draws together the racial and utopian motifs of earlier fiction, and builds upon works such as *A Woman of Mars* and *The Electric Gun* by not only dramatizing their themes, but also providing a fairly rigorous exploration of them.

Vandals of the Void (1931) recalls *The Coloured Conquest* inasmuch as both novels rely upon suspenseful action-packed plotting. *Vandals of the Void* is the better work, however, for whilst the pacing of *The Coloured Conquest* sometimes stands in the way of the full exploration of theme, *Vandals of the Void* is conceived as pure entertainment and generates no thematic concerns to clutter or impede the narrative.

Tomorrow and Tomorrow (1947) is the most serious-minded and ambitious novel of the three. The scientifically fictional elements of *Out of the Silence* are used chiefly to colour and heighten the plot (for Cox could just as easily have explored his themes in a realistic setting), and in *Vandals of the Void* the future is used solely for its ability to provide escapist exotica (such as space ships and aliens). But in *Tomorrow and Tomorrow* the future is *the future*: it is the destiny toward which the present may be heading – it is today writ large. Thus, of the three novels represented in this section, only *Tomorrow and Tomorrow* is "science fiction" in the truest and purest sense, for it is the only one of these three novels which *demands* a futuristic setting in order to articulate its theme.

From Erle Cox's *Out of the Silence* (1925; Westport, Connecticut: Hyperion Press, 1976) I have used Chapters XIX and XX (pp. 229–53); from James Morgan Walsh's

Vandals of the Void (1931; Westport, Connecticut: Hyperion Press, 1976), I have excerpted Chapter IV – "The Wreck in the Void" and Chapter V – "The Guard-Ship" (pp. 38–58); and from M. Barnard Eldershaw's *Tomorrow and Tomorrow* (Melbourne: Georgian House, 1947) I have taken pp. 3–11 of Chapter I.

> # Andax and Odi
> *from*
> Out of the Silence
> *Erle Cox*
> *(1925)*

*Finding a huge metal dome buried beneath his rural property,
Alan Dundas begins to investigate. The dome houses a huge
underground complex bristling with machines and gadgetry
of a highly advanced nature, and Dundas begins to spend
more and more of his time exploring. After roaming five vast
"galleries" exhibiting the artistic and scientific wonders of
some lost civilization, Dundas comes to the sixth gallery —
and discovers that its exhibit is the body of a woman in suspended animation.*

*Enticed by the woman's beauty and entranced by the
eerie fascination of his discovery, Dundas solicits the help of
his good friend, Dr Richard Barry, and together they revive
the woman. Several weeks of recuperation follow, and during
this time the two men learn nothing more about the girl than
that her name is Earani.*

It was at the end of the third month that Earani began to tell
them of the mystery of her being, for she reserved the revela-
tions until Barry was there to hear them. It was one afternoon when the three were seated together in the "temple",
and the talk had touched on the subject of geology. Barry
had hazarded a second-hand opinion on the length of time
that life in any form had existed on the earth. "Ah, Dick, my
dear boy," (she had long adopted Alan's form of address),
"how wildly they guess, those scientists of yours. Come: I
will show you." She took Alan's atlas from a table near by,
and with it a volume from the library. Then she called them
both to the couch beside her, and with the books on her lap

to illustrate her meaning, she told them of the world's past. "You remember, Alan, how you showed me this map on the day after you recalled me to life?" and here she turned to the map of the world. "Strange as it was to me then, I knew what it meant, although the chart I was used to was so different. See, here it is," and she opened the other volume. "Before my eyes were closed in the long sleep in which you found me, this was the world I knew. See, although it is so altered, many of the lines are familiar." Their three heads bent over the maps before them, and with her dainty fore-finger Earani traced the many places, still almost the same, on both charts.

"Do you mean, Earani, that since you knew the world it has altered so?" asked Alan.

"Indeed, it has altered, this old world. Can either of you wise ones tell me the cause?" She looked smiling from one to the other.

Dick shook his head. "I pass — Alan, I leave it to you."

"And you, Alan?" Her soft white hand fluttered to his arm. "Tell this Dick, who knows everything, how this old world was wrecked to build a new one in its place." She smiled into his eyes.

Alan shook his head in turn, but before Earani could speak again he broke in: "Wait, though. It may be that I can guess. Some of our men hold that at one time the axis of the earth has moved, and that the shock must have dislocated the whole of the surface. I have always thought this theory fantastic, but it may fit."

Earani laughed softly, and nodding her head, she turned to Barry. "Ah, Dick! You see Alan can use his head as well as that great strong body of his. My teacher is worthy of the office."

"Was that really the cause, Earani?" asked both men to-gether.

"That, indeed, is what happened. Ages and ages ago the world was inhabited by a race of human beings just as it is to-day. It was a race that had gone through all the trials and struggles through which yours had passed and is passing. Some day I will tell you of it; at present let it suffice that the race had attained to the greatest heights humanity is capable of when the great calamity befell."

She paused for a moment, as though the picture of the great lost past saddened her. Then she spoke again, and her voice came in a little more than a whisper. "Our people knew of the blow that threatened long before it fell. They were too great to fear for themselves; but they knew that on the ashes of the wrecked world another race would arise. They knew, too, that the new race would have to pass through the same great trials before it won to its own high place. What they mourned was that all the great works of their brains and hands should perish utterly. That their race should vanish was a small thing compared with the danger that all their great ideals should vanish with it.

"Can you think of what it meant to those who had helped in the great work, and the men who knew the value of it? A little perhaps you can understand, but very little, unless you knew the people of the lost world. Oh, so long ago! And yet it seems to me so very near."

Then after a little silence she spoke again. "And so they determined on a desperate effort to preserve their knowledge for the benefit of the people that were to come again. They had but two hundred years in which to work. Little time enough for their work, but it sufficed. On each of three carefully selected spots on the earth they built a great sphere such as the one we are now in. In the building of them they brought to bear every grain of the great lore they had, to win their purpose and make them invulnerable against the great calamity. Into each of them when all was ready they gathered together a specimen of all their art and science. The means of holding life suspended had been known for many generations, though it was but little used. Then it was determined that into each sphere one person should be placed to form the link between the old world and the new."

"Why only one in each?" asked Alan, who was following the story with burning interest.

"The question was deeply debated at the time," she answered. "Although we knew that for any ordinary time the body could be kept in a state of suspended animation, yet there was no certainty that the ages that must pass before reanimation took place, if it ever did, would not cause the attempt to fail. Our people did not wish to condemn more than would be necessary, to the risk of a terrible fate. There were so many and such terrible dangers for the chosen ones to face. So in the end three were chosen."

"How chosen?" asked Barry, eagerly.

"In the first place," she answered, "volunteers were called for. Thousands answered the call. It was no thought of self-preservation that brought them forward. Each one knew that there were dangers to be faced by those who were selected that were worse than the death that the race had to meet, but none of the old race feared death. To them it was but an incident. No; each one was animated by the hope that in the end it would fall to his or her lot to carry the light from the dying race to the race unborn.

"All over the world councils were held, to which the candidates were called, and the most fitted were sent forward to a central council, where the final choice was made; and so it fell out in the end that I, Earani, was thought worthy of the great honour. Why? Fate, I think; for amongst so many there would be but small difference."

"Earani — tell us," broke in Barry. "You say there were three great spheres. The others — what of them?"

She rose to her feet and walked to the keyboard that had been her first thought on the day she had awakened. Turning, she faced them. "The master builders who contrived this work left nothing to chance. This keyboard is in everlasting connection with those in the other two. Only absolute destruction could break the tie. Listen!" Her fingers moved swiftly on one section of the board. Then she stood still watching them. No sound broke the silence. After a moment she spoke. "There is no answer to that call, and so I know that one has failed to stand the strain of the wrecked world." Again her hands fell on the keys, and this time a deep clear note of a bell answered her touch. "You hear," she cried. "So Andax lives and waits for his release."

Dundas and Barry looked at her in silence. The news of the existence of a second sphere affected them both deeply, but in different ways. To Barry, the news that another being of the type of Earani could be brought to reinforce her, increased the feeling of uneasiness that had already gained hold of him. Alan, however, saw in the news only a threat against his love for Earani. "What," he thought, "would happen were a man of her race to appear on the scene? Surely he would be her fitting mate in every way? What chance would I have against such a rival?" The thought sent a feeling of blind jealous rage through him. It was he who broke the silence. "Tell me, Earani — this Andax you speak of. Is it the name of a man or woman of your race?"

Earani left the keyboard and walked towards them. "Andax," she said thoughtfully, as she paused before them. "Well, Andax is a man." She looked from one to the other and smiled. "He is a man, too, who would be difficult perhaps for you to understand without knowing him." She sank into a great carved chair facing them. "When I said that volunteers were called for, for the long sleep, I did not make myself quite clear. It was decided one hundred years before the great disaster fell that one of our race should occupy each sphere, and from that time until the selection was made our race occupied itself with the idea that fitting representatives should be ready when the time came.

"Each generation was watched with increasing care. The welfare of the unborn was almost a religion with us, aye, it was a religion with us. Some day it will be so with you when your eyes are opened. Every rule for the blending of human blood had been laid down long before, and we knew the type of man we wished to breed, and worked for it." She turned in her chair and looked down the "temple", where the curtains were drawn wide, out into the gallery beyond at the statue that was framed in the doorway leading to the ante-chamber. She waved her hand towards the statue. "That was the man who first laid down our laws of race making, and Andax is directly descended from him. Ah! he was a man, and Andax is an improvement; he is twenty generations of careful breeding better. Alan, why are you looking so angry?"

Alan pulled himself up. "Truth to tell, Earani, I don't like that face; it looks absolutely pitiless."

She nodded slightly. "Yes, perhaps you are right. The breed had little weakness about it. But that breed did great things for our world. All of our best carried the strain. I have it on both sides, not much, but enough to tell, and the blood of the old doctor holds it in check; but in Andax it is almost pure. I grew up with him and know him well. He has intensified in him all the characteristics of the breed. In appearance he has the same high forehead and sparse hair, the thin nose and the wide nostril, the straight, lipless, mouth, and the steel bright eyes." She gave a little laugh. "Not one of the race ever had a heart. They carried an organic pump in the thorax that was no use except to keep their brains alive."

Barry listened with a sense of fear he could not control, but, hiding it as best he could, he said: "Your picture isn't exactly fascinating, Earani; I should imagine he would not be altogether a genial companion."

She nodded. "Andax would not appeal to many people. He tolerated me. He regarded me as a useful fool; in fact, he told me he did. He was my tutor in surgery for my year's course, and afterwards I had two years under him for engineering. He was angry about that. He said that if I would let him graft one lobe of his brother's brain on to my brain he would put me through the course in one year, and I refused." She laughed lightly. "It was then he told me I would never be anything more than a useful fool, and he was furious because I took up law and literature instead of government and domestic science." She paused a little. "Pitiless was perhaps the right word, Alan. Cold, passionless, and calculating, all of them. Absolutely inflexible. They saw one goal ahead, and went straight to it. There was no thought of self-interest with any of them and no desire for power or authority for its own sake. They looked on our world simply as one great experiment for them. They were unflinchingly honest even with themselves. Andax there would have vivisected me or anyone else without anaesthetics if he thought the result would ultimately benefit the race, and at the same time he would have sacrificed himself just as surely. And mark you, my friends, there are stories of their doings I could tell you that are not good to hear, but there was never an act of theirs, however terrible, that did not bring a greater blessing in its train."

For a while there was silence; each of her hearers was busy with his own thoughts. The picture Earani drew of the other being awaiting release affected them both deeply. Then Barry spoke. "This other sphere, Earani; you know where it is? Can you find it?"

"Yes," she answered; "there will be no trouble about that. Wait, I will show you." She took the two maps to the table and bent over them. "From your maps and ours I have worked out the alteration of the axis; the rest is easy." She paused now and again with closed eyes, as though mentally calculating. Then — "Yes, that will be about it, roughly, about 74 east and between 36 and 37 north. About here." Her finger indicated a point to the north of India. Alan turned to the map in the atlas and ran his finger over it. Then he gave a low whistle. "Pretty spot, isn't it, Dick? Right in the middle of the Himalayas, about four hundred miles north-west from Simla."

"What kind of country is it, Alan?" asked Earani.

"In the world's greatest range of mountains. Almost impossible country amongst eternal snow, and only partially known. Earani, a search there would be hopeless," answered Dundas, with rising spirits. "Why the sphere might be buried beneath the mountains a thousand feet."

"It is likely you are right," came the unruffled answer. "Indeed, it is almost sure to be so, for before the disaster that spot was a great tableland. Still our work will be simple. Once we reach the locality I can ascertain the position of the sphere with absolute accuracy, and the rest will be easy."

"Even if it were buried?" interposed Barry.

"The depth is of no importance. A thousand feet or ten thousand, I have the means at hand. You will understand later." Her calm assurance left both her hearers hopeless. She dismissed the matter with a gesture of her hand. "Time enough to talk of Andax. First I must be ready to tell him all he will want to know, and believe me, he will be hungry for knowledge when the time comes." Barry looked bewildered, and Earani, noticing his expression, smiled. "Oh, Dick! There are so many things you do not know yet. What troubles you?"

"I was wondering at the moment how old Andax is, or rather was, when he started the long sleep."

"We were born in the same year," she answered. "He is just twenty-five. The twenty-seven millions of years don't count," she added laughing. "I don't look my age, do I?"

The two men gave a gasp. The figures stunned them, but there was another matter that was beyond their comprehension. It was Alan who gave it expression. "How is it possible that at that age he was your tutor in your studies, as you say, in surgery and engineering?"

"It is simple when you understand the mental powers of the man. By the time he was fifteen he had gone through every course of science we knew. For generations his brain had been developed. Perhaps" – she turned quickly to Barry – "you have seen my brain, Richard, and your own. Now I can give you an idea. His brain is comparatively more developed over mine than mine is over yours. If you can realize that you can realize what I mean. A mental effort that would wreck your mind would pass his unnoticed."

Dick nodded. "I see," he chuckled. "It took me six years to go through my medical course. I wonder how long it would have taken him? About a month, I suppose."

Earani looked up. "Indeed, Dick, judging from your brain, you must have worked very hard to do it in the time." The comment was made so simply and was evidently so free from malice, that Dick joined Alan in the shout of delight that followed it, and for the time being they forgot their forebodings.

It was in this way that Alan and Barry obtained their first knowledge of the past of the dead world, and the glimpse, slight as it was, only whetted their appetite for more.

That evening, before they finally separated, the two men were thoughtfully silent. It was only at the last moment that

Dundas said, "Dick, I don't like the idea of Andax. He seems a pretty large order to let loose on the world."

Barry realized his friend's real reason for disliking the idea, but passed it without comment. "I like it even less than you do, Alan, but it's my opinion that our desires in the matter won't be considered. Our only hope is to try and use our influence for the best. For the rest it is on the lap of the gods. Good night," and he passed into the night in an odour of petrol.

"If I tell you the history of the three statues you will have an outline of the history of the race." Earani spoke in answer to a question from Dundas. "Those three men left the greatest marks on its development of all who ever lived, and each in an entirely different way."

"Faith, Earani," said Barry, "from the look of the old gentleman in the rags, I should say the race left some marks on him in return."

"We own it to our shame, Dick." They were standing in the great vestibule before the sculptured group, and from where they stood the face of the statue stared over their heads with its frozen expression of misery and pride. The master hand that had wrought the stone had given all but life to the figure, with its bowed shoulders, weighed down with intolerable wrong and suffering. "Yes," Earani went on, "he was judged and condemned as the greatest criminal our world had ever produced." They turned together, and she led the way to the "temple", and there went on with her story.

"His name was Odi, and until he committed the deed that altered the whole course of humanity he lived unknown as a poor schoolteacher. At the time he lived (you must remember it was about three thousand years before the great disaster) our world had advanced even then beyond what yours is now in development. To a certain extent it was, however, much as yours is today. We were far more advanced in art and science than you are now. We had commenced as you did in ignorance, pestilence, and war. We had been split into groups and nations with as many languages. The groups and nations gradually coalesced, and with them grew up a common language. War had practically ceased, and from that cause and also from the advance of medical science the increase of the population of the world came to be a serious factor in our history for more reasons than one. The great problem, however, was the problem of the coloured races.

Mentally and in everything but physical endurance they were beneath us. They could imitate, but not create. They multiplied far more rapidly than we did, and, led by ambitious men, they threatened to exterminate the white races by sheer force of numbers. In some places, where the two races lived side by side, the position became acute, and everywhere they demanded as a right an equality they were unfitted for. Perhaps you know faintly what I mean."

"We understand, Earani. The problem is not unknown to us," put in Barry.

Earani nodded. "I have read of your problem, Dick, but it was as nothing compared with the one the world had to face then and the one Odi solved. There were at the time over three thousand millions of people on the globe, of whom more than four-fifths were of the lower race. They had all the benefits of our science, and were protected by our laws, but as time went on the bitterness grew on both sides beyond all endurance. They learned the power of numbers, and grew arrogant and overbearing. In one place the mutual jealousy flashed up into a short but fierce and bloody war, the first that had happened for over two hundred years. It was a quarrel over territory; territory that meant existence to one race or the other. That fight resulted in the obliteration of a white outpost of over two million people. Strange as it may seem, very few, except those in actual contact with the coloured races, realized even then the danger to the white."

Dundas smiled a little, and interrupted. "I suppose, Earani, there were plenty who preached the doctrine of up-lifting the coloured races and treating them as brothers?"

Earani nodded. "That was as it happened, Alan, mostly through the teaching of the priest class; those not directly in contact with them opposed reprisals. They talked evolution, education, and brotherly love, and, I have no doubt, meant it. They argued that it would lower them in their own eyes and in the eyes of the coloured people if they inflicted punishment. 'Why plunge the world again into the crime of war?' shouted the priest class. 'Example on our part will teach them better.'

"But there was one man who read the signs aright. He was Odi, the obscure schoolmaster, living on the fringe of the white nations. All his life he had studied the question in silence. Then it fell out that some of his inventions brought him enough wealth to enable him to live at his ease, and he gave the whole of his time to research.

"It has never been finally decided whether his great discovery was the result of accident or of deliberate experiments with the one object in view. Practically everything he possessed was afterwards destroyed, and his name and the secret of his power alone survived. The secret was afterwards known as the 'Death Ray'." Earani broke the thread of her story. "What you know as electricity we knew more of then than you would dream now."

"We know precious little about it, anyhow," said Barry.

She laughed and went on: — "That's an honest confession, Dick. There are a few links missing in your chain that I can supply in good time. But to return to the 'Death Ray'. I have often thought of that man, with his terrible secret locked in his heart, and setting about his work absolutely unmoved by the thought of the consequences of his actions to himself or the millions of other lives it involved.

"The first knowledge the world had of his power was that an unknown and appalling disease had broken out amongst the coloured races in the most thickly populated part of the world. At first it started in one city, and from that centre spread in an ever-widening stain. Almost from the first it was noticed that the whites were absolutely immune. But that this was from design never entered even remotely into the speculations of the horde of workers who gathered to fight the plague. Remember that when it once started the disease was no matter of months or weeks in action. It was a question of days. The coloured people, old and young, went down before it with appalling certainty. The unseen death missed none. It swept through the country in an ever-widening wave, the course of which could be marked in a clearly-defined line as it advanced. In vain the whole world fought the growing terror. Every nerve was strained, and every resource of science was used to the uttermost. Fight as the scientists would, the death defeated them. There was not one single instance where a person attacked recovered, and inside the line of the advancing tide there was not one single instance of a coloured person escaping or a white man being affected. I can only make you understand the awful magnitude of the blow that fell by the records of mortality. In the first eight weeks from the outbreak, over one hundred and twenty millions had perished."

The two, who had been listening intently, looked incredulously at Earani. "Why, Earani, apart from anything else, the disposal of such a multitude of dead should be impossible, and delay must have meant an epidemic through the world as bad as the disease that killed the blacks," said Barry.

"That is so, Dick," she answered grimly. "The records of the time showed how fully alive the people were to the danger. Indeed, they left the coloured race in the end to fight for its own salvation in order to cope with the new horror that threatened. Indeed, there were a few small outbreaks, but the world was prepared, and beat them out before they obtained any hold. You must remember, too, that our race was better equipped to deal with such a crisis than yours is now.

"Then a strange thing happened. Just as suddenly as it appeared, the plague stopped, and the world breathed in relief. It seemed as if the danger had passed. There was a month of respite, and then, to the horror of all, it commenced again with redoubled violence in a new quarter. This time in the heart of the territory of the coloured races. What had gone before was as nothing to the fresh outbreak. It swept everything before it, but in the densely-populated districts it killed more swiftly, and spread more widely than formerly. Even now it is difficult to think of that time without a shudder. Five times it ceased and broke out again, and towards the end the word ran through the coloured races that the whites were exterminating them. No vows of innocence, no attempts to reassure the terror-racked multitude, were of any avail, and the horror was added to by a bloody internecine upheaval, in which the doomed race fell as swiftly before the arms of the whites as before the destroying disease.

"The sixteen months that the terror lasted are on record as the most awful period in our history, and when they were passed the coloured races had ceased to exist. Out of two thousand millions, not half a million were left scattered amongst the extreme northern and southern parts of the world, where the disease had not penetrated."

"Good heavens, Earani!" exclaimed Alan. "Do you mean to tell us that this appalling thing was the work of the man Odi?"

"Just so, Alan; his work alone, and even in the end his part might have gone undiscovered but for the determination of a few scientists to probe the matter to the bottom.

"Several remarkable features were recorded apart from the disease itself. In each instance the disease started from a common centre and spread rapidly outwards. When the records were made up it was noticed that in charts of the affected countries its boundaries were a clearly defined circle, except in the later outbreaks where the edges of the circles were broken by already ravaged country. Then again, it was noticed that the intervals between the outbreaks were subject to some regularity. It was by summing up slight details that the investigators came to the conclusion that the intervals would just permit of the perpetrator of the tragedy moving from centre to centre. Even then it seemed a far-fetched hypothesis to assume deliberate human action. Gradually, however, the evidence piled up, and the question became from 'Was it the work of a man?' to 'Who is he?'

"Then Odi spoke up. Openly and fearlessly he announced himself the perpetrator of the deed. Even then the world was incredulous, but in the end there was no room for doubt. He proved to the astonished investigators beyond all chance of contradiction the means he had used. He had discovered an electrical ray that passed the white skin, and only acted through the pigmented skin of the coloured people. After only a short exposure to its influence, a general paralysis of the nervous system set in, and death ensued in from twenty-four to thirty-six hours. The gradual spreading of the havoc from its centre was caused by a proportionate weakness, according to the distance from the power itself. When he had exterminated all within reach, he simply moved his plant to another site and repeated the process. You see the ray was silent and invisible, and passed through all natural obstacles as if they had been non-existent. It did its work swiftly, silently and undetected."

Earani paused in her story, and Barry broke in: "That was a hellish deed, an infamous act, and yet you say that your people honoured him as a benefactor. Earani, they could not do it."

The woman smiled her soft, slow, unemotional smile, looking at Barry as an elder would look at an angry child. "Not at first Dick. No, they did not honour him. They looked on Odi's deed in the same light as you do now. That is, when they had time. At first they were too busy seizing the vast vacant territories. The few great national confederations were on the verge of flying at one another's throats to see which could seize the most, until they realized that there was plenty even for their voracious desires."

"But Odi!" asked Alan. "What became of him?"

"The fate of the daring reformer," she answered. "What else? From one end of the world to the other the priest class raised the outcry against him. We had ceased to punish crime. We cursed the criminal. He was outcast and branded. The very children baited him in the street. He was shunned, excommunicated in the true sense of the word. His goods were declared forfeit. His name was held up as one accursed. At first he answered his accusers boldly and justified his deed on the ground of the good of humanity. He pointed out that the confederations where the priest cast held the greatest power were those that had benefited most largely already, and in time to come would benefit more. Aye! it was true, but none the less they howled him down — spat upon him. In spite of all they did he held his head high. Poverty and outrage were his lot until the end, but they did not break his spirit."

"And the end?" asked Barry.

"A fitting one for the stormy life. One day he penetrated to a gathering of the priest class and their followers, and there he stood before them and spoke his mind to them. Aye! but it was a speech. Some day I will read it to you; we have it word for word in our archives, an inspired prophecy, and when he had spoken the children of the peace took the apostle of death and stoned him before their temple. That statue in the vestibule was wrought from the only picture we had of him, and that was taken as he spoke his last words.

"Look, my friends, even as he had said, it happened. After about two hundred years here and there arose an apologist. The world was infinitely more prosperous and infinitely more peaceful. The locked-up treasures of Nature that had gone to nourish the unfit were directed into proper channels. There was room to breathe in what had been an overburdened world, and the world knew and recognized it. At first shamefacedly, and then openly and honestly it was acknowledged that the deed of Odi was the salvation of the civilized races."

Barry rose to his feet and commenced to pace slowly to and fro. The uneasiness in his mind had taken definite shape during the story. "It may be as you say, Earani," he said, "but to my mind the means could never justify the end — no matter if the result were all you say and more. The crime would be unpardonable."

Earani watched him quietly with her elbow on the arm of the chair and her chin cupped in her palm. Looking at Barry she spoke to Dundas. "Alan, tell Dick what you do with weeds that grow up amongst your vines — the weeds that draw the nourishment from the soil, that would undo the work of you hands, and cramp the development of the fruit. What do you do with them, Alan?"

"Plough them under," said Alan briefly.

"Just so, plough them under," repeated Earani. "Dick, has

your world not yet recognized that there are weeds of humanity as well as of vegetation?"

"That is no parallel, Earani. I say it was a crime – a hideous crime. There is no more justification for it than there would be for killing a man to steal his money. The fact that it was done on a colossal scale only makes it so many million times worse."

"You can find no palliation?" Her statuesque calm was a strange contrast to Barry's agitation.

"None. It is unthinkable."

Still unmoved, Earani said quietly, "Tell me, Dick, this country of yours you are so proud of – who owned it before your people came here, if I remember rightly, not much more than a hundred years ago?"

Barry stopped abruptly in his restless pacing as though the question had petrified him. Earani sat upright, and pointing an accusing finger at him. "Answer me honestly, Dick. Have you ever once in your life given a single thought of remorse for the thousands of helpless, if useless, aborigines that were exterminated by the ruthless white invasion? Yet can you honestly declare that you think they should have been left in undisturbed possession? Morally, your fathers and you are on the same plane with Odi."

Barry threw back his head and answered defiantly, "Again, Earani, the parallel is not just. In this case it was the survival of the fittest."

"Sophistry, Dick, sophistry. The Death Ray, or rum and disease – aye! or firearms – what difference? The result is the same. Your people are in undisturbed possession of their land, and they are exterminated. Read your own world's histories. Your international morals are the morals of the jungle. Brute strength and nothing but brute strength, spells safety. Alan, what do you say?"

" 'Pon my word," said Dundas, who had listened half-amused and half-serious, "I don't think we in Australia can throw any stones at Odi, neither can anyone in North America, for that matter. The fact that the people of the United States imported a worse problem doesn't affect the fact that they settled their first one à la Odi, although they were more gradual about it."

"Do you support the theory of the Death Ray, Dun?" asked Barry, perturbed by Alan's defection.

Dundas drove his hands deep into his pockets and leaned back in his chair. "Dick, honest Injun! I feel that the world would be better and cleaner if some of its races were to become extinct. Take, for instance, the gentle Turk. I'll say this, that if I knew of an impending catastrophe that would wipe the whole of that race off the face of the earth, and could prevent it, I wouldn't."

"You mean you think you wouldn't," put in Barry, "whereas if it came to the point you would probably do it if it cost you your life."

"I'll be hanged if I would, Dick. No, I mean it absolutely. I would think no more of it than you would of cutting into a malignant growth. You talk of parallels. Well, the Turk is a cancer on humanity, and nothing else. He would have been wiped out fifty years ago if the big nations were not afraid of one another."

Here Earani interrupted. "Can you tell me the present proportion of black to white, Dick?"

Barry shrugged his shoulders. "Afraid I can't," and he looked inquiringly at Alan.

Dundas rose from his chair. "I can't say, but I expect 'Whittaker' can. I had to get a copy to satisfy Earani's appetite for facts and figures." He took a volume from a casket and turned its pages rapidly. "Humph — here we are!" Then with his pencil he jotted figures on the margin of the page. "Here's what I make of it. Total estimate of human races — One thousand six hundred millions approximately. Caucasian, six hundred and fifty millions, leaving a balance of about nine hundred and fifty millions coloured. Roughly five to three against the whites."

Earani looked up. "You see, Dick, even now it is five to three, and the odds will go on increasing."

Barry looked at her in dismay. "Earani, for God's sake, say what is in your mind."

She answered calmly. "Nothing as yet, Dick — but think — were Odi's deed to be done again, would it better be done now or when those numbers were double, and when you think, remember too, Dick, there is no place in the world for the unfit."

Barry shook his head. "My profession is saving life, not destroying it. Are there none amongst the whites who are unfit? If you follow your theory to its conclusion where does it stop?"

"We found the means to eradicate the unfit, even amongst the white races," came the answer serenely. "But it took a man who could stamp his will on the world before it could be done. Dick, your ideas strike me as being absurd. You would hold in honour as the greatest of your citizens a soldier who would lead his countrymen to kill another people by hundreds of thousands and send as many of his own to their death, merely on account of an international squabble, right or wrong. He is a hero. A national demigod almost. But is he any better than Odi, or any different from him, who dared to save a civilization? To my mind Odi is the better man. He had a reason for his death ray. As often as not your soldier is wrong in the cause he fights for. Even putting the best construction on his deeds he frees the world of an overburdening population, only the worst of it is that the finest type of man is killed in warfare, and the weeds are left to breed. Pity you couldn't form your armies of the unfit."

"Earani, I don't surrender, I merely won't argue with you any more," and Barry sat down, pursing his lips sourly.

The woman walked to his side, and laid her hand lightly on his shoulder. "Wise boy, Dick," she said gently. "Come, I must put you in a better humour. Why should we quarrel because millions of years ago some people died? Listen to this and forget your worries." She moved to the keyboard, and a moment later a burst of heavenly music throbbed through the great gallery. It held the listening group spellbound while it lasted, and when the last grand notes had echoed away there were tears in the eyes of the two men. There was a long silence, as though no one cared to break the spell, until Earani spoke. "That was one of our greatest choirs and the work of one of our master musicians. Tell me, Dick, was the price we paid for that, and all it means, too great? That is but an infinitesimal part of what we owe Odi."

Barry made no answer, but rose to leave, and at a gesture from Earani, Alan followed his example.

When they walked from the shed to the homestead that evening Dick spoke very soberly. "Dun, God send we have not done an evil thing for the world. If I could read her mind my own might be easier."

"I don't think we have cause to worry, Dick, though I'll admit she looks at things from a different point of view. Earani would be influenced by us in her actions."

"I'm not thinking so much of Earani as of that cold-blooded devil in the Himalayas. How far is he likely to be influenced by us?"

"Sufficient to the day — let us hope that Andax can't be found. It seems a pretty tall order to me."

Barry shook his head. "Dun, if Earani says she can do a thing, she can do it, and I'm perfectly certain that she can and will resurrect that damned friend of her youth, and, what's more, we can't stop her."

Richard Barry's fears are well-founded, for as time goes on it becomes perfectly clear that she has both the scientific means to locate Andax and the fixed resolution to join with him in wiping out those who are deemed unfit to live. To make matters worse, Alan Dundas is falling ever more deeply in love with Earani — and with her ideas.

In desperation, Richard Barry goes directly to the Australian prime minister and reveals Earani's plans. The two men agree that Earani must be stopped — even if this means killing her in cold blood.

Unluckily for Richard Barry and the prime minister, Earani's super-science allows her to eavesdrop on conversations taking place in any part of the world — including the office of the Australian prime minister — and so she is able to foil this betrayal. It seems that Earani's plan is about to succeed when Marian Seymour, Dundas's jilted lover, ends Earani's life with the stab of a knife.

Dundas takes the body into the underground fortress and presses the building's self-destruct button.

Entombed in a dome beneath the Himalayas, Andax is left to wait for all eternity.

(See also pp. xxiv–xxv).

The Wreck in the Void
from
Vandals of the Void
James Morgan Walsh
(1931)

In the twenty-first century, thanks to the discovery of the lunar mineral rolgar (which is used to fuel space propulsion engines) man has established an alliance with the inhabitants of Mars and Venus, and is seeking to explore the outer planets of the solar system as well as the still unexplored inner planet, Mercury.

Space Captain Sanders, an operative in the elite Inter-planetary Guard, is travelling to Mars aboard the space ship Cosmos *when he receives a coded signal from the Earth Council of the Inter-planetary Guard. Strange things have been happening in outer space: ships have been reaching port with all communications paralyzed, and in every case the trouble has occurred in open space and has been preceded by an inexplicable onslaught of intense cold.*

Ordered to be alert for further incidents of this kind, Sanders uses his Guardsman status to command the skipper of the Cosmos *(an Earthling named Hume) to inform him immediately if anything unusual occurs. The mysterious attacks, however, are occurring in deep space, and the* Cosmos *is due to land on the Moon to refuel, so Sanders can look forward to a few days of relaxation . . .*

(See also pp. xxv–xxvii).

I have spoken of the Moon as airless, yet that is not strictly correct. Habit, however, is a hard thing to cast aside, and one clings stubbornly to old beliefs even in the face of the newer facts. Our satellite, as we have known for centuries, lacks atmosphere such as we possess, and its day and night, each of fourteen Earth days in duration, swing from torrid heat in the one to the extremes of perishing cold in the other. But in the rifts and hollows and the abysmal depths of the craters air still lingers, tenuous and all but unbreathable to us, but air nevertheless. Such life as there exists on the Moon lives mostly underground, or did until the advent of the rolgar mines.

To counteract the extremes of heat and cold, and secure a constant supply of air at earth pressure, huge buildings have been erected. Each mine is practically an enclosed city, entered through air-locks. It was on one of these air-locks that the *Cosmos* had come to rest; one of her ports was jointed to a port in the air-lock, forming a sort of enclosed gangway, through which passengers ascended and descended.

Apart from the mechanical ingenuity that aided the embarkation there was nothing to see of any interest. Give me a landing in the free air every time. From where I stood I could see through the quartzite side of the promenade deck above and beyond the air-lock, while I was able at the same time to run a speculative eye over the passengers leaving and arriving. Those taking off were mostly Earth miners, rough, rugged fellows, with an odd Earth official with them, and, of course, my acquaintances the Venerian family of Mir Ongar.

There were not so many coming on board. Mostly Venerians. A couple of those ubiquitous planet-trotting Martians with them to add a leaven to the dish. We took on no Earth-men. When one comes to think of it, it is a curious thing that the Moon should hold least attraction for those who are closest to it. If it had not been for the Venerians and their discovery of rolgar I believe we would have been content for ever to sheer past it into space. As it is the Moon – or rather its rolgar mines – gives us the means of holding the balance of Peace in the Universe; the sinews of inter-planetary war are to a great extent ours, and none can fight should we decide to cut off supplies.

Our stay on the Moon was only of short duration. An air-port inspector or two donned oxygen helmets and made a thorough examination of our landing gear and gravity screen apparatus before passing us out. As soon as that was done and our clearance had been issued our port was sealed and disconnected from that of the air-lock, the signal given, and the lift begun.

Beneath us Archimedes dropped away until the black circle of its crater was no more than a shrivelled ring Mars flared up redly ahead, though presently we shifted our course a little as though we meant to leave it to our left. This, however, was due merely to the fact that we were in a sense circle sailing. It must not be forgotten that if we were travelling in space, so too was the planet of our destination. Our course was set exactly for that point in the void, where, according to our astronomical charts, our orbit, if one can use the expression, and that of Mars should intersect. A ticklish job, you must understand, is this of space navigation, requiring a remarkable intricacy of calculation and cross-calculation.

So the days passed. Once we sighted a meteor heading, it seemed, directly for us, but our repeller ray sent it rocketing off on a new path.

A finger touching me lightly on the shoulder brought me with a jerk out of the depths of sleep. I touched a button at the wall side of my bunk and the light tube above my head glowed brightly. I blinked. Gond, the first officer, was standing beside me. Seeing that I was awake:

"Quickly, Mr Sanders," he said in a half-whisper. "The skipper wants you."

"What is it?" I queried.

"I don't know. Something I sighted out in the void of space. It was my control hour. I called him, he sent me to call you."

"I'm coming." I slid out of my bunk. "I'll be there — control-room, I suppose? — as soon as I can dress."

"Quickly, quickly," he breathed again. He knew not what it was he had sighted — some wandering mystery of space, no doubt — but that the urgent need of my presence had been impressed on him deeply enough it was plain to see.

"I won't waste a minute," I said. "You can go back. I'll follow almost on your heels."

Indeed, I was half dressed before the door shut on him. A Guard sleeps often in his clothes; when he does not he can get into them with a minimum loss of time.

It wanted two seconds to the minute I had allowed myself when I slipped through the door in my turn, fastening buttons as I went. At that hour no one save the officers and crew was likely to be about; I need not fear that, half-clad, I would run into any of the passengers.

Hume himself awaited me, dressed only in tunic and shorts. The control-room was warm enough to make up for any deficiencies of costume.

"What is it?" I asked the moment I stood beside him. He did not reply but motioned me to the screen that communicated with our look-out "eyes".* The screen darkened momentarily, then flashed into light as the beam from our searchlight shot out and picked up the object that had occasioned the alarm.

For some seconds I was not quite sure what it was. Possibly because it was drifting towards us end on, I thought for a moment that it was a meteor, but the slowness of its approach should have warned me from the start that it was not that at all. Then as we swung round and I could see it broad-side on it looked more like a space-flier. That indeed was what I would have felt satisfied it was but for the absence of lights on board. A long cigar-shaped object, tapering to a point at one end, made blunt and warty at the other by the discharge tubes that clustered there.

"Can you get her name?" Hume whispered to me.

I could not. But I made sundry adjustments to the scale knobs at the side of the screen and the projection of the space-flier seemed suddenly to leap forward and become closer.

With some little difficulty I at last picked out her name. "M–E 75 A/B," I read from the line painted near her prow.

"Mars-Earth," Hume amplified. "Carrying A and B class traffic, passengers and freight. Um. This is your job, Sanders, I think. I wonder what's gone dead in her?"

"That's yet to learn. How did you pick her up?"

"Our locator positioned her long before we were able to see her. We – Gond, that is – thought it was another meteorite. But you see it isn't."

He paused and looked at me.

"Sanders," he said abruptly, "I am in your hands. What am I to do?"

"I'd like a look at her, a closer one, if I may. Can we lay alongside?"

"We can board her if you wish."

"I'd better. I wish you'd give the orders."

He threw me a smile at that. This big bluff man had his weakness, and I played on it that night, partly from a sense of courtesy, partly because it was policy. As long as I did not interfere with his command, just so long as I asked him as

* The look-out "eye" is a selective lens that has the power of picking up an object in the same fashion as the human eye, and reflecting it on the screen. It is a very complicated piece of mechanism for all its small size, and the secret of its construction is closely guarded. Invented by Lodz in 1993.

favours what I was entitled to order or demand, he was my grateful warm-hearted friend. Something of his appreciation of my consideration, my care not to humiliate him before his own officers showed in his face.

I left it to him to give instructions, and set myself to watch the craft itself. We had veered a little, our speed was slackening, yet we would have to move round in a wide circle before, perhaps in another half-hour, we could come back and sheer in beside the stranger craft. Our engines, which had for a while been silent — for in free space once a certain pace is reached impetus and freedom from friction carry us onward — took up an odd pulsation, just enough to steady us.

Momentarily I lost sight of the derelict, picked her up again and again from all sorts of odd angles as the movable "eye" mounted on our prow swung round as we altered our course. Then abruptly I saw the length of the derelict looming large beside us, a black bulk that almost filled the vision screen. Came there a slight jar and I realized that our attractors had caught and held her.

Word came up from the port control that we were connecting and that our air-tight extension had been sealed against the derelict's nearest port.

As I turned away from the vision screen Hume caught my arm.

"Can I come?" he whispered in my ear. "I'm interested . . ."

I nodded. "Certainly. I'd like a witness, and someone to check my own observations. What are her tests?"

He spoke into a tube, then turned to me. "Normal interior air pressure," he reported. "Temperature 28 degrees Fahrenheit."

I whistled. Four degrees below freezing point. Something queer there. Either she should have dropped to absolute zero, or else maintained the normal interior temperature. What in the name of the Universe was holding her constant?

I took down one of the emergency coats from a hook, a heavy fur-lined fabric that covered me from chin to ankle, slipped my feet into the insulated boots one of our helpers held towards me, and drew them thigh-high. With the coat drawn in and its bifurcations buttoned tightly round each leg I was insulated against cold. I could even feel the warmth of the heater wires in the fabric as the current from the battery fixed to the back thrilled through them. I drew on my gloves and someone clamped on my air helmet, sealing it temperature tight on to the metal collar at the neck of my coat.

Each helmet contained a radio attachment that provided means of communication with each other and with the ship if necessary. I tried mine. It sparked, and a fraction of a second later I heard Hume's voice burring in the receiver at my ear. Sealed against air and temperature variations, we could yet converse as we chose.

"Ready, Sanders?" he said, and when I answered in the affirmative he led the way down the direct ladder to the connecting port.

The connecting port, really a long metal tube that could collapse in on itself telescope fashion, had been extended to the wall of the derelict and clamped there. The door of the latter's port had been opened mechanically, but the blasts of normally heated air the fans were sending through our craft pulsed along the connecting tube and kept the temperature there from diminishing perceptibly.

The moment we stepped through the open port of the stranger vessel, however, we sensed the change. Despite our heated emergency kit the cold air lapped round us, clutching our limbs with icy fingers. For the moment the grip of it, no less than the inky blackness of the ship's interior, halted us. I had a feeling that the cold was not so much the absence of heat as a sentient thing in itself.

Hume touched the button of the portable light at his belt and I followed suit. The white beams sprang out, filling the place with a light akin to natural daylight.

There was nothing to see here, but then neither of us expected that there would be anything. It was up in the control departments and the living quarters that we hoped — or feared; neither of us was quite sure which — to make our discoveries.

The direct ladder that led straight to the upper control department seemed clear, and with my place as an Interplanetary Guard to sustain I took the lead. The trap-door was closed, but it opened at a touch and I climbed into the compartment, then turned to give a hand to my colleague. A moment later we stood together, staring round the cabin.

It was nothing like as modern as its equivalent on the *Cosmos*. From some of the devices it seemed the craft was at least ten years old. I made for the log book. Search brought it to light in the drawer of the captain's table, and a comparison of dates showed that it had been written up within twenty-four hours. Therefore whatever had happened to render the craft derelict had occurred within the measure of one Earth day.

Both of us had naturally expected to find some trace of humanity in the control-room, bodies, if not living creatures. But there was no sign of anyone and no sign of a struggle. For all we could see the men on duty might have walked out the door in as orderly a fashion as though they were going ashore.

"What do you think of it?" I asked Hume.

His voice buzzed with a perturbed note in my ear. "I don't know what to think," he said. "It's weird, uncanny. It's – " Whatever else he was going to say he pulled himself up with a jerk.

"We can't form any definite opinion about anything until we've searched the ship from control to keel."

"Quite so," I agreed, but as he made a move towards the door I stayed him.

"Let us read the dials before we go," I suggested.

He moved towards me again, and we studied the indicators. The engine dials showed an ample supply of fuel, and the stud had been pushed over to "Stop". No question about that then. The engines had not run down or been brought up automatically. Human agency or something akin to it had been at work here.

Mindful of what Harran had told me I turned to the heating machinery indicator. It showed that the apparatus was still running. Yet here we were in an atmosphere at present a few degrees below freezing point, whereas the thermometer should actually have registered something between sixty and seventy degrees Fahrenheit.

Curious on this point I turned to the wall thermometer. The glass was shattered, the mercury had vanished. From the way in which the glass had broken it was impossible to say whether the damage was deliberate or due to excessive cold. If it was the latter the control cabin itself must have at one period endured a temperature of at least forty-four degrees below zero!

Hume clutched my arm convulsively.

"What is it?" I asked, starting.

"I thought . . . I felt," he spoke in a strained voice, "as though someone . . . or something . . . had just come in."

I swung round sharply. The door, which a moment or so before had been closed, was now open a space. Even as I stared the gap seemed perceptibly to widen.

As a man I am no braver that the rest. I know there are more things in the Universe than we have as yet managed to tabulate, forms of life, abodes of intelligence, that may appear monstrous to us, just as perhaps we appear monstrous to them. But as against this I believe — and experience has yet to prove me wrong — that everything there is must face dissolution sooner or later, that it can indeed be killed suddenly and violently, provided only that one can reach a vital spot.*

My courage was oozing from the tips of my insulated boots as I turned towards the door, and I was already aware of an uncomfortable, prickly sensation about the region of my backbone. Nevertheless the fact of another's presence gave me comfort, so, taking my ray tube in my free hand, I swung the door wide open with the other, and sent the beam of my lamp searching down the dark passage outside. I saw nothing. No visible entity appeared. My audiphones, which would have recorded the sound of any movement, however faint, remained stubbornly silent. Only a wave of cold that threatened to bite through the warmth of my emergency coat seemed to flow in on us like a living thing.

"Nothing there," I said in a tone meant to be reassuring.

"Nothing," Hume repeated, and I could have sworn to a faint note of relief in his voice. "I'll tell you what, Jack," he ran on, "it's the uncanniness of this place that's giving us the creeps, that's what it is. The sooner we pry into every nook and corner the better. We're losing time as it is and letting our nerves get the better of us."

There was sound good sense in that, but oh, how I wished we had brought some others with us. I would have given much then to have had a couple of my own sturdy, hard-headed Guards beside me. Something of what I was thinking must have impinged on Hume's consciousness, for:

"It's a pity we didn't bring a man or two with us," he grumbled in his helmet.

---

* Mr sanders stresses this point, probably because when the first Earth-men reached the Moon they found there in the central caverns actively inimical forms of life that it seemed almost impossible to kill. It was not until Borendeler's invention of the ray tube in AD 2000 that they were finally exterminated. It is now known, of course, that they were endowed with a natural armour that effectively protected their vital parts, though for long the legend that these lunar animals were immortal persisted on the Earth.

"And have them take a risk we don't care to face?" I countered.

"Oh, well, there's that to it," he answered. "Let's get ahead before we start thinking over things."

He tried to push past me, do doubt in the hope that in action he would find a spur to his own courage, but I stayed him. These space-captains may rate themselves as highly as they please, but when it comes to facing the dangers of the unknown it is the Guards' privilege to lead. I think he guessed my motive, for he flung me a whimsical smile, plain to see through the glass front of his helmet.

I shut the door carefully behind us. I was more or less sure now that some unnoticed motion of the vessel had sent it stealing open, but I had no mind in case I was mistaken that I should be taken unawares. If that door should open again I would know of a certainity that there was an intelligent agency at work.

As we traversed the passage to the promenade deck my mind played round what was to me the most significant feature we had so far come across, the utter emptiness of the control-room. I could not imagine any officer of the Inter-planetary Service leaving his post unless there was good reason for it. And everything pointed to the supposition that the desertion, if such it could be called, had included everyone on duty in its scope.

Our beams wavered down the line of the promenade deck, fell on the chairs spread about the space, and simultaneously we stopped dead, and looked fearfully at each other.

"Did you see it?" Hume whispered.

"See what?" I asked, for I wanted corroboration of the reliability of my own eyesight.

"The people sitting in their chairs . . . still . . . lifeless."

So I was not dreaming. Hume had seen what I had seen.

"Hume," I said abruptly, "we haven't thought of it before. We've taken certain things for granted. But there should be buttons about the wall here . . . lights . . . better than our own portable lamps. Perhaps after all they may be working."

He swung the beam of his own lamp round, then his mittened hand closed over a stud and drew it down. Instantly the length of the promenade deck sprang into light. I shuddered. Row on row of chairs, most with occupants, met our eyes. They sat as stiff and still as figures carven from wood. Dead, it seemed, without a doubt.

I leaned over and touched the nearest figure, a woman,

on the cheek, and even through the heated thickness of my gloves her flesh struck cold. I drew back with a gasping sigh.

"Hume," I said, "This is beyond us. We must know how these people died, if they're dead; if not, what's wrong with them. And that's a doctor's job."

"That's what I'm thinking," he agreed. "I'd better call him up?" He looked to me for approval.

I nodded.

He adjusted his communicators to the ship's, and purely out of curiosity I listened in on him.

"That you, Gond?" I heard him say. "Good. It's Hume speaking. Send Dr Spence over at once. What's he to bring? I'm sure I can't say. Oh, yes" – I'd whispered to him – "say it may be suspended animation, or cold exposure. That's data enough for him. And, yes, better send two men with him. The most reliable. And give them a ray tube each. They can reach us through the control-room. No, nothing yet . . . of any importance."

I liked that. He was not giving anything away, forgetful, no doubt, that with the stranger ship's lights on and the two craft riding side by side the deck we were on would be plainly visible. Thanks be it was during the sleep-hours, else we would have had eager, excited, curious, perhaps fearful passengers peering at us across the gap from the quartzite windows. I thought of that, thought too what might happen if some sleepless individual began to wander along the deck, saw, gaped, and went off to wake his friends.

"Tell Gond," I cut in in a quick whisper, "to close his shutters on the promenade deck. Else we may be watched. What we have to do may be better done without curious onlookers."

He put that through, and I heard the click as he cut out.

"We'd better wait," I said in answer to Hume's unspoken question. "More may turn on what Spence can tell us than we think." Nevertheless I put in some of the time of waiting by looking about me. It seemed that everyone had been frozen into immobility as he or she sat. The thing itself had come upon them suddenly, for there was nothing either of surprise of horror in any face.

The doctor came with his attendants, stared at the still figures, made such tests as he could, then straightened up and cased us. In the white light of the vessel's deck I could see his face show blank through the glass front of his helmet.

His hand went up to make some adjustment of his audiophone before he spoke.

"Frankly," he said in answer to my question, "I can't tell you what it is. They've been frozen, that's what it amounts to, but several of the characteristic signs are absent."

I guessed what he meant. I'd looked closely for the blue and purple splotches, the other signs of a man frozen to death, and had failed to find them. Frozen they were in a sense, yet perhaps turned to stone more nearly described them. A little bead of perspiration trickled from my forehead down my nose; the glass front of my helmet seemed to be clouding a little; there was a feeling of warmth that I had not noticed before beginning to permeate my body under the emergency coat. Of a sudden the meaning of it came to me.

"Hume, Spence," I called through the audiophone, "It's getting warmer. Can't you feel it, both of you?"

Something akin to a blank consternation showed for the moment in Hume's face; the doctor looked interested, albeit a trifle puzzled.

"Don't you see," I ran on, "this cold's disappearing? The heaters are beginning to make themselves felt. All the time they've been warming up the air, not perceptibly until now. But it's a big lift from forty-four degrees below zero up to the twenty-eight it was when we came on board. That means that from the time this happened — whatever it was — until the moment we stepped aboard the heaters had raised the temperature a matter of seventy-two degrees, from minus to plus, a tremendous lift. What's more, they're still doing it. It must be getting back to normal now."

"But why," said Hume, puzzled, "didn't the heaters freeze out too when this happened?" He made a clumsy gesture of his mittened hand to include the figures on the chairs.

The answer to that hit me almost the instant he asked the question.

"Simple," I explained. "The heater plant runs in a vacuum. External cold couldn't effect it."

"Of course." His voice was tingling. "I should have thought of that before."

"I didn't until just now." I put my hands up clumsily and caught at the fastenings at the back of my helmet.

"Steady, man, what are you doing?" Hume said agitatedly.

"I'm beginning to roast. Perhaps we can take our kit off now. At least I'll be the first to try."

"But the air," Hume's voice was vibrant with warning. "We got a normal pressure, but there may be something in it, something inimical to life."

"I'll take the risk," I answered. I had seen something out of the corner of my eye, something that looked a mite uncanny. I preferred not say what it was – yet. But it made me think that the air was safe, breathable at any rate.

I fumbled at the fastenings myself, for Hume mumbled he did not want what might happen on his conscience if anything went wrong, and in the circumstances I was not inclined to press him to help me. But I saw the doctor was following my example, though the two men waited to see what their skipper was doing first.

The helmet came off at last and the cool air hit my face. Cool air, not cold. The temperature, as I had surmised, was lifting degree by degree as the heaters struggled with and overcame whatever it was had caused the cold. The air was breathable. At least I could sense no foreign element in it, nothing to account for that abrupt drop in temperature.

In a moment I had stripped my emergency coat, leaving only my boots. They did not matter so much. The doctor was free of his trappings by this, too. He took one gulp of the air, and looked across at me, then I saw his eyes widen.

His glance had travelled past me to the chair at my back. I whirled round. The woman whom I had first examined was stirring, yes, visibly stirring. Her bosom rose and fell, gently at first, then more rapidly as she gulped in the air. Her eyes opened . . . wide. She stared about her. Her glance fell on us. One expression after another chased with the rapidity of light across her face – astonishment – incredulity, fear, I thought.

An inarticulate cry, a sort of strangled scream, issued from her lips, and her head dropped forward in a faint. Spence sprang to her aid.

But the little cry, almost soundless though it was, might have been some signal already agreed upon. All over the deck figures were stirring. It seemed that one surprise on another was being stacked up in front of us.

Hume, with his helmet off and himself half-way out of his coat, uttered an exclamation. I gasped as I followed the direction he indicated. A tall man with the insignia of an Inter-planetary skipper on his collar and coat-sleeves had

risen languidly from a chair some distance down the deck,
coming to his feet slowly, with a bewildered expression on
his face, as though he had just been roused out of a sound
sleep.

His expression changed as he saw us. Surprise, anger at
this seeming alien invasion of his vessel, seized on him. He
made a quick movement forward, then came striding down
the deck towards us.

"What's . . . what's the meaning of this?" he demanded.
Then a puzzled look came into his eyes and he passed one
hand across his forehead.

"How . . . how did I get here?" he said bewilderedly.
"The last I remember was in the control-room, thinking it
was getting rather on the cold side, wondering if anything
had gone wrong with the heaters."

I took his arm. "Captain," I said, "there's a mystery here.
With your help we'll solve it. We came on you, floating in
free space, without lights, you . . . your people stretched
out apparently dead . . . as you were just now."

"Who . . . what are you? From what ship?" he asked
quickly, the light of an odd fear in his eyes.

I slipped my fingers in a pocket, found my badge and
extended it flat in my palm towards him.

"You're safe . . . in good hands," I said. "Whatever you
have to tell, you can say without fear."

For the moment he hesitated, staring away from us
through the quartzite windows of his ship at the black
shadow of the shuttered bulk of the *Cosmos* floating a few
yards away.

"My officers, the men who were with me . . ." he said a
trifle incoherently, running his eyes down the long lines of
chairs.

The passengers were stirring now, coming back to life, all
a little bewildered if one could judge from their expressions.
The woman who had fainted had now revived, and it struck
me that she was the only one of the lot who had shown any
sign of fear on regaining consciousness. Could it be that she
alone of all that company had seen something? At least I
was not minded to leave the ship until I had had a chance of
questioning her.

"Good," I said, "your first duty is to your officers.
I think you'll find them all here, on this deck." You see, I
was beginning to have a glimmer of what had happened,
though the precise motive behind it all eluded me. "Get
them together, bring them somewhere where we can talk.

All that were on duty when . . . when whatever it was happened."

I dropped my voice an octave, came a little closer to him. "Captain," I said, "Don't look round. But tell me quick, who is that woman just behind us?"

He turned slowly as though looking down the run of the deck. I could have sworn his eyes did not so much as touch the woman in passing, but:

"A Mrs Galon," he whispered back. "An Earth-woman, she says, though I take leave to doubt it. Why?"

"We'll want her," I told him. "After we've talked with you. But see she doesn't move away. I'd rather she had no opportunity to speak with the others in the interval."

"As you wish," he said deferentially. There was magic in that little badge of mine, a magic that made me proud to belong to the Service it represented. After all, we Guards may hold up schedules, and interfere much in many ways, but it can never be said that we use our power at any time for anything but good. Perhaps that is in the long run the secret of our power.

"Better," the captain shot at me in a whisper, "better get your men to tend her. Mine . . . I don't know . . . Everything's bound to be disorganized."

I gave the cue to Hume, and he passed the word to his two men. I gathered they were to cut Mrs Galon out a moment after we left, shepherd her after us, and keep her waiting in the outer room until we were ready for her. As it was while the skipper was rousing the watch on duty the others of us unobtrusively slid between her and the rest of the passengers.

I don't think she noticed it, or if she did she gave no sign. Her interest seemed centred on Spence, perhaps because the was the first of our company with whom she had come in contact, the only one at any rate who had paid any sort of attention to her. That it had been purely medical attention did not, I felt certain, matter in the least.

A moment it seemed and the space-ship's captain came striding back to us, behind him a little straggle of his men.

"I'm ready now, gentlemen," he said, "if you will follow me."

He led the way along the deck, but it struck me in the instant's glimpse I had caught of his face as he passed that he seemed of a sudden to have grown worried and a little afraid.

The Captain of the M-E 75 has good reason to be afraid, for his craft has become the latest target of the vandals of the void. But Mr Sanders is correct in his deduction about Mrs Galon; she has indeed "seen something".

Before the paralyzing cold reduced her to unconsciousness, Mrs Galon saw eerie, almost invisible nine-foot tall aliens descend upon the space ship. Pressed to describe these beings in great detail, Mrs Galon asserts that they were transparent and "seemed to flicker".

This proves to be the crucial detail. In time Sanders is able to prove that the aliens (who came from unexplored Mercury) are able to render themselves invisible by means of a device which sets their molecules vibrating at such a speed that they can barely be detected by the human eye.

But the aliens are pressing home their attack. Venus is already under siege, ships of the Inter-planetary Guard are coming under fire, and it is only a matter of time before Earth and Mars are threatened as well. Can Sanders render the aliens visible, and then destroy them, before it is too late?

Thanks to the ingenuity of Sanders' Martian fiancé, Jansca Dirka, the answer is yes. In one of the earliest space battles in science fiction, the Mercurian invaders are repulsed.

Aubade

from

Tomorrow and Tomorrow

M. Barnard Eldershaw

(1947)

The following excerpt comprises the opening pages of
Tomorrow and Tomorrow. *It illustrates the novel's literary
qualities through the rhythm of the sentences, the precise
and appropriate imagery, and the distinctive diction. Mood
and atmosphere are manipulated in such a way that they
reflect the central character's state of mind; we know Knarf
is melancholy and disgruntled.*

*Just as the overall structure of the novel plays an import-
ant part in the enunciation of its theme, so certain structural
devices are employed to significant purpose in the excerpt.
Knarf (a citizen of twenty-fourth century Australia) is first
glimpsed at dawn, caught between the two realms of
darkness and light, just as in his own life he is caught
between his own era and the past (for he is writing a novel
which recreates life in the period from 1920 to the 1950s).*

*The body of the excerpt offers a twenty-fourth century
perspective on Australian history, tracing the displacement of
the Aboriginal "First People" by the settlers. In addition to
providing an insight into the tenor of the authors' social
analysis, the excerpt also presents Australian sf's first
sensitive and sympathetic account of the Aboriginal way of
life.*

The first light was welling up in the east. In the west a few
stars were dying in the colourless sky. The waking sky was
enormous and under it the sleeping earth was enormous too.
It was a great platter with one edge tilted up into the light,
so that the pattern of hills, dark under a gold dust bloom,

was visible. The night had been warm and still, as early autumn nights sometimes are, and with a feeling of transience, of breaking ripeness, of doomed fertility, like a woman who does not show her age but whose beauty will crumble under the first grief or hardship. With the dawn, sheets of thin cold air were slipping over the earth, congealing the warmth into a delicate smoking mist. Knarf was glad to wrap his woollen cloak about him. Standing on the flat roof in the dawn he felt giddily tall and, after a night of intense effort, transparent with fatigue. Weariness was spread evenly through his body. He was supersensitively aware of himself, the tension of skin nervously tightened by long concentration, the vulnerability of his temples, the frailty of his ribs caging his enlarged heart, the civilization of his hands . . . Flesh and imagination were blent and equally receptive. The cold air struck his hot forehead with a shock of excitement, he looked out over the wide sculptury of light, darkness, earth, with new wonder. For a few moments, turning so suddenly from work to idleness, everything had an exaggerated significance. When he drew his fingers along the balustrade, leaving in the thick mositure faint dark marks on its glimmering whiteness, that, too, seemed like a contact, sharply intimate, with the external world where the rising light was beginning to show trees dark and grass grey with that same dew.

Behind Knarf the lamp still burned in the pavilion and the dawn had already diminished and sickened its light. Only one wall, the west, was folded back. It was empty save for the low broad table with its piles of manuscript, a chair in the same pale unornamented wood, the tall lamp, and a couch where Knarf sometimes slept on a summer night with all the walls folded back, like – he told Ren, but his jest had fallen flat – an antique corpse under a canopy. There was no colour except in the bindings of the books piled on the table and spilled on the floor. The frame of the pavilion stood up dark against the golden sky and within the frame the lamplight, at variance with the new daylight, was clotted and impotent. The vapours of a night of effort and struggle could not escape. The empty room was like a sloughed skin. Knarf had been born from it into this new day of which he was so keenly aware.

In this pause between darkness and light he was between two worlds, a reality between two ghosts, a moment of sharp individual consciousness in the drift of centuries. His imagination had been living so vehemently in the past that the

present had become only half real. He was standing at a
nexus of time. Four hundred years ago, a thousand years
ago, dawn among these gentle hills would have seemed no
different, to any living eye that had seen it, than it did to
him. In a few minutes, so quickly was the light growing, the
world of to-day would be back, incontrovertibly, in its
place. But now, for a moment, the old world, the past,
might lie under the shadows just as easily as the present.
A thousand years ago the country had been covered with
bush, a thick mat of it, unending, breaking into natural
clearings, closing in again, a shaggy pelt existing for nothing
but itself, unknown except to the wandering tribes of the
First People, and they, measured against the world they lived
in, were newcomers and sojourners. They lived in it according to its terms without changing it or penetrating it. The
pattern of their lives wound, like a kabbalistic sign traced in
water, through the bush. Their apparently free roaming had
followed a set tide. Their food supply, since they did not
intervene in nature save in the spearing of game, was bound
upon the seasons. Within this cycle of nature was the human
cycle, the pattern of contacts, the linking invisible trade
routes, the crossing and recrossing of tribe with tribe, the
circulation of thought and knowledge as natural and
primitive as the circulation of the blood in the body. Within
the human cycle was a mystic cycle, the linking of rites and
places, of ceremonies that were symbols of symbols
forgotten even in the beginning of time but that continued to
draw men through old, remembered ways. He thought of
the anonymous and indecipherable tracks of the First People
which had lain so lightly on these hills. Far away, reduced
by distance of time to outline, theirs was only another
arrangement of the eternal pattern, of eating, communicating, and reaching out into the unknown. They were gone,
completely and utterly, nothing was left of them but a few
rock drawings, a few spearheads in rosy quartz, some
patterns incised in wood, the words of some songs, soft,
melancholy, their meaning forever sealed. Their dust was
in this dust, nothing more. In the north, where they had
not perished but had been absorbed, their docile blood had
mingled without trace and no overt memory of them remained.

Four hundred years ago this country was stripped bare.
The delicately moulded hills were naked to the sun and wind
and rain, their hoarded fertility broken into and flowing out
of them. Knarf remembered the old barbaric name of the

river – Murrumbidgee. It had not slipped quiet and full between canal-like banks, tame and sure, as it did today. It held
the rich lands in a great gnarled claw, its red banks sculptured
into canyons, carved, pillared, eroded, littered with the flot-
sam of old floods, an ancient tribal river that ruled like a god
in these parts. The countryside had been called the Riverina,
a gentle fruitful name, a propitiatory name perhaps, much
better than Tenth Commune; Knarf would have liked to see
the old name in use again. To divide up the earth into squares
with a ruler was too arrogant. This earth was not like any
other earth, it had its spirit still, even if old god Murrumbidgee was tamed and made to serve it. All that happened
was written in the dust, it didn't end and it wasn't lost, it
was woven in.

The river had been a frontier. At the beginning of the dark
ages, there had been a migration along and beyond it, – the
people who would not make terms thrust out by the pressure
from the coast. They had mustered their flocks, piled such
goods as they could salvage on to their trucks, and with their
families sought the interior. It was here, probably almost at
this every spot, that their final decision had had to be made.
The waterways had been secured so that they could no
longer push along the comparative safety of the river fron-
tages. From here they had struck west and north for the
safety of the bad lands. When the trucks had foundered for
want of petrol, which happened sooner or later, (nowadays
whenever a farmer turned up a rusted shard of metal in the
paddocks by the river, he'd claim it was from one of the
abandoned trucks – they must have been pretty thick about
here, like the detritus of a routed army) they had taken off
the wheels, cut down the famous Murrumbidgee gums, the
old-man trees, and made themselves rough drays to which
they harnessed their horses or their bullocks and they had
gone on. No one pursued them, but their needs drove them
further and further out. As they reached poorer country
they needed more and more of it for their sheep. They could
not stick together, they had to scatter. It was every man, or
every family, for himself. The years of the migration were
good, the country was in good heart and so were the men.
They were the descendants of a peculiar people called the
Pioneers and, only two or three generations earlier, their
forbears had gone out into the wilderness, had come down
here from the coast and the city, and, driving out the First
People and cutting down the bush, had made a life for themselves. It had been hard and many had perished but others

had prospered, grown wise, tough, and rich. They hadn't been afraid of the country and its irregular rhythms. The sons thought they could do it again, or rather they wouldn't believe that they couldn't. They were the great-grandsons, the grandsons, and even the sons of Pioneers, so close was the end to the beginning. History melted down the years between and these followers of a forlorn hope became one with their successful forbears, and were also called "The Pioneers". They left their foundered, mortgaged runs, where they had been feeling the long wars like a drought, and set off in a sort of cheerful desperation. If they lost a lot they got rid of a lot too. What had been done once they could do again — but this time it was different. There was not only no way back but there were no resources behind them. For a year or two it was not so bad, while the few things they had brought with them lasted and the seasons were good. Then the situation began to tell on them in earnest. At first they shore their sheep but there was no market for the wool. It decayed and stank and burned in bark sheds. A little of it they made shift to spin into yarn for their own use. Several risked a journey to a southern port with a drayload or two, but it proved too dangerous and unprofitable. They could dispose of the wool readily and secretly but there was little or nothing they could get in exchange. It was useless to keep the flocks save a few small ones to provide meat, yarn, leather, and tallow. They let them go, it was better than con-fiscation. The sheep wandered over the fenceless pastures. They lambed and wandered on. Their fleeces grew and blinded them, the burden of wool dragged them down till every morning there were some that could not rise and must starve where they lay. Summer and drought pressed hard on them. The waterholes dried up. The sheep died in hundreds and then thousands. Dumb and helpless death was every-where. The Pioneers had great difficulty in keeping alive the small flocks that were necessary to their own survival. Beside that the death of a myriad sheep meant nothing to them. Even on the coast where there was water and feed people starved and went in rags. One dry summer was enough for the sheep laden with wool.

The men were much harder to break. Others had come after them, a motley crowd of the dispossessed, the angry, the frightened, the hungry, but they had had no staying power, they began to die like the sheep as soon as they had crossed the Murrumbidgee. But the Pioneers endured, long and incredibly. Like the First People, they learned to move from scanty resource to scanty resource, they valued nothing but water and food and perhaps the antique fetish, liberty, but that would not be a word they ever troubled to speak. It was something they could not help having and for which they had no use. They were as tough, as thin, and almost as black from the sun, as the First People had been, but, unlike the First People, they had no festivals, no corroborees, no old rites. They were scaled down to something below that. It is said that as a people they stopped breeding.

They could not or would not return and no effort was ever made to bring them back. Such people were useless for the building of a new world. A few may have straggled back, but very few. The great majority was lost. After twenty or even thirty years there would be a few survivors, madmen living in caves with their phantom dogs beside them, men gone native with the last of the tribes, gone crazy.

That wasn't the history you found in history books, it was local legend. Knarf believed it and Ord said it was true. He had known it for a long time but only this morning did it seem completely real. He was smitten, he supposed, with imaginative convictions. It was often like that. Knowledge lay dead in his brain, so much ready-made merchandise on its shelves, and then, often for no obvious reason, it quickened and became part of the small, living, and productive part of his mind. In the shadowy morning light he could trick himself into seeing the Pioneers moving down to the river in neutral coloured cavalcade, flocks of sheep travelling over the brown plain beyond in a haze of dust, tall, brown, laconic men in dusty clothes, their heterogeneous belongings piled on the makeshift vehicles already weathered to drabness, the slow flight into country without cover. . . . There were people far out west, in the next commune, old or lonely or simple people, who in unguarded moments told stories of the Pioneers. Solitary travellers had seen camp fires in the bush. When they approached, the fire had been burning bright with a skeleton sitting beside it, bushman fashion, on his heels. Their ghosts are thick round waterholes, and if you spend a night there you cannot sleep for the rattle of hobble chains and the stamping of horses that will have left no trace in the morning. The strange dog seen at twilight is no mortal dog but the mythical folkdog, the Kelpie, "too faithful to die", as they say. When cattle stampede in the night they say "It's the Pioneers". Sometimes, it is said, they pass through on a moonlight night, you hear the rustle of sheep's feet in the dust, the creek and clatter of riders, and even men's voices singing in an archaic dialect, and in the morning there will be broken fences and eaten out paddocks but not a mark in the dust of the road or a single dropping of dung. . . . But no one ever caught up with this legend, it had always happened farther on. It was like the Hosting of the Sidhe, Ord said, thrusting it farther back into the world that was his own province.

There must be a good deal of Pioneer blood about here still, Knarf thought. He'd often noticed, though it wasn't a thing anyone talked about, that the inlanders were taller, looser, leaner than the men on the coast, with less of the orient in their faces. Blood mixed slowly even after all this time.

With his back to the east Knarf had been straining his eyes into the west. The light had grown imperceptibly. It collected on objects like dew. The river was already a broad silver band. At his feet there was still a well of darkness, a well full of sleep, but farther away the white houses of the square and along the bank of the river were visible. By concentration, sight could rescue the dark lines of trees and even pick out, across the river, the black and grey pattern of the irrigated orchards and gardens. As yet there was no colour, only assembling shapes. The river was quicksilver between dark banks.

In a few minutes now the past would be buried again under the present. The scene he knew so well and loved so deeply would cover and supersede the figment of his imagination which had had for the moment the intense overstrung reality of things that pass. He would see, not the shaggy olive green hills of the beginning, nor the bare hills of the twentieth century with their chromatic swing from the new green of the rains through silvers and browns to the naked brown purple of the earth, stripped and compressed by drought; not the irregular wasteful pattern of land overdriven and under-used, but the lovely design of safe and steady fruitfulness. It was a bright picture, where there had never been a bright picture before. If a man of the First People had stood here he would have seen only a monotone, or perhaps no more than the mazing pattern of narrow leaves against the sky. To the Pioneer it would have been a variation in pale colours, country under threat, a threnody for the wind. And yet – it must have been lovely. It might even have had something the present lacked. Eyes that had known it would be homesick to-day. Man might turn away from surfeits to pine for hard and meagre fare. To think of the Pioneers as a people who had ravaged the country, left it denuded and helpless and then had gone out, irrationally and obstinately, to die with the country, to become in the last resort place-spirits, the half-evil genii of the soil, was a poet's conception. Life was lived as fully then as now, now as then. This, that looks so sleek, is only an approximation too.

The Australians, of whom the Pioneers were part, had been the second people. They had been so few, never more than eight or nine million in the whole continent. They had been a very strange people, full of contradictions, adaptable and obstinate. With courage and endurance they had pioneered the land, only to ruin it with greed and lack of forethought. They had drawn a hardy independence from the soil and had maintained it with pride and yet they had allowed themselves to be dispossessed by the most fantastic tyranny the world had ever known, money in the hands of the few, an unreal, an imaginary, system driving out reality. They had their hardbitten realism and yet they co-operated in the suicidal fiction of production for profit instead of for use. They thought of Australia as a land of plenty and yet they consented to starve among the plenty. They lost the reality of their land to the fantasy of the Banks. They looked always to Government for redress and assistance but they were always scornful of their governments and with a persistent lawless streak in them. They loved their country and exalted patriotism as if it were a virtue, and yet they gave a greater love to a little island in the North Sea that many of them had never seen. They were hard drinkers and yet had puritanical prejudices and made difficulties against the purchase of their drink. Inherent gamblers, they legislated against gambling and then broke their own laws systematically and as a matter of course. Lovers of horseflesh, they had no feeling for the animals, sheep and cattle, by which they lived. They praised the country but lived in the cities, or they grumbled eternally of the land but would not leave it. There was no measuring their pride and yet they were unsure. They tried to live alone in the world when their whole civilization was in the melting pot. They called the North the East and the Near North the Far East and it was to them an unknown place of mystery and menace. They were a fighting people — but not at home. They settled their differences at home by other means. The small people was prodigal of its armies; generation after generation, they swarmed out to fight and die in strange places and for strange causes. Tough, sardonic, humorous, they were romantics the

like of which the world had never seen. Crusaders without a
crusade, they fought for any cause that offered or for the
simulacrum of a cause. They went to South Africa to fight
against a people small and liberty loving as themselves. They
fought in France and Flanders, Egypt, Palestine, Mesopo-
tamia, for an imperial design from which they themselves
sought to escape. Within a generation they were fighting
throughout the world, for what they scarcely knew, for brave
words and a coloured rag, for things that were only names
being already lost. They fought with tenacity and elan, the
bravest of the brave. Or was that the incurable romanticism
of history? Knarf didn't think so, there were facts and figures
to support it.

All that, and yet they weren't a belligerent people. It was
as if there were two people, indistinguishable in peace time,
the fighting tribe − the Anzacs, as they came to be called −
and the others who didn't fight. At the first drawing of the
sword the cleavage showed and apparently they accepted it.
The armies were volunteer, both sections of the community
joined together to refuse conscription. It was one of their
gestures of freedom, the curious truncated liberty to which
they held.

Knarf could think of the Australians as living in a
perpetual high gale of unreason. Their whole life was stormy
and perverse. They were city-dwellers and their cities were
great vortices of energy that carried them nowhere. They
strove enormously for the thing called profit. In competition
men's efforts cancelled out, one against another; they could
succeed only, one at the expense of another, but when competition merged into monopoly they were worse off, for as
the forces became more powerful they were more destructive. A terrible logic worked itself out. There were those who
saw the end coming and cried their warnings, but helplessly.
When a man is caught in a conveyor belt he is not saved by
realizing his danger.

Part 2

The Present

The stories in this section represent the current Australian science fiction scene, and illustrate its range of style and subject matter. Each of the writers represented here is still writing science fiction, and thus – with the exception of the items by Frank Bryning and Wynne Whiteford – each one is represented by work published after 1975, to allow the writer to be judged by recent work. Frank Bryning is represented by his 1956 story, "Place of the Throwing-stick", because its dramatization of the contrast between Aboriginal and European cultures supplements the account of the Aborigines in *Tomorrow and Tomorrow*. The Wynne Whiteford story, "One Way to Tomorrow" (1957), has been included because it exemplifies the "typical" time travel story, and as such provides an interesting contrast with the time travel stories by David J. Lake and A. Bertram Chandler.

Jack Wodhams' story, "One Clay Foot" (1979), is a rebuttal of films such as *Star Wars*, in which spacecraft engage in "typical World War II fighterplane duelling, complete with sound effects". Writing that he was "dismayed and depressed" by *Star Wars*, Wodhams offers a more probable account of space combat. By contrast, Philippa C. Maddern's "Inhabiting the Interspaces" (1979) remains down-to-earth in both its setting and its social concerns.

The stories by George Turner and Damien Broderick both invite the reader to come to terms with the attitudes and motives of non-Earthly (though not necessarily non-human) beings. Turner's "In a Petri Dish Upstairs" (1978) provides a methodical and serious demonstration of the social impact of technological change, and the prose style – appropriately – is impersonal and subdued. Damien Broderick's story, "A

Passage in Earth" (1978), is more playful in intention, there-by allowing the author to employ a more florid experimental prose style.

Publication details of these stories are as follows: Frank Bryning's "Place of the Throwing-stick" first appeared in *New Worlds Science Fiction* (March 1956); Wynne N. White-ford's "One Way to Tomorrow" first appeared in the *Australian Journal* (1 May 1957); A. Bertram Chandler's "Kelly Country" first appeared in *Void* magazine no. 3 (1976); Jack Wodhams' "One Clay Foot" first appeared in *Alien Worlds*, ed. Paul Collins (St Kilda: Void Publications, 1979), with Wodhams' comments on *Star Wars* forming part of a preface to the story; Philippa C. Maddern's "Inhabiting the Interspaces" first appeared in *Transmutations*, ed. Rob Gerrand (Melbourne: Norstrilia Press and Outback Press, 1979); and Damien Broderick's "A Passage in Earth", David J. Lake's "Re-deem the Time", and George Turner's "In a Petri Dish Upstairs" each appeared first in *Rooms of Paradise*, ed. Lee Harding (Melbourne: Quartet Australia, 1978). The text of Broderick's story includes corrections made in the 1981 Penguin Books edition of *Rooms of Paradise*, and Lake's story has been revised slightly.

The stories in this section are not presented in strict chronological order, though there is nevertheless a sense of chronology maintained throughout Part 2. Frank Bryning, A. Bertram Chandler, and Wynne N. Whiteford have been placed first not only because of their seniority in years, but also because their work shows the influence of the style, tone, and stance of the 1950s. In the case of A. Bertram Chandler, however, I have selected a story written in 1976. In terms of seniority and the evolution of style, Jack Wod-hams, George Turner, and David J. Lake should probably follow, yet the Lake story neatly complements the two time travel tales that come before it, and so it has seemed only sensible to place Lake accordingly. Damien Broderick's prose style makes him a "newer" writer than David J. Lake (even though Broderick has been writing sf for longer than Lake), and – with only a few stories to her credit – Phillipa C. Maddern is undoubtedly the "newest" writer in this collection.

Place of the Throwing-stick

Frank Bryning

(1956)

Munyarra had his first sight of the monster he had come to slay when the creature's pointed snout, beyond the horizon, flashed back the light of the setting sun.

Instantly he dropped flat amongst the dry grass tussocks. His exultation at having run his quarry to earth at last was held in check by his instinct for caution if he were to take the monster unawares. So he lay without moving a finger or toe until the gleam of light — from the monster's eye, no doubt — died away, and darkness came.

When he did arise his naked black body was invisible in the night. Without hesitation he set off, to travel in a great half-circle until he was due east of the monster's position, and still beyond its horizon. There, in a shallow depression, he laid down his great war boomerang (which could break a man's leg) his two light hunting spears, and his deadly shovel-nosed spear. With his spears he laid also his woomera, or throwing-stick, notched at one end like a crochet hook to take the haft of a spear, and so add its length and leverage to his throwing arm. From his waistband he released the corpse of a thirty-inch bearded dragon, encountered early in the afternoon, which would provide his meal.

With bare hands he scooped a meagre trench in the dust and set his economical blackfellow's fire with a few handfuls of dry saltbush twigs. He made fire by twirling a stick between his palms in a cleft in a small piece of wood held by his great toes. Then he transferred a smouldering wad of shredded grass to the sticks and breathed them into flame.

His meal of broiled lizard finished, Munyarra lengthened his fire trench a few feet and spread the glowing coals along it. When they had become grey ashes he scooped them out, took their place on the heated earth, and slept.

In little more than thirty days Munyarra had travelled on foot thirteen hundred miles from his home territory between the Timor Sea and the Gulf of Carpentaria. He had come to where, according to smoke signal, "yabba-stick", and word of mouth, white men were making powerful magic with a monster that flew through the air like a spear with a haft of fire, and roared with a voice of thunder.

In him, *allatunga* — head man — of the *Warraimulluk*, his tribe's mightiest warrior and hunter, the blood of his fighting ancestors had stirred. Time had come again for a man to do as the mighty Grungrunja had done in the days of the Old Ones.

The songmakers of many tribes still chanted the defeat of the white man's horned monsters by Grungrunja, *allatunga* of the *Arunta* people, and greatest warrior of *his* day, though his left arm was but a stump at the elbow. Even the song-makers of the white people had made a "paper-yabba" of the story,* Munyarra had been told. For Grungrunja alone, and with his one mighty arm, had driven back the first white men to invade *Arunta* territory with their herds of bellowing, horned monsters which ate out the grass and starved the timid kangaroos and small game upon which the black man lived.

In the generations which followed, by force of numbers and their terrible weapons, the white men and their herds had taken all the country. Until, at last, in shame, the white men's own tribal councils had forbidden them that most nor-thern peninsula in which the *Warraimulluk* and neighbouring tribes still lived in the ancient ways. And there the blood of old and young alike still quickened at the song of Grung-runja's victory.

Grungrunja, armed for battle, had been on the trail of a marauder from the south. He was close upon his quarry in the territory of the *Dieri* when he ran into the first herd of cattle he had ever seen, coming straight at him through the scrub and trampling the trail he was following. In a haze of dust, with a menacing, many-throated lowing, armed with a myriad spears which sprouted two-by-two from their heads, they came on at walking pace.

From behind the herd Grungrunja could hear the frequent crack of a stockwhip, and over the tossing head-spears and

* "Desert Saga" by William Hatfield, to whom the episode retold here is gratefully acknowledged. — F. Bryning.

undulating backs of the monsters he could see the ridiculously adorned and headgeared white men on horseback.

Mounted white men he had seen before, from a distance. Several of his fellow spearmen had been slain, and he had lost his left forearm by the sting of the shrieking bees launched against them by throwing-sticks that merely pointed, puffed smoke, and cried "crack!" like the sounds he could now hear beyond the monsters.

Grungrunja found that the herd had already outflanked him. He would have to flee across open ground in full sight of the leading monster – a huge, long-horned steer – and, no doubt, also of the shrieking bees whose sting was death.

Flight was his only chance, he knew. But his bush lore told him that as soon as he moved and became visible, running, he would be pursued. So that same lore bade him take desperate advantage of surprise and momentary, feigned attack.

From the shadow of a clump of *mulga* Grungrunja threw his heavy war boomerang with all his strength. Then sweeping up his spears he leapt into full view – his three and a half limbs spreadeagled in the air – and yelled his bloodcurdling battle challenge.

The boomerang gouged out the leading bullock's left eye and tore the left horn from its head at the moment Grungrunja's cry made the air quiver. Bellowing, the beast reared up, swung round on to the horns of the one behind him, and charged back into the mob. In twenty seconds the entire herd, lowing and milling, was working up to stampeding speed, back the way it had come, with the white men in pursuit.

Grungrunja, already in full flight in the opposite direction, had been astonished to find himself the victor. He stopped to see the havoc he had wrought, until cattle and horsemen had disappeared. He retrieved his boomerang – and picked up the bullock's horn, which had remained with his tribe as a potent magic long after the spirit of Grungrunja had entered his totem brother, the *brolga*, to soar freely for ever on slate-grey wings . . .

Munyarra was of the *brolga* totem in his own tribe, as Grungrunja had been in his. He had often fed upon the wild descendents of the white man's cattle, and he knew they were not so fearsome as they had first appeared to his people. Now he was deliberately stalking the newest monster of the white man, to prove it, likewise, vulnerable.

This creature, the bushland intelligence had informed him, possessed only one horn — albeit a mighty one. Indeed, it was said that its horn and its body were all one. And it had four wings which it used either to fly with or to stand upon, upright and motionless like a bearded dragon on its hind legs and tail, simulating a sapling stump or a branch on a fallen log.

So Munyarra had journeyed south across the dry "dead heart" of Australia, from Arnhem Land in the north, bearing the flint-tipped and fire-hardened wooden weapons of a by-gone age. He came to do battle with the leader of the white man's new herd of monsters before they could encroach on the last remaining territory of his people . . .

He had passed in friendship through the lands of the *Mangari*, the *Anula*, the *Binbinga*, and the *Warramunga*. In that lush Gulf country he had fared well on flesh and fowl and fish, on water-lily roots and wild honey — all taken "on the run" without deviation from his course.

Unseen by any white man, and by few if any black men of the Centre, he had come one evening to the little town of Alice Springs, and had marvelled at the immensity of the white man's "camp". That night he had gazed in wonder at the unwinking, brilliant fire the white man used to light his square-windowed *gunyahs* and the broad, straight trails through his camp.

By night he skirted the little town, and in Grungrunja's *Arunta* territory, now gameless cattle country whose one-time warriors' bushcraft had become the craft of horse and cattle men — and beggar-men — he slipped like a wraith be-neath the Overland Telegraph line.

Then he came upon the railway. All that night he skirted the endless, snake-like rails of the single track, making many tentative approaches, until the dawn. In the early light he screwed up his courage and hurdled the rails in one prodi-gious leap.

That same eventful day, during an interval when no dust cloud from the white man's whining monsters that ran without legs could be seen from horizon to horizon, he flitted across the transcontinental motor road.

So he entered the depopulated *Aluridja* country to the west of salt-crusted, bone-day Lake Eyre. South and east he kept on through the no less deserted *Arabana* and *Wailpi* lands, towards the monster's lair.

Through the desert he had fared, not sumptuously but adequately, on lizards and snakes, and an occasional rabbit or kangaroo-rat. Those who eat reptiles do not grow fat, but the bushman knows they nourish. And all the way Munyarra had been heartened by the frequent sight of his totem brother, the big, crane-like *brolga,* or "native companion" as the white men call him. In one of these, sooner or later, Munyarra knew, his own spirit would reside for ever — even as that of the great Grungrunja.

Thus he had come at last, in good, lean, fighting fettle, and unobserved by men, by instruments, or by patrol air-craft, to the place where the white men flew and tended their roaring monsters — the place the white men had named with a blackfellow name — *Woomera,* the place of the throwing-stick . . .

At dawn Munyarra lay concealed in a shallow trough behind a tussock only seventy yards from the monster. He had left his camp in the night, bearing only his war boomerang, his shovel-nosed spear, and his *woomera.* He had stalked the monster from behind — where, he had observed early, there was no eye on its smooth, shining skin.

Despite its size the monster was a stupid thing, for it had taken no advantage of the dark to conceal itself. It had stood starkly amidst the brightest fires Munyarra had ever seen — some fixed on the ground, some carried around by the whining lesser monsters on which the white men rode — and all incredibly bright and unflickering. In all this light, for some hours, Munyarra had studied his adversary.

Like the horn of a bullock — like the point of a spear, broken off — it stood on its four legs which were also wings. Unmoving, it was, but none-the-less alert — truly as a sham-ming lizard might stand. He was not fooled by its immobility, although he was appalled by its size.

He could not, he realized, strike at its head, as Grungrunja had done, to knock off the single horn surmounting it. Thrown from below, a boomerang could only glance off the horn without damaging it. A throw from farther back, to strike across the point, would be impossible.

But Munyarra had discerned a more vulnerable place — the monster's groin — the place where, beneath the lizard-like body, the four wing-legs came together. His estimate of the vital nature of this region was confirmed by his observation of the care with which many of the men serving the monster ministered to the orifice he discerned there. There, he felt, was the place to strike. There, even if his hard-thrown boomerang failed to kill, it must surely maim and cripple . . .

With the rising sun behind him Munyarra watched the servants of the monster withdraw in their whining, wheeled beasts, leaving it alone on the desert while they went inside their low stone *gunyahs* in the distance beyond.

Five minutes longer he lay watching. Then, weapons in hand, he crept stealthily to within thirty yards . . . Beneath the monster he could see the vital orifice, a wide ellipse now, with thin, fin-shaped appendages . . .

Leaving spear and throwing-stick at his feet, Munyarra straightened up, boomerang in his left hand.

Unknown to him, one of the servants of the monster, in the reinforced concrete *"gunyah"* a quarter-mile away, was chanting . . . " – eighteen – seventeen – sixteen – "

Balancing on the balls of his feet, Munyarra took the boomerang with his right hand, hefted it, swung it across in front of his knees, and then back for the throw.

" – seven – six – five – four – " chanted the monster's servant.

The heavy war boomerang left Munyarra's hand below chest height, swooped, spinning, down to knee level, then swung suddenly upward between the two nearer legs of the monster.

Straight up into the orifice it went, to clatter against the fin-like appendages, buckling one and remaining there, jammed between them . . .

Neither cry of pain nor quiver of movement came from the monster. Munyarra who had swept up spear and throwing-stick as he recovered from the throw, felt a pang of chagrin at his failure.

But even as he puzzled the monster roared – and belched fire from his bowels!

For an instant Munyarra knew a wild ecstasy at the thought that he had rent the monster asunder. Then the hot blast of flame seared him like a thousand camp fires, and in an instant singed off his sparse beard and the hair of his head and body. The roaring of the monster rose to a howling scream that tortured his eardrums, made his bones ache and vibrate, and the earth beneath him to quake. Beneath his upraised, eye-shielding arm Munyarra saw the monster lift all four feet off the ground at once — and leap into the air!

He fled . . . The monster screamed and howled — behind him at first . . . then from above.

Snatching a terrified glance upwards Munyarra saw the monster in flight, truly a spear with a haft of fire, and still screaming shrilly.

He ran on, but a change in the voice from the sky made him look again. Higher yet, still riding its flaming tail, the monster was weaving its nose about in ever-widening circles — plainly seeking its attacker. Munyarra stopped in his tracks, so as not to attract attention by his movement.

Too late! The circling, questing nose came down. The fiery tail came up like that of a charging crocodile. The monster was coming his way!

Munyarra knew he must stand and fight. Spear haft found the notch of his *woomera* as he took his stance. He would throw as soon as his enemy should come into range. Then, as he was skilled in doing, he would leap aside at the last moment, just too late for the other's aim to change.

Yet all Munyarra's skill in the manoeuvre of evading spears had never given him experience in evading a missile flying faster every second and every yard from the moment it was launched towards him. The muscles of his throwing arm had barely tightened . . . his *woomera* had driven the spear haft a mere four inches while the monster travelled the last fifty yards . . .

There was a blinding flash of light and an earth-shaking detonation. There followed two secondary explosions and a leaping fire. The rocket range technicians swarmed like ants from their reinforced concrete bunkers, climbed into fire-fighting vehicles, and headed for the pillar of fire and smoke.

A jeep peeled off to approach the scorched take-off area. Two men got down from it to investigate a small yellow flame which flickered on the ground.

"Good God Almighty!" swore one, as he stamped out the flames and turned over with his boot the charred bent object. "A boomerang! What do you suppose . . . ?"

The other did not reply. Both stared in puzzlement across to the burning rocket.

Beyond the smoke a *brolga* spread its six feet of slaty wings upon the air and swung away towards the north.

Kelly Country

A. Bertram Chandler

(1976)

I don't like it here.

It's no worse, I suppose, than where (when?) I really belong, it's just that it's . . . different. There are similarities, but they don't help any. Just when I kid myself that the situation (at last!) is coming under control I trip over some damned discrepancy and fall flat on my badly battered face. I thought at first that making a living — after I was discharged from the mental hospital — would be the least of my problems; even though I am a displaced person there's been no need for me to learn a new language. But it hasn't been easy. I had in mind a series of articles on my life and hard times — my life and hard times, that is, before I came here — but it didn't work out. Every newspaper editor whom I approached said that he wasn't interested in fiction, and every magazine editor told me that he wasn't interested in science fiction. Sf, for some reasons, just hasn't caught on in this country, and the only fantasy that ever gets published is rehashings of Celtic mythology.

I've tried to track down Siebert, of course. He would be able to help me. But where is he? Two Dr Sieberts I did find, but one is a gynaecologist and the other a dentist. It's Siebert the theoretical physicist I want, but he must still be in his native Austria or Germany or whever it was that he came from. If I had the money I'd take a trip to Europe to try to find him — but money in a sufficiently large amount is what I haven't got and probably never shall have.

I never have had much, but I was getting by, selling the occasional short story and, now and again, a far from successful novel. Freelance journalism provided the bread on which to spread the precious butter derived from creative writing. I'd get an idea and sell it to one of the editors whom I knew, then scratch around for the material for the series of articles or profiles or whatever. *The World Shapers* was the series that I was working on when I met Siebert. It dealt with little-known scientists and engineers who might well change, improve even, our way of living. I'd interviewed Dr Canning, who'd made what was essentially a Stirling engine using solar radiation as the external heat source. (It worked, too, and generators so powered would have done much to resolve the energy crisis.) And there was Colonel Remington, a retired army engineer who was an authority on one aspect of aviation. It was Remington's contention that the airship should make a comeback — and this, too, tied in with the fuel crisis. Why burn oil to proceed from Point A to Point B *and* to stay up when you need burn oil only to proceed from Point A to Point B? He had a beautiful little — not so little, actually — model dirigible, helium filled, with electric motors, radio controlled. He let me play with the controls and fly it over a couple of figure eight circuits. I hope that he finally found somebody to put up the money to build a big ship . . . And there was Wellaby, with his thoroughly worked out and costed scheme to tow icebergs from the Antarctic ice barrier to South Australia during times of drought. The fresh water so obtained, he convinced me, would cost no more than fresh water from more conventional sources. And Wellaby tied in with Dahlgren, who had revived the idea of a Central Australian Sea, using nuclear explosions to blast out the basin.

Oh, they were all off-beat, but none of them outrageously so. I wanted a real Mad Scientist to round off the series, somebody with a foreign-sounding name for preference, a refugee from the comic strips. And yet his ideas would have to possess a glimmering of credibility and would have to be capable, if put into effect, of reshaping the world. After all, such people have, now and again, shaken our planet to its foundations. The mildly eccentric, violin-playing Albert Einstein, for example . . .

So there was I, with the series almost completed, and I had a good market waiting for it and once the money was in the bank I'd be able to carry on with the research for what I hoped would be *the* Australian novel. All that remained was the Mad Scientist profile. Luckily (unluckily?) I have a retentive memory. I recalled a tongue in cheek interview in one of the dailies with a then newly arrived Dr Siebert. Siebert had been unwise enough to mention the possibility of

Time Travel. The interviewer had the time of his young life playing around with all the usual paradoxes — going back through time to murder his grandfather before he as much as met his grandmother, going ahead to read tomorrow's papers and then making a fortune at the races or on the stock exchange . . . If you're at all familiar with a certain type of American science fiction you'll know all the plot gimmicks.

Without too much trouble I was able to get hold of a copy of that paper. It was a little more trouble for me to run Siebert down, but I managed eventually through one — my only one, if you must know — of my academic contacts. The scientific community, I gathered, regarded Siebert no more seriously than that young reporter had done. But I got his address — an old but well preserved and not too blatantly tarted up terrace house in Paddington. He wasn't on the telephone, so I wrote to him. I got no reply. After making due allowance for Post Office inefficiency I wrote again, this time enclosing a stamped, addressed envelope. Again there was no reply. If it hadn't been for that stamped, addressed envelope I'd have dropped the idea of interviewing Dr Siebert and found somebody else. But it was the petty meanness, as it seemed to me, that got my back up.

So I went out to Paddington fairly early on a fine winter's morning. I knew where the house was, of course; I'd located it during the preliminary hunt down of my quarry. I hammered on the old-fashioned brass knocker of the front door. I was on the point of giving up and leaving when I heard footsteps approaching over an uncarpeted wooden floor. The door opened, but only a crack, only to the extent of the chain. I looked down at Siebert and he peered suspiciously up at me. He was a round little man, bald except for the bushes of grey hair over his ears. My immediate impression was of a rather bad tempered koala bear.

I asked politely, "Dr Siebert?"

He countered in a voice that just missed being squeaky, that held strong traces of some middle European accent, "Who else would it be? Your business?"

I tried to put him into a good mood. I apologized for not having made an appointment, and added that it wasn't easy to do so as he wasn't on the 'phone. He told me that telephones are time wasters. By this time my own good mood — such as it was — was fast evaporating. I said that I had written to him, twice, but received no reply. He said that he neither replied to nor even read unimportant correspondence. But he did ask me again what my business was.

I told him my name, took a card out of my notecase and handed it to him. It carried, under the *John Carmell*, the magic word *Journalist*. For some reason the sight of that word makes most people ready and willing − often too ready, too willing − to talk. But not Siebert. "A journalist," he told me contemptuously, "knows less about more things than anybody else on this planet." He thrust the card back at me. I took it, put it back in my notecase. He told me to take my foot out of the door so that he could shut it.

But I can be stubborn. I tried to explain to him that I was a freelance, not directly employed by any of the newspapers. I told him about the series of profiles that I was working on. I name dropped. Obviously he had heard of Canning and Dahlgren and I sensed that he was weakening. I mentioned Kraus, the anti-gravity man, who was also in the series. That did it. Siebert, it seemed, knew Kraus. Not only did he know him, he didn't like him. I realized that if I didn't take my foot out of the door I'd finish up with a bad bruise, if nothing worse.

Then it happened. From inside the house, the hallway, came a sharp *pfhht!*, a sort of soft explosion. From where I was standing I could just see a low table − and on that table had suddenly appeared a wire cage, with something pale moving inside it. There was something else on the table − a white oblong. The animal in the cage chittered loudly. I knew then what it was. A white rat. A laboratory rat.

Siebert seemed even more surprised than I was. He left the door, went to that low table. He picked up the little white oblong. He looked at it. He returned to me.

He said, "It would seem that I did − will − let you in. It would seem that I will stage a demonstration for you. This is your card . . . "

I said, "Is this some kind of conjuring trick, Doctor? You gave it back to me . . . "

He said, "I am giving it back to you again."

I looked at it. It was my card all right. I put it back in my notecase.

He said, "You now have one more card than when you left your lodgings this morning."

I said, "Unluckily I don't know how many cards I should have."

He said, "No matter. Come in."

He shut the door briefly to release the chain, reopened it wide. I followed him through the narrow hallway. The white rat chittered at us as we passed it. He said to it, an odd note of affection in his voice, "Do not worry, Adolf. There will soon be only one of you again. . . " So Siebert had a device for duplicating rats, I thought. Big deal.

He opened a door at the end of the narrow hallway, switched on the light. It was the machine that first caught — compelled — my attention. It could have been a crazy mobile welded together by some futuristic sculptor from junkyard odds and ends. There were wheels, set at odd angles to each other. There was a control panel with switches and dials and a cathode ray tube. And the perspective of the thing was . . . wrong.

Under it was a low platform. On the platform was a wire cage. In the cage was a white rat.

"Adolf," said Siebert as though making an introduction. (Well, he was, I suppose, doing just that.) "He is in a — how do you say? — paradoxical situation. He is coexisting with himself."

That didn't make sense to me. There were, obviously, two white rats, one out in the hallway, the other in this laboratory.

I said, "There are two rats, Doctor."

He said, "There is one rat. Very shortly I shall use the . . . temporal displacer to send Adolf back through time and over a distance of a few metres. You saw him arrive in what is now the Past. You cannot deny that."

I said, "But one solid body cannot occupy two spaces at the same time. That makes sense, doesn't it? Or doesn't it?" He looked at me quizzically. I went on, "It's that axiom. You know. Two solid bodies cannot occupy the same space at the same time. I just sort of reversed it. . . "

He asked, "So you have some knowledge of mathematics, of physics, Mr Carmell?"

"Only what I learned in school," I said. "And I've forgotten most of that."

"What do you know about gyroscopes?" he demanded.

"Don't they always stay pointing in the same direction?" I suggested.

He allowed himself a slight smile. "Rigidity in space is one of the properties of the gyroscope. Another one is precession. . . "

"Like in the precession of the equinoxes?" I hazarded.

He ignored this. "Imagine a spinning gyroscope. You press down on one end of the axis and it resists the downward pressure. But it does move. It precesses, swings to one side at right angles to the applied force, in the direction of the rotation. . . "

"I see . . . " I said doubtfully.

"The rotors of my machine precess," he went on, "but not through any of the dimensions of normal space. But they precess, nevertheless, within the Space-Time continuum."

"Through Time?" I demanded, unbelievingly.

"Temporal precession," he assured me.

I didn't say anything, but my disbelief must have been plain on my face. He laughed. "And now, Mr Carmell, the demonstration . . . " He started to fiddle with the dials on the control panel. The rat chittered loudly. "Poor Adolf," he muttered. "He knows what I am doing. He has made the journey, longer journeys, often, but still he is frightened . . . " He turned to me. "But wait. Your card . . . "

"Any card?" I asked.

"Whatever card you take from your notecase must be the right one," he said.

I gave him the oblong of cardboard and he put it on the platform beside the cage. Then he switched on and the machine, the Time Machine, came to life. The rotors started to spin, slowly at first, then faster and faster. The sound of it rose rapidly from a low humming to a high, almost supersonic whine. In the cathode ray tube was what looked like a revolting circle of green light, but not an ordinary circle. It was somehow important that I think of the name of it. It came to me suddenly. A Mobius strip . . . And the wheels, the rotors . . . They were spinning, gleaming, tumbling, fading, seemingly always about to vanish and yet never doing so.

There was a sharp *pfhht!*, the sound of an implosion. The rat was gone from the platform, and with it my card.

Siebert stopped the machine then. The rotors slowed, the high whine deepened to subsonic hum, stopped. Again there was the *pfhht!* The rat flashed into being, chittered at us. But there was no sign of my card.

I asked Siebert where it was.

"But I gave it back to you," he told me, "just before I let you into the house."

I tried to work things out, but gave it up. I asked instead, "What does this thing *do*, actually?"

He said, "I sent the rat back through Time."

I didn't say "Impossible!" right out loud, but Siebert must have read my expression. He snapped, "You have seen, and yet you doubt."

I said, "Time travel just doesn't happen."

He said, "But it does. We are all Time Travellers, proceeding at a fixed and steady rate from the cradle to the grave..."

"From the womb to the tomb," I amplified. "From the sperm to the worm. From the erection to the resurrection."

He glared at me, then permitted himself a frosty smile. "You have a sense of humour, Mr Carmell," he commented. "But permit me to finish. We are all, as I have said, Time Travellers. But I have discovered how the rate of travel may be accelerated, or reversed. I have given you a demonstration. Think carefully, now. Could there have been any trickery?"

So I thought carefully. Siebert, I decided, might be a conjuror — but if he were he was a highly professional one. I had seen the rat — *and* my card — arrive in the hallway, allegedly from what was then the Future. I had seen the rat — or *a* rat — vanish from the laboratory, allegedly into the Past, and then return. Just to make sure I went to the door, opened it and looked into the narrow hall. The low table was empty.

All right, I thought. I'll play along. Siebert may or may not be a fake, a charlatan but, in any case, there're the makings of a good article here.

"How did . . . Adolf get back here?" I asked.

"Imagine a piece of elastic," said Siebert. "Imagine that it is stretched, temporally as well as spatially, with Adolf, in his cage, on the end of it. The force to stretch that elastic emanates from the machine. When the machine is stopped, the elastic snaps back. It is as simple as that."

Oddly enough, it did sound simple. I was beginning to *feel* the principles of Time Travel, although I was still far from understanding. That machine — that Time Machine — looked capable of anything, especially when it was working.

Siebert looked at his watch. He said, almost diffidently, "At this hour of the morning I usually take refreshment. Would you care to join me?"

I had no objections, of course. I was expecting tea or coffee, but he produced a bottle and two glasses. The bottle contained Schnapps. He served it without ice cubes or water. I'm a beer man myself and that first drink was much stronger than I'm accustomed to. So was the second, and the third . . . Siebert wasn't exactly twisting my arm, but it would have been ill mannered of me to let him drink by himself.

Nonetheless, I made some attempt to get on with the morning's business. "All right, Doctor," I said, "I'll accept that your temporal displacement device does work. Then why don't you use it to travel into the future? Not far, only a day or so, just to get a look at tomorrow's papers. And then you clean up at the races, or on the stock market . . . "

He smiled rather sadly. "I am not a practical man, Mr Carmell," he told me, "but I like money. I have already given thought to doing as you suggest. But the future is . . . dangerous . . . "

"So is the present," I said. "So is — was? — the past."

"Not in the same way," he told me. "You see, it is like this. From every passing second, every microsecond, even, there branch out an infinitude of possible *and* divergent futures. From every passing second in the past other infinitudes of alternatves have branched out. My machine will send you into one of those possible futures — but, so far, there is no way of knowing which one it will be . . . "

Send *you*, he had said. Send *me*? Not bloody likely. Although I should like a look at tomorrow's papers . . . Perhaps a dog, I thought, trained to pick them up from people's front lawns and bring them back . . .

"Adolf," Siegel went on, "has had his predecessors . . . " The white rat chittered at the sound of his name. "Some of them I did send into the future. Two returned dead, without a mark on their bodies. Unfortunately I am not a veterinary surgeon so I could not determine the cause of death. One, obviously, had died in a vacuum. One, one only, returned alive. All the fur was burned from his body. I had to kill him, in pity."

"Oh," I said. "Oh."

"The past," he said, "is safe. The railway tracks, if I may use a simile, are already laid down. There is no possibility of the Time Traveller's being shunted into one of the alternate universes."

I began to suspect a line of sales talk. I said, "You mentioned that only *some* of Adolf's predecessors were sent into the future. What happened to the ones you sent into the past?"

"They are dead," he told me. "Both of them."

"And you say the past is safe!" I expostulated.

"It was their present that was not safe," he said smugly. "They survived their temporal voyages unscathed. And then one, the first one, escaped from his cage and was killed by the cat that I used to keep. A few weeks later the second one also escaped and ran out into the road. He was flattened by a passing car."

He poured more drinks. Was he trying to soften me up? That thought did flicker across my apology for a mind, but only briefly. But there was some sort of nigger in the wood-pile, I couldn't help feeling.

I asked, "If the past is all that safe, Doctor, why haven't *you* travelled back through time? Think of the historical novels you could write, with every detail dinkum as all hell. You could make money that way, as a writer ... "

"But I cannot write," he said sadly. "I know my limitations. Too, somebody would have to — how do you say? — mind the shop. I have no assistant trained to operate the machine during my absence ... " He paused. "But you ... ?"

"No thanks!" I told him hastily. "Not me. I haven't a mechanical mind. Any machine that I as much as lay a finger on, goes on the blink."

He said, "That is not what I meant. *You* are a writer, Mr Carmell. And a reporter. There is so very much that you could write about. An eye witness account of the Crucifixion ... "

I told him that I wasn't a religious man.

He went on persuasively. "Then, perhaps, the Battle of Waterloo? No? Or the Battle of Gettysburg? One of my ancestors was there. As you know, quite a number of European military officers served with the Union forces ... "

"No ... " I said.

"Ah," said he brightly. "I think I see. Those battles are not Australian history. Then the landing at Gallipoli?"

"No," I said again, but he sensed that I was weakening. He asked just what and where and when was it that I wanted.

Like a mug, I told him. I earbashed him about the novel that I'd been meaning to write for quite some time, on which I had already done preliminary research. He was rather surprised, I think, at my choice of place and period. He said, "But this Ned Kelly ... I have, of course, heard of him — he was no more than a robber, a — how do you say — bushranger."

This annoyed me. I said that Ned Kelly was more, much more than that. He was a freedom fighter, a guerrilla leader, with a charisma that has survived to the present day. He might have been much more than a hunted criminal if the cards had fallen a little differently ... I ran down, out of breath, refreshed myself with a gulp of Schnapps, then went on. "It was the Siege of Glenrowan that I wanted to see," I said, "with that great, armoured figure tramping through the low mist like some huge robot, striking terror into the hearts of the cowardly policemen ...

"I want to see Ned Kelly played by himself, not by Mick Jagger!" I concluded.

"And why not, Mr Carmell?" asked Siebert softly. And even more softly, "It is time that a human being made the journey, not some mere rat . . . " Then, briskly, "The time and the place, if you please. The temporal and spatial co-ordinates?"

"Glenrowan," I told him. "The early morning, at about half past two, of June 28, 1880 . . . "

He said that he would have to find out the exact latitude and longitude, and left me. He gestured towards the bottle and my empty glass as he walked, just a little unsteadily, out of the laboratory.

I helped myself to another drink. The bottle was so nearly finished that it seemed pointless to leave anything in it. There was nobody to talk to except the rat, Adolf, in his cage, so I talked to him. He seemed to understand what I was saying. I told him that I should have a mascot with me for my voyage into the wild colonial past. (I used to keep white rats when I was a kid, and still rather liked them.) I managed, after a struggle, to get the door of the cage open. I stuffed Adolf into my breast pocket just before Siebert came back. Adolf didn't seem to mind. And the learned Doctor didn't notice that the cage was empty.

He was putting on a bit of a whinge, in fact, complaining that although he had charts and maps for all over the world Glenrowan was hard to find. He fussed around with the controls of his machine, setting the dials for the coordinates of my destination. I remember hoping that he was sober enough to get things right, not to send me back to watch the building of the pyramids or the construction of the Great Wall of China or something else in which I wasn't interested. Not that I was all that sober myself. If I had been I'd never have climbed on to that platform, under that assemblage of cock-eyed flywheels in that distorted framework. But, as I've said, I was feeling no pain. I even made a joke.

I said, in what was meant to be a German accent but probably wasn't, "You may the count-down commence, Herr Doktor!"

Siebert stared at me bewilderedly, then suddenly realized that I was trying to be funny. His imitation American accent was no more convincing than my German one had been. "All systems Go! Go! Go!"

His finger stabbed a button. Over my head those blasted wheels started to turn and the rotating circle of green light appeared in the cathode ray tube. The low humming of the gyroscopes rose rapidly in frequency to a thin, high whine, painful to the ear.

And . . .

And I was alone, and I was cold, and I was sober.

And I was frightened.

I wondered at first if Siebert's sums had come out wrong, landing me in the middle of Siberia in mid-winter. It seemed cold enough. I was wearing only a light summer suit. I opened my eyes, dreading what I might see. There was a railroad track — the trans-Siberian railroad? — and, not too far away, a tiny cluster of yellow lights. A lopsided moon hung high in the clear sky, indicating but doing little to illuminate the shadowy masses of trees and bushes. Some nocturnal bird was kicking up a raucous racket. In the distance a dog barked, the sound carrying clearly in the still air. Also carrying clearly, but not loudly, was the music of a piano accordion. It seemed to come from that little huddle of lights. It sounded like an Irish jig. Well, I thought, at least it wasn't Russian . . .

There was another light and it was unsteady, moving, approaching me. Somebody was walking along the track, from the village, carrying a lantern. I stood there, waiting for him. He didn't see me until he was almost on me; he had been too engrossed in making his way without tripping over the railway sleepers.

And then he looked up and stared at me.

"Who are you?" he asked in a shaky voice, in a rather soft English accent that I couldn't quite place.

I thought that I knew who he was, but I had to be sure. I asked, reasonably enough, "Where and when am I?"

He asked, rather angrily, if I was mad or intoxicated. I repeated my question.

He replied shortly, "Glenrowan, of course." Then he went on, angrily, "Out of my way, sir! Ned Kelly and all his gang are in the hotel, drinking and singing, waiting for the special train. They've torn up the tracks on the other side of the village. I must stop it, or God alone knows what will happen!"

I said, "So you are Thomas Curnow . . . "

"And who are you, sir?" he demanded. "Are you one of *them*?"

I was standing with my back to the moon so that my face was in shadow. He raised his lantern so that he could see me more clearly. He raised his lantern — and gasped, and dropped it. There was a little crash of broken glass, a brief flare from the exposed wick, the stink of spilled kerosene.

"A head . . . " he muttered, "looking out of your pocket . . . Two red eyes . . . "

For a second or so I was as frightened as he was, then I remembered taking the white rat from Siebert's laboratory. "It's only Adolf . . . " I said soothingly.

"Adolf?"

"He's a rat. A white rat. A sort of pet . . . "

"The train . . . " he said.

The train . . . Yes, it was coming all right, and coming fast, the chuffing rattle of the old steam locomotives carrying loudly over the rapidly diminishing distance. There had been delays, I remembered, and the drivers, urged by Superintendent Hare, would be trying to make up time, to reach the township of Wangaratta before the Kelly Gang rode away to continue their depredations elsewhere. (They had ridden away, of course, and were actually at Glenrowan – but Hare did not know that. Yet.)

And what else did I remember? Curnow had carried a red scarf as well as a lantern. And there was a good moon . . .

Curnow took his stance in the middle of the track, the red scarf in his hand. The man had courage. He stood there – and I, like a bloody fool, stood there with him. We could see the train now – the pilot engine in the lead, its headlight dim by today's standards but, no doubt, considered dazzlingly bright in that day and age. There was a ruddy glare from the firebox as the door was opened, illuminating the smoke and steam billowing from the funnel. There was a shower of sparks.

We stood there, while that steel, fire-breathing monster roared closer and closer. We stood there, with Curnow frantically waving that scarf. The driver must have seen us. Perhaps he thought that we were Kelly supporters attempting to delay the special train still further. But whether he saw us or not it was clear that he had no intention of stopping.

Curnow stood his ground – or would have if I hadn't dragged him with me as I jumped clear at the very last moment. We rolled on the rough gravel, bruised, clothing torn and skin scratched and bleeding, as the train rattled past – the pilot engine first and then the locomotive with its short string of coaches. I heard horses whinnying in answer to the piercing blast of the leading engine's steam whistle.

Then there was comparative silence. I scrambled to my feet, helped Curnow to his. We started after the fast diminishing red rear light on the guard's van. It drew level with, then passed the little cluster of lights that marked Glenrowan.

He said bitterly, "God alone knows what will happen now. It could be what I have been dreading, a revolution. The wild Irish against the English squatters . . . "

Beyond Glenrowan there was a crash — but not as loud as I had been expecting. There was another crash — and that came up to my worst expectations. It was a series of crashes, actually. I could visualize the locomotive of the special train itself ploughing into the overturned pilot engine, the coaches jackknifing . . . Whatever else has changed, train wrecks still follow a well established pattern. And we could hear the shouting and the screaming — more screaming than shouting, of horses as well as of humans.

We started to run along the track towards the wreck but neither of us was especially fit and, in the uncertain moonlight, we were stumbling over the sleepers. We slowed to a walk, as rapid a walk as we could manage in the circumstances. We passed the hotel; its door was wide open, the yellow lamplight streaming out. The place seemed to be deserted.

Ahead of us there was gunfire — rifles and revolvers it sounded like. So some of the police had survived, were putting up a fight . . .

They were still fighting when, at last, we stumbled on to the scene of the wreck. The air was heavy with acrid powder fumes, with smoke from the burning wreckage, and through this mist moved the figures of the outlaws, seemingly invulnerable to the fire that was being directed at them.

They were still fighting, although the battle was almost over.

Curnow and I approached one of the splintered coaches in time to see a giant figure discharge his revolver into the face of a bulky man in civilian clothing — and that was the end of it, although some of the injured horses were still neighing.

I heard one of the outlaws say to the giant, "Ned, the poor horses . . . "

"We shall have to shoot them," was the reply.

"And there are women here, Ned," went on the smaller man. "Dead . . . "

Women? Inspector O'Connor's wife had been aboard that train, I remembered, and a Miss Smith, her sister. I remembered, too, that Ned Kelly had boasted that never had he harmed a woman . . .

"Women ... " said the giant, his voice muffled and distorted by the cylindrical steel helmet of his armour. "This time we have gone too far. But we have to fight on ... Perhaps the bold Fenian men in America will help us ... " Then he said heavily, "It had to come to this."

I couldn't resist the temptation. I said, "You aren't supposed to say that until you're on the gallows, Mr Kelly."

He swung to face me. His eyes glared at me from the slit in the cylindrical helmet. His heavy revolver came up to point at me. I knew that I'd have to talk hard and fast and convincingly if I wished to escape the fate of Superintendent Hare. But I never had a chance to.

That moonlit scene with the wrecked train, the dead policemen and the living outlaws, flickered out like a snuffed candle. I was conscious of the thin, high whine of Siebert's machine. But there was something wrong. The sound was unsteady, oscillating. And there was a *twang*, like suddenly snapping a violin string.

Bright summer sunlight hurt my eyes. When I could see, I found that I was staring into a ruddy face, a man's face, rough, with mouth agape in amazement.

"And where the hell did *ye* come from?" he muttered. "An' is that a rat in yer buttonhole, or am I seein' things?"

I ignored his question. There were so many that I wanted to ask myself. Where was I, and *when*? I was not back in Siebert's laboratory, that was for sure. I was outside, on a hot summer's day. There was a crowd around me, men in slacks and brightly coloured shirts, gaily miniskirted women — but only that drunk seemed to have noticed my arrival. There was music, a military band approaching, and the air was familiar enough. It was *Waltzing Matilda*.

So I was, at least, in the right country.

And I was on the waterfront. It was almost familiar. The shoreline that I could see over the rippled blueness of Sydney Cove — if it was Sydney Cove — looked like Kirribilli. And Bennelong Point looked as Bennelong Point had looked before the building of the Opera House. But there wasn't any Opera House, although there was a bridge from Dawes Point to Milsons Point — but not *our* bridge, not the familiar coat hanger. It was a great suspension bridge, a scaled down version of San Francisco's Golden Gate. But there were ferry piers along the Circular Quay and on the western shore of the cove was an overseas passenger terminal, and alongside it a big, grey ship.

The band was close now. I could see the uniformed

players through the crowd. Scots? No, although they wore kilts, *yellow* kilts . . . But hadn't the Irish once worn kilts, saffron kilts? Kilts they were wearing, and bright green tunics, and breastplates of polished metal, and odd, cylindrical helmets, and the soldiers who marched after them were similarly clad.

"Three cheers, me boys!" somebody shouted. "Three cheers for Ned Kelly's Own!"

When the cheering had subsided I turned again to the man who had seen me arrive. I tapped his arm. I said, "Excuse me . . . "

He turned and regarded me owlishly. "There'sh no excuse," he said with drunken solemnity, "for a man who comesh from nowhere *an'* wearsh a white rat in hish buttonhole."

"Please, where am I?"

"Ye mean ye don't know Shydney when ye shee it?"

"Please, what date is it?"

"Ye're drunker than I am, mister, an' I've had a skinful. 'Tis Deshember the twelfth — or ish it the thirteenth? I'm not too sure meself — 1975 . . . "

I persisted, although he was beginning to edge away from me.

"Those soldiers, marching to the troopship . . . Where are they bound?"

If I hadn't by this time taken a firm grip on his elbow he would have got away from me.

"Vietnam," he muttered. "Where elshe?"

"But the war's over," I said.

"The war over? Ye must be mad. The war'll never be over long as there'sh a shingle, Christ-hatin', Commie bastard left alive . . . "

He angrily shook his arm out of my grasp and melted into the crowd. Looking after him I saw the light breeze lift the folds of the huge ensign at the stern of the troop transport. It was a green flag, with the stars of the Southern Cross, in gold, at the fly, and a golden harp in the upper canton.

One Way to Tomorrow

Wynne N. Whiteford

(1957)

Joe Buller let his anger work up to a white heat as he strode down the street, kicking savagely at a piece of wood that lay in his path. As he passed the last of the hops he caught his reflection in a strip of mirror, and the red, aggressive face that peered back at him from narrowed eyes pleased him. He looked like a man who was used to getting his own way.

His knock on the door of the shed was thunderous.

"Coming," called Mallinson's voice from within.

"Make it quick. It's me — Buller."

Footsteps. The door creaked open, and Mallinson, tall and stooping, pushed his lank black hair back from his forehead as he peered short-sightedly out. "To what do I owe — " he began.

"I want some of my money," said Buller brusquely. "Look — I don't like doing it this way, but I've got to have it. Had a big loss this week. They're sticking the fangs in."

Mallinson hesitated, then pushed the door wide. "Come in."

Buller strode into the shed. He noticed that Mallinson had rigged up a switchboard with multiple power-points fed from it. He wondered if he'd had an electrician check it. Probably not. And if anything went wrong, who was responsible? The owner of the shed — Buller. He set his jaw into line of battle position.

"Just what are you doing here?" he boomed.

Mallinson began rolling a cigarette with lean, nicotine-stained fingers that shook incessantly. "You'd never believe me if I told you."

"Just tell me. I'll tell you if I believe you."

Mallinson tilted his head back, focussing his eyes on

Buller. Lighting his cigarette with a cheap automatic lighter, he took a quick, nervous draw on it and gestured with it to a complex mass of mechanism in the far corner.

"Any idea what that might be?" he asked.

Buller looked at the thing. Some resale value in the electric motors, anyway — say a tenner each. And the coils of copper wire — worth a bit, any time. The vacuum tubes might be expensive, or they might be junk — he knew nothing about radio.

"Suppose *you* tell *me.*"

Mallinson tapped the ash of his cigarette into an empty jam tin. "Suppose we put it this way. We live in a universe that has four dimensions. In other words, a four-dimensional continuum. A continuum which has, to put it crudely, three dimensions of space and the other — well, you might call it time. Only that wouldn't be quite correct. Better call it the time-space interval. Are you with me?"

Buller shook his head. "No, sport. I lost you right back at the start."

Mallinson coughed. "Put it this way, then. Everything is composed of particles. Each particle, plotted in a four-dimensional continuum, is a line. A world-line, as we call it, extending in the direction of the time-stream. Got it?"

"Look, there's one thing I *haven't* got, and that's my money."

"I'm coming to that. Now listen. All your life, you — the host of particles which make you up — travel along the time-stream, always at the same steady speed. Get that?"

"Yes. So what?"

"I can alter the speed, with that machine. I can accelerate or decelerate the speed of movement along the time-stream of anything within the machine's field. Watch."

He stepped over to the machine, getting up on a platform surrounded by screens of wire mesh — he had to close one of them after him like a door. He set a couple of electric motors spinning — Buller noticed with some satisfaction that they were battery-powered, not using the mains current through his meter.

"I want you to wait for me here," said Mallinson. "I'll be some time."

He moved the central lever on the control panel slightly to the right.

Buller stared. He gave a hoarse shout, ran forward a couple of paces, then stopped. The hair on the back of his neck seemed to be trying to stand straight out.

"Mallinson!" he bellowed.

But the room was empty. He rushed to the door. Outside, the morning air was fresh and sunlit and real. He ran right round the outside of the shed, then went slowly back inside. Was he going off his head? There *had* been a machine in that corner, hadn't there? And Mallinson — he *had* been there — hadn't he? But where had he gone?

Overwork. That was it. Overwork and worry. Making a man see things. He must have thought he'd seen Mallinson here — just thought it.

Suddenly there was a taste of fear in his mouth like metal. Over on the bench, a wisp of grey smoke from Mallinson's cigarette-butt still rose from the jam-tin.

Buller sat down on the one chair in the room. He felt much less sure of himself. Much less sure of everything. Time machines! Bah! Lot of damned rot. Why, if a man could skip backwards and forwards in time, he could go back to yesterday and meet himself.

Then what would happen when the two of them had been knocking round for the odd day, and came up to today again, to the time when he'd gone back? That'd mean they'd both go back, and then you'd have four of them, wouldn't you?

He tried to think it out from a different angle. This was as bad as the one about "brothers and sisters have I none, but this man's father is his brother's uncle", or whatever it was. Then, like a bursting bomb, the solution struck him.

Hypnotism! That's what had happened. This Mallinson character had hypnotized him.

That was the only answer. There wasn't any machine. Never had been. Mallinson had hypnotized him into believing a lot of twaddle, then simply walked away while he was out of it.

Angrily, he jumped to his feet. And then the room was filled with a ringing crash of sound.

Mallinson and the machine were back. Back in a flash, solid and real and moving, the motors humming, Mallinson in the act of taking his hand off the control lever, then stepping down and striding across the room to the bench as though he had just walked in through a door. He picked up something from the bench and grinned.

"Forgot my lighter," he said to Buller, who was suddenly finding it hard to breathe. Striding back to the machine, he stopped in mid-step. "What's the matter?"

Buller waved his hand feebly. "Nothing. Take no notice of

me. I've only gone mad. That's all. Off my nut. But it's nothing. Nothing at all."

Mallinson stepped closer to him. "Listen," he said, "I only made this little demonstration to convince you I was carrying out serious experimental work. The last thing I wanted to do was upset you in any way."

"Upset me? Upset me, he says. Does something that's plain damned impossible, right in front of my eyes, then asks me if he's upsetting me."

"Listen, old man, you'd better get a grip of yourself. Come here."

Buller rose to his feet in a daze, and Mallinson led him across to the machine. He held the wire screen aside for him.

"No!" shouted Buller.

"I just want you to get a closer look." Mallinson stepped up on to the platform. "Come here a minute," he said.

Buller's curiosity got the better of his wisdom, and he stepped up beside him. Mallinson pointed to the alarm-clock on the bench across the room.

"What's that clock say?" he asked.

"Ten-fifteen," said Buller, and as he spoke Mallinson flicked the lever to the right and back again. A crash of sound, a sound almost too deep to be heard, a sound that Buller felt through every atom of his being – and then silence again, except for the hum of the motors.

Buller shivered. He felt like a man who has just had an electric shock. The shed was still there, with the long bench and the broken chair and the piles of junk – but something was wrong.

The light was wrong. It was coming the wrong way for morning sunshine, and it looked reddish and dusty. And something was wrong with the clock, too – the hands, which a moment ago had pointed to ten-fifteen, now showed twenty past five.

He sprang off the machine and rushed to the single small window, pulling aside the piece of sacking that served as a blind. Late afternoon sunlight slanted redly against the trees.

"God!" he gasped. "What's happened to the day?"

"You've missed it," said Mallinson. "I wouldn't worry, though. You should live just as long. Maybe a few hours longer, from the viewpoint of the people out there. You've jumped through seven hours of time in a fraction of a second – that's all."

Buller flung the door open. A step or two outside, he

halted. A group of men standing a dozen yards away whirled to face him.

"There's the swine," roared one of them. "He's been in there all the time."

They strode menacingly towards the door. Buller didn't wait to ask to which swine they referred. In a flash, he was back in the shed, the door slammed.

"They're all here together," he said.

"Who?"

"The blokes who are sticking the fangs in."

The door shivered on its hinges. Buller saw one way out. In half a dozen strides, he was on the platform of the machine.

"No!" screamed Mallinson, but the word was chopped short as Buller swung the lever as far to the right as it would go . . .

He felt weightless, dizzy. A high-pitched, droning hum pervading everything, and an endless vibration throbbed through him. A flickering light played about him, its flicker almost too fast to be seen — fifty, perhaps a hundred flashes a second. Then, abruptly, it was lighter all round.

He had the feeling of being in the open. A bright arch of light swung up and down the sky like a skipping-rope. Buller looked at the controls. Better not touch the ones he didn't understand. The long lever was marked with a plus sign on its right, minus on its left. So you pushed it right to go forward in time, left to go back. Fine. He'd wait until the crowd outside the shed were tired ot waiting, then go back — but not quite all the way back, just back to some time after they'd gone away.

Suddenly, he realized he didn't know how fast or how far he'd travelled. With a sudden chill, he recalled Mallinson's quick flick of the lever — an inch to the right, then back. At that rate —

He swallowed. The flicker — that was the flicker of day and night. The arch of light was the sun, moving too fast for him to see; and that skipping-rope swing of the arch of the light was the swing of the sun from summer to winter and back. A year every second or so. Hey, wait a minute . . .

With a quick grab, he centralized the lever. He shut his eyes. It wasn't true. It couldn't be true . . .

But it was! It was all there when he opened them again.

The shed was gone. The road had gone. There were still trees about, but they were in different places, and some of them were different kinds of trees.

He was in a walled garden, with walls of a shimmering golden substance that looked semi-transparent. A building out of an ultra-modern architect's dream towered above a hedge of strange plants with huge exotic flowers. And walking along a path was a girl.

She was tall and willowy and brown, with silver-green hair piled in a fantastic style, greenish make-up, and vivid violet lips.

She was dressed only in a bright-patterned plastic skirt and transparent high-heeled shoes. Seeing Buller, she stopped in her tracks and screamed.

A shout sounded from the house, and a hairy, blonde young giant with a physique of an all-in wrestler appeared round the end of the hedge. With a roar he wrenched a plastic stake from the garden and rushed towards Buller like a charging rhinoceros. For the second time, Buller coped with the situation by moving the lever.

He moved it to the left, to go back. But something went wrong. No flicker of days and nights. Only a dimming of the light. The fellow with the stake was still there, apparently arrested in mid-stride.

But not quite arrested. He still came forward in a horrible slow-motion, muscles rippling as he swung the stake slowly, very slowly backwards to strike. Buller didn't wait. He pushed the lever to the right again, and set everything humming and flickering once more.

He began to do some solid thinking. Jumping forward in time had got him out of an awkward spot twice, but he couldn't just keep going on and on. People he met seemed to become harder and harder to get on with.

Sweating, he tried moving another lever on a circular dial. The hum of the machine became higher-pitched, the light steady and even. Some kind of building sprang into being instantaneously a short distance away, then collapsed bit by bit into a heap of ruins that were soon nothing more than mounds.

A forest of trees came and went, and a river swung beneath him so that for a time the machine was poised over water. Then the reach of the river receded and built up grassy flats below him. He centralized the lever and let the machine fall to the turf.

Hot. Hot and tropical. The edge of the river was fringed with palms, and away beyond it vast buildings of outlandish design towered in a complicated chaos against the sky, a lambent haze of light playing about their soaring pylons.

Buller took his coat off and hung it on the end of the control panel, mopping his forehead with his handkerchief. Damn Mallinson and his machine. How would he ever find his way back to his own time from here? Or was it from now?

He turned, his eyes taking in countryside that had changed beyond all recognition. A hundred yards away, a broad strip of green metal ran past like a highway, and along it ovoid metal shells were whipping past at meteoric speed. Evidently vehicles of some kind, although they were without wheels or wings − it looked as though some magnetic force held them above the metal strip.

Buller suddenly realized that he was hungry. Hesitantly, he began to walk towards the strip. Why not hail one of the passing vehicles? Perhaps these people would be interested to meet him.

He held up his hand. One of the metal ovoids stopped, hovering, then sidling off the road, dropping to the ground near him. A door opened.

"Oh, no!" shouted Buller, as something started to get out. Something blue, with a pointed head and double-jointed limbs . . .

Buller didn't wait. He must have covered the hundred yards back to his machine in little more than ten seconds. As he grasped the lever, though, a flexible-fingered blue hand whipped over his shoulder and pulled away some of the wiring at the back of the control panel. He threw the lever across, but nothing happened.

He stood frozen, looking down at the blue prehensile limb resting on the panel near his elbow. He tried to make himself look round to see just what was standing behind him. But he couldn't. He blacked out . . .

He awoke in an immense room, lying on a flat surface of cold metal. Above, irregular pillared walls soared into an iridescent mist of light. A tingling sensation prickled his skin.

"All right," called a voice with an outlandish accent. "Cut the radiation."

Buller cautiously looked round the room. To his relief, the first living being he saw was at least human − a man in skin-tight white overalls, big and fair, with a massive head and shoulders and long legs. Next to him were two of the blue, pointed-headed creatures, looking at Buller with slitted yellow eyes. Then he saw the fourth member of the group. A girl.

A redhead. Dressed in a brief, sarong-like thing, she would have made any twentieth-century film star look like a peasant. Even with her crazy hairdo — one side of her head was shaved bare, the other a mass of tumbling coppery waves. When she saw Buller awaken, she glided across the metal floor towards him, looking back at the tall man.

"I like, Mal. I may?" Her voice made Buller a little less anxious to get out of the place.

"Safe now," commented the man called Mal in a booming voice.

The girl helped Buller to his feet and led him across to the others, who were standing near a bewildering array of electronic gear. Buller looked hard at the tall man, to keep his eyes from straying to the blue things with the pointed heads. He couldn't take that part of it yet.

"I'm Malzon Karu," said the tall man.

"Malzon?" Buller extended his hand, letting it fall as the other man merely looked at it curiously. "That sounds familiar."

"Lots men called Malzon," said the girl. "After the Great Malzon. He invented the time-modifier, back in the days before space-flight."

Karu introduced Buller to the blue things. Buller absorbed the fact that they had unpronounceable names, and came from an unpronounceable place.

"Then — this is really the future." He gazed at the apparatus. "Listen, I came here from the year 1957."

The others exchanged glances. The tall man did some calculations. "But that's ridiculous. That's four years before the Great Malzon patented the time-modifier, on the old time-scale."

"Anyway," persisted Buller, "I'd like to go back, if I may."

"Back?" echoed the girl.

"Bok?" said one of the blue things. He made it sound like an axe biting into a log.

"How d'you mean, back?" demanded Malzon Karu. "You know how the time-modifier works? You can exist in time-stream at high intensity, so that external events pass you slowly, or at low-intensity, so they race past you quickly. You must know that!"

"But — look, how do I get back to 1957?"

"1957? How can you get back there, man? It's past. Finished with. What a ridiculous idea — making time go backwards. What about cause and effect?" Malzon Karu looked round at the others. "Why, if you could reverse time, you could go back to yesterday and meet yourself." The girl and Malzon Karu laughed, and the two other beings shook with a chirruping sound.

"That's right," said Buller slowly. "Funny thing is, I worked that out for myself, a long time ago."

"And think of historical events," persisted Karu. "The signing of Magna Carta, the Wrights at Kitty Hawk, Norden's landing on Mars. If it were possible to go back in time, those places would be stiff with tourists."

The girl gave a peal of laughter. Suddenly she patted Buller's arm. "I like your crazy ideas, Red-Face; they're stimulating." Abruptly she frowned. "1957. Did you ever know the Great Boola?"

Buller stared blankly. "The Great — you said, Boola?"

"Yes. First man who actually travelled by time-modifier. There's a statue of him at — "

Suddenly she broke off, walking round Buller and looking at his profile. Malzon Karu looked at him from the other side.

Joe Buller drew himself erect, chest thrust out.

"My dear girl," he said with sudden dignity, "I *am* the Great Boola."

Re-deem the Time

David J. Lake

(1978)

When Ambrose Livermore designed his Time Machine, he bethought him of the advantages both of mobility and of camouflage, and therefore built his apparatus into the bodywork of a second-hand volkswagon. Anyone looking in at the windows, such as an inquisitive traffic policeman, would have taken the thing for an ordinary "bug" with a large metal trunk on the back seat. The large metal trunk contained the workings of the Time Machine; the front seat and the dashboard looked almost normal, and the car could still function as a car.

When all things were ready, one cold afternoon in 1984, Ambrose got into the front seat and drove from his little laboratory in Forminster to a deserted field on a South English hill. A white chalk track led him to the spot he had chosen; further along there was an ancient British hill fort, but not one that was ever visited by tourists. And this gloomy October day there was no one at all to be ruffled by his extraordinary departure. Applying the handbrake, he looked about him; and at last he smiled.

Ambrose did not often smile, for he was a convinced pessimist. He had seen the way the world was going for some time, and in his opinion it was not going well. Energy crisis was followed by energy crisis, and little war by little or not-so-little war, and always the great nations became further locked into their unending arms race. Sooner or later, the big bang was coming; and he wanted out. Luckily, he now had the means for getting out . . .

Briefly, he wished that general time travel were a real possibility. One could then go back to the Good Old Days — say, before 1914. One could *keep* hopping back, living 1913 over and over and over again . . . Only of course the Good

Old Days weren't really all that good; one would miss all
sorts of modern comforts; and besides, the thing was impossible anyway. Backward time travel was utterly illogical, you
could shoot your grandfather and so on. No: his own work
had opened up the escape route, the only escape route, the
one that led into the *future*. There were no illogicalities
involved in that, since everyone travels into the future at all
times. The Livermore Accelerator merely speeded up a
natural process — speeded it up amazingly, of course, but . . .

But there it was. He would hop forward a century or so,
in the hope of evading imminent doom. Surely the crash
must come well before that, and by 2100, say, they'd be
recovering . . .

Ambrose took a deep breath, and pressed the red lever
that projected below the dashboard.

The sensation was bewildering. He had done it before, of
course, behind locked doors in the laboratory, but only for
a subjective second or two, little jumps of a couple of hours.
Now years were flashing by . . . Literally flashing! There was
a blinding light, and the ghostly landscape seemed to
tremble. Shaken, he looked at his dials. Not even the end of
the century . . . and yet, that must have been It. The Big
Bang, the War. His forebodings had been entirely right . . .

He steadied himself, his fingers gripping the lever. The
landscape seemed to be rippling and flowing, but there were
no more explosive flashes. As he approached 2100, he eased
the red lever towards him, slowing down, and now he saw
things more clearly. The general outline of the hills and the
plain below were not greatly altered, but at night there were
very few lights showing. Forminster from up here used to be
a bright electric glimmer. He smiled grimly. Civilization had
been set back, all right! Probably they were short of power:
you can't get electricity from nothing. But, what luck!
This countryside hadn't been badly hit by bombs or lasers,
and there were still small towns or at least villages dotted
about. Yes, he would certainly emerge here and try his
luck . . .

Now for immediate problems. As he slowed to a crawl, he
saw that the surface of this hillside meadow had dropped by
a few centimetres. No worry about that, it was better than a
rise! And a hundred metres away a wood had sprung up, a
sparse copse of beeches that were rapidly unleaving. It
looked deserted, too. A perfect place to hide the car while he
reconnoitred. As October 2100 ticked away, he pulled the
lever firmly back, and stopped.

The car dropped as though it had just gone over a bump in a road. It fell those few centimetres, and shuddered to complete stillness. He had done it!

Almost, you might think, nothing had changed, apart from that wood. The same downs, the same cold cloudy autumn afternoon. Somewhere in the distance he heard the baa of a sheep. It was a comfortingly ordinary sound; even though, come to think of it, there had been no sheep in these parts in 1984.

Ambrose smiled (that was becoming a new habit). Then he drove the car deep into the wood.

The village of Ethanton still lay at the foot of the hill. He had driven through it several times in the old days, looking for a safe site for his great evasion: it had then been a crumbling old place, half deserted, its population of course drifting away to Forminster or London, half its cottages converted into desperate would-be-tourist-trap tea-rooms. There had been a railway-station a couple of miles off until the economic crisis of 1981; when that had gone, the last flickering vitality had seemed to forsake the place. But now –

Now, to his surprise, Ethanton seemed to be flourishing. There were new cottages along the road. At least, they were new in the sense that they had not been here in the 1980s; otherwise he'd have said they were old. Certainly they were old in style, being mostly of dull red brick with slate roofs, and one even displayed black oak beams and thatch. That one, certainly, had the raw look of recent construction: he peered at it, expecting a sign saying TEAS – but it wasn't there, and indeed the whole front of the house had that shut-in appearance of a genuine cottage. For that matter, there was nothing on this road to suggest tourism: not a single parked car, nor a motor cycle. And the road itself, which led after a dozen kilometres to Forminster – it had deteriorated. It was no longer smooth tarmac: it was paved through the village with some lumpy stuff that suggested cobblestones.

He moved cautiously on into the High Street, and came opposite the Green Dragon Inn. And here he was struck motionless with surprise.

It was not much after four o'clock, and yet there was a small crowd of men milling about the inn, some nursing tankards as they sat on the benches outside. The whole dusky scene was feebly brightened by an oil lamp swinging over the main inn doorway; there was a lamp-post on the pavement nearby, but that was not functioning, and indeed three or four workmen seemed to be doing something to it while the village policeman looked on. The clothes of all these people struck Ambrose as curiously antiquated; one drinker in particular boasted a high collar that might have been in the height of fashion in the 1900s. There were no motor-cars anywhere along the street, though there was one odd-looking bicycle leaning against the inn wall, and beyond the lamp-post stood a parked horse carriage complete with coachman and harnessed horse.

As Ambrose gazed at the scene, so the scene began to gaze at him. In particular the policeman stiffened, left the workmen at the lamp-post, and strode over towards him.

Ambrose braced himself. He had anticipated some difficulties, and now he fingered the gun in his trouser pocket. But that was the last resort. He had done his best to make himself inconspicuous: in a pair of nondescript old trousers and a dark grey jersey he thought he might not be too unsuitably dressed for England in 2100. And he had to make contact somehow.

The policeman halted directly before him, surveying Ambrose through the half-gloom. Then he touched his fingers to his tall blue helmet.

"Beg pardon, zur," he said, in the broadest of broad bumpkin accents, "but would yew be a stranger in these parts, zur?" The dialect was more or less appropriate to this county, but almost stagily exaggerated, and in details stagily uncertain, as though the policeman had worked hard to study his role, but still hadn't got it quite right. "Be you a stranger gen'leman, zur?" he repeated.

"Well — yes," stammered Ambrose. "As a matter of fact, I am. I — I was strolling up the hill up there when I had a bit of an accident. Branch of a tree fell on me — nothing serious, but it dazed me, and I don't remember very well — "

Suddenly the policeman's hand shot forward and he seized Ambrose by the shirt collar. Normally when this sort of thing happens, the piece of garment in question is used only for leverage; but strangely now the hand of authority began holding the shirt collar up to the light, and feeling its texture between its large fingers.

"What, what — " spluttered Ambrose.

"Ar, I thought as much!" exclaimed the policeman grimly. "One o' them Anaky fellers, you be. Well, m'lad, you'll come along o' me."

Ambrose clawed for his gun, but the policeman saw the move and grabbed his wrist. By now the workmen had come up, and they joined in the fun, too. Ambrose was seized by

half a dozen heavy hands, he was pulled off his feet, and the
next moment the policeman had the gun and was flourishing
it, to exclamations of "Ho, yes! One o' *them*, he be! 'Old
'im, me lads – 'e's a bleedin' Anaky, 'e is!"

Suddenly there was a new voice. "Now, now, constable:
what exactly is going on here?"

Higher Authority had arrived.

Ambrose was marched into a small back room of the
Green Dragon, where he was guarded by the policeman, and
interrogated by the gentleman who had taken charge of the
proceedings.

Dr Leathey had a trim brown beard, intelligent blue eyes,
and a kindly expression; like Ambrose, he seemed in his early
thirties. He was dressed very neatly in a dark suit, high collar
and tie of pre-World-War-I vintage. The room where he conducted his investigation was dimly lit by candles and an oil
lamp, and boasted in one corner a grandfather clock. There
was something about that clock that specially bothered
Ambrose, but at present naturally he couldn't give his mind
to that.

"So, Mr Livermore," said Leathey, "you claim loss of
memory. That is droll! Loss of memory is no crime whatever,
on the contrary, it is extremely virtuous. But I am afraid
amnesia will not explain the semi-synthetic texture of your
clothing, nor the forbidden make of your automatic pistol.
Now really, Mr Livermore, you had better come clean. If I
were to hand you on to the County authorities it might go
hard with you, but here in Ethanton *I* am the authorities: I
am the JP, the doctor, and the specialist in these matters, and
I have certain discretionary powers . . . Come, let us get one
thing clear, at least: where do you come from?"

"From – from Forminster," stammered Ambrose.

Leathey and the policeman exchanged glances. Leaghey
sighed and nodded. "Mr Livermore, that is practically an
admission of guilt, you know."

"Eh?" said Ambrose.

"Come, why pretend? You must know that for the past
sixty years that town has been officially re-christened Backminster – for obvious reasons. A shibboleth, Mr Livermore, a
shibboleth! Forminster, indeed! I put it to you, Mr Livermore – you are a BA."

"PhD, actually," murmured Ambrose. "In Physics."

"PhD?" muttered Leathey dubiously. "Oh, well, I
suppose that's still permitted; I must look up my annals,
but I believe those letters of yours are still within the letter

of the law. So — *Dr* Livermore, I presume? Quite an intellectual. But really, this is surprising! Do you really come from
Backminster?"

"Yes," said Ambrose, sulkily. He glanced past Leathey at
the grandfather clock, and hated it. "Yes, I did come from —
er — Backminster; but that was some time ago."

"Many years ago?"

"Yes."

"Curiouser and curiouser," said Leathey, with a little
laugh. Then he seemed to turn serious. "Dr Livermore, I
rather like you. You are an intelligent man, I think, and
certainly a gentleman, and that counts for something these
days — and of course will count for even more by and by.
If you will confess and submit to purgation, you might well
become a useful citizen again. You might indeed become a
power for good in the land — a perditor, or a chronic healer
like myself. Will you submit, Dr Livermore, and let me help
you?"

A disarmed prisoner has very little choice when faced with
such a proposition. Ambrose thought for about half a second,
and then said yes.

Leathey rose. "Good. I knew you would see reason. But
let us continue these conversations in more agreeable
surroundings. Simkins," he said, addressing the constable, "I
shall take Dr Livermore to my own house, and I will be
answerable for his security till tomorrow."

Then they were escorting him from the inn to the horse
carriage, which turned out to be Leathey's private convey-
ance. As they passed, Ambrose noticed that the workmen, by
the light of swinging oil lanterns, were carrying off the lamp-
post which they had uprooted from the pavement. It
wouldn't be much loss, he thought: it was a very old-
fashioned looking lamp-post.

Suddenly, with a kind of horror, it came to him what had
been wrong with that grandfather clock in the inn parlour.
Its hands had been pointing to somewhere around seven
o'clock — several hours wrong; and they had been moving
anti-clockwise.

In other words — *backwards.*

As the brougham gathered speed and rattled over the
cobblestones, Ambrose leant toward Leathey, who sat
opposite. "What year is this?" he breathed.

"1900," said Leathey calmly. "What year did you think it
was?"

Ambrose was too overcome to reply. He slumped back with a groan.

Dr Leathey was evidently a well-to-do bachelor; his house was large, stone-built and ivy-covered, and was staffed by several men and maid servants. These people found Ambrose a bedroom, laid him out a nightshirt, and in general saw to his comforts. A valet explained that in the morning, if he wished, he would shave him — "You being, I understand sir, not quite up to handling a razor yourself." Ambrose soon got the point: safety razors did not exist, so he, as a prisoner, could not be trusted with such a lethal weapon as an old cutthroat blade.

The manservant made him change his clothes completely. Luckily, Ambrose was about Leathey's height and build, so an old suit of the master's fitted him quite well. The high starched collar was damnably uncomfortable; but at least he was presentable, and was ushered in to dinner.

He was Leathey's sole guest. "Let's not talk now," said his host, smiling. "Afterwards, sir, afterwards . . . "

It was a very good dinner, of a somewhat old-fashioned English kind. The vegetables and the beef were fresh and succulent, and there was a very good 1904 Burgundy. Leathey made a joke about that.

"Glad the URN don't object to wines of the future, within reason. I suppose you might say four years isn't Blatant. But I like my stuff just a *little* mellow."

Ambrose gazed at him and at the bottle in a sort of stupor. Then suddenly he saw the point, and nearly choked on his roast beef.

"Drink some water," said Leathey kindly. "That's better. You know, Dr Livermore, you are the strangest Anachronic criminal it has been my lot ever to run across. Mostly they're hardened, bitter, knowing — you're not. And therefore I have good hopes of you. But before we get to the heart of the matter, let me get you to admit one thing. We live well, don't we, we of the Acceptance? Do you see anything wrong with this village, or this house, or this dinner, anything sordid or unwholesome?"

"No — " began Ambrose, "but — "

"There you are, my dear feller. The whole world is coming round to seeing how comfortably one can live this way. As that great old reactionary Talleyrand once said, it's only the *ancien regime* that really understands the *douceur de vie*. You BAs are only a tiny minority. The proof of the pudding — ah, talk of the devil! Here it comes now, the pudding. I'm sure you'll like it. It's a genuine old English suet, carefully researched — "

"But it's all insane!" cried Ambrose. Forgetting his manners, he pointed with his fork. "That clock on the sideboard — why is it showing four o'clock and going backwards?"

"My goodness," said Leathey, looking astonished. "You really must have amnesia. Protest is one thing, stark ignorance another. You really don't *know*?"

"No!"

After the meal, Leathey took him to his study, which was fitted with half-empty bookshelves and a huge black wallsafe. Over the safe was hung a painting in a rather academic eighteenth century style, showing some sort of goddess enfolded in clouds; between that and the safe an oaken scroll bore the florid inscription: "She comes! she comes!" Leathey waved Ambrose to a comfortable arm-chair, and offered him a cigar.

"No? Cigars will still be all right for quite some time, you know. And separate smoking-rooms for gentlemen's houses are not yet compulsory. I do my best to get these things right . . . All right now: let's begin."

Ambrose leant forward. "Tell me, *please*: are we really in the year 1900?"

"Of course," smiled Leathey.

"But — but we can't be. Reverse time travel is a stark impossibility — !"

"Time travel?" Leathey's eyebrows shot up; then he laughed. "Ah, I see you're well read, Dr Livermore." He got up, and took from a shelf near the safe a slim hard-covered volume. "*The Time Machine*," he murmured. "Dear Mr Wells! We'll only have him for another five years, alas, and then — into the big safe with him! Freud went this year, and *he* was no loss, but one will miss dear old science fiction. Well, *officially*." He brought his head close to Ambrose, and gave a confiding chuckle. "We are acting for the best, you know; but if you join us, there are — compensations. Behind closed doors, with blinds drawn, I can assure you, Dr Livermore, there's no harm in *us* occasionally reading cancelled books. And you can't lick us, you know, so why don't you — Pardon me; you get my meaning, but I believe that's a cancelled phrase in this country. I must learn to avoid it."

Ambrose gulped. "I am going mad — "

"No, you *are* mad. I am here to make you sane."

"You are not really living backwards," said Ambrose.

"Dammit, you don't take food *out* of your mouths, your carriages don't move in reverse, and yet — . Hey, *what was last year?*"

"1901. And next year will be 1899, of course. Today is the 1st of March, and tomorrow will be 28th February, since 1900 is not a leap year."

"Of course!" echoed Ambrose hysterically. "And yet the yellow leaves on the trees show that it's autumn, and — How did this insanity happen? I really do have complete amnesia, you know. In my day time was added, not subtracted — "

"In your day?" said Leathey, frowning. "What are you, Rip Van Winkle? Well, it may help you to emerge from your delusion if I give you a sketch of what has happened since the Treaty — "

"What treaty?"

"There you go again . . . Well, to start with, after the Last War and the Time of Confusion, it became obvious to the surviving civilized peoples of the world that the game was up: the game of Progress, I mean. The earth was in ruins, its minerals exhausted, most of the great cities devastated. If we were to try to go that way again, it would be madness. Besides, we couldn't do it even if we wanted to: there was little left, almost no fossil fuels, no minerals, no uranium even. We couldn't even keep going at the rate we'd become accustomed to. There was only one thing for it — to return to a simpler way of life. Well, we could do that in one of two ways: by a controlled descent, or by struggle, resistance, and collapse. Luckily, all the leading nations chose control. It was in 2016, by the old Forward Count, that the Treaty was signed by the United Regressive Nations. And forthwith that year was renamed 1984, Backward Count; and the next year 1983, and so on."

"So we really *are* in 2100," said Ambrose, breathing a sigh of relief.

Leathey fixed him with a severe look. "No, we really are in 1900, Backward Count," he said. "It is only you Blatant Anachronics who call it 2100. And, by God, we are *making* it be 1900! We are removing all the extravagant anachronic wasters of energy — this very day you saw my men getting rid of the last gas-lamp in the village — and so it will go on. It is all very carefully programmed, all over the world. One thing makes our plans very easy, of course — we know exactly *when* to forbid each piece of technology, and when to replace it with its functional predecessor. Our Ten Thous-

and Year Plan will make all Progressive planning of the bad
old days look very silly indeed."

"Ten Thou — " began Ambrose, staring. "You're mad!
Stark, raving mad! You don't really intend to revert all the
way — to the Stone Age!"

"But we do," said Leathey gently. "Metals won't last for
ever. And agriculture has to go too, in the end — even with
the best of care, at last it destroys the soil. But not to worry.
Polished stone is very useful stuff, believe me, and one can
learn to hunt . . . By then of course the population should be
down to very reasonable limits. Oh, I know there are some
heretics even among our Regressive establishment who think
we'll be able to call a halt well before that, but they are
simply over-optimistic fools. A halt would only renew the
fatal temptation. No, there is no stable resting-place half way
down this hill: we must retrace the whole enterprise of hope-
ful Man."

"There must be a way out," said Ambrose, "there *has* to
be — "

"There is no way out." Leathey laughed bitterly now.
"Believe me, I know how you feel. I, too — we all have our
moments of rebellion. If only, one thinks, if only the Pro-
gressives had handled things differently! When the earth was
theirs, and the fullness thereof, and the planets were within
their grasp! You know, you can pin-point their fatal error,
you can place their ultimate pusillanimity within a few years
of the Old Count. It was during the Forward 1970s, when
they had reached the Moon, and then — decided that space
travel was 'utter bilge', as one leading light of an earlier time
put it. If they had gone on, if they had only gone on *then* —
why, we would now have all the metals and minerals of the
asteroids, all the wealth of the heavens. Perhaps by now we
would have reached the stars . . . and then we could have
laughed at the decline of one little planet called Earth. But
no: *they* saw no immediate profit in space travel. So they
went back, and turned their rockets — not into ploughshares,
but into nuclear missiles. Now we haven't the resources to
get back into space even if you Anachronics were to take
over the world tomorrow. We are tied to Earth for ever —
and to the earth, therefore, we must return. Dust to dust."

"But — the *books*," cried Ambrose, waving at the half-
empty shelves. "Why are you destroying *knowledge*?"

"Because it's too painful. Why keep reminders of what
might have been? It is far, far better to make do with the
dwindling literature suitable to our way of life, and not

aspire to things that are for ever beyond our reach. We ate of that apple once — now, steadily, we are spitting it out. And in the end we shall return to Paradise."

"A paradise of hunter-gatherers?" said Ambrose sarcastically.

"Why not? That is the *natural* human condition. Hunter-gatherers can be very happy folks, you know — much happier than agricultural labourers. Hard work is wildly unnatural for humans." Leathey stood up, yawned, and smiled. "Well, so it will be. Back to the womb of the great mindless Mother. In our end is our beginning (I hope that's not a cancelled phrase). I'm glad, of course, that the beginning won't come in my time — I would miss all these creature and mental comforts." And he waved at his books. "Now, Dr Livermore, it's been a hard day, and the little oblivion calls — I suggest you should sleep on what I've been telling you."

The next morning after breakfast Dr Leathey gave Ambrose a medical examination, paying particular attention to his head. After several minutes, he shrugged.

"Not a trace of the slightest contusion. And yet you still have this complete amnesia?"

"Yes," said Ambrose.

"I am afraid I find it hard to accept your story. Don't try to shield your associates, Dr Livermore: I know there must be a cell of yours, probably in London. If you confess, I can promise lenient treatment — "

At that moment came an interruption. The maid brought the message that Simkins the policeman was at the door.

"And, sir," she said, her eyes goggling, "he's got a Thing with him sir! I never saw — "

"What sort of Thing, Alice?" said Leathey, getting up.

"A thing on wheels, sir. A sort of an 'orseless carriage . . . "

"Let's go and see it," said Leathey, smiling gently.

"May — may I come too?" stammered Ambrose. He had a frightful presentiment . . .

"I'd rather you did. Perhaps you can throw some light on this Thing."

And so, on the drive before the doctor's house, Ambrose beheld it. It was his rather special Volkswagen all right, with the policeman and several yokels standing by it — and, horror of horrors, one yokel *in* it, in the driver's seat!

Constable Simkins was explaining. "We found this 'ere motor-brougham, sir, up t'wards the Old Camp, in Half-Acre Wood. Jemmy 'ere knew summat about the things . . . "

Jemmy, from the driver's seat, leaned out and grinned.

"Used ter be a chauffeur back in old 1910, sir, an' I soon worked the workin's out. Nice little bus she is, too, but mighty queer in some ways. Wot's this little red lever, I want ter know − "

Ambrose screamed, and instantly was clutching the man by the shoulders and upper arms.

"Ah, so it *is* yours," said Leathey, shaking his head. "Naughty, naughty, Dr Livermore! A Blatant Anachronism if ever there was one, I'm afraid. That model's been forbidden for all of my lifetime, I think."

Ambrose was sweating. "Get − get him out of here!" he choked. "He could do terrible damage . . . "

"All right Jemmy," said Leathey easily. "don't touch anything else. You've done very well up to now. Now, just get out."

As Jemmy emerged, Ambrose leapt. Before anyone could stop him, he was into the front seat of the car, and jamming down the red lever.

The world grew dim.

For quite some (subjective) time, Ambrose was shaking with the remains of his fright, his hand jammed down hard on the red lever. Then as he recovered control of himself, he realized that he was soaring into the future at maximum speed. At this rate, he'd be going on for thousands of years . . . Well, that might not be too bad. Leave that insane Regressive "civilization" well behind.

He eased up on the lever. Where was he now, nearly two thousand years on? It must be quite safe now. Regression would surely have broken down long ago of its own insanity, and the world must be back on the path of moderate progress; chastened no doubt, wisely cautious, climbing slowly but surely . . . That might be a very good world to live in. Now, what did it look like?

Rural: very rural. The village had disappeared. Below him was a flat green, and around that clumps of great trees, broken in one place by a path; along that way in the distance he glimpsed a neat-roofed building, low pitched like a classical villa. Over the trees rose the bare green downs, apparently unchanged except at the old British camp. There the skyline was broken by wooden frameworks. Skeletons of huts? Perhaps they were excavating. Ah, archaeology! That, and villas, certainly indicated civilized values. And right below the car's wheels − it was half a metre down, but that wouldn't matter − the green was flat as a lawn. Doubtless this was parkland. A good, safe spot to emerge . . .

He jerked over the red lever, and was falling. The car struck the green surface —

But it struck with a splat. There was a bubbling, a sliding . . .

Suddenly, with horror, he knew it. That greenness was not a lawn, but a weed-covered mere. And he and his Time-car were rapidly sinking into it.

He got out of the pond somehow, and when at last he stood on dry land, people had appeared from the direction of the house, which was not after all a stone-built villa but an erection of wood and thatch, rather sketchily painted. The people were half a dozen barefoot folk dressed in skins, and they jabbered at him in some utterly foreign tongue. Some of the men were fingering long spears. And, as he looked back over the green slime, he saw that his Time Machine had sunk without trace into that weedy womb.

The savage men were in process of taking him prisoner, and he was submitting in listless despair, when a newcomer appeared on the scene. This was an elderly man of a certain presence, escorted by a couple of swordsmen, and dressed in a clean white woollen robe. He stared at Ambrose, then interrogated him in that strange tongue.

Ambrose jabbered helplessly.

"Hospes," said the man suddenly, "profuge aut naufrage squalide, loqueris-ne linguam Latinam . . . ?"

And so Ambrose discovered that Latin was spoken in this age, by some of the people at least. Luckily, he himself had a reading knowledge of Latin, and now he began to make himself brokenly understood. He was also even better able to follow what the wool-draped gentleman was saying. His name was Obliorix, and he was the local magistrate of the tribe, its guide, philosopher, delegate to some federation or other — and protector of the Druids.

"I see that you have met with some accident, stranger," said Obliorix, wrinkling his nose, "and yet, beneath your mire and slime, what extraordinary garments! Bracae might pass, but that is no sort of authorized mantle, and those boots on your feet . . . " He looked grim. "Could it be that you are a Resister of the Will of Chronos? A belated *Christian*?"

A madness came upon Ambrose then. "Domine," he cried, laughing hysterically, "what year is this?"

"Unus ante Christum," said Obliorix seriously. "1 BC. And therefore, since last year it is decreed by the United Tribes that all Christians shall be put to death, not as misbelievers but as anachronisms. The Druids on the Hill keep their wicker-work cages constantly supplied with logs and oil — you may see them from here — so I fear me, stranger, if you are a Christian, I cannot save you. To the pyre you must go."

"I — I am not a Christian," said Ambrose truthfully but weakly. He was doubled up with helpless laughter. "1 BC," he repeated, "1 BC!"

"And next year will be 2," said Obliorix. "What is so funny about that? Truly, it will be a relief in future to number the years by addition." He began to smile. "I like you, absurd stranger. Since you are not a Christian, I think I will make you my jester, for laughter begets laughter. What, will you never stop braying?"

And so Ambrose became at first Chief Jester to Obliorix, magistrate of the tribe of the Oblivisces in southern Britannia; but later he went on to greater things. As Ambrosius Aeternus, he grew to be a respected member of the tribe, and on the death of Obliorix he succeeded to the magistracy and the United Tribes delegateship. In 20 BC he went as envoy to the Roman Governor of Gaul, who, of course, was gradually unbuilding Roman towns for the great withdrawal that would take place in the fifties. And throughout his long and restful lifetime, Ambrose would from time to time break out into helpless laughter, so that he became known in Britannia as Ambrosius the Merry.

It was an added joke that, when he was able to persuade the Oblivisces to drag a certain weedy pond, the Time Machine proved to be rusted beyond repair, and only good to be beaten into spear-points. But for that Ambrose cared nothing; for in any case, what use was a Time Machine which only progressed backwards into history?

And besides, he told himself, he knew what lay in that direction; and he didn't want to get there any faster.

One Clay Foot

Jack Wodhams

(1979)

I was not entirely a neophyte when I was transferred to his fleet. I already had three kills to my credit, one in particular that had earned me a commendation "for courage and innovative enterprise". That phrase might have caught the eye of Commander Beeschopf Praze. It was known that he tried to cull only the most promising to his squadrons. What was not so well known was how he spent that promise.

He did not keep us waiting long before putting us to the test of duty. We were assigned our craft and were going through familiarization and briefing within two hours of our arrival. It was quite hectic, deliberately made so. We had been chosen; we were supposed to be a little better than most; therefore we should be able to adapt more readily than plebeians.

When we reached our first sleep-slot that day, we welcomed it, believe me. But hardly had we rested, it seemed, than the reveille was playing quick alert, to hurry us up, and out, and away, to perform our first patrol as an arm of Beeschopf's Buccaneers. The title suited him, his group. It was an openly cultivated facade of swashbuckling.

The sector battleground was the notorious non-world of Breaker. As armies might have once fought to possess a starkly unproductive crag for its sole use as a dominating eminence, so our military now fought to lay claim to the veritably useless but strategically vital territories that could be employed as bases to guard the passes of the Universe.

Our first two patrols were anti-climactic. Our brushes with our enemy were distant and unproductive of contentiousness.

However, our third outing was more demanding.

Praze took us by a circuitous route, curbing the exponential of our acceleration, bringing us in behind the smaller of Breaker's two moons. We stayed with him all the way, so close that we could maintain twinkle visual contact, which was always curiously comforting.

Human psychology has its amusing side. *Everything* could be done on the boards, by the comps, and possession of an actual visual ability was not at all necessary. Yet it was there, incorporated to satisfy a need, and no craftsman ever came into The Web blind, for instance, even though sights could play no part in our docking. Likewise, every craft continued to be stocked with some surface armament, short-range direct line-of-fire pieces purely intended to enable an astro, force-landed into some hostile environment, to ward off any ground-crawling horrors. We even still carried a Beamer, presumably just in case a craft should be sent to some area where the technique for reflecting deadly rays had yet to be perfected, or even thought of. I am sure that we still also would have carried parachutes if some legitimate rationalization could have been conceived to suggest their retention to be advisable.

It seemed strange sometimes how mobile everything was, how mobile everything *had* to be. Mobility meant survival. Yet here we were, as though by mutual consent, descending to dispute ownership of a huge immobile.

It had to be. We had no choice. *They* had no choice. The desolate world trapped us both, to dictate the terms of limitation.

We hung high. Always, it seemed, there had to be a hesitation, an instinctive reluctance to go in. I felt that our relative speed was not fast enough. But Praze gave no hint of any such sensitivity. Certainly the panels read out no warning signals of detected anomalies in our immediate huge arc of the heavens.

Space was beautiful. The machine was a powerhouse and a cocoon, to represent an ultimate in security. Perversely we deliberately sought to place it under threat.

Now I guessed that Praze was going to take us down, to where there *was* a down. Down towards the planet, down to experience some drag of gravity, even down into some of the restricting density of an atmosphere perhaps.

My mouth went dry in anticipation. I took some gluquen to moisten my throat. This was where the big boys played. The closer to the planet, the greater shield it provided our opponents, if any. The closer to the planet, the slower we must be obliged to go, a complex balancing of forces to directional desirability, compellingly mandated by *it*.

I was right. Praze did decide, was decided, to close with the planet. Here the nerves tightened up, and the senses became hyper-alert. Breaker loomed, a black blob wearing a crescent of orange that reflected one of its year-long days.

We all knew Breaker by repute. There had been times when one side or the other had gained ascendancy, and had attempted to construct ground installations. It was not known how many tunnels had been drilled, how much secret equipment shipped in, how advanced either side might be in some well-concealed location. It was not known how much might have been destroyed, just how long it might take to convert Breaker into a defendable bastion. Or perhaps it was known, which was why it was fought over so fiercely.

We slowed and slowed, until at less than five-squared-tens out we were doing no more than a world-relative pace that would surface us in an hour. Praze instructed a release of three decoy cappacks on a specific comp delay of 145 minutes. It was a significant clue to his anticipations.

And still we closed. I sucked more gluquen.

We angled to slide into the upper fringes of the atmosphere, Praze running us along an edge below a sighting of Breaker's sun. Lower and lower, and slower and slower, we descended into the near-permanent rim of dawn-twilight of the world below. Praze's mastery of pace ensured that our craft warmed less than dull red, to afford scant chance for any visual sighting of our presence. All our negatives were full on, of course, yet we all felt that these precautions were more a ritual to be performed rather than truly effective counters to detection. *They* would know that we were here. We were *expected* to arrive here, perhaps not known precisely when and where, but any gain of surprise was ever marginal, tactical, fleeting.

Speed — so much hinged on speed. The right speed, at the right time, in the right direction. And we seemed to be travelling awfully slowly now, the world beneath making us feel that we were standing still, ten kays above its surface, dawdling across *its* face at a mere couple of three-squared-tens.

I didn't like it. It made me feel clammy, waiting to be struck by God-knew-what, my boards being rendered half-blind by the blocking mass that we were circling. Breaker was bigger than Old Home Earth, so I understood, but only by a factor of a shade under .1. My blooding had taken place at a much smaller point of contention, at a brief but intense Moon of Icarus Conflict. The atmosphere on Breaker was much like that encountered during training at Home. I had felt the envelope of gas to be an encumbrance then, and I felt Breaker's vapours to be a hindrance now. Although I had the theory, I had never actually known combat under conditions that added such an invisible soup to the considerable tug of a planet's attraction.

Situations can have unreality, and unreality is linked to dreamtime. Tenseness maintained becomes unreal, and cruising, follow-my-leader, blunts the edge of personal perception. Follow-my-leader creates the bad habit pattern of waiting for orders, of unconsciously placing too great a reliance upon a leader's assumed superior responsibility. Our previous patrols had provided little to sharpen me.

Before me the code read $50° -45-43$, and for a vital moment it did not register. An automatic, startled re-check with the visuals, and the screen was empty. The boards were displaying my comrades rapidly spilling away, and in one more second I should be alone.

Just short of panic I took full control of the overrider, and slammed my craft onto its new bearing. Now my tenseness was of a different calibre. Now I became sharply aware, and swore at myself for being lulled by an hour's idle-seeming drifting. Contact! I swore again. Such a lapse of concentration could carry a deadly price.

They knew we were coming. Even as we knew that *they* would be here. I wondered if *they* felt much the same as we did, whether *they* knew the fear. I wondered if *they* were wishing themselves elsewhere, acid in their stomachs, afraid to face off, but even more afraid *not* to face off.

My comps registered them, and our comcomp totalled our opposition to outnumber us by two. The chart registered two fanning into my sector, with another two periph to be presently of secondary consideration. No hope of visual here. We were lost to each other but on our coded grids.

The leader had led. Now we were alone, booted out hellbent that we might ourselves try to prove the advantage of his ploy.

They were coming at us from the dark side.

This was interesting. More, was fascinating. My absorption in the boards before me became complete. Within the sphere each controllable object had its own relative horn of mobility, a bent cone that could itself pass its outermost curve through $360°$. The limits of this curve were dictated by

its angular velocity in respect to another object, and to the
degree of control that might be placed upon that velocity. In
the trade, to have "Cs", or CornuCopias, was to have horns
aplenty; that is to say, was to possess more than adequate
directional choice, to have the whole blown-out umbrella as
a field for selection. The craftsman's art was to keep available the wide part of his own funnel, the maximum options,
for himself, while seeking to curtail an opponent's outlet to
as narrow a pipe as could be engineered.

It was a fascinating business. Every curve was a straight
line. Every straight line was a curve. Speed was so very
important. I believed that Praze had brought us in too close
to the planet; its pull and friction constituted a minor irrita-
tion. But my angle, the course Praze had proposed, presented
me the initial course of action that I might take.

Again I cursed the inattention that had cost me a vital two
seconds of self-determination. Praze could not have guessed
that it would be my luck to have to engage two at once on
this sortie.

They were mine. Even at this distance it was more than
instinct that told me that they had jointly chosen me for
their prey. Perhaps, with that finesse won by successful com-
batants, they had spotted my late break from our pack, to
gamble on my being but a fledgling, and perhaps just that
little more twitchy than most. How strangely the brain
works.

Speed, planet, atmosphere, fledgling. I read my boards,
and I could read theirs. My computers said everything and
knew nothing. Only the superior computer that was my brain
could convert their messages into sense. *They* were not
coming in fast enough.

I deviated and picked up, to effect evasion, to hope at
least to draw one side only. And they picked up and mutuali-
zed in an outswinging that might lead them to triangulate me
ideally.

It is very difficult to explain the emotions felt, the
singularity of being involved in so intimately dangerous a
pastime. My mind summed up so many things with greater
than lightning speed, and I made adjustments, and checked,
and corrected, and re-corrected, without really thinking
about it, virtually automatically. But it came from my own
inspiration, and ever less from training.

Now I was not scared. I had no plan, no concept of an
end result, and yet I had a knowledge, a subconscious certainty of... of what? Of survival? Of superior craftsmanship?

What was I doing? I was watching my boards and playing. It was an electronic game. The one who got the highest score was the winner. I was good at electronic games.

I read the factors, and was surprised at my own coolness. The periphs had gone, and the other engagements had become much too distant to record with my area. Just the three of us.

Speed, deflection, shadings. I could read their boards as though I were sitting in their cocoons. And to read their boards was to read *them*. Finesse. Fledglings do not make master touches. Now I had worked them up to as fast as I might hope them to allow their eagerness to overcome their caution. Another delicately precise course correction fractionally tightened my gradually descending curve into the atmosphere, and they now had me almost in range, and surely could taste my blood, as surely as their risk would seem minimal.

Now I de-acced even more, to tighten my long downward curve even further. Speed. My combat experience in atmosphere was limited; my experience in factors was extensive. Fear=escape=speed — to get the hell out, back into the safety of space in the greatest hurry. To slow down, to actually drop towards the increasing density of the hostile world below was either very foolish, or . . .

One of them had a sense of smell and almost imperceptibly altered tack, enough to instantly tell me that he wanted to buy just a little more time. The other came on, correcting his arc even as I hugged into my curve further yet, forcing him to adjust, adjust, adjust, fighting to line me, to de-acc sufficiently. I could almost see his fingers flying and his lips cursing as he strove to achieve what quite suddenly had become less of a likelihood.

The margin was very slim, but it was an irrefutable margin nonetheless. And now *I* chose to show some spite. Here I dropped an already well-programmed missile of my own, and it tracked beautifully, slanting ahead of me, racing ahead on my course, and concealed by my own emanations. And he unleashed at me, while his partner on reappraisal slewed away to detour, to seek an improved approach. To cover the curve of my grenade, I swirled my seat as I plus-acced, up away from the planet, to even congratulate myself upon my timing, that the stress forces upon my physique at no time so far had been severe.

Judging from my board readings, my leading foe at least was not so fortunate. He appeared to be making the most strenuous efforts to correct his errors. In fright, and anger, perhaps, he was inclined to over-correct. From my reading I could guess that he was subjecting himself to a maximum of inertial distortion. His speed was excessive for a grazing contact with the atmosphere, quite likely to impose some unwanted and agonizing counter-thrust upon his strained frame, and also possibly to flare him off, to mangle his communications during the period he strove to regain control. Could I have spared the time, I would have liked to have tried to visually spot his glow, but the luxury of such a break in my concentration was something that I simply could not afford.

He had ambitiously launched a double-double salvo, the second as back-up maybe to repair blunders made by his first. Neither pair posed any real problem to me, for however he had programmed them, he was in no condition to give full attention to any modifications that their guidance might require.

I suffered no such handicap. My missile was on course, surely to be showing on his monitors by now. His partner might have spotted it sooner, but if any warning passed between them, I saw no effort being made to take evasive action.

I was on full plus-acc now, weaving out to that partner, straining to match him and to claim equal advantage before he could shape to dress me with any form of pre-emptive.

There is a point passed by two converging chunks of matter at which a lethal rendezvous may no longer be avoided. It was awesome, and therefore irresistibly distracting. On my panels my missile and my foe became irrevocably fated to cohabit a pool of detonation. He had been incredibly slow, or blind, or stupid. At the last he tried a fiendish twist, but was far too late.

I was happier to be going away from the planet. A star appeared on my board. Again I had no time to spare for visuals. One missile. A low-cost victory indeed. So many favoured multiple-missile attacks that they tended to launch more than they could handle. A single missile at times might not be too easy to spot, especially if its deflectors were aided by some ground radiation. Lucky. I had been lucky.

Now how might I deal with his friend? But his friend had changed his mind. He altered his course again, and on my charts I saw him drawing out of the arena, treading on plus-acc to get himself out of the field. I did not know whether to be glad or disappointed. I toyed with the thought of giving chase — everybody does — but I was suffering more from

Breaker's drag than he was and, unless he stopped to fight, I could not catch him before pension time.

So he quit. This was no disgrace to him. This was flattery to me. Having deceived and wiped out his friend, I must be someone other than a novice. The thought was tickling. A reaction from stress.

I bottled my elation and returned to my boards. I opened and scanned the limits, to try and deduce how others might be faring elsewhere, that I might take my presence to where it would be most helpful. I stayed high and prickly, vectoring for anything loose. A good mood was dangerous. I determinedly remained sober, to save the champagne for when I got back to base.

By sheer chance I contacted Rede Scylia, who seemed to be having some trouble holding his own in a duel on the dark side. I arrived too fast to be actively helpful, but my appearance scared off his opponent, who made a creditably exact exit that defeated any attempt to impose restraint.

With Rede catching up, I hunted further but, though we traversed the planet once-and-a-half, we encountered no more argument. What others we had luck to contact were off on token pursuits, or were returning to base.

This was the way it was. We could not stay. To go down to land upon the planet was not recommended. There was no rest to be had down there. Down there was to be a stationary target that would be sure to receive some sort of attention within the hour. We brawled, to prove that we cared, and then we went home to The Web, to wherever it now strove to be inconspicuous as well as indestructible.

We used Rede's clocked coordinates for The Web, and I covered his tail as he led the way home. We caught up with nobody, and nobody caught up with us. It was nice to be Out There again, and free, leaving combat behind, especially after a satisfactory engagement.

I was quite relaxed and smiling by the time we reached the outer check-points of The Web.

Praze, too, was relaxed and smiling, the same light deprecating smile that seemed never absent from his face. He had, it appeared, made yet another kill. With my hit, the score had been three to two in our favour.

One we had lost was Yahi Kahiki, and this at once robbed my success of its savour, subduing my good humour. Yahi had been a big, amiable fellow. We had done a lot of learning together; had been of the same induction. We hadn't exactly been special friends. Rather, he had been the type to treat those in his peer group as friends regardless — an outgoing, undemanding man who gave first, but left nobody in debt. He had played a very fair board.

An overlapping record showed Yahi engaging an opponent. He went off the periph in a deadly chase, never to be seen again. It pained me to lose him. He had been a tempering force. Our other loss was a man called Bab Washitt, or Washill. He hadn't been a newcomer in my contingent, and I had hardly known him.

Yahi gone. It hurt.

Beeschopf Praze was talking in the mess. He had his admirers. And he *had* made yet another kill. Wonson Moy was passing him a drink, and asking him how it felt to gain such mastery. Stupid question. But Wonson played a defensive board. He would never understand aggression that was directed against the strong rather than the weak. Yahi had died. Wonson Moy had lived that he might try to find with questions those answers he could not find with guts.

"I am not a hero, Ablethree Moy," Praze said, reflecting his calculated geniality, "I am a psychopath." It was an underemphasized admission. "I enjoy it Out There. I welcome the challenge. I enjoy having Death at my shoulder, that I may borrow his scythe."

"We have seen the replay of your action, sir," Moy said. "It was quite *brilliant.*"

"It was elementary," Praze mildly disparaged, "although it is not easy to convey this sense. I have tried to teach, but you must possess the talent in the first place, and developing the knack is almost entirely a matter of experience. Some are more temperamentally suited to the role than others."

"Your action was so smooth, sir, your positioning so perfectly timed." This was Garrald Frandby. He sounded a mite envious. "It seemed so . . . so *cool*, if I may say so, sir. *Are* your nerves really uptight at the time?"

The lips smiled, the eyes derided. "I have seen men crack up. Some of them have been quite good but, after a few or a number of sorties, they got jumpy, and began to drink too much, and to talk louder, and to laugh longer at sillier and sillier jokes. When you get such symptoms, I shall tell you. When *I* get such symptoms, *you* can tell *me*." And he sipped his drink and viewed us with that friendly cynicism that discounted our chances of ever equalling his own qualities.

"I'm sorry we lost Yahi Kahiki," I said. "He was a good

man, sir." I don't know what I was looking for. Acknow-
ledgement, maybe. Some concession to the dead man's
ability, perhaps.

"He had some promise," Praze conceded with unchanging
affability, "but he made a foolish mistake. We could see that
he had not overcome their equality. They probably made
him eat the cheese in his own trap. And it has cost us a
valuable craft."

As I said, I didn't know what I expected. After all, Praze
hadn't really known Yahi who, like me, had been a newcomer. Lost on his first real action. Praze could hardly have
been effusive with sympathy, and yet, somehow . . .

The taste in my mouth at the end was sour.

I did not enjoy dinner that night.

There were more patrols, but there was a period just then of
fewer skirmishes. Such states occur from time to time. Sometimes their cause would seem to be a psychically shared
reluctance by both warring parties to push or shove too hard
for a while. At other times its cause could be political, the
word going out to keep rattling the sword, but not to slash
too nastily for the moment.

I did not have another kill for some time. What engagements I did undertake proved abortive. On three separate
occasions encountered opponents consented merely to spar
with me from a judicious range, only to decline to accept any
lure to a more serious confrontation. I concluded that the
other side probably had more Wonson Moys than we had.

And in the debriefings it was I who suffered most from
Praze's seemingly well-meant advice. While nodding at the
efforts made by others, Praze would suggest that *my* tactics
might have been improved if I had done such-and-such, that I
might have stalled a getaway if I had tried *this,* that I might
have surprised my opponent by attempting *that.* He acquired
the habit of preferring to use the record of *my* mission to
demonstrate various points of error, and to indicate what
might have been.

He was never savage with me, never bit too deep, and
never used blunt teeth. I am not sure that even he knew what
he was doing. On the one hand he did not appear to comprehend my style, my method, my necessary individuality at all.
At the other extreme, it was possible that he understood too
well.

A special mission came up, and I was included in the group assigned to carry it out. It was an intercept that was to take place so far from our home area that two sub-bases had to be introduced to serve as RRR — re-orientating, relay, and rest-stations. These served a vital function to short-hoppers. The Universal scenery was never still and, when travelling great distances, virtually always over previously unspanned regions, it was by no means impossible to get lost. A constant trick practised by both sides was star-blotting, and "star"-making, or shifting, to screw up crucial navigational fixtures.

The intercept was a very carefully planned and quite intricate procedure. A great deal depended on the craftsmen. It was anticipated that our relative speeds might differ so acutely that communication between our sections would be too delayed to be useful.

Broadly, what was to take place was a shepherding hunt pattern. My task, with two others, was to jump the escort and keep them occupied, while frightening the key fish to plus-acc the hell out and seemingly escape on his way. Others would then intercept *him* on the road, knowing where to look, and what for, to hopefully frighten him still further and sheer him into a desired direction. His actual taking was to be done by Praze, who would no doubt receive most of any congratulations that fell due.

I didn't think much of *our* part. It was the most danger-ous, as the initial encounter, and was the most likely place where the whole plan could fall apart. In my opinion, it was where Praze *should* have been. If all went according to plan, it would not require an expert to deliver *his* coup de grace. The escort would not be composed of amateurs.

It was a most unusual attack — Out There. It made all the difference knowing exactly where and when our target would be. If our intelligence was accurate.

We three interceptors each adopted a star, to wear a matching radiation to our fore. The three-point triangulation of our alignment would curve us in like spokes to meet the party of the third part. It was considered that our disguise was to be effective right down to the advantage of close-range surprise. Providing that our intelligence was a hundred per cent correct. Any deviation from the itinerary and our quarry would soon remark three strange new stars in the heavens, and the joke would be on us.

Frankly I did not think much of the scheme. The impon-derables of advancing successfully behind a star facade per-suaded me to the greater odds that some minor misplacement would simply make us look like idiots coming forward behind flashlights. But my view was discounted, and Praze himself expressed disappointment at my misgivings. Vigilance Out There was customarily slack, he averred and, in the time allotted, differentiating between real and dummy stars, and their purpose, would itself cause sufficient confusion to be to our benefit as we pressed home our attack. We were not to take the key fish. We were to split the escort from its charge, to prevent any re-uniting, and to drive at least one of the escort back rather than to annihilate them all completely.

Skulduggery was going on there.

In the event, it took us over 140 hours to get into position, and we spent another thirty checking and re-aligning, and winding ourselves up for the showdown.

I disliked the entire affair. We hung Out There, and Breaker's sun was but a midget. I wondered if we were being missed over that scarred landscape. The giant red they called Gumboil looked nearer, almost the size of a red little fingerprint. It was extremely deceptive. Nothing else was nearer. Except the fish and its escort.

We hung Out There — what an odd expression, but very common. This was always the way it *seemed*. For matter has, of itself, no intrinsic capacity to go anywhere. Matter itself lacks the quality of mobility, is a static substance always, and has motion that may only be measured in its relationship to *other* static matter. Light has a finite speed, so it follows that matter must possess a finite inertia.

I hung Out There, sensationally, obviously, going nowhere. Actually, I was tangentially leaving Breaker's sun — or it was leaving me — at close to 200,000 kps. It was leaving me. That's how it looked on my sub-major board.

And the fish was coming. And according to us he was pretty near right on schedule, and giving us our cue to start building up a nice plus-acc of around .5 to press us comfortably into our seats.

Starshine. I plotted, and plotted, and double-plotted to perfect my arc to their sighting of my chosen start. Identifying them positively, I stringently monitored *their* progress, grudgingly admiring the quality of the espionage that could so exactly pinpoint a time and place in nowhere. I shivered. It was uncanny. It was unfair. Their security Out There should have been inviolable. A traitor had betrayed them with a most vicious precision.

Inexorably we closed with our target. Speed. It is the speed of matter in relation to the speed of other most local matter which is important. We closed with our quarry at an optimum of 10,000 kph on reverse acc, Rede Scylia fractionally tardy.

Eight blobs on the board — our three, and their five — one large, one smaller, and three scragwagons. Time running out. Comp-identification labelled the large one as a Crevillion, an armoured supply and planet blaster, a spoiler that could throw out missiles like confetti, and which carried enough techs to steer sufficient of these to make life interesting. This had not been mentioned in our briefing. The Crevillion's main disadvantage, as with most fat things, was its poor manoeuvrability. Even if all its personnel were properly seated in their gyros, the difference in potential between one end of the craft and the other, and even from side to side, could be critical in an emergency.

The lesser craft was decided to be a sixleaguer, a sleek and special vessel of a type favoured by the wealthy, a trader's flagship, a minister's public-yacht.

Time, speed, closing. Distance to range perimeter narrowing. Which one was the fish? The Crevillion could not match our acc — therefore we were unlikely to chase *it. It* would stand and fight. The sixleaguer, on the other hand, was probably sprung-tubed for super-acc. Given a break, it could probably pump itself up to leave us without actually popping out the eyeballs of all on board.

The sixleaguer was the fish, had to be. So many things in so few moments. Pity.

They held unvarying course, totally unsuspecting. The temptation was too great. I risked to attempt a visual sighting. Sheer useless, wishful, human stupidity. Folly. God! but it was always the way. A "ping" announced a missile launch, and it was not one of ours. Two, three, four, five missiles in quick succession from the Crevillion. On the board, in range now, just.

Swearing. But the missiles, though in a defensive pattern, were clearly headed only one way. It was Otterheim who had been spotted. Five missiles only. A detected anomaly. A reaction less alarmist than cautionary automatic. They were too late; we were in.

I slammed off five shots of my own, timed to perfection. Then I was swinging in my seat, and was sweeping away, monitoring them home at my ease, and already second-guessing ahead to just how long we might play the Crevillion. Scylia also had unleashed, and was running clear. Otterheim had only let go two, and even this early his concern to take evasive action was apparent on the board.

It was not fair. I felt sorry for the scragwagons. Their astros could have been reading, or listening to music, or visually playing chess, or using their boards in coded competition, or tubbing in the black slot with an exerciser, or . . . or anything, even sleeping. They didn't have a chance. Scylia and I covered any slim avenue of getaway, and our boards registered two double strikes and a single. Otterheim's shots slid by unattended. He was angling and gaining, and was plainly unhappy to be singled out so soon for retaliation.

One of our spare shots was sent to spark the sixleaguer, and the remaining four were curled into the Crevillion.

I feared our surprise to have been too complete. The six-leaguer was supposed to get away. We had eliminated the outriders. Our victims' response to the panic button appeared to be sluggish.

But now the Crevillion bristled. Anti-missiles snapped out of her in profusion; panic indeed, and by no means quite soon enough. I viewed my boards. It was tremendous how impersonal a man could feel at a time like this. I could well imagine their goggle-eyed horror at being so unmercifully caught.

The sixleaguer was putting on pace at long last. I was obliged to destroy *their* missile from its destiny. It surely had come close enough to give them grey hair and an incentive to spurt more lively. With luck they would credit the Crevillion for the intervention.

Otterheim had just about shaken his worrisome but over-excited pursuers, had depleted his own arsenal to eradicate the most persistent. His position placed him to be the one most suited to take up the hunt of the sixleaguer. So this he was coded to do, as convincingly without success as possible.

This left Scylia and I like sharks to circle and hamper the whale, and to decide just how much more damage we might inflict. For one missile had completely breached its defences, and another had been halted so near that it had registered on the board as a rattler, or indeterminable.

The Crevillion Class were built to withstand some tough punishment, and our armament was never intended to be deployed against so prickly a fellow. The Crevillion was compartmented and had a multi-layered skin, and possessed a capacity to absorb blows by peeling and crushing, to then stagger through with whatever might be left, and to continue in menace. A crew of six, possibly eight, possibly augmented by specialist techs, super-cargo, ordinary cargo, anything. It had the room to accommodate any number of extras and modifications.

It was after us. A trifle belated, but otherwise I could not fault its choice of course, to interpose itself most ably between us and the departing sixleaguer. Now things were working out more as we desired. The Crevillion *was* crippled. The sixleaguer would surely leave it behind to hold the rear. Otterheim was the sixer's only danger. With him the sixleaguer would have to take its chances.

The Crevillion shaped over to challenge *us*, clearly displaying that it had no intention to run. Speed, the squaring of the circle, the coefficient of the straight line that was a curve. Everything was a straight line. Everything was a curve. The right speed, the righ acc, was always so crucial. Closing with an opponent, his speed was my speed, and my speed was his. It was acc that made the difference, that determined the sheer physical limits of possible manoeuvrability.

Misjudgment meant missing. The faster the meet, the greater the probability for error. Everybody wanted to in and kill fast. Everybody wanted his opponent dawdling nicely on matched full acc, a sitter with limited forward options. It could never be done. The computations were marvellously limitless. An astro always had at his disposal a combination that had never been used before.

I coded Scylia. I did not care to underestimate the Crevillion. In fact, the more I thought about it, the less I relished again entering its protective orbit.

The sixer was now off the action boards, with Otterheim wrapping his guts around his backbone trying to match pace. Already the Crevillion was beyond rejoining its charge in any near-future time. But we had to make sure. And this meant harrying the monster a little, and drawing it even further aside. Had we a planet beneath us, our task would have been somewhat easier. Gravity imposes its own uncompromising demands upon bulk. Out There, the Crevillion was less fettered. I could not recall any incident where one had been attacked Out Deep before. There was novelty about the whole affair. And such novelty could be dangerous.

They were awake now all right. They countered our pattern, and we altered our offensive line, thinking again.

Our hits seemed to have slowed the brute, but nevertheless the boards showed it building up a rush. We matched, keeping our distance. It had no hope of catching us, not with anything. We, on the other hand, had no real desire to win glory by trying to shard it into meteorites.

It was a stalemate. And anyway, our instructions permitted for survivors. But *they* did not know that.

It was gloriously free Out There. Small as we were, we posed a threat. We had an enormous amount of room. We decided, Scylia and I, on wide-ranging teasing runs, and truthfully it turned out to be quite fun, an exercise in maximizing our superior mobility. We tantalized and drew fire that fell short of creating anxiety, and we seized the opportunity to ourselves practise steering single missiles through the defensive systems of our adversary. And we had more luck than our foe. We each scored another rattler.

Altogether the engagement transpired to be a very rewarding experience. When we finally wearied of the game, we simply broke off and went home. And here I remembered the sixleaguer, and wondered whether the rest of the enterprise had gone so well.

"It was the wrong choice," Praze said. "You didn't think it out well at all." He was never acid in his censoring, just maddeningly chiding.

"It was my decision, *sir*," I said. "In my view, the scragwagons could have made the outcome completely indeterminate. Their astros wouldn't have been novices."

"Agreed. But you had the advantage of surprise. A tussle with them would have been logical, and to have broken off leaving a survivor or two would have been sensible." He should have clucked. "You missed a golden opportunity."

"I didn't see it that way, sir."

"Obviously. The Crevillion was a gift on a platter. Your initial concentrated fire could have wiped it. It could have been seen to have *been* your intended target. You could legitimately have overlooked the sixleaguer slipping away, to take on the scrags for a spell, but to be content to quit, having achieved your objective. You could have made it look so much better."

"If we had taken on the scrags, there might not have been *been* any survivors."

"That's not a real possibility, is it?" he discounted. "Anyway, you would have accomplished your mission, which was the most important thing."

"We *did* accomplish our mission, sir."

"Yes, yes, I know," Praze smiled, "but the Crevillion" —

he shook his head — "that was a bonus that should never have been passed up. It was bound to have been carrying . . . other important people, most probably a key officer or two. What a chance." He sighed. "Never mind. It's done now."

He was so regretfully pitying without rancour, that I could feel myself beginning to choke. They had wanted the other side to have a survivor. Logic dictated that that should be the strongest. I had decided the Crevillion to be the most likely to get back. God damn my hide, if they hadn't worried too much if *anybody* got back, why hadn't they said so?

Disgruntled, I made my excuses. Disgruntled? Away from the group I seethed. It was infuriating. And Praze, of course, had nailed the sixleaguer properly. He had had it driven squarely straight into his arms, and he had hit it with a neut-pack, to take the craft intact. The entire project was a part of some clandestine scheme that I guessed would involve sub-stitution of the original occupants of the sixer for purposes beyond the imaginings of ordinary mortals.

Blast him! The golden opportunity had been to test the Crevillion out. Our unhindered engagement had provided us an invaluable exploratory exercise. Blast him again!

I spent more time in the Simulator than most. I worked out several patterns, and a couple were especially promising. The Conical Corkscrew was one of my devisings.

As with tic-tac-toe, the Conical Corkscrew required a first "X" to be in the right place in order that the rest might be aided to be put in line. It was several sorties later that a suit-able opportunity occurred.

We had sparred, this scragwagon and I, and he was no fool. He must have known that I was no fool either. However, he concluded that he just might be able to take me, and he took up an interesting acc in a sweep that must have flattened his bellybutton, to give that extra little punch to his launch. And he only sent out two, and his chosen deflection was not at all bad.

It was a good fight. We were in orbit over Breaker, with clear perimeters on our boards and interruptions unlikely. At once the situation had a familiarity, and I was reminded of my ploy.

I could evade his two, and I programmed my anticipations, while he, also anticipating, started taking appropriate defen-sive action even before I fired. Practised, knowing what I was doing. I punched out the sequence and launched my three in two seconds flat. I smiled as I guessed his puzzlement at an oddity in the pattern I chose. I could hopefully presume that he might think that at least one of my shots was malfunctioning.

Speed, always speed. No calibrations can be prophesied perfect. Had his reaction been as unorthodox as my launch, my game would have been much harder. But — one — he had two of his own to home in on me, and — two — with two of my shots apparently already going wide, his need for concern was not great.

He made the mistake I wanted him to make. He took the most obvious evasive action against my most threatening warhead. Good. I cut my margins to hold his interest, taking an avoidance angle that might excite him and hold his attention, and to help me judge how good his coordination was.

His coordination was very fair. His position on my boards was approaching ideal. He evaded my first easily. It was likely that he thought I was being kept too busy avoiding *him*.

We danced, his missiles and I, and I realized here that one fault in my plan was that playing a goat could become tedious. He had had seven passes at me to my one at him, before he noticed my second shot curling in. Like my first, he found it easy to evade. I was worried that he might knock it out, for it passed through a clear area of vulnerability. But he let it go, fearing it not.

Now I did my most spectacular change of pace and direction, crushing the breath out of me and realigning to a vector that would force him to twinkle his fingers if he were not to lose me altogether. And at the same time my third pacer came back into play, and it was fast and true, and he plus-acced to get out of its way, persisted to chase me, and found my first coiling back into him.

From here it was about all over. I calculated him to be on full plus-acc which, normally, was a satisfactory enough breakaway manoeuvre. But, rather than criss-cross, I had bracketed him with a tightening variable three. On plus-acc he only had forward options.

Awake to his peril, he opened up. I modified my weapons accordingly. My triple spirallings began to shrink.

I felt sorry for him. He abandoned his shots. I could imagine him suddenly being very fully aware of his danger, to be anxious all at once to get away. But my shots tracked him with a matching magnetism, the fastest wide, the slowest shallow, projecting a defeat of whatever speed he elected.

The four formed a funnel of doom. He blasted out counter-shots, but their speed at point-blank was too great, and they whisked away worse than useless. He de-acced frantically; the whip of his seat could have uncoupled his brain. I was poised and ready, and transmitted duplication in an almost simultaneous split second.

I don't know if the de-acc killed him first. Plastered back in his seat, I do not know if he started screaming. All I saw, on my board, was that he made no more variations. The Conical Corkscrew ended in an inevitable point. It was sobering.

I did not look too hard for more trouble before going home.

Beeschopf Praze felt sorry, sometimes, too, but with him it was different. *I* thought it was different.

As he spoke of his latest conquest, his dry, insincere empathy churned my stomach. We listened because he was our mentor, and our respect for him was to assist him in his indoctrinating instruction. He ran the replay and pointed out each telling feint.

"From the very outset, as you can see, he displayed a curious mixture of tentativeness with bravado," Praze said. "So I did a run, to test him out, and to encourage him. He had read his text-books. He was obedient to the rules."

Already I could see the picture, the story that the boards were beginning to tell. The perpetual self-effacing smile grotted me. Even here I could sense what was coming.

"He was a very good student. As you can see, I began to take him through his paces." Praze paused. "He presents us with a fine example of the difference between knowledge and intelligence. Demonstrably he had the knowledge. His tactics, indeed, are difficult to fault; are the moves advised by the best manuals on the subject, complete with recommended variations. If nothing else, he appeared to have a very good memory."

I watched the board, and my palms were moist. It should not have been so. I was never as tense as this in actual combat. Copybook. As Praze said, his opponent had slid from move to move, virtually, patently, agonizingly as might be according to the Regulations of Orbital Engagements.

"My successive counterings of his moves should have told him that he was up against someone . . . capable." Praze reflected a fainty despairing incredulity. "Had he been intelligent, at this stage he should have been well awake and backing off. He must have attributed my passive subjection to his vain overtures to his own skill at intimidation. He perhaps persisted in thinking of me as a running novice, attributing his near-misses more to my good luck than to his inexpert judgement."

I glanced at the others. They, too, were watching fascinated, but open, seeing no deeper than the lesson being detailed.

The boards continued to tell the remorseless story. Praze turned patsy, leading his foe on, taking him through every ritual that he might know. And then, in a subtle, masterly, refined, and superbly executed manoeuvre, the hunter and the hunted changed roles.

It was sickening. On the excuse of "demonstrating", Praze toyed with his victim. Where he had let the man run the gamut of assault practices, now he led him through the variety of defence procedures, noting the faults of each such manoeuvre, countering, and keeping on the pressure. I wanted to scream for the idiot to use his own brains, but the fool persisted in taking evasive action like a robot, standard specified reaction, as though he had nothing else to turn to, as though he had to believe that only by saying the stipulated prayers would his promised salvation ever come to pass.

The numbskull. He filled my gorge.

"As you can observe, after trying everything that he knew, and nothing at all that he didn't, his position finally became quite hopeless. I felt sorry for him. I could imagine him being young, and by now utterly exhausted. For a fleeting moment I knew compassion — a twinge, a thought to spare him."

Liar! I looked away, that Praze's eyes might not meet mine.

Praze went on: "But in that same instant I knew that if I allowed him to escape he would at once become more dangerous, to become at once more experienced, to become at once a more wary and less careless an enemy, and so to become a much greater threat than he was before. A tyro excused is a learner survived to take a further step towards becoming truly knowledgeable. He would have become less of a tyro against *our* tyros."

I watched the boards, the glims sliding to an irrevocable climax, a last humiliation, a classic Golden Corridor, a run through a lethal gauntlet that only a dumb amateur would permit to happen. Those who live by the book shall die by the book.

"I had to finish him off." Praze was wry. "I felt some reluctance, as I say, after such intimacy, but the risk of him having another chance to think for himself was too great."

The glims closed. I sat in the fool's seat and could see him gibbering, his dreams of glory imminently to be snuffed.

Praze had tortured him. Praze could have taken him in the very beginning. Certainly Praze could have taken him at any time during the later stages. It knotted my guts. It was sadism. As a salutory illustration to *our* beginners, he was so clever, the Simulator could have been programmed to perform the entire schedule. No doubt Praze considered a real-life orchestration, with himself the fearless maestro, to be more significant and efficacious.

The scragwagon became a broken egg, to be scrambled and shredded, to become meaningless particles in an abyss. It nauseated me.

I never said anything. I never did. *He* was a living superlative. Others discussed aspects of Praze's engagement with him afterwards, but I took my leave as soon as I could. I always did. They could call it conceit if they liked, to jibe that I thought that there was nothing more that I could learn. *Me.* I spent more time in practise than any four of them put together.

The only thing that I kept learning from Praze was of the ruthless superiority that more and more made his facade of modesty insufferable. The fool could have got him. Just by using a little bit of gumption, the fool *could* have got him. It upset me. It had been for real. I had ached to have been able to take over – *ached.* Poor green bastard, he had never earned such contempt.

Strange effect. Whether from this or another cause, I took ill, and had a 48 on sick leave.

Maybe I chose the wrong time to go broody. Commonly after an energetic sortie there came a period of relative calm, for the licking of wounds and yet another reassessment. The next two or three patrols would be quiet, the sparring somewhat mutually token and warily resentful.

This time it was different. Whether my presence would have altered things is purely speculation, of course, but the news at once made me regret my absence from the fray.

To make up the complement, Mirkiss Gourboudin, a newcomer, had been led out on his first foray over Breaker by our glorious leader. Beeschopf Praze had personally had him under his wing. But Praze had not kept him there.

I could read the boards. Their initial intercept had been a single. This meant a reconnaissance, a lost sheep, or a trap. Praze read it to be the former. Even at that stage I read it as the latter.

Some easy meat to practise on. Praze detailed Rede Scylia to take care of the solo, and coded Gourboudin to accompany him and assist.

Rede left the formation. Gourboudin followed. The solo was no lost sheep. At best it was out spotting. I had worked often enough with Rede to know that he, too, smelt a rat. It was instinct. The replay on the boards was impersonal, expressionless pinpoints. But shadings in change of position, a zeroes-one shift in angular degree, to me spoke volumes.

The solo took evasive action. It was to be expected but, again, a slight imperfection in choice of course did not fully maximize his escape opportunities. A minor carelessness, was it? There were some clever ones who flirted with dangers, possessed of a confidence that sliced thin margins.

Scylia recognized him so, it seemed, and adroitly, slyly compensated, almost in a reflex action. Already their play had told them much about each other.

But Gourboudin was not so wise, and here he made an elementary mistake, plus-accing suddenly over and away towards what he saw to be an obviously more advantageous shepherding position. He meant well, not needing to be told, not deeming it necessary to get a coding from Rede. And shortly now, crucially, the rest of the patrol slid off the work boards.

Rede coded Gourboudin, correcting, trying to make the best of the move. Gourboudin complied. The solo made good use of the error, and tacked himself to swing even further out.

Rede Scylia wanted to let him go. I knew Rede. The odds were too even. The craftsman in the scragwagon was no dummy. He was taunting, rather than shaping up for a fight. The whole thing was screaming.

They held a fateful delaying pattern, and the coding flew between Rede and Gourboudin. Gourboudin hungered to prove himself, and Rede hedged, unable to explain his *feeling* of their situation. Only to at last relent, and almost savagely punch the keys to programme a lure and attack approach of his own.

The plan that sprang from Rede's fingertips gave full value to the meaning of the word "experience". It was there on the boards — the proposal, the alternatives, the modifications, the corrections, the counters, counter-counters — summed up and outlined in an instant display of perception and utterly professional grasp. This was what it was all about. Patience and determination. They would hunt the damned scrag-wagon, and give him something to be clever about.

It might have worked. But then the others appeared. There were eight all told, and their timing was faultless. They popped over the periph within seconds of each other, and they commanded the sphere coordinates at speeds established by their decoy.

Such things happened. I could swear even as I watched. Neither of ours should have stood a chance but, as with controlling missiles, numbers can sometimes be a hindrance. They *all* wanted to taste blood.

Never had I known Rede to be so brilliant. He could have got away had he wished, and here he was most foolish. Here he directed and took over Gourboudin's frantic play, to mesh it with his own, decisively double-integrating, to himself create a hole through which Gourboudin might crack his bones in reverse-acc and escape, howling head-shredded. Rede Scylia was still fighting when the play left Gourboudin's board, but he was doomed.

He did not return. Rede Scylia did not return. Instead we had Mirkiss Gourboudin still with us, and already he was behaving like an overworked veteran, and had a bad tic in his left eye. It was a poor exchange. Rede had been a reliable comrade, a first-class craftsman. I felt his loss bitterly. It should never have happened.

Beeschopf Praze took leave to be with a favoured mistress while she gave birth to his brat. I went back on patrol, leading the patrol, back into the routine, and *now*, for a while, contentiousness abated.

I fretted. I wanted someone to try to lure *me* into a trap. I wanted *action*. I wanted things to *move*, to be challenged, to have my claim to dominance defied. Maddeningly, our enemy declined to oblige.

We roamed 'way above Breaker, sunside, nightside, spoiling for trouble, and being unopposed. We? *I*. Perhaps I was too keen. At what contacts we did make, I deployed my forces in so gritty and businesslike a manner that my would-be opponents were deterred from going beyond the formalities. It was the wrong temper for success, and was a departure from my own stated accent upon wiliness.

It was a period, having responsibility for the group, that I was adapting to, just beginning to get familiar with, and to appreciate its potential, when Praze restored himself to us, and resumed his pre-eminence. Ideas that I had begun to develop became aborted. Methods that I had worked out, that we might try, became so much psychological mumbo-jumbo again. I could not communicate with Praze. He had his way of doing things and, from past experience, I knew his reaction to any novel approach that I might suggest.

I chafed, enormously frustrated. There was nothing I could do. There was no ear that I could gain, to bypass this man. He was the authority here, the acknowledged and proven expert, one of *the* most famous and outstanding craftsmen of the war, modest, still insisting on going out with his men, still insisting to lay his life on the line for The Cause. He was a formidable force, a living legend. What could I do? What *could* I do?

Action was consuming. Engaging an enemy freed me. Every problem extraneous to the play became totally irrelevant. And on this particular patrol there was enough confrontation to satisfy the most ardent knight.

For a start we met *them* head-on, a most unusual circumstance that must have surprised them as much as it did us. Secondly, we were both travelling comparatively low over Breaker, both seemingly using it as a shield, that we both consequently had our speed somewhat governed thereby. We were like two people who were trying to sneak up on each other upon opposite sides of the same wall.

Initially, unbelieving, there was a strong tendency to panic. To add to the confusion, I hit the buttons to code procedure orders, instinctively, forgetting that I was no longer commanding, and simply *knowing* the fastest, sanest, coolest thing for us all to do. This encoding tangled with that issued just as immediately by Praze, and which detailed a divergent line that contained few coincidences. It could have been disastrous but, in the event, the uneven break-up of our pattern did not suggest disorder so much as evidencing individual decision, a calm unpredictability that our opponents might not have found heartening.

Their reaction was quite some seconds slower and, as we

closed, they were behind us in their countermandings, and an idiot on their side had already launched three torpedoes that would not have a hope. Whatever advantage there was to be gained was ours.

At this stage both patrols were virtually still complete and converging from both sides of the key-board, twenty-seven in all, fifteen of ours to twelve of theirs. It was incredible. I had never seen anything like it. If we all remained confined to the same area, and we each launched five missiles, this would produce a fantastic interplay of one hundred and thirty-five shots. My God! What boards *those* would be!

But it could not happen, of course. A head-on convergence was startling, but was not by any means a desirable angle to approach battle. Looping back failed shots was too time-consuming and telegraphic to be worthwhile. Already both formations were mushrooming out, and I became obliged to centralize myself in my own sphere.

With what seemed remarkable rapidity we were upon each other, and going through each other, with a curiously mutual amazed helplessness. Our proximity was such that I scanned for visual contact, but was disappointed, naturally. It was nightside but, even so, the distances between us were still great. It was strange that, in the very midst of enemy scrag-wagons, I felt it perfectly safe to take time out to try and actually *see* my opponents. It was the situation. At that point there was not much that either of us could do.

But the shock was wearing off, and the boards began to shape up even as the contestants continued to disperse. There were the runners, and the chasers, and those willing to snarl and bare their teeth.

The numbers on my board dwindled to nineteen, to fifteen, to eleven. They scattered up and down and sideways, to slide off my perimeter and into exclusive zones of their own.

Like a cheetah, I had selected my target from the outset. The processes that prompted my choice would be impossible to define; there was some "click" that took place, that determined that I should concentrate on *that* one. His movement, his line, his speed — there was *something* there that triggered me. I never failed to intrigue myself with my own mystery.

He knew that I was after him. Only nine on my board now, and *his* moves were most pertinently related to mine. And he was slowing, and steadily dropping into Breaker, into atmosphere.

I felt an odd sensation in my gut. A scragwagon chasing

me fired a couple of poorly judged shots, which he did not follow up very well, and which amounted to little more than a gesture. I fancy that he did not care for the mass of Breaker, and the steady slowing of his comrade and myself, for he turned away, possibly nervous of two more of *our* side between him and the security of Out There.

This was the way it was. One minute full boards, and the next hardly anybody. My choice was not running from me. If vulnerability is sought, then it has to be offered. Again the sensation in my gut. What conceit. It was more than possible that *I* was *his* choice.

And so it proved. I learnt a tremendous amount that day. He was quite exceptional. He put Breaker to his service in a manner that I had never imagined. Twice I failed to compensate adequately for the added force of Breaker, and was constrained to abandon the missiles concerned. Passes became limited by Breaker's nearness. It was like a flat plate that cut off the bottom of our sphere of operation, a plate that *gave* us a bottom and a top, a gigantic impassive material presence that was ever ready to snatch us to itself should we but be so careless as to lose control.

Slower and lower. Again I knew that unfamiliar sensation. Instinct, instinct — *instinct!* My fingers flew even before my conscious mind could dictate the reason why. I guessed his attack fractionally before I was totally committed, and was evading fast, and countering fast, my mind yelling me to plus-acc the hell away, my will clamping me to an unreal lucidity that held me to match him still, to lower yet.

The sensation was fear. My face and neck were damp, my palms moist. Fleetingly I was concerned what it would be like to lose; in actuality, whether it was possible. Lower still. We were locked. To try a breakaway meant doom.

The atmosphere felt like glue. It was really not so thick but, after vacuum, its effect was subtle and somehow not pleasant. We were some five kilometres above the surface. It was intimidatingly close. And my opponent knew the terrain. Never before in battle had I been brought to consider mountains. Such things have no significant consequence upon the normal boards. And he was taking me lower.

I escaped his shots by twin margins that I could hope never again to need to shave so fine, and the sweat dripped from my chin, and *he* was hunting *me*, and now I was taking a desperate refresher course in ground appraisal, and was incorporating the information into all other considerations.

And from terror I clawed out to anger, and from anger to an icy concentration that was not to leave me.

He had beguiled me, and he had very nearly succeeded in nailing me. It was a prepared trick, admirably performed. Did he have another trump? I doubted it. Thinking, thinking, learning. Now he launched a salvo of five at me, and I nearly shouted my elation at the sight. He had missed his certainty, and his salvo told me that he knew anxiety and that I might yet elude him.

It was his error. He had the advantage of me, but the five would betray him, would be too much. I would *make* them be too much, to switch his preferences until he was dizzy. And better yet, I sank further towards the planet, now testing *his* nerve, and making *him* sweat.

High risk. I turned back into the mountains, and he had to pull his shots high as I careered along valleys. It troubled me to lose his shots from my board where the ranges intervened. Higher than me, I could imagine him programming a reception to meet me where I might most likely come out.

Now I hit the skids, zapping my body about and laying on the pressure as much as I could bear. Had I nicked my chin shaving that morning, my whole damned skin would have peeled back. I arced, angling hard and fast to complete the split-second move, to gamble a choice to skim a peak on a side opposite to that which might have been anticipated. It was a hair-raising switch executed with calculated precision by a man who demonstrably had not yet lost his nerve.

Still climbing, the full field came back onto my boards, for his play to at once become more apparent, and I spun again, to complete my "S", to re-match him, not to lose him, to show him that I had plenty of fight left. His shots were off-beam, were very well placed to cover every manoeuvre except the one that I had taken. Near misses took longer to retrieve and re-programme than wider swings, and even the best tended to be too eager in their closing of the gap between shot and target.

He was not happy. He loosed off a couple more grenades. Now he had seven to manage. I judged him to be tiring, not panicking, but harassed into doing a lot more work than he desired. I had only two missiles out, both lurking wide and waiting to be coordinated to a play that even then was formulating in my mind.

But just at that moment, into our sphere, a third party appeared, high, and detecting us, altering course, to slide down to examine the situation and plainly to join us.

I swore. The pattern was broken as surely as a mirror met by a rock. My opponent broke just short of conforming to an enfilading corridor that I might have exercised, to virtually abandon his play temporarily, recognizing discretion to be the better part of valour, and preferring not to take on two of us at once. For the fresh intruder was one of ours. It was, indeed, Beeschopf Praze.

It was extraordinary. It was uncanny. It was a strange and uncommon eventuality. It bumbled me to be coded, to be distracted just as I was about to go into my end play.

Praze took over. My opponent, my honourable opponent, should never have had such bad luck. Praze came in pouncing upon a wearied man. He coded me orders. He was my superior. He was Our Commander. My play was shattered. Praze's play supervened, brisk, decisive. Between the two of us, the poor bastard never stood a chance.

We brought into play an extra two shots from me, to make it four shots each. In view of our combined skill, this was a fifty per cent excess in deployed armament.

Our opponent was no greenhorn. In short order he was made aware that his chances of escape had become negligible. I knew him. I sat in his seat and could comprehend the behavioural reaction that prompted his signals of defiance that registered on my boards. He was concerned. He was dangerous. He would prove it.

He let go everything he had left, plus recalling his wanderers, to give him a total of eleven weapons ranging. He had hope, perhaps, to confuse his way out.

Praze was deadly. I could sit in his seat also, and I knew that he was smiling. There was an authoritarian note in his codings, and I received the impression that he was attempting to encourage me, even in one part to urge me to relax, and to say that everything was now under control.

Instructions. He kept telling me what to do. It was not my play any longer, not in any way. I had become a supernumery. Now it seemed that I filled the role of a rescued useful aide and, if I attended closely, I could be shown how to participate in a butchery.

I cannot describe my feelings. I went onto automatic, doing what I was told, so far relinquishing concerned personal involvement as to be sharply warned to properly correct the pace and deviation of my shots. Curiously, for a while, I became a dispassionate observer of myself, watching myself obey, seeing myself paying attention.

Our foe's eleven shots were not so badly placed after all,

for they came curling in in a novel criss-crossing formation, concentrating entirely on Praze, and creating a cover to separate himself from me. Praze was diverted. I was interested. It was a bold extravagance surprisingly well unified considering the numbers involved, and had his target been a lesser man than Praze, his strategy could well have succeeded.

It was an understandable error. Praze had not been on the boards long enough to be read. My man knew *me*, possibly thought that *I* was still commanding the play, and so had chosen the newcomer as likely to be easier to cripple. I could pity him for his sheer bad fortune.

Praze steered through the storm, eluding disaster by narrowly trimmed margins, and for a while I did not know whose side I was on. Then Praze was through, and our opponent spent out, and we had nothing left to do but hunt him down with our own unopposed eight.

Our nominated enemy sloped down towards Breaker, seeking thicker atmosphere, perhaps in a last vain hope to find some kind of sanctuary below. Relentlessly we pursued him, Praze at leisure having us bracket him with our shots, with an exactitude of patient savagery, to savour the moment, to linger to relish the absolute inescapability of our hexoid squeeze.

I felt nothing at the triggering, not any least sense of exaltation, or triumph. Nine points of reference on our boards coalesced into one, which in turn powdered out into stardust, a spreading, fading cloud.

Praze was well pleased. The bombardment had exhilarated him and given licence to his viciousness. He coded me: "One of the fellow's Ms was almost a rattler!" He said other things, but my replies were desultory. I could not share in his shop talk, not with the attitude that his words revealed.

Then I caught something. He mentioned a malfunction. I queried this. The code came back. It was nothing serious. He had had a slight drop in cabin pressure, which he had so far been unable to restore, but which appeared to have stabilized adequately.

What prompted me to express concern, caution, I cannot say. Instinct. An intuition to pay heed, entirely spontaneously. I coded him my reply, reminding him that we were in atmosphere, which could be providing a compensating density that would lower the stress placed upon any plugged leak. It was possible that he had been badly holed by the near-rattler that he had experienced. If such was the case, and the gash was severe, a blow-out could occur Out There and, depending upon its location, could have some crippling effect that just could be disastrous. I told him that it was worrying that it was his cabin pressure that was affected, and suggested that it might even be better to land, to check, to see if repair could be managed.

Landing on Breaker did not appeal to him, but he stayed in atmosphere, even to dropping a little lower, retesting his systems. I followed him, closing the distance between us.

I signalled him that we could both ride in my craft if we decided that his was unserviceable, but he was unenthusiastic about scrapping his machine, which was the most super-latively well-appointed fighting craft in the fleet. In his opinion, if he were holed, the ritepunc-gunc would be unlikely to tear out, would be like cement already, and any further leakage would be minimal.

I said okay, but conveyed my continued unease, and further suggested that I might approach near enough to make a visual inspection. I could scan him, I proposed, to probably be able to detect if, and just where, he might have been hit. He was agreeable, and apparently amused to indulge the fussing anxiety of a grateful disciple.

The situation was unreal. Two craft never drew so close to each other, not even in formation.

I picked him up on my visual, and he grew and grew. I was in full forward alignment. It has a strange psychological effect, to actually *see* a craft travelling ahead. It never happened in fighting. It was something that I regretted, something that I always missed. The opponent was always anonymous, even as a craft. To actually witness a disintegra-tion, a result, was never more than a poor resolution of one bright light.

Praze hung before me. I brought the cross-hairs of my visual targeter into play, to examine his hull, to measure the location of any discovered flaw. The manual sighting, the range-finding, was quite absorbing. My remembering of an unused technique was surprisingly complete and satisfying.

I was very close now, and slowed exactly to matching, and he filled my screen. I said that I could spot a defect already. And my fingers keyed to pass details and to hold his atten-tion, while my mind, as in a separate compartment, con-sidered many other curious things. There were The Others, those who never did survive to become peers. Rede Scylia.

Praze would see me killed also before ever I should challenge
his rank. A legend. The ground weapons system could be
manually operated, to so bypass the flight record. The
Crevillion was recalled. Ground weapons were not checked
unless the craftsman requested it. It was a maintenance chore
left entirely to the degree of a craftsman's wish for total all-
round mental comfort. My premature assumption to give
orders surely would occasion reproach. Oh, Big Yahi Kahiki.
A mistress and another baby. An opponent snatched from
me, an honourable opponent, who became almost literally
crucified by our shots, to be so ignobly despatched.
Beeschopf Praze.

The circumstances would never occur again. Such opportunity would never again arise. I opened the ground-weapons
ports. To use such in a space action was unthinkable, ludicrous. The limited range, the straight-line firing pattern, was
purely for platform shooting at a fixed target. No one would
ever use such weaponry against a distant and highly mobile
foe. To shoot another craft into oblivion by such means
would be totally unbelievable.

The range was precise, the cross-hairs centred upon a most
vulnerable spot. I triggered the guns. Point blank. I saw the
shells punching holes in him, and for critical seconds he hung
there, soaking up my primitive barbs. Then he heeled, quite
suddenly, to fall away to my left, and down towards Breaker,
sucked by gravity.

I went down after him, keeping him close in my visual,
loosing more fire at him, not wanting him to get away,
letting him have everything I had, seeing pieces begin to fall
off him. And he began to roll, slowly at first, over and over,
and to pitch into a steeper curve yet towards Breaker's
surface.

It was then that I knew positively that he was finished.
I felt most odd. I followed him down. He seemed to fall forever, a silent spiral plunging to the planet beneath.

When at last he struck, he smashed and burst, and the
inner command capsule wrenched out like an egg, and
bounded off on its own, to crunch and slam and batter itself
into a grotesque distortion.

I landed. I dug into my emergency kit and suited up. I
went out to inspect the crash site.

The legendary figure was truly dead.

I collected those items of his personal identity that I
could retrieve. These would be souvenirs. I did not dawdle.
The surface of Breaker was dangerous. The wreckage was

sure to be blasted again as a precaution against subterfuge.

I lifted off, took a last look, then headed for Home Base as fast as I could.

I had done a service for The Cause. The replay, *my* replay, would show our engagement with an enemy. The replay would show his close call. The replay would recount his malfunction, and my concern. Then the replay would show him going out of control, and not responding to my call any more.

The replay would end with a splatter. The rest would be supplied by me, my account of what I had been able to see on the visual. Even use of my ground weapons could be excused, if it were claimed necessary, to ensure certain destruction of our specialized equipment, records, etcetera, that they might not fall into enemy hands. Yes. I would do a King David. I would lament. I would be most distressed. I would be the instigator of, and the first to chip in credits to, a memorial to the legend.

The legend should live. I could see to that. It could be useful, very useful, I knew him; he was my friend. He taught me all I know. He was the greatest. Or *one* of the greatest. There was room for me, now. And there would be a little more discipline, and a little more training, and a lot more survivors. Just as soon as I came to take over the command.

In a Petri Dish Upstairs

George Turner

(1978)

When, some fifty years after the Plagues and The Collapse, Alastair Dunwoodie put the first Solar Power Station into synchronous orbit over Melbourne Town — that is, some 38,000 kilometres above it — no warning angel tapped his shoulder to whisper, "You have created a fresh culture and rung the knell of an old one."

It would have been told to mind its own celestial business. With solar power now gathered by the immense space mirrors and microbeamed to Earth for network distribution, the Golden Age was appreciably closer. With a Station in Heaven, all was right with the world.

Remarkably soon there were seventeen Power Stations in orbit above strategic distribution points around the world, sufficient for the needs of a planet no longer crawling with the famined, resource-consuming life of the Twentieth Century. The Plagues and The Collapse and yet less pleasant events had thinned the problem.

Dunwoodie was a builder, not a creator, his ideas had been mooted in the 1970s, some eighty years before, but had not come to fruition when The Collapse intervened. It was, however, notable that even in those days, when social studies of crowding and isolation had been to the fore, nobody seemed to have considered what changes might occur among the first people to live out their lives in a steel cylinder in space.

And not for a further eighty years after the launching did the Custodian of Public Safety of Melbourne Town begin to consider it — when, for the first time in three generations, an Orbiter proposed to visit Earth. When he had arrived at the vagueness of a possible decision, he visited the Mayor.

"Do you mean to give a civic reception for this brat?"

The Mayor of Melbourne Town was unenthusiastic. "It's an event, of sorts. A reception will let Orbiter vanity preen while it keeps the Town's society belles from claiming they weren't allowed to meet him. I hear he's a good looking lad."

The Custodian seemed uninterested in that.

The Mayor asked at last, "But why? After three generations they send a youngster — nineteen, I believe — to visit. What do they want? Why a boy?"

"A boy on a man's errand, you think?"

The Mayor's expression asked, *Why are you wasting my time?* and he waited for explanation.

The Custodian went at it obliquely. "The Global Ethic," he said, "the Ethic of Non-Interference — do you ever question it?"

The Mayor was a very young man, the Custodian an old and dangerously experienced one. The Mayor went sharply on guard but his expression remained as bland as his answer: "Why should I? It works."

The Custodian's authority outweighed the Mayor's — Mayoral duties were social rather than gubernatorial — but he had no overt power to punish. But advancement could be blocked or privilege curtailed without open defiance of the Ethic as it operated on Departmental levels.

The Custodian surprised him. "You should, James; you should question continuously. Particularly morals, conventions, habits, regulations — and ethics. The older and more ingrained, the more questionable."

Stiffly, "Those are matters for Global League delegates."

The Custodian grinned like a friendly skull. "You needn't be so damned careful; I want your help, not your scalp. Review some facts." He flicked a raised finger. "First: the Power Stations as originally flown were rotated about the long axis to afford peripheral gravity." Another finger. "Second: when the final Stations were flown, the seventeen formed themselves into the Orbital League." Third finger. "Then they made unreasonable demands for luxuries, surplus wealth, cultural artifacts and civic privilege under threat of throttling down the power beams. That was seventy years back."

"School is a year or two behind me," said the Mayor coldly, "but basic history remains familiar."

"I'm selecting facts, not lecturing." Fourth finger. "So the Global Council of the time authorized use of a remote-action energy blind, a — call it a weapon — whose existence had not been publicly known. The Orbiters threatened our micro-beams, so *we* blinded the internal power systems of Station One from a single projector in Melbourne Town. After a week of staling air, falling temperature and fouling water they cried quits and — " fifth finger " — the Orbital League has made no such further error since."

"So for once the Ethic was ignored."

"Oh, but it wasn't. We took suitable action, harming no one seriously, to preserve the status quo. That was all."

The Mayor said, "It was *not* all. The Stations had been earning extra revenue with their null-g factories — perfect ball bearings, perfectly formed crystals and so on. Earth stopped buying, limiting Orbiter income to the Power Charter allocation. That was reprisal and un-Ethical."

"Earth protected herself against wealthy Stations accumulating the means of further blackmail."

The Mayor was contemptuous. "Semantic drivel."

"It was a Council decision. Do you dispute it?"

"Yes," said the Mayor and waited for an axe to fall.

"Good, good, good! So you see, the bloody Ethic means whatever you need it to mean."

The Mayor retained caution. "Most realize that, privately. Still, it works."

"Because *laissez faire* has become part of our cultural mentality. But what of the cultural mentality Upstairs?"

"Well, we know they have developed non-Terrene conventions and behaviour. There's been little physical contact since they cut themselves off."

"Quite so."

Silence dragged while the Mayor wondered had he said more than he knew. What the Orbiters had done was to stop the rotation of the Stations and give themselves over to a null-g existence. When you thought of it, why not? To live in utter physical freedom, to fly, to leap, to glide, to dispose for ever of the burden of the body . . . the wonder was that they had waited so long to grasp delight.

It followed that the first generation born in space was cut off from Earth. Once muscle structure and metabolism had settled into null-g conditions, exposure to gravity became inconceivable, possibly disastrous . . . ahh!

"This young man, this Peter Marrian — how will he deal with weight? Power-assist harness?"

"I must tell you about that," said the Custodian. "You'll be fascinated . . . "

The no-nonsense Orbiters preserved no fairy tales from their Earthly heritage but they had formulated a few austere anecdotes for the very young. One concerned a super-virile Orbiter who married a Terrene heiress and brought her home to live in orbit.

Peter heard the tale when he was not quite three and already absorbing Orbiter lore with a mind the commune nurses noted, in their giggly fashion, as destined for Upper Crust privilege.

" — then, when he'd defeated all the schemes of the rich girl's wicked father, he joined with her in a church as they do Downstairs. Then he brought her to the Station with all her riches and the Commune Fathers awarded him such extra privileges that he lived happily ever after."

It did not occur to him then (or later, for that matter) to ask how *she* lived ever after. His interest was in the early part of the story, which told how the young Orbiter became big and powerful in order to face the monstrous Terrene weapon, Gravity. Now, how was that accomplished?

He spat at the nurses who said he would understand when he was older. They had no idea, for they were only third-women and not educated beyond their needs, and such rearing facilities did not then exist. But soon would.

Such facilities, *all* facilities, cost money. The Commune's only money-wealth was the cynically limited income derived from the Power Charter, kept at a "reasonable minimum". The Orbiters were welcome to pride and null-g freedom — at a suitably cheap rate.

The first generation had tried blackmail and learned a rapid lesson.

The second generation had reasoned that conditions were humiliating rather than unbearable — and in fact provided much which Earth could not — and could be endured until better opportunity offered. The important thing was to acquire money with which to buy — well, facilities.

By the third generation the Commune Fathers had grown longer sighted and the first cheese-paringly sequestered funds were being transformed into a huge centrifuge at about the time young Peter asked his question. Cutting gravity and so cutting culturally loose from Earth had been a fine gesture but there could be advantage in a squad of Orbiters who could move comfortably on Earth's surface. And recommencing rotation was out of the question for the older folk.

"I hate it!" — shrieked and repeated to exhaustion — was the reaction of Peter, aged four, to his first experience of the centrifuge. Even the fiddling 0.2 g was outrage to a physique which had come to terms with mass and inertia but knew nothing of weight, nor wished to.

On the second day, after a bout of desperate clinging to the doorgrip, he was allowed out after ten minutes, bellowing, while the thirdwomen giggled at his aggressiveness. It would be a useful trait in the future planned for him.

After a fortnight of systematic lengthening of his daily accustomization — allowing internal organs to realign gently to a vertically weighted structure — increase of the g factor began. His rages evolved into arrogant self-confidence as the psychlinicians worked with cold devotion on the boy's emotional fabric.

At age six he lived most of his day in the centrifuge, a series of belts round the internal circumference of the Station and large enough to accommodate a considerable cadre now that a method had been established. With his weight at 0.5 g (he was the only one as yet on the fastest belt) he looked forward, under psychological prodding, to greater conquests. Signs of muscular shape, as distinct from subcutaneous muscular structure, were discernible.

The Commune Fathers allotted him the personal name of "Marrian" — a joke of sorts, and their first mistake.

"Since the Orbiters set aside wedlock and the family system, second names have been allotted on a descriptive basis, focusing on job or personal attributes. What does Marrian describe?"

The Mayor had been, as promised, fascinated by the facts but more intrigued by the Custodian's possession of them. "I'm sure I don't know, and I know even less how you came by this knowledge. You have excellent informants."

"If you mean spies," the Custodian said comfortably, "say spies. I haven't any really. Only shuttle pilots and a few delivery agents visit the Stations, but their tattle and observations add up to this and that."

"So they penetrated the nurseries to learn bedtime stories and discovered the centrifuge nobody else knows about — and didn't, er, *tattle* even to their best friends?"

"Well, they told *me.*"

"They thought bedtime stories worth a custodial report, these most unofficial agents?"

"Perhaps I should admit to some literary licence in fleshing out the picture." The Mayor, played with, shrugged and was silent. "Am I so inept? Must I tell the truth?"

Administrative secrets can be slippery, but curiosity had carried the Mayor too far from retreat. "It would help," he said coldly and the Custodian's instant grin warned him that he shared the pool with a shark.

"The Power Stations talk to each other. I listen. I don't hear deadly secrets, for they aren't stupid. Only occasional indiscretions and errors come my way. It has taken fifteen years to form a picture from scraps."

"They talk in clear?"

"By line of sight laser."

The Mayor saw appalling involvements opening but the hook was in his jaws. "Transceivers would be shielded, and you can't tap into a laser beam undetected."

"Who can't?"

It was not really a shock, only one more privacy violated by nameless men. The Custodian offered a spinoff comment: "The intention of the Ethic is preserved by continuous distortion of the letter."

"Semantics!" But the repetition was half hearted.

"The price of language. Now you know some secrets. There's a price on those also."

"Which I pay at once?"

"There is an action to be taken and I must not be implicated. Public Safety must not seem interested in Orbiter affairs. Less obvious people are needed — like those uniformless couriers of yours who fix giddy-gossipy eyes on Town affairs and keep you informed of the social fluxes you so gently do not seem to guide."

The Mayor said uncomfortably, "I rarely interfere — "

"But how could you? The Ethic, the Ethic! But I want to share your knowledge of everything Peter Marrian does on Earth and every word he speaks here."

"My boys aren't equipped — "

"They will be. Sensitized clothing and sound crystals at the roots of the hair. They'll be walking audio-cameras."

"This is all you want?"

"For the moment."

There it was, the — no, not "veiled threat", but . . . that phrase the pre-Collapsers had used . . . the "rain check" taken out on him. "Am I to know what we are looking for?"

"The reason for Peter Marrian's visit."

A part of the Mayor's very considerable intelligence had been worrying at the question since first mention of the name and had reached a conclusion. He thought, In for a credit in for a bust, and said, "But we know that, don't we?"

The Custodian smiled, at last like a man rather than a skull. "We do?"

"The Orbiters, if what formal communication we have with them is a reliable guide, have developed lazy habits of speech. They drop unnecessary final consonants, like g and f and h — sendin, mysel, strengt. Peter Marrian's name refers to his job, but has been misunderstood. Peter Marrying."

The Custodian laughed like a madman. "Do you imagine they'd waste resources preparing a brat to come Downstairs to get married? They don't even recognize marriage."

"But we do. And isn't that the whole point of the bed-time story?"

The Custodian calmed abruptly. "You'll do. It took me several years to realize that. The reason for it all?"

"Money. If you can't earn it, marry it. All Orbiter property is, I believe, communal."

"Good, good. And so?"

"This visit is, perhaps, exploratory, perhaps the opening move in an Orbiter campaign for . . . " He trailed off. "For what?"

The Custodian stood to go. "That is what I asked the Global Council to consider. They are still considering. Mean-while it is up to you and I to see that Petter Marryin, how-ever often best man, is never the groom."

2

It was unfortunately true that the Custodian's information derived mainly from Orbiter indiscretions and errors. Much escaped him entirely; much was filled in only after the affair was over.

He did not know, for instance, that Peter Marryin's face was not wholly his own. Orbiter technicians, observing the TV shows of Melbourne Town's entertainment idols (whom they despised utterly) with special attention to those who brought the young grovelling in ill-concealed sexual hysteria, spent two years designing the face; surgeons spent a further two creating it. The result was coldly calculated to turn the heads and raise the blood pressures of a prognosticated ninety per cent of Melbourne Town females between the ages of thirteen and thirty — a carnally desirable young lout with something for everybody and a dedication to its use.

Such thoroughness would have scared the Custodial wits out of him, more so if he had realized that the target had been narrowed to this one city on Earth.

Peter should have gone to Earth when he was eighteen, in that era an ideal age for a beginner at wiving, but the Commune Fathers were a committee and had fallen into the committee traps of indecision, vacillation and name calling without in nearly twelve months selecting a plump enough fly for their spider.

There were too many possibilities. One of the more disastrous outcomes of the planetary Ethic of Non-Interference had seen economic expertise, enhanced by psychelectronics, carve obese fortunes out of the re-industrialized planet; young heiresses were available in a wealthy world where small families were still the cautious habit of a species which had once already come within an ace of starving itself to death.

The Commune bickerings had ended with the death of old Festus Grant, right under their feet, in Melbourne Town. In wonderment they totalled the fabulous holdings – Rare Metals Research, Lunar Constructions, Ecological Rehabilitation and Exploitation, Monopole Ramjets, Mini-Shuttles Corporation, Sol-Atmos Research and Reclamation and more, more, more – The list rang louder bells for them than all the Jesus Cult cathedrals in history.

And all – all – all went to Claire Grant, only child of the dead widower.

The haste with which they groomed, briefed and despatched the casually confident Peter was worse than indecent; it was comic and contemptible. And thorough.

At nineteen the boy had all of the traditional Orbiter contempt for Earthworms, amplified by the hundreds of teleplays he had been forced to watch in order to become familiar with customs, speech idioms and etiquette. (He still did not really understand their drama; third generation Orbiters were unable to comprehend the preoccupations and philosophies of people not reared in a steel tube.) He had also an instilled awareness of being a cultural hero in embryo, the bedtime-story-boy who lived happily ever after in a swagger of privilege.

By Terrene standards he was paranoid (by Orbiter standards arrogant) but had been coached in adapting his responses to an Earthworm norm. The coaching, brilliant in

its fashion, allowed insufficiently for unpredictable encounters (encounters were rarely unpredictable in an Orbiter
tube) and the shuttle was scarcely spaceborne before his
furies stirred to Earthworm insolence.

The pilot was a jokey type, all bonhomie and loud mouth,
saying, "You'll find old Earth heavy going, feller," and laughing madly at his obscure pun based on an idiom not in use
Upstairs – one which sounded to Peter like a mannerless
criticism. And: "Watch the women, boy! They'll *weight* for
you to *fall* for them. Get it? *Weight* for you to – "

"I get it, thank you. Now mind your own damn business
and watch your disgustin tongue."

"Hey, now!"

The co-pilot dug him in the ribs to shut him up and
grinned sympathetically at Peter, who interpreted the grin as
zoological observation of the freak from Upstairs and
returned a glare of rage. The co-pilot shrugged, adding fuel to
a conviction of insulting pity.

The fool at the landing field, who mocked his strength by
offering to carry his luggage, was saved from assault only by
a memory of teleplays showing the planetary obsession with
menialism – free intelligences actually *offering* service! He
relinquished the bags with contempt and began to focus his
accelerating dislike for things Terrene on the unfortunate girl
he had been reared to meet. *She* was responsible for the
shame and insult he must bear in the course of duty.

In his anger he forgot even his irrational fear that Earth
gravity would be mysteriously different from his experience
in the centrifuge – that "real" weight would be something
else. By the time he noticed that it was not he had calmed
sufficiently to go through the mental balancing routine laid
down for him by the Orbiter psychlinicians.

It was an excellent routine, devised by men who knew
more about his mind than he ever could. By evening he was
ready – "debonair" was the word he favoured – to face the
Reception at the Town Hall, the first in line of the haunts of
the rich bitches. The Grant had better be there; he was not in
dawdling mood.

It was the Mayor, now, who sat in the Custodian's office; the
audio-crystals and the transcripts Englished from them were
politically too touchy to risk outside a secured area. The tape
they had heard had been prepared from a crystal lodged at
the root of a hair on the head of a shuttle co-pilot. How the

Mayor had achieved that, far outside his sphere of authority, the Custodian had the good taste not to ask; he was certain that this young man would go far and successfully.

"An unpleasant little shit," he said.

The Mayor (who, if age were the only factor, could have been the Custodian's great-grandson) was beginning to feel at home with the old exhibitionist. "I think that the Orbiters are what we have made them."

"Yes. Be properly glum about it."

"If he looks like bringing off a marriage — "

The Custodian said harshly, "He won't."

"But if?"

"Very well — if?"

"We might engineer small events, derogatory to his self-esteem, to push him past his restraints, allow him to erupt in public scenes which will make him socially unacceptable. Then we could look down our official noses and send him back Upstairs with a complaint of his behaviour."

The Custodian laughed and asked, "Are you ambitious?"

"In two years I will be thirty and no longer eligible for minor civil office. If I am not selected for a further Supervisory career I must fall back on commerce. The last Mayor of Melbourne Town is now a factory hand. This youth-decade in Social Administration can be a trap for the unprepared."

"I wouldn't worry too much."

They understood each other exactly.

But they did not understand Orbiters at all. Deny how they might, they shared in the recesses of their minds the common opinion that Orbiters were peculiar, backward and hardly to be taken seriously. In a perilously easygoing culture the problems of underdogs — their sense of grievance and drive, not for equality but for revenge — were little comprehended on realistic levels.

Nor did either understand the drive for achievement latent in a moneyed nonentity. They had thought, when assessing the field, that Peter would certainly be snatched up by the glamour crowd, and little Cinderella Claire lost in the crush.

3

The hall was crowded. Not, of course, that one cared a damn for the barbarian Orbiters or their peculiar tribalisms, but one was justified in observing a Social Curiosity.

Amongst the crowd Festus Grant's daughter was strung taut, breathless at her own projected daring, at what she intended to do tonight. When this ball was over she would be the envy of the smart set, even a centre of scandal, but for once she would have shone as "the girl who dared".

She was a social nobody and knew it. She would, at age nineteen in a year's time, attain her majority and control of the greatest fortune in Australasia, but that meant nothing to the Pleasured Classes; after a certain number of millions money became an environment rather than a possession and simple quantity no ground for eminence.

That she was intelligent, good hearted and socially more willing than able counted not at all against her plain features, washed-out eyes and too-plump figure. The physical defects could have been surgically corrected but among the Pleasured Classes this was Not Done; the struggling masses might falsify and pretend but One Was Above That.

Worse, she lacked taste. She was wickedly overdressed — with too much jewellery, a too blatantly fantastic hair arrangement, a dress too brightly red and too ornate and — and without the subtlety of choice which could subtract and adjust and transform her into what she wished to be.

All she had was useless money. She was accustomed to the attentions of men who pursued her prospects rather than herself and, as one who could buy any number of husbands, despised men who could be bought.

She danced with one of them to pass the time. *He* would not appear until just before the Protocol Dance, the fourth. While the eager young man found her unresponsive, in her mind she rehearsed her move. As the richest heiress present (and this was a point of etiquette wherein money *did* count) she would automatically take place next to the Lady Mayoress and be the second person presented. If *He* had been married, some wealthy matron would have been in the place of opportunity; it paid to know the rules and to be prepared to use them.

Colour and sound died as the orchestrator left the keyboard, and she rid herself of the eager young man.

When at last *He* arrived — he was anticlimactic.

Secretly she had hoped against commonsense for something strange, exotic (so, secretly, had they all), an outworld fantastication of dress, an oddity of manner or unexpectedness of appearance —

— anything but the too-ordinary pale and slender young man, in commonplace Terrene attire, who hesitated at the door as if taken with yokel surprise at the spectacle of Melbourne Town's Pleasured Class frozen in the half-bow and half-curtsy of welcoming protocol, then came uncertainly down the hall, guided by the traditional Visitor's Escort of Police Controller and Aide, whose dress uniforms outshone him utterly.

He was a mistake, a nothing. Her scandalous resolution lapsed; he was not worth it.

Then he came close. The escort fell back as he halted the correct four paces from the Mayor. At least, she thought, he had been coached in the observances. The Mayor stepped forward and the Orbiter lifted his face to the light.

Disappointment vanished before the most vitally handsome man she had ever seen. He was the epitome, the gathering, the expression of every media star and public idol who had ever roused her fantasies. He was The Orbiter — unearthly.

She scarcely heard the formal exchange; she ached to have done with it and with the visitor's formal round of the floor with the Lady Mayoress, so that she . . .

Peter bowed to the Lady Mayoress as the introduction was made, but the matron did not offer her arm.

They talked.

With the orchestrator's hands poised, waiting, over the keys — they talked.

Claire was furious. The woman was waiving the protocol of the first dance. Orbiters might be socially backward, but this was diplomatic insult.

Then the Mayoress took a pace back, terminating the exchange, and still the orchestrator waited on the Mayor's signal.

Claire saw a faint uncertainty in the Orbiter's fixed smile and knew that this was the moment. A public prank became an act of rescue.

She stepped quickly forward and he, perceiving the movement, half turned to her. She made the formal half-curtsy, knew she did it awkwardly and cared not a damn for that, and asked with a clarity that shivered to the doors of the hall.

"May I request the Protocol Dance?"

There was a stillness. She saw fury on the Mayor's face, instantly veiled. She sensed rather than heard an intake of half a thousand breaths — and realized the meaning of the disregarded dance, the substitution of formal chat. Gently the Protocol Dance had been passed over in consideration of

a visitor who in a weightless community could never have
learned the Viennese waltz.

Through the petrification of her shame she heard the
voice that could have charmed demons: "Why, thank you,"
and felt the slender fingers take hers. Lifted from the curtsy,
she gazed into the smile that had been sculpted for her to
gaze into. He said, "I shall be charmed, Miss Grant." But it
was she who was charmed that unbelievably he knew her
name, and it was she who triumphed over Mayor and
Mayoress, escort and orchestrator and all the Pleasured Class
as he added, "I have taken delight in learnin your ballroom
antics."

While he cursed the Freudian slip behind his plastic smile
she treasured it as the needed oddity, the otherworldliness
that made him truly a visitor to Earth.

If Claire Grant and Peter Marryin made a less than graceful couple, the swishing of tongues outmanoeuvred was balm
to the ugly duckling's waltzing ego.

Sensitized areas on the couriers' jackets did not make the
best of cameras. Subject to crumpling and difficult to aim
with accuracy, two of them yet caught Claire's expression at
different times during the ball.

"She's in an enchantment," said the Mayor.

"She's on heat," said the Custodian, to whom romance
had suddenly become a dirty word. "He's had brat's luck."

"Or good preparation."

"Meaning what?"

The Mayor ran back through the audio tapes. "This."

Peter's voice murmured in midair, "Ugly ducklin? What is
that? You have charm."

"You don't mean that." She was coy, ecstatic, flirtatious
and pleading all at once. ("Thank sanity we don't stay
young," the Custodian muttered.)

Peter's ghost voice said, "I do mean it. Men appreciate
charm in a woman."

"They appreciate money in a woman."

"I don' understan you."

"You don't understand money?"

"Intellectually I do, but not as an attraction. We don' use
money Upstairs."

Then he talked of other things as though money were of
no interest.

"Neat," the Custodian agreed. "Made his point and left it at that. Even stuck to the truth."

"But not to the truth behind the truth. He has been very well prepared."

"Fortunately, so have we."

The Custodian was wrong about that. On his fourth day on Earth Peter Marryin proposed to the infatuated, richest girl in Melbourne Town, was accepted by her and married to her (with housekeeper and maid for witnesses) by public data-record plug-in, a terminal of which was, quite naturally, located in her late father's study.

Capture and consolidation took something under fifteen minutes, whereas the Custodian had relied on an Engagement, a Round of Gaiety and a Splendid Society Wedding for time in which to generate a dozen subtle interferences. Against Peter's precision and speed no bugging system could do more than record the outwitting of science and power.

The Mayor was silently amused at the old man's raging against defeat. The backward barbarians Upstairs had foreseen opposition and surveillance and designed a lightning campaign to outflank both. He began to respect the barbarians.

But the old man stamped and raved in gutter language that stripped away the cool superiority of his public persona. It was altogether too humanizing. Embarrassing.

The Mayor raised his voice to drown the performance. "She's under age. The marriage can be annulled."

The Custodian snarled at him, "Only if her guardians demand it. Do you think they give a damn while they control the money in trust?"

"There might be means to persuade one of them — "

The Custodian calmed suddenly. "All right, you're trying. But we can't do it. Undue influence? Try and prove it! Even the newscasts are squalling 'the starstruck love story' a bare hour after the event, telling the world romance is alive and throbbing. Public opinion will see interference as bias against Orbiters. Nobody gives a damn for Orbiters but everybody loves lovers, and bias will be elevated into accusations of racialism or exoticism or some bloody pejorative coinage. And if interference were traced to me — " He shuddered.

And certainly not to me, thought the Mayor, who now had an assured future to protect.

The "starstruck lovers" honeymooned brilliantly around

the Earth for a month before Mr and Mrs Peter Marryin left
for the Power Station.

A structure two thousand metres long and five hundred in
diameter, floating below a battery of thousand-metre solar
mirrors, is immense by any standard, but nothing looks big
in space until you are close enough to be dwarfed and awed.
Dwarfed and awed Claire Marryin surely was, gasping at her
beautiful husband's ambience of marvels.

She had never been in space. (After all, who had, save
those whose work took them there? Nobody would *need* the
stars for generations yet.) So she played with null-g, bruising
herself a little and laughing at her own clumsiness, while
Peter fumed and was darling enough not to show it. When
the shuttle entered the vast lock in the Station's anal plate
(they actually called it that, she found, with a smothered
laugh) she calmed down and set herself to be a stately
matron of eighteen, worthy of a wonderful man.

From the passage opening on the interior of the Station
they came quite suddenly – he guiding her, at times a little
roughly, because Orbiters made their topology connective at
any angle instead of in terms of up and down – to a platform
from which was displayed the whole panorama of the Power
Station.

She looked along a huge tube whose walls were chequered
with little square boxes which she only slowly recognized as
dwellings, grouped around larger boxes which were community buildings and surrounded by neat squares and circles
of lush green. In the gravitational centre of the tube hung a
great disc whose visible face seemed to be nearly all window
glass and which occupied perhaps a third of the inner diameter. But it was nearly a thousand metres distant and did
not at a glance seem so big, any more than the boxes two
hundred metres below and above – *around, away* – seemed
large enough for dwellings.

She clapped her hands and cried out, "It's like a toyland!"

"Toylan!" On his face an expression she had not seen
there before – anger, revulsion, contempt – slipped into
bleak control. He said stiffly, "Your toylan is the home of a
fine an proud people," and led her to the conveyor belt while
she held back tears for her stupidity. Then it seemed he
remembered that these were new and fabulous sights for her
and set himself to be kind, and within minutes she was asking
shy questions, trying not to have them foolish ones.

"The disc? The factory, we call it. It's empty."

She asked timidly, "But why?" and thought he considered carefully before he answered.

"It was part of the original Station, a complex for the manufacture of artifacts which could be perfecly formed only in null-g conditions. But the Station grew too rich for the comfort of Earth an an embargo was placed on our goods. The factories have stood empty for more than seventy years."

"But that's unfair!"

"Yes!" The one word, with again the blank look of emotion repressed.

So there was a tiny cloud of resentment of her Earth. Best to ignore, allow it time to disperse. There was much to exclaim at here; for instance, she had not expected moving streetways, with railings. There were, in fact, railings everywhere. Strange for dwellers in free fall, free flight.

"There are free jump areas," he told her, "above roof level. There people may break their bones as they please. Once you take off you can' slow down or change direction, an in collision no weight doesn' mean no inertia. So in public places you ride an hang on, for the sake of others."

There was a touch of explanation-to-the-child-mind about that, and some impatience as he said, "I suppose you busy Terrenes don' think about such things."

Her loving tongue babbled, "Why should we, dear? It isn't our way of life."

She did not know she had just told a paranoid hero that Orbiter affairs were not considered interesting. Or that were it not for her nearing nineteenth birthday and the Grant industrial holdings he could have wished her dead. The stupid, yammering bitch!

The Station observed a twenty-four hour routine for metabolic stability, and that "night" Peter played host. Claire understood that social customs must alter and evolve in a closed community and that personal contacts might come uneasily until she found her niche, but the function left her bewildered.

The "party" was held on the lawns surrounding their "house" — their living-box — like a green pool. The box itself existed for privacy; in the weatherless Station life was conducted in public.

There was nothing for her to do. A fleshy, shapeless

woman appeared, requisitioned by Peter, to prepare snack dishes, and Claire's attempts to talk to her were balked upon grunted variations of "I'm only thirdwoman an don' know those things", making it plain that she was there to work and wanted only to get on with it.

What was a thirdwoman? A junior wife? But the Orbiters did not marry. They had some manner of temporary liaison for early child care but she, Claire, was uniquely the only *wife* on the Station. She could not question this clod but later must ask Peter.

At eight o'clock the major lights dimmed throughout the tube. Streetlamps remained and some freefloating clusters of coloured globes and rods and planes that she found restful to watch. The Orbiters' artificial night had its own soft charm.

Nothing else did. The guests arrived in male and female groups, never mixed. They congratulated Peter on his bride — and hesitated over the word or pronounced it with a sly grin or could not recall it until reminded. They seemed to regard the marriage as a triumphant joke.

After they had congratulated Peter they stared uninhibitedly at her. When Peter introduced them, most seemed not to know what to say to her; the men in particular seemed resentful at being expected to make conversation at all.

Even the women, grouped together and apart from the men, seemed interested in her only as an exotic display piece. And well, she thought, might they stare! Plain on Earth, here she was a beauty. These shapeless females, all flesh and rounded tubes of muscleless limb, were like talking grubs. She swore she would exercise, go daily to the centrifuge and *never* let herself fall victim to null-g.

The men were as bad as their women, pipestem roly-polys; Peter alone looked like a real human being. And even he, she thought with a touch of dispirited spite, was no physical match for a real Terrene man.

Perhaps in her isolation and disappointment she had drunk too much, and had become afraid of vertigo in weightlessness, for she showed no more than a dumb resentment when a massive pudding of a woman dragged her into a disapproving group to hiss at her, "Stop tryin to talk to the men. Sexes mix in private!"

Even Peter seemed only occasionally to recall her presence. The "party" dragged interminably and she did not remember going to bed.

She woke to a hangover and a furious Peter dressing with

compressed lips. She scarcely believed she heard him mutter, "Drunken bitch!"

Over coffee she gathered courage to ask what a third-woman might be and he snapped at her, "A bloody servan, trained for that an nothin else."

The words were plain but she did not understand the threat in his eyes.

He said, "I'm goin out. Stay here. Don' leave the house. I'll be an hour."

Desolate and uncomprehending, she drifted through the living-box, with its neatness, its compactness, its accessories to comfortable living. To efficient living, she amended; the Orbiters were not a comfortable people. She recalled the ill manner of last night, the resentment scarcely repressed, the smiles that were silent laughter.

And was suddenly afraid. And as suddenly more afraid that it was too late for that.

Peter returned within the hour, in more cheerful mood, ready to kiss and play. She responded with silly relief, as if a smile could cancel ill-will already delivered. He had "pulled strings", he told her, made an arrangement which only her special circumstances could justify.

"The Psychlinic will take you immediately."

She fled from his arms, too affronted for fear. "I'm not ill, Peter!"

"No, no!" He laughed, soothing and conciliating and as handsome as all hell and temptation. "It's a teachin group. It isn fair to toss you unprepared into our ways and customs so I've arranged an implant, a rundown of all the special social conditions, etiquettes, things you need to know so as not to stub a social toe every time you step out."

She cried a soft "O-oh!" for a gift without price. Much of her education had been by psycho-implant and she knew what was involved. He had given her a ticket to painless knowledge she would have been months in achieving.

And a man who could command the time of a Psychlinic was no mean husband.

The clinic was absurdly old fashioned, its "chair" a cocoon of electrodes and leads and handles to be gripped and precision clamps and heaven knew what else. On Earth the whole thing was done with a single helmet and a hypodermic.

Perhaps her amusement showed, for the Psychlinician explained, in a tone stiff with non-apology, that the Station used its original equipment, that there was no money for new models from Downstairs.

Claire said with her friendliest smile, "Then I shall buy it for you", and sat herself firmly in his ancient chair.

An unreadable expression came and went as he said, "Why, I'm sure you will."

It might be their mode of thanks, but it lacked gratitude. She felt a mild numbness in her thighs, shifted slightly to ease it and realized that the whole buttock was losing sensation.

In sudden, frightened anger she cried out, "You've used a penetrant narcotic! In the chair seat!"

He said bluntly, "Yes", and winced as her voice rose to screaming pitch.

"That's treatment for dangerous criminals and violent lunatics. I'm not – I'm not – "

He said forcefully, "Sit back an shut up!"

And, since that was the nature of the drug, she obeyed. In the few minutes of mental freedom left her she peered into hellmouth.

What they did with her occupied several days. They fed her the acclimatization material, of course, since she was to dwell here permanently and not be a clumsy nuisance. Then came the establishing of submissive reactions, no simple job on a mind accustomed to freedoms which to the Orbiters seemed sheer anarchy. Only then could they begin the deep probing necessary to planning the personality split. When that was done they designed and imprinted the controlled schizophrenic balance that could be tipped either way with proper triggering. It was necessary that a superficially "normal" personality be available if Melbourne Town should send an envoy who would demand to talk with her when the inevitable questions came to be asked.

Aside from that, the Psychlinic found her a fascinating study; relaxation viewing of Terrene teleplays had not prepared them for the revealed truths of Earthworm culture.

"Effete and decaden," said the Chief, "floatin over realities and never seein them. Gravity or no gravity, it's we who are the strong. *We* are the human future."

4

On her nineteenth birthday a healthy and self-possessed, if unwontedly serious Claire Marryin contacted her guardians by visiphone and made her wishes known. They argued against the control of immense wealth being taken out of Terrene hands; they pleaded, stormed and stalled until she threatened to settle the matter by simple deed of transfer. She behaved throughout with polite but weary stubborness.

The Commune Fathers of Power Station One became the administrators of the Grant interests.

"That," noted the Mayor, "makes them owners of just eight and one quarter per cent of Melbourne Town and unhealthily concerned in mining estate and development from Mars to the solar corona."

"It was expected," said the Custodian, "but what will they do with it? We know better now than to guess at Orbital thinking."

What they did was unexpected in its naivety. They tried to play the market. They not only lost a great deal of money but wreaked some small havoc with those lesser Grant holdings they chose for their experiments in finance.

"Economic stability is threatened," said the Custodian, with a perfectly straight face. "It is time to return their visit."

5

The seventeen Spokesmen of the seventeen Station Commune Councils were in session on Station One when a delivery receivals clerk chattered over intercom that the Custodian of Public Safety of Melbourne Town was in the anal corridor and demanding entry.

"How large is his party?"

"He is alone, Alastair Father."

"Delay him five minutes, then escort him here yoursel."

"Yes, Alastair Father." The clerk returned to the corridor where the lean and lined and very patrician old man took his ease without benefit of handhold, as to the manner born. In a Terrene that seemed obscurely insolent, as did the silent waiting for the clerk to speak.

"I am to escort you to the Father, but firs there are matters I mus atten to. I won' be — "

The Custodian delivered arrogance with a polite smile. "I am sure you have nothing more important on your hands than my visit."

The clerk said, "That's as may be", and turned towards his office. *Snotty Downstairs bastard!* Orbiter insularity overcame him. "Stationhans don' take orders from Terrenes."

"Pity," said the Custodian equably. The clerk withdrew, wondering was that a subtle Terrene threat.

Alastair First Father, who had been Alastair Dunwoodie, swept them out of the room like children. Before his immense prestige the communards made no attempt to argue but sought invisibility in the nearest dwellings. All, that is, save the inevitable youngest-promoted, still inclined to display intransigence rather than sense.

"Refuse him! Sen him about his business!"

"He is about his business." The First Father urged him towards the door. "It is too soon to invite reprisals, as I am curious to see Charles again."

"Charles! You know him?"

"We were friens once. Now, go!"

The youngest-promoted went, bemusedly reckoning the Father's age.

Were friens? It was an uncommonly wistful thought for Alastair. And now? Loyalties had come between. He punched an intercom number and said, "There's a Terrene envoy here. Prepare Claire Thirdwoman."

The Chief Psychlinician despatched his Physical Training Authority, Peter Marryin, to the hydroponic garden where the girl would be making the daily harvest of fruit and vegetables, a faintly stupid smile on her face. She was plump now, and losing shape, but seemed contented enough; it had been necessary to repress most of her emotional reaction-strength in order not to blur the edges between personalities by creating a too-obtrusive secondary.

The code phrase which brought her original persona to life was cruel to the point of obscenity but served its purpose of reaching deep into the preconscious. Peter, who had never conceived of her as more than a means to an end, gave no thought to brutality and outrage as he said distinctly into her ear, "Peter Marryin loves Claire Grant".

The young Charles had worked in space and knew the rules of null-g movement, and the old Charles had wisely spent fifty hours in the shuttles reconditioning himself before facing Alastair. He would not lose face through physical incompetence.

He even managed to inject a hint of swagger into his slide-

and-shuffle entry into the Council Hall where the old man stood alone at the head of the long table with its — yes, seventeen chairs. All present and correct — then hurriedly got rid of while an impudent clerk obstructed.

He said, "You're showing your age, Alastair," and gave his skull grin. "Old as God and no doubt twice as crafty."

Alastair flowed to greet him in a movement which seemed to glide him, upright, down the length of the room, making Charles's swagger mere bumptiousness, and held out his hand. "Well, ol frien!"

The Custodian returned the grip gently and allowed himself a bare sentence of old affection: "I have always remembered you, Alastair." Then, as they measured each other with uncertain and wary smiles, "I bring not peace but a sword."

Alastair, too, had been a Cultist in the old days. "To set man against his father an daughter agains her mother? Not on the Stations, Charles. Our conception of relationships does not allow internecine frictions."

"Not Terrene against Orbiter, those brothers on Earth and in Heaven?"

"The chance of brotherhood is gone by."

As simply as that the lines of battle were drawn.

They sat at the table, using the bodybelts that allowed movement and gesture without reactive floating, and the Custodian launched his attack directly.

"The Governance of Australasia suggests — " he laid the lightest of stresses on the verb, " — that a Committee of Advice be appointed to guide your financial handling of the Grant holdings."

"There are no Grant holdins. I suppose you mean the Orbital League holdins brought to the Communes by Claire Thirdwoman."

So the whole League was in it; not really news. The final words penetrated less swiftly, then shockingly.

"Thirdwoman! Alastair, that's slavery!"

The First Father smiled thinly. "What could she be good for but manual labour an childbearin? Your children of wealth learn nothin useful to an Orbiter. I assure you she is not discontented."

"I want to see her!"

"You shall."

"Good." *Some double dealing there? Be watchful.* "Now, the holdings — "

"No Committee of Advice, Charles!"

"You're amateurs. You'll go broke."

"Our economists are learnin. We buy expert advice now from Earth. Terrene's have little that can' be bought, includin allegiance."

"I know damned well what you buy. I also know that your first attempts to deal in millions caused a minor recession in Melbourne Town. If you succeed in bringing down the whole Grant empire there'll be economic chaos."

"We aren' stupid."

"But you are inexperienced. We must protect ourselves."

"No Committee, Charles!"

"It is already set up."

"*Un*set it. We won' obey it." The Custodian's expression gave him pause. "The Ethic, Charles! You can' interfere." The skull grin threatened to engulf him. "*What have you done, Charles?*"

As the declaration of love unlocked the sleeping persona, Claire burst from within herself like an emerging butterfly. Life flooded her face; her lips parted and smiled, her spoiling body straightened and she looked into her lover's eyes with an instant's joy that faded into apprehension and loathing.

He had seen it all before, was turning away when she asked, "What do they want now?" and answered over his shoulder, "Firs Father wans you. There's a Terrene envoy here."

Envoy! Hope was immediately quenched. No envoy could free her. In a moment they would give her the injection and tell her what to say and do and there she would be, gabbling that she was happy and had no desire to leave the Station, that everyone was so kind and that she had fulfilment here such as Earth could never offer and more and more gushing, lying rubbish.

She asked, "Why should I bother?"

"What?"

"What's the use? I don't want to see him, to tell force-fed lies and build myself more unhappiness."

He faced her furiously. "Listen, girl! You're an Orbiter and what Firs Father says, you do."

In the rare periods of personality release, such as the visiphone communications with bankers and enquiring relatives, her hatred had been born in the schizophrenic hell of the submission drugs. During the long weeks of thirdwoman regression her subconscious mind had been conjuring powers of viciousness the little Claire Grant could never have roused from her psyche. Now, in these moments of hyper-euphoria, between the awakening and the drugging, she was uniquely herself, undrugged and unregressed — a creature of misery and rage.

She said, with a menace he did not hear because in his thinking it could not be there, "Don't talk to me like that."

"Come on; don' waste my time."

She goaded, "Your time is nothing to me."

"Bitch!" He put out a grasping hand and she struck it away, hissing, "Don't touch me, you filth!"

It was stunning. No woman spoke to a man like that, *no* woman. Nor would a man dare use such words to Peter the Culture Hero. And she had struck his hand! Outraged self-love rose like a scald in the throat, and his fingers hooked into claws.

She said, making sure of him, "If you touch me I'll kill you."

She needed to kill someone, and who better than the man who had married for her money the girl who despised fortune hunters? As his hands reached for her she casually took one in hers, dragged the arm straight and kicked him in the elbow, breaking it to the obbligato of his screaming. It was easy. Orbiters knew little about aggression or defence; both were difficult or embarrassingly ludicrous in null-g.

The screaming unleashed joy in her and she knew that she *would* kill him. Others in the street had heard him and heads were turning but they could not save him. She, Claire Third-woman, slave, dupe and Earthworm, was about to murder the Culture Hero before their eyes.

They could not realize how simple it was for her. A year of null-g had made her competent in the leaps and anglings of free fall, and her Earthworm musculature made it possible for her to achieve take-off speeds and endure landing collisions no Orbiter could match. Even her centrifuge-reared "husband" was not her equal.

She caught his arm and he shrieked again, and hooked her foot under the moving-way guide rail. Figures now leapt towards her, too late. Taking him by wrist and smashed elbow she flung him, howling, against the wall of a dwelling twenty metres away. He hit it face forward, sprawling like a spider, and she launched herself after him, turning in mid-air to strike with her feet at his spine, and heard it crack.

She had her moment of murderer's ecstasy, sexual, blood-deep, complete. Let the surgeons and biochemists revive and rebuild him (as they would), but she had cleansed herself of shame and hatred.

Then reaction set in and with a crippling weariness of spirit she turned to defend herself . . .

"Done?" the Custodian echoed. "I have set up a Committee of Advice. Nothing else."

"Unacceptable."

"But there are, of course, alternatives."

"Which are?"

"One is that you should re-assign the League holdings to Claire Grant and return her to Earth."

The First Father laughed, but uneasily because the breath-taking impudence of the demand spoke of threat behind threat. "You're out of your min."

"We can take the money from you, you know."

"Not by way of Claire. She gave it to us. I feel you will have a record, verbal and written, of the whole transaction."

"I have, Alastair. And an expert psychological report on her speech and behaviour patterns during the exchanges with her administrators, showing a ninety per cent certainty that she was under submission drugs. I can recommend that the Marketing Court freeze your assets while the transfer is re-examined."

"You can' prove druggin."

"You don't deny it?"

"Or admit it."

The Custodian felt less regret for that old friendship. Neither was the same man he had been eighty years ago, and both were centenarians, patterns of biochemistry and geriatric technique, with interests and loyalties eight decades divergent. He found himself caring not a damn for Alastair's needs so long as Melbourne Town survived. The perilous honesty of chauvinism at least left him unrepentant of hard hitting.

"You'd have to kill the girl to prevent me getting the truth. Would you do that, Alastair?"

The First Father's smile was deep winter. "No. I don' wan the Global Council puttin a military prize crew aboard my Station."

They came from all sides, angling up towards her. Almost lethargically she struck with her feet at the first comer, a

squealing firstwoman spitting anti-Terrene rage, and used her
mass to change direction and clutch at the jump-halting rail
on a dwelling roof. The rest fell into a confusion of collisions
and reachings for any anchored mass. Their babbling anger
and shock sounded ridiculous; they lived such ordered lives
that in emergency they flapped and fluttered. If they caught
her they would kick and hit and pinch and threaten but in
the end she would still be thirdwoman in the hydroponic
garden. And Peter reconstructed. And nothing changed.

Then why not let them take her? There was no freedom.

For an instant, looking upward, she saw where, five
hundred metres away across the diameter of the cylinder,
final freedom lay, and reflexively launched herself towards it.

At once she knew she had been stupid, that it was better
to live. There could always be the unexpected, the reversal of
fortune. In panic she began to struggle, but what Peter had
told her was true: once in free fall you cannot stop or slow
down or change direction.

Her launch had been deadly accurate, a simple straight
line with no gravity-fed trajectory for miscalculation.

The end of Claire Thirdwoman, crying and clawing for the
inaccessible sides, was entry into the twenty-metre maw of
the Station disposal unit, the vast mouth that could swallow
machine complexes or obsolescent building units without the
need for laborious dismemberment. She died at once as the
heat units sensed her, felt nothing as the grinders shredded her
contemptuously in a spurt of gears and in seconds was a mist
of molecules expanding into invisibility in pressureless space.

6

In a right little, tight little island in the sky there is small pre-
cedent for announcing the neo-death of a local hero and the
dissolution of his killer. Inexperience blurted out the news
breathlessly in front of the Earthworm stranger.

For the second time during the affair the Custodian
exploded in ranting fury, cursing Orbiter and Terrene
stupidity alike, reducing himself to manic gutter level, until
he saw that the First Father watched him with the bleak care
of a duellist who sees advantage.

He checked himself abruptly. In an access of intuition,
even some residual affection, he pondered the needs and frus-
trations the Orbiters had brought on themselves when they
sought the pastures of heaven by casting away weight.

He said, "We need truth, Alastair, both of us. Neither was ready to move; now we must."

The First Father bowed his head. Concealing a smile? At any event, he made no attempt to argue. In minutes the Custodian knew all he needed, including the business of the League meeting his advent had dispersed – the secret buying of weapons, offensive and defensive, from men on the five continents Downstairs who would sell honour, history and the future for money.

That was bad enough. Worse was that the First Father did not fear him.

Feeling all his years, he sat down with the other old man – friend, enemy and gameplayer – to plan a fresh tomorrow.

Emotion subsided; perspectives revived; Claire's death became a tactical weapon each sought to grasp. They circled, testing defences, until a confident Alastair made the first lunge.

"Charles, you can no more risk investigation of this affair than I can."

The Custodian sighed inwardly. It had been, he supposed, inevitable that Alastair, despite his remoteness from the social psychology of the Earthworm, should recognize that.

Still, he must try. "*You* certainly cannot. Your League is no danger to Terrene culture yet, but this last year holds the proof that you will be. Some day. Even soon." He added easily, "You will be stopped, of course."

Too late; that hand was already lost. "How, Charles? How will Earth explain retributive action a secon time? Attemp it and I, *I*, will tell the story of how Claire Marryin died. I will tell the trut, all the trut. And your Earthworms will discover how their precious Ethic has created a poverty-stricken ghetto in the sky, but one that intens to kick the Ethic to pieces rather than continue as the unseen slaveys of some Victorian servan quarters in the attic Upstairs. Revenge on us may be swif but public scrutiny of the Ethic *and* of its manipulators will be pitiless. It will be the end of the Ethic."

The Custodian had seen from the beginning that he was caught. It was not easy even to go down fighting. He said lightly, "But everybody questions the Ethic in his heart. It is an elaboration of good manners, pointless in essence but providing a permanent framework of behaviour for discussion without bloodshed."

Alastair laughed at him. "It mus be one of the great jokes of history that Earth has based its firs planetary culture on good manners, then created an offshoot with none. An a better joke that the collapse of a lie nobody believes in could plunge you into cultural anarchy. All your international relationships balance on it. You won' take the risk."

Of course he, and Earth, would not. Bluntness now would serve as well as anything. "What do you want?"

"To be rid of you."

That was unexpected; he said nothing at all but waited for Alastair to continue.

"You can' blow us out of the sky. Too un-Ethical and too revealin. But you can pay us to go away. And we'll go." He grinned with sudden savagery. "Like the classic barbarians on the Imperial boarders."

That was staggering. The Custodian groped for words, any words to stall for thought. "The power supplies − "

"Automated platforms to replace the Stations. The plans are ready. Ten years from keel to full operation."

That was worth a sour laugh in return. "We've had automation plans of our own for the pasty twenty years. The problem has been what to do with you. Now you tell me you'll go away. Where to? Let me guess at your view of the matter."

He ruminated.

Alastair said, "There's somethin you should see. Come along."

They floated out of the hall to a moving-way which carried them up the curve of the hull, through little nests of the living-boxes and the lawns and gardens in their patterns of cultivated brilliance. All growing things were a passion of Orbiters. Their natural art form, perhaps? They could have chosen more coldly and worse.

He said, "I think I have it. The basic need was money. First for armaments in case Earth did indeed become provoked into violence by the demands you would some day make. Second for *material* to implement whatever design you have in mind. Behind this is a determination to cut loose from Earth once and for all. The cultures have diverged to the point where neither understands the other or needs the other. Cultures which don't understand each other despise each other, have no use for each other, no matter how they pretend otherwise. Am I doing well?"

"Very well."

They left the moving-way and Alastair opened a door. Inside was nothing at all, an empty room.

"Total isolation breeds its own neuroses, Charles. Our psychologists set up this room years ago. People come here to soothe their tensions, pacify their resentments, defuse their aggressions."

He touched switches; the room became black dark. A slit twenty metres wide glimmered faintly in the floor, opened like a vast eye, and gazed at the stars.

The Custodian understood only vaguely. "The galaxy means little to me, but for you it has come to have psychological significance. Is this where you will go?"

"Eventually. Not yet. It is a long dream."

"And now?"

"Firs, Jupiter. You can pay us to mine the satellites and the atmosphere."

The Custodian knew he should have foreseen it but the politician in him asked, "Why should we?"

"Because in a century or so you will have another population-an-resources crisis Downstairs, and you can use somebody to prepare the alternatives for you. By then we will be wealthy enough an self-sufficien to engage the universe on our own terms. There are eighty thousan people in the Stations now; we mus plan for a million. Ten Mother Islands and a hundred minin scows for a start. The resources out there will cover your nex dozen population explosions; you'll find us a good bargain. And what remains of the Ethic can seek virtue in Non-Interference with our cultural destiny."

"The impudence of it all is breathtaking. All I need do is lay the idea before the Global Council and they'll collapse like cards before your diplomatic acumen. It will need more than a silver tongue to sway them."

"Let the Ethic sway them!"

The Custodian swallowed a sound like a smothered laugh. "Blackmail, Alastair!"

"But mos Ethical, Charles, within the Terrene meanin of the word. By the way, did you know that the original twentieth century intention in suggestin space platforms was to establish free colonies in space?"

"Was it indeed?"

"Indeed. I have always said that we learned nothin from the Collapse. We've simply taken a little longer to arrive were they wished to go anyway."

Several hours later, when the Custodian was preparing to return home, the First Father glanced fortuitously overhead to where, across the diameter, a disposal gang loaded a day's garbage into the vent, and felt a twinge of guilt.

The Custodian, following his gaze, wondered aloud if everything was recycled.

"Not quite everythin."

"No? Oh, yes, of course, that — Tragic business; tragic . . . " He was busy formulating his approach to the Global Council.

7

The version retailed to the Mayor was perhaps a little slanted. He was impressed. "You know, we'll be well rid of them."

"For the time being."

The Mayor's eyebrows rose.

"Nothing ends, James. Alastair First Father is quite aware that as Lords of the Solar System one day they'll come home again — as barbarians at the ancient gates. But you and I won't be around to worry over that."

A Passage in Earth

Damien Broderick

(1978)

I grew her in a pod, and she was my sweetling, my darling,
the best baby I ever made. The big collapsicle field was shut
down by then, on our last slowing skid back to Earth, which
might explain why she didn't come out raddled like the
earlier tries. Or maybe it was love, for I put that child together with doting devotion, blended her nucleotides with
the passion of an *haute cuisine* autocrat. Delicious enough,
yes, yes, to be gobbled down on the spot. But that's Shaun's
diction, concupiscent and lipsmacking, lustful-eyed and car-
nivorous, and she was never meant for Shaun. Not my
Mahala, bright birdsong for the ear's ravishment of austere
Shem.

Which is being gallows smartass after the fact, of course.
When I started growing Mahala I knew she'd be my benedic-
tion to an altered Earth, spinning sixteen solar years ahead
and to one side of our cruddy battered prow. But the details
were up for grabs. You can't trust humans to sit still, even
when they're riding an *e* exponent rollercoaster. I knew
they'd have changed in ten thousand years, Mahala's distant
genetic cousins, but I certainly didn't guess then that they'd
have done the demi-god thing: wound up strutting out their
own archetypes. Maybe (in the limit, as we analytic types
say) it was inevitable.

"Cloth Mother," she asked when she was eight, smartass
herself, "will I have a prince to love when we get there?"

I stopped cuddling and tried to sound stern.

"Fiddle-faddle, long shanks. This is a vessel of the People's
Anarchy and I'll have no backsliding on *my* bridge."

She did that thing with her nose which everyone except a
parent considers sickeningly cute, and went mercurial eight-

year-old scornful. "It would be *nice* to have a prince, Captain, and if you're going to go Hard-Wire on me I think it's purely a *shame.*" The little beast had got to H in the biography matrix and kept mixing Freud up with Harlow, largely to get a rise out of me (see what I mean?). When she was sixteen and stepping out on Earth, Mahala was innocent and bashful, if she felt like it, as peach blossom, but at eight she just powered away like a savage with every joule of the five sigmas of savvy I'd woven into her nucleic acids.

We came down without much noise but with fine star-bursts of fiery light to the Versailles they'd made of temperate Earth. They'd forgotten about us, as predicted, having long since shed interest in the rest of the universe. There's no game to compete in drawing power with immersion in the archetypes. I ferreted out the way of it and congratulated myself cordially on my forethought in having prepared my pretty spanner to throw into their dreary stock repertoire of byzantine elaboration. Then I shot back up to orbit without opening the front door — while Mahala blinked in surprise at her mirror, getting her hair ready — and there I mused for a while.

"We'll nip in the back way."

"All right," she nodded without complaint, trusting me. She was a generous, utterly beautiful young woman, and I loved her far too much to toss her into the lap of some whirligig god prince. (Shaun was ruling at that time, but I didn't much like the looks of Shem either. Both of them needed a good hefty boot in the tail.)

I decided to give a wide berth to all their stupefying crystal towers and grandiose pleasure domes and deer-browsed ecological pastures, the chocolate-box stuff. On the other hand I wasn't just being perverse; there was no percentage in squatting down on the Gobi desert (they'd left it alone) and twiddling our thumbs. I needed a place with a measure of natural hostility but not wholly denuded of people.

This time we snuck in over the new South Pole and I dropped us inconspicuously in a mess of crowberries and bilberries on the basalt crags of Heimaey Island, near the remains of the Whorled City of Vestmannaeyjar. The big magnetic polarity flip-flop had been in the offing when I'd left Earth, and the massive soft-iron spirals of Vestmannaeyjar were nearing completion. Obviously it hadn't worked. I guessed that those gritty argumentative utopians who'd built my vessel had been zilched when the ozone layer blew off.

It was crazy cold, just the same. Plate spread had ripped Iceland up somewhat, and the geysers boiled heartily in new locations, but snow was in the air and ice on the ground. We'd frightened a mob of reindeer and there was quite an amount of filthy exhausted complaint coming from the grubby exhausted locals who'd been herding them into a sort of rudimentary corral outside a mean little village whose construction might well have antedated the Vikings. There was a coarse lilt to their obscenity, as befitted poets and scientists down on their luck, and I knew I'd come to the right place. I bundled my dear pet up in thermal undies and synthetic furs and sent her out to find true love.

Mahala hesitated on the top step and looked doubtfully back at my warm, food-scented interior.

"Last stop, sweetheart," I told her. "All out." It broke my heart, of course, but you have to see these things in perspective. I induced a warm current in her coffee-brown cheek, for a parting kiss, and wrapped her in a long tight pulse for a hug. "Good luck, my darling. Now don't fret," for her lashes shone with tears, "I'll keep watch. Off you go, Mahala, the real people are waiting for you." They were, too, shin-deep in slush, gawping and gaping and muttering scornful couplets to one another to keep their nerve up.

"Who shall I ask for?" she said in a small appalled voice, staring down at their red-tipped faces.

"It's simple, honeybun. You must look for your beloved, the most miserable of men."

I thought she was going to bolt back in but she just stood there for a time blinking slowly, her throat moving in the shadow of the furs. Then, "Oh, shit," she said, and went gracefully down the icy steps to meet the outcasts.

Did Mahala believe I'd be able to keep her under observation wherever she went? I don't know. She had trust in me, of that I'm certain. But I had never told her about the hefty cloned neural net I kept fed and watered, welded behind a bulkhead, flesh of her flesh, supine and mindless but resonating to her awareness and consciousness. My own sensory electrodes were anchored all through the net, so I was able to monitor Mahala (and, though for ethical motives I'd never done it, evoke ideas in her brain) at any distance on the planet's surface. So I pursued many billion thises and thats while she slogged through the snow to their rocky shacks and kept a small but sufficient part of myself tuned to her adventures. If anyone were brutish enough to lay a finger on my baby without her permission I'd zap him hard enough to fry his balls.

As it happened, the only animosity Mahala met was sour and envious looks from some of the outcast women, but she had even them charmed fast enough. She seemed so fragile, and was demure with the men, and the information she offered freely was meat and drink to this community. None of them had been as far off-planet as the moon. Mahala herself, of course, had not been with me to the edge of the universe but I'd provided her with a liberal education.

"Actually I've just eaten lunch," she told them, but they seemed so disappointed (and at least one grey old bag so close to a resurgence of snoot) that she smiled nicely and ate their reindeer milk curd with glistening bilberries and mango from the greenhouse. The men whose beasts we'd put the wind up sat with her at the long bench and chewed with gusto on roast steaks, tossing bones to gigantic gentle dogs with far more hair than manners. Mahala declined the meat.

"The quasars *are* intelligent?" asked a biologist, a gaunt lined woman with intent eyes.

"Much more than that," Mahala said, putting her empty bowl aside. "They're ever so old, and very wise."

Triumphantly smiling, the biologist cried: "I knew it! For centuries I've been telling that asshole Kerala — "

There was hubbub; one of the herders seized Mahala's wrist with unreflective eagerness. (I did not kill him. My jealousy is under perfect rational control.) "Could you communicate with them? What did they tell you?"

For a moment she allowed his grip, before drawing her hand away. I detected the ambivalent shock of alternating current: never before had she known a human touch.

"Of course, I wasn't born then. But They spoke to the vessel, to the Holistic Cybersystem Executive. I don't think sh'he wanted to come home after that, but They told shim it was sher duty."

Silence, abruptly, was total. Wind whined about the broken walls. The herder cracked his knuckles, looking at the rough grain of the table. He said: "Child, what did They convey to the cybersystem?"

"Well the main thing, I guess, was the secret of the universe."

Everyone stared at her, and I could sense the ion balance

tremble in the room. They had all been exiled here from the courts and great places of the world because asking questions about large enigmas had gone out of fashion when Shem was deposed. The air shivered with intellectual greed.

"Tell us," a faint shriek. So she did. Arctic twilight (or was it now Antarctic?) draped the windows, and logs fed the fire. A dog nosed closer to the hearth and began to snore. People sighed as she spoke, and snorted in angry disbelief when treasured hypotheses tumbled with the logs into the flames, and were shushed by their fellows. Mead and spirits went into glasses and down throats, and I had to make some minor adjustments to Mahala's hypothalamus to prevent her getting completely sloshed. She loved the attention from this lot, grotty as they were; there might be no princes among them but they all had brains like razors (even the poets) and Mahala had always been a bright kid.

When she finished, a young pregnant mathematician heaved herself up from her cushions near the heat and eased in next to my own baby. "You're saying that the entire universe is a single matter-wave, weaving backwards and forwards through spacetime from one singularity to the other? *One* elementary particle only?"

Mahala nodded, and sipped at her mead. "Exactly, Belina, a smeared standing wave. The state vector collapsed, specifying this particular reality, when It sort of opened Its eye and, well, regarded Itself with approval. Do you mind if *I* ask a question now?"

"My god. My god." Belina closed her eyes and placed her hands on her bulging uterus. "Mahala, what can we possibly tell *you*?"

My baby glanced around the rapt table, at all of them, shyly, and said: "How can I find the most miserable man in the world?"

In the incredulous interval, Nigel's serrated laugh caused her to jump. He was one of the poets, dissolute and haggard, with irises the colour of the polar sky at noon. "We can tell you where the bastard is, my lovely, but not how to find him."

"But I must find him," cried Mahala in alarm. "He is my beloved!"

There was a lot of confusion for a while, the scientists not having the faintest clue what was afoot and the poets seeing instantly and not liking it, each moiety trying to shout the other down, and my dove bursting into pissed tears in the midst of it. Nigel muscled in at once and led her aside to the fire, speaking into her ear.

"I don't know why you want him, when you could go to the high places and find your welcome in Shaun's plump bed — or stay here with us, and share mine — but I'll tell you where you have to go. Maybe your big metal friend up there on the hill can get you in to him." And he told her where the Prisoner was held: the whole world's most wretched creature, bitter in defeat, ancient in the cycle of victory and loss and now at the nadir of his fortunes: yes, the lord Shem, patron and betrayer of knowledge, incarcerated in his brother's fastness at the centre of the world.

I hadn't expected Mahala back on board quite so soon, if at all, if ever; the advice They'd given was heuristic, not a point-by-point flowchart. I'd shut the habitation environment down to standby. Shucking off her furs in my soft yellow light Mahala shivered, dazed by the booze, the wind belling outside, her expectation.

"Come right in, darling," I said. "I'll make you a mug of hot chocolate." I nuzzled her broad nose and got a flowered filmy thing for her to wear and popped her into bed, and by the time she was asleep I'd lifted in a sub-orbital parabola, heading for daylight and old gloomypuss.

As she slept I wrought that small miracle which I saw was necessary, touching her brimming ovaries and, releasing a single egg, prepared her womb for its nurturance. This much I had expected to come about in the course of nature; now I understood the urgency of our passage in Earth. And I was filled with a dread I put down to a parent's pre-nuptial jitters.

We fell without sound across the lush grasslands of the drained Med, across the early spring thaw-brawling rivers plunging through that immense canyon, hovered finally above his place of bondage: Aethalia, a fist thrust from the ancient seabed. I settled at the peak of Monte Capanne and gazed down with my magnified vision on the shabby roofs of his villa, old San Martino, restored a hundred times by the look of it and a hundred times gone again into decay. In the ample grounds male birds of paradise scratched and strutted, wing plumes like segments shaved from the golden apples of the sun, their chubby bodies emerald in the morning light. Drab females scurried in the long shadows of heraldic topiary wild with seed, dragons bristling beards, cancerous lions, the

slower shrubs still brown and scrawny. Nobody cared. I
waited until Mahala had woken, draped her this time for the
milder air and the breathless hope of her love in cloth insub-
stantial and translucent as ectoplasm, tucked tight beneath
her lovely breasts and flowing like a comet's veil behind, and
I gave her a glass of milk and sent her off down a path I
cleared through the dead vines and brambles to the villa.

She passed through the dusty portrait-hung hallways without hindrance, her heart pumping fast, me interposing
between the dreadful tools of mayhem his captors had contrived. Charges shorted like rainbows. I'm swift and I'm
powerful and I know more than they did (for they had never
hung enraptured under the torrential glory of Those Who
watch from the rim of the universe), so she was safe from the
inanimate, no matter how terrible.

Entering the final sanctum, the air itself tugged at her like
the surface of a fluid, a meniscus. Her garments floated,
pressed the firm shape of her body for an instant like wet
clinging muslin, floated again. Shem stared at her with con-
stricted eyes from his escritoire at the centre of a room of
spiteful mirrors (every surface hard, curved, brilliant as
mercury, throwing his infinite images and, now, hers), his
left hand slowly lowering a quill cut from a pinion of the
dazzling birds outdoors, his right hidden at his lap. With a
voice like some old industrial mechanism he told her: "It is
too soon. Nobody is here. Go away." But his hidden hand
jerked in a spasm.

"I'm Mahala," she said, poised on one foot, baffled by the
repetitions of light and the million dark retreating icons, and
then, focusing: "Oh! Oh you poor man, what have they done
to you?"

Shem, black as obsidian (obverse, yes, of his absent mar-
moreal twin), rose to his shackled feet and leaned towards
her across the polished desk. His strong left fingers crushed
the pen; his withered right arm flopped. The skew of his
spine was not deformity but adjustment to the ruined spindle
which was his left leg below the knee. Beneath his flaring
nostrils (broader than hers, and flatter) the notched, botched
curve of his harelip writhed.

"It is my own doing," he said. "It is the punishment I
inflict upon myself, in failure." His speech appalled her.
Tenderness opened within her heart. "Our specialists diag-
nose a carnifying psychosomatic conversion. They cannot
decide if it is precipitated by shame or guilt." He laughed
horribly. "Bone and nervous tissue melt into flesh. It'll get

worse before it gets better. I can live in the knowledge that when his thousand years is up my father Shaun shall sit here witnessing *his* body rot." He strained toward her, muscles bunching uselessly against the shackles at his feet, hands scattering the sheets of vellum. In puzzlement he glared at her. "Or do I mean my brother Shaun? My son?" He lifted the escritoire and slammed it shatteringly against the mirrored floor; the floor failed to shatter. "Are you really here, then, girl? Come closer, let me touch you. It is — not — " he ground in agony, palatals blurred and lost, " — *time*."

Tremulously, she crossed the blinding floor and caressed his maimed face. He shuddered, right claw contracting.

"I seek the most miserable man in the world, for he is promised to me as my beloved."

"Jesus," Shem said. He turned his dark cheek into the curve of her hand. "You've come to the right place."

"Your poor feet!" Mahala cried, stooping, her breasts falling forward to his voracious gaze. With the knowledge I had given her she touched the shackles here and here and they fell from Shem's feet. He reeled, crashed, tore then like an animal at her garments and his own, while she looked up in pain and absolute incomprehension into his grotesque mad face, her love turning back like a poisoned barb to enter her body and burst her heart, and his seed gushing like flame into her womb. Mahala, my baby, my gift to those who had made me, did not cry out. In her shock and betrayal she convulsed like a deer slain for sport, while his seed coursed within her secret places to the ripe, waiting egg, and the breath blocked in her throat like ice.

I watched her ravishment in a rage violent as madness. I stormed within my metal prison. For ten million millionths of a second the Earth hung at the balance of oblivion. In my grief I activated the collapsicle fields; the ship, for a nano-second, crashed into infinite density and sucked at the world. For that period the world convulsed with Mahala's hurt. Monuments shivered and broke. The pleasure domes of the high places split, cracked, yawned. Oceans heaved; birds fell stunned from opaque air. Then my grief attained perspective. I shut off the fields and took the walls of the villa San Martino in my grasp and hammered them to a vibration of titanic speech.

"Shem, once lord of this Earth, what has thou done? For thy foul work this day, man, thou art curst. Stand back from the woman Mahala lest I smite thee into unending agonies."

My baby got to her feet as the man drew back to his knees, to his hands. All her lovely things were torn and smeared; she pulled them about her. Great sobs broke within Shem's chest, tears flooded from his eyes. He rose, staring at his multiple selves, wiping the tears away as they fell with his perfect right hand, standing straight on his straight legs, opening without cry or whimper his curved, sculpted lips. He could not elude her image in the silver walls. Sinking to the elegant chair he allowed his beautiful face to drop onto folded arms, and there Mahala left him to his belated, wracking remorse as she walked painfully away from that place and stumbled up the hill to my useless, bitter ministrations.

She did not tell Shaun that she was pregnant, and nobody in that lustrous, sterile city asked. The handsome people took her up as a bauble, the season's premier diversion. Masques, balls, prodigies of cloud-sculpture in her honour enzymatically illuminated: you name it. Her misery was deemed decorous. Remorseless in their appetite for frivolous titbits from my voyage across the universe in an optional black hole, they expressed a marked indifference for anything of substance. The lord Shaun was not himself stupid, precisely, yet he saw himself as a practical man, in love with mighty engines whose gizzards he delegated to underlings, a man born for conquest (but so too had Shem viewed himself, and would again), manfully dedicated to gaming and hunting. So predictable; I hung in that lonely orbit to which I'd removed myself and seethed with boredom. In feminine moods I knitted booties. At other times I raged anew and vowed vengeance. Mahala, meanwhile, ate lightly of their pastries but put on weight. She maintained her reserve and her chastity, to the veiled derision (and covert gratitude) of the court's ladies.

When her confinement was near Mahala made her announcement, to a minor flurry of astonishment, and suffered no lack of commentary arch, wry, languid, sardonic and scornfully droll.

"Are you hermaphroditic, then, my dear?" inquired Maureen O'Darlene de Raylene y McYamamoto, a porcelain matron nimble enough in the raising of her own skirts. "We've heard no faintest whisper of gentlemen at your bed-chamber, and surely you were alone in the vastness of space?"

Mahala regarded her coolly. Her ankles were swelling and an anguish of perplexed love frayed her nerves.

"The children have a father, Madam."

"More than one little piccaninny? How delicious."

Mistress Maureen O'D. drifted away to the needless shade of a huge-leafed tree. The babies struggled, kicking, and my own darling child pressed her locked fingers on the drum of her belly. In the open compound Shaun and the hearties of his entourage were superintending the harness for their day's hunt. Autumn was well along, bright enough but smoky; soon the ground would be too cold for the vast gastropods. One of the fine men, chivvying his mount with an excess of vigour, slipped in a trace of the great snail's mucus and went arse over tit, to the raucous glee of his colleagues. The beast's behemoth head swung down and its forward tentacles extruded, eyes moist and sad. The fellow's swagger-stick came up in a brutal stinging slash, and the snail recoiled into its richly textured shell. For all the mass it mounts on its mutated vertebral bracing, *Helix horribilis* is a timorous animal. Handlers came out shouting and cursing. The snail's master stalked off to restore his splendour, and Mahala watched from her isolation as the animal slowly came about and glided away, ten metres of damp leather and armour-plating skimming as many centimetres of glistening slime.

Shaun was waiting at her elbow as she withdrew.

"Fine creatures, aren't they, my dear? Won't you change your mind and ride to the hunt? The experience is exhilarating — nothing like it! — and I promise you it's smooth as silk, can't possibly harm your . . . condition."

"My lord, I do not approve the way you treat the animals — these snails, and those you hunt. Besides, there is always the chance, no matter how remote, of an accident." Somewhere, fallen leaves were roasting in a fire, sweet to her flaring nostrils. And decision came upon her, crystalline, unheralded. Mahala touched the gloved wrist of the tall pale man and looked directly into his eyes, into a gaze equal to that poet's on the cold southern island. "The babies are your brother's children."

There was no motion in his body. At last he said:

"Shem's heirs?"

"Yes."

"Impossible." Then, "Do you understand? Now I must have you destroyed. If there is any chance," said he, fully conscious of irony, "no matter how remote . . . "

"My babies and I are safe," Mahala said with composure.

"We have the protection of the cybersystem."

In fury, he lashed his open hand across her face. "You stupid gravid bitch!" I waited, poised to kill him, and knew I *must* not, not yet, if ever. Wormwood. I watched as he stood there, regal in his martial kilts, as he spoke at once through his devices to men and machines deployed across the tamed globe.

I watched as he looked into the image of that empty mirrored room.

He took Mahala through a hushed, distraught throng to his throne room and showed her the millennial history which was there. She was not afraid. My darling child knew (and I knew she knew, through the anchored neural net which was part and not part of her) that she had stepped beyond history, beyond myth, into that dislocation which ends an age and sees another born. The babies kicked and kicked. Soon her labour would begin.

"Ten thousand years!" Shaun roared. Yes, now he was roaring, now it was coming home to him authentically. The tapestries and friezes seemed to shake to his wrath. "A cycle fixed in eternity! Do you imagine that I rejoice through all those days of my thousand years of exile, through my mutilation and the envy which gnaws at my entrails? Is it easy to share this throne with my other self, with my father, my brother, my son Shem? It is *not* easy. I tell you it is not. But it is the way the world must be, it is ordained, it is *duty*, goddamn it, you swollen sow witch."

Tones shrilled the air, lights pulsed, phantom figures came and departed without physical presence. Shaun's machines were hunting, scouring the earth.

"Besides," he told her, his face mottled like bloody marble, "the thing is impossible. You have allowed his escape, but he cannot be the father of your bastards."

He was here, an apparition told him. And later here, said another. There is furtive mobilization of men and weapons, reported a third. Nausea afflicted Mahala; panting, she found a chaise and lowered herself to its comfort, lifting her tired legs. Contractions began. She called out to me, silently, and I dropped from orbit like a bomb to wait for her demand.

The interstellar vessel hovers above the palace, a phantom informed the lord of the world. We cannot bring it down. We advise caution with respect to the woman. Midwives are standing by in the anteroom. Her time is close at hand. He brushed them aside, insensate, prowling electronic corridors for his enemy brother.

"This is *why* it is impossible," he explained in tight, bitten words. "He is sterile, as am I. It is a consequence of our joint nature." He took her jaw in the grip of his fingers. I began to burn through the roof and the defences of the palace, careful not to damage the art. If he started getting really rough I had faster techniques at my disposal.

"We are like the snails you viewed with such disdain today in the compound — bred to a purpose, monstrosities outside and above nature, yes, but the end of our line. Our seed is defunct. I have had a million women; their wombs have never quickened. Woman, I say you are a *liar*."

The lord Shem has begun his march, the shades cried in panicky voices. His war machines are bearing down on us, and we are caught unprepared.

"The babies are Shem's," Mahala stated quietly.

A spasm shook her, then, and she cried out. Fluids broke upon the ancient stone paving. I peeled open the Michelangelo ceiling above them and lifted her into my waiting body.

There was blood, tearing, a gonging in the earth too profound for human ears. Blood there was, and lacerated flesh, and the lamentation of orphans. Shem came into the high places mounted on a giant lizard, his hands blazing with hot blue flame. Shaun stood atop his burning palace, in the stinking confusion, and his shields dazzled like the sun's face. I hung above it all, at the moon's orbit, and wondered at the terrible duty I had discharged. I longed for the balm of Those Who burned without conflagration, there in the frozen darks at the occlusion of space.

The babies howled.

Mahala, my child, held them to her swollen breasts, hugged them to her, and wept with love and grief.

The twins are girls. I saw to that.

Inhabiting the Interspaces

Philippa C. Maddern

(1979)

The important thing was to take notice when things changed, because changes meant danger of discovery. One had to be very sharp-eyed and careful; the nightly tour of the building was enjoyable, but also a necessity — the room-by-room, step-by-step, space-by-space check that everything was as it had been.

She had a routine of her own, and that in itself was pleasant. It was good to feel the same slight regret every evening at leaving the comfort of the three-cornered cave behind the display boards stacked against the conference room wall. It was reassuring to go down, every night, and get the lumi-torch from where it sat on the window ledge of the men's toilets every day, soaking in the light to give back at night. To be sure, the torch had come into the building with her, and was not now as efficient as it had been; but then mostly she knew the building well enough to do without it. It was security, too, against the odd time when there was up-heaval in the building, and she had to take to the dark spaces in the ceilings and behind the walls.

Then it was time to start the night's first purposeful potter along her own laid-out track, starting from the base-ment, through the canteen (picking up the odd slice of kabana or bread or soy-bean munchie along the way), up around all the offices, rifling quickly through the desks, hunting the kitchen fridges for milk, nosing among the office memos and rubbish bins, absorbing bits from the small stores of biscuits, chocolate, sugar, brandy, vitamin pills, apples in bottom drawers along the way, up to the calm carpeted rooms on the fifth floor with their nuleather chairs and wooden desks. It was a slow progress, and demanded time and concentration; yet it was reassuring to search out food bit by bit, in inconspicuous nibbles and swigs, to ponder information, snaffle forgotten keys, search the workshop for handy bits and pieces.

There were not many places she could not get into. The hidden safe in the biggest office (but that was electronically keyed to palm print and voice control) and one or two filing cabinets, whose keys she had never found and whose locks had no space for the slip of plastic which worked well elsewhere — but that was all. The rest was her territory, unchanging and manageable.

After the prowl, there might be time for racing round the building (eight minutes by the basement clock was her fastest time, locking and unlocking as she went). Or she could go to one of the offices, sit in its desk chairs, and read its in-trays, letters, and diaries; or there was the maintenance room to go through (not of course using the machines, which would be noisy, but just touching up keys with a file, or sharpening the stolen chisel which she kept in the leg pocket of her jumpsuit). Then again, there were food caches to replenish, and a wash every few nights was a good thing; a person depending heavily on their sense of smell cannot afford the distraction of their own stink.

So the night passed and, at the end, she would replace the torch, and go down to the basement, locking herself into the workroom cupboard and dozing quietly while the cleaners came and went. Then, after she had heard them shuffling and joking and bye-byeing their way out, it was time to go back to the cave in the conference room; to lie on its furry floor, watching the blade of light on its straight wall strengthen and broaden as the day grew; to drowse through the hours, waking sometimes to the tramp-shuffle of feet, the drawing back of chairs, the slap of papers on the table, and the argument of the day-people's voices; until the dark came, and it was time to start again.

Once upon a time (so the story in her head ran), a girl like her had walked briskly through the daytime doors, into the lift, up to the second floor, into the personnel manager's office. There she had had her papers stamped, and walked out, falsely calm, marginally cool, intelligence thinly overlaying terror, into yet another office, after another regulation forty-day lay-off, into another regulation twenty-day work shift. In despair at the constant sickening shifts of living, she had approached the console, been assigned a desk — and found there, for the first time in such a situation, traces of the previous occupant. There on the wall, beside the chair but below desk-level, was a collection of pictures, cuttings, and extracts — all size-reduced, it is true, and taped very inconspicuously to the cool cream plaster, but nevertheless evidence of some continuity, some stability.

She spent the rest of the day dropping hand-scanners and sheets of paper and trays of clips so that, in pretending to search for them, she could read, gradually, the whole collection. It was fortunately eclectic rather than sequential. A few details stuck in her mind still; ingenious limericks, a series of cartoons about the consistent hopelessness of a child playing baseball, a small poem about mice and men living in the spaces left vacant by each other. But mostly it was the underlying premise that continuity was possible that she remembered. Outside, in the sliding networks of the world, people moved endlessly from city to city, following the miniscule regional rises in job placements, restless anonymous conglomerate crowds. Here beside her desk was stability.

It was, indeed, a seminal time in her life, a time when all occurrences clicked neatly into one implication, without volition on her part. One day there was a momentary power failure, and she saw the office for a moment safe and calm, all its efficiencies and activity smoothed out by the weight of the dark. Another time, at tea break someone commented on the strange coincidences of his coming back here as a clerk when he had been a cleaner here last year. Someone else asked what the cleaning shift was like, and he said, not bad, except for the hours — having to get to work at five-thirty every morning nearly killed him. Potential difficulties solved themselves at every step. Utilitarian fashions were in, so it was easy and inconspicuous to buy a well-pocketed black jumpsuit. A notice appeared on the fridge at work —

THERE HAVE BEEN COMPLAINTS IN THE PAST WEEK OF FOOD THEFTS FROM THIS FRIDGE; IF THESE DO NOT CEASE THE FRIDGE WILL BE REMOVED

— but everyone said it was only a threat, because these things worked themselves out with change of shifts. Every day, it seemed, new motivations appeared. Newsprints reported moves to shorten working shifts and promote longer and more varied lay-offs, in view of the rising production/population ratio. A friend died; he had gone swimming while on a high, and his companions reported that he had said, "The deep sea is beautiful", then simply closed his eyes and sank as if by will-power. Not realizing what he was doing, and being somewhat high themselves, they had failed to rescue him.

It was easy, after that, to imagine him sliding beneath the nervously shining surface of the sea, deeper and deeper into the green space beneath, trails of perfect silver bubbles marking his path downwards. Always in her mind the bubbles rose quickly at first, and then increasingly slowly, and at last stopped; and they and his body hung suspended in a great stillness.

So one night before the end of her shift, this girl, instead of leaving the building, had locked herself in a cupboard, and waited for the lights to go out. Afterwards, she had wandered, panicky and exhilarated, around the few rooms to which she had access. Early in the morning, she had walked out unchallenged, and spent the rest of the day in the carpark, in the company of four sleeping meths drinkers.

At the end of her shift, she bought an expensive new lumitorch, told all her acquaintances that she was going to spend her forty days bush-walking around Hattah Lakes, and hinted that she was thinking of taking off for Central Australia. On the last day, she walked into the building carrying a limited-life plastic bag with a supply of food, the torch, a screwdriver, and other odds and ends which she thought would be useful. Most of them proved instead to be useless, and were ditched. The few good choices she carried around with her all the time. A lot of the food was eaten by mice (she cached it in the wrong places). The bag, dropped from a window, sat tangled in the sun for a few days before degrading into invisibility, and she disappeared from the unstable glare of her daytime life.

She still thought of that girl often, not exactly for the pleasure of the memory, but because the contrast between her inefficiency and clumsiness then, and her present wisdom and knowledge and skill, was comfortingly sharp. That first girl's life, for some weeks, had been full of alarms, noisy mistakes, unseen opportunities, missed information. Now, her life had settled, for the first time ever, into a constant routine, every day and every night the same, for ever and ever.

Fairly regularly she revisited the picture sequence by her original desk, noting with some pleasure the failure of attempts to clean it off (the original compiler had cannily used bond-tape, which was now firmly integrated into the plaster) and the occasional small additions (moustaches on the cartoon figures). But this time, as she faced it; an inkling of more serious unfamiliarity with her surroundings made itself felt. The sequence, on closer inspection, proved to be the same; but something in the room was different.

Switching off the torch, she sat back on her heels, and considered. New sounds? Draught? Temperature change? Smell — smell, yes, there was a whiff of something unusual here. By licking her finger and rubbing it on her nose, she brought it up stronger — a metallic, chemical smell, not immediately threatening, but suspicious. Careful prowling tracked it down to a desk at the opposite end of the room; the smell was printing ink from a newsprint lying open on the desk top, the cheap quick-drying ink of a tabloid print-out, very rarely smelt in the office.

Now that she had identified it, she could afford to be curious. Opening the torch, she played the light over the page. At first, it was disappointing, nothing but fuzzy pictures with meaningless captions; then her eye caught the paragraph scanned in red to mark the reader's interest. It ran:

HUMAN MOUSE-TRAPPED. Mice? Rats? or just a new life style? London police reported today the capture of a man they claim has lived in an office building for eight years unknown to regular workers.

"He must have been a regular human mouse, stealing food, sleeping in corners," said one of his "trappers".

Message for any other mice is "Watch Out", though — I hear there's new kinds of traps getting ready for them.

Otherwise — who knows? — might be just the life for some of you "mousy" types out there . . .

And so on, filling up space with a lack of information.

She stood for a while, pondering over it, and whether it might be a threat. On the one hand, it was in London, which was a long way away, and it had nothing really to do with her. On the other, the whole article began to seem like a little eye, peering up at her inquisitively from the desk top. It made her angry; what right did they have to take someone out of his home territory? But then again, what could she do about it? She never moved papers on desks; that was asking to be found out. For a moment she thought of putting it into the shredder. Would the owner think the cleaners had taken it? Or would he simply forget about it? It depended, of course, on how important it was to the owner (H. Jorgensen, according to the panel on the desk). But how was she to know? It was scanned, so Jorgensen must have requested it, but why? For passing curiosity? Or, if not that, for what possible other reason?

She dithered for some time but, in the end, left the paper untouched. Instead, she went down to the maintenance room and resharpened her chisel, feeling somehow that it was the safest thing to do.

Next evening, when she went to check H. Jorgensen's desk, it was properly empty, and only the faintest whiff of tabloid ink lingered above it.

The following night, she knew the instant she crawled out of the cave that there was something wrong in the building. Crouched dead still at the entrance, she searched through all the impresssions coming to her out of the dark for the one who had alerted her; and, at last, heard again the ominous sound. Footsteps. Footsteps; not close, a floor away, maybe. She raced silently for the angle in the corridor which sheltered the heating pipes, and put her head against it. Down the pipes from the floor above, the echoes came plainly. Pace pace pace, stumble, clang. Shuffle. Pace pace. Silence. Pace pace pace.

She thought. Once or twice there had been people in the building at night, but mainly in the big offices of the half-time permanents upstairs, but never for long. This might be the same, though it did not sound so. Neglecting the lumitorch, she ran for the stairs and went up them as quickly and silently as a draught. The room on the corner had a window which overlooked the office where the footsteps sounded. Opening and closing the door with hardly a click, she moved in, avoided the table, and crept up to the window. If it was a day-person, there should be a light showing.

There was no light. All the long windows of the office were as blank as black paper in the thin gloom of the city. Worried, she moved to the corner of the room, near the pipes, and listened again. For a moment there was nothing; surely the person could not have got out so soon? But then, clear and loud, she heard the steps again, coming towards the near door of the office. As they halted, next to her but for the wall, she held her breath and heard, over the thumping of her own heart, the breathing of the person in the office, then the snap of the lock turning, then the door dragging over the carpet, and then the steps again moving out into the corridor.

There was a row of low seats along the corridor wall of the room, and she was under them in a fraction of a second, in case the intruder should come in. But, listening at the skirting board, she heard the steps go faltering on down the corridor, right to the dead end at the west wall, and come back again, and veer off towards the stairs.

She lay a moment to give the person time to move on, and to consider what to do. If it was only a day-person, it would not be long, but then day-people very seldom walked in the dark. Always before, she had been able to trace their progress through the building by the lights switched on and off, until they lit themselves safely out the door. But what if the person were a burglar? But then not many burglars worked in complete dark, either. A burglar would not be hard to cope with — she could avoid anyone like that all night, easily — but what would be the consequences? Quick to see the worst, her mind leapt to a picture of burglar alarms attached to every door. That would make things very difficult; not impossible, because she could dismantle some alarms, but difficult. Or what if the intruder were a security person? But there seemed no sense in having so slow and inefficient a security check.

She could simply keep out of the way all night; but then she would never know what the person had come for. Ignorance was dangerous. In the end, information could be more important than food. She wriggled out from under the chairs, and listened at the pipe again. The footsteps were still going down the stairs, but very faintly now. It was safe to come out of the room, and go fast-pace through the office and out and down the back stairs, to check on the intruder's route through the lower floors.

All that night she shadowed the intruder, at first at a distance, and then, as she became sure of her own skill against the newcomer's ineptitude, closer — once or twice, so close that she could catch the body smell, and be almost sure it was male. In one way it was so easy that it bored her; he fumbled slowly through the dark along a very small circuit of the building, while she ran in beautiful clever circles around him. Yet in another, it was uncanny, frightening; for he neither worked nor stole, but only walked, heavy-footed and alien, around her territory. In the end, he stayed so late that it was nearly dawn when she watched him out of the front door, and she had no time to scrounge before the cleaners came.

Standing, hungry and tired, in the basement cupboard, she thought ahead for the day. There was no reason that she could immediately see why an intruder at night should mean an upheaval in the day. But there might be a link that she did not see; the cave might not be safe. But the cave held her best cache of food, in a sealed niche under the floor. It would still be possible to hole up in the ceilings for the day, but she had no extensive food caches in the ceilings, because of the mice. Also, the ceiling hide-outs took time to reach; she would have to dislodge a light fitting and replace it behind her. There would not be time to do that and raid a food cache.

But the ceilings were undoubtedly safest; and thinking around all the hide-outs, she decided at last on the one reached through the washroom. That at least would leave her time for a drink and a piss before the day. For food, she would have to rely on the handful she always carried in her pockets, and whatever she could gather from the small ceiling caches; all right, as long as she could stock up tomorrow.

So the night did not end at its usual time, and was not restful, anyway. Standing balanced edgily on a wash basin, she prized out the light fitting, hauled herself in, and replaced it loosely behind her. After that, there was still the task (risky and slow without the lumi-torch) of inching through the ceiling fittings to retrieve food caches.

Even when she had finished, and lay uncomfortably in the cold stuffiness of the ceilings, there was still the future to be considered. The longer she thought, the more unusual and potentially dangerous the intruder seemed. Irrational happenings like that often meant large-scale disturbances in the building and, in case of one occurring now, the only thing to do was to collect resources and retreat almost wholly to the ceilings for some time. It was not a pleasant thought, and would mean a lot of hard work in the coming night; but, having thought it out, she felt a little less anxious, and at last, hours into the day, could fall asleep.

When her time-sense woke her at about nine that night, she was at first bewildered at the unexpected black dark, and hard angular surroundings. The edges of bad dreams were still cutting at her attention, but there was no time to think of them. She had her programme worked out — first, check for possible intruders, then general forage, and lastly, the demanding job of cleaning out food caches all over the building.

At the door of the washroom, she stopped to listen, and clenched her fists in anger as she heard, again, the slow footsteps of the intruder. Now she would have to check where he was and what he was doing before starting the night's heavy work. From the sound of it, the man was in the office on her own floor. Visualizing it, she remembered that the ceiling there was beam and presspanel, not always well laid. That would probably be the best place to spy on him. She ran for the lumi-torch, then back to the washroom, and went up into the ceilings again.

With the torch, ceiling work was much quicker. It took only a few minutes to reach the space over the office and find a crack beside one of the beams. She put her ear to it and listened; the sounds of someone in an unfamiliar place still came up clearly. Almost shutting off the torch, and angling the beam through the crack so that it just faintly lightened the dark, she squinted down. Nothing but a slice of desk and carpet. She moved to the next beam and, luckily, a slightly wider crack. Here, she could just see a blob and a curve, which resolved themselves, in a few moments, into the foreshortened arm and shoulder of the man. Then, as he took a step sideways, he swung into full view. She saw his head bent over something in his hands and, as he moved again, the thing became clearer — a long tube, almost like a very old gun, but thicker, with something that might have been a dial at one end. The man was swinging it round gradually, checking the dial every few degrees. Once he moved it up until it pointed almost directly at the ceiling, and she saw the faint grey circle of its muzzle clearly; then he clicked his tongue, and returned the tube to a level, and moved on a step, so that she lost sight of him again.

Whatever he was doing was incomprehensible, and therefore worrying, but it was slow. Also, it was not immediately threatening. A little reassured, she snaked back to the washroom, shut the torch, and fled off to the canteen, to collect waterproof containers, ferry them back to the washroom, fill them, and stack them one atop the other in rows in the ceiling.

She worked harder and faster that night than ever before in her life. She brought out her complete bunches of keys, raided the big refrigerators, recklessly pocketed whole chunks of cheese, packets of biscuits, cartons of bean-meal.

At first she stopped every few minutes to listen to the man working his way ponderously through the office, and its adjoining rooms. Later, the manic urge for speed and thoroughness almost overcame caution, and she went from floor to floor, rifling through the desks, taking quantities that she would never normally venture on (but in a time of office upheaval they would not be missed). Sweating, she raced up and down the stairs from cache to cache, clearing them all — the cave, the lift well, the locked filing-cabinet drawer whose one key she had stolen long ago.

Late in the night, she came at last to her best cache, large and safe, hidden in the angle between two cupboards, boarded in (her own work) with slats stolen from the workmen who built the cupboards. It was difficult to reach, accessible only if one practically crawled inside one of the range of cupboards. Also, it was some time since she had checked it, and the slats had stiffened into place. Knowing that there was not much time, she wrenched at them roughly, aware of the noise it made only as a subsidiary factor, less important than the need to dismantle the cache.

So she was unprepared, as she backed out of the cupboard with hands full of food packages, to see the man standing in the centre of the room, pointing his metal tube at her.

Unprepared; but she had long ago learned to be quick. Before the packages had hit the floor, she had seen that he blocked her way (there was no second door to this room), and seen too that, though he had found her, he seemed hardly able to see her — standing stock-still, looking straight at her, as if he had never learned the trick of seeing sidelong in the dark.

The chisel came easily into her hand; she leapt just to the left of the man, slashing out and downwards, feeling the blade catch on cloth, then on flesh, then drag free. But the man himself had sprung back, quicker than she expected. He landed backed up hard against the door, one hand still grasping the tube, the other raised in defence, but still peering uncertainly through the gloom.

The thing might be a gun. She stopped, crouching, chisel still poised for stabbing. The man said something, and she snarled at him; belatedly, the words became meaningful, if not sensible.

"Wait; it's all right, I'm a friend."

She did not answer, her mind crowded with plans for getting him away from the door, for killing him, for disposing of his body.

"I'm a friend," he repeated. The tube wavered in his hand.

No point in killing him. If she hid him in her part of the building, he would stink her out, and if she put his body anywhere else, there would be an investigation. But what to do with him? She snarled again, and feinted with the chisel.

He dodged, and his head thumped against the door.

"Out," she said, gesturing.

"I only wanted to see — "

"*Out.*" The first time she had raised her voice in the building. The ring of it, down the corridors, through the pipes, the lift shafts, the ceiling spaces, terrified her with its noise and unfamiliarity.

"I won't hurt you," he said, moving sideways, trying to keep an eye on her.

"What's that?" She gestured to the tube.

"That? Oh, that's all right. I'm sorry. It's not a weapon or anything. It's only an infra-red detector." Then, when she did not answer, "Really, it's all right. I made it myself. You can look at it if you like."

He reached it out to her. She struck at him, and he jumped back, dropping the tube on the floor, where it bounced harmlessly.

They faced each other, still and tense in the dark.

He began to speak again, the words slipping out of his mouth so fast that her unpractised ear missed patches of them.

"Look, I saw this article, and I thought I'd . . . interesting . . . try for myself . . . study . . . the other night, did you know? . . . okay, you're scared I . . . won't stir things up . . . find you . . . "

She laughed, and gestured with the chisel towards the door. "Out."

Cautiously, he backed through the doorway, and she followed, shepherding him down the corridor, out to the east stairs where the gloom was already lightening, down and around and down and around towards the exit.

At the stairs, he bravely turned his back to go down forward. Once he said, "I'm not going to stir things up for you, you know that, don't you?"

Unable to think of any of the terms of abuse she had once known, she flung out at him, "*Jorgensen*", the only human name she could remember.

He half turned, in surprise. "How did you know?"

"Get out."

"What's your name?"

But she did not answer, having forgotten it long ago.

On the ground floor, two squares of pale grey light were already lying on the entrance tiles before the door. The cleaners would soon come in. He turned on the threshold, and said, "I could be useful, you know. You don't know, but there are ways they could find you out. You might have to move, and you wouldn't know where to go." In the light from the door, the sticky patch on his dark shirt where the chisel had caught him was plain to see. She hesitated, unwilling to approach the door; but the sight of him, braver, feeling safer now he was near daylight, was too much for her. She feinted to his left, then doubled back neatly, and drew the chisel in an elegant line across his face from one cheekbone to the opposite jaw. Blood sprang out to meet the blade, and he cried out, crouched hands to face, humiliated; then turned, scrabbling for the door, and stumbled out.

Shivering, she watched him run 20 metres from the building, looking back in case she was following. Then, appalled by the near daylight, she turned herself, fled upstairs, grabbed the metal tube (no time to worry about its possible dangers) and raced for the ceiling.

All the years, all the days, all the hiding, the careful secrecy, wasted. "You only have to be wrong once." Who had said that, long ago? On what work shift had that ultimate arrogance terrified her? For it was true; forget once to look around, and you could be discovered.

Nothing lasts; not memories, nor time, nor place, nor safety, nor secrecy. Nothing will keep, and nobody cares about it as she does. "It'll be all right," they said when she wept and begged not to grow up, for childhood to last. "It's wonderful for you young folks," they said, "nothing like all the unemployment when I was young" — dragging her from one job, one building, to another and another and another. "I'm a friend," they said, tramping carelessly through her territory.

Nothing will keep.

Perhaps if one made a world, right from the start; built it piece by piece, space, stars, planets, sea, land, plants, animals, humans, cities, all with one purpose; embedded in it everywhere directives that would last for all time; all to provide one niche for its creator, a place exactly appropriate, where nothing would disturb her and she would disturb nothing; perhaps then one would be safe, one would be left alone.

But she had left a mark on someone; they knew about her now.

The metal tube fitted awkwardly into the ceiling. Squinting down at the dial, she saw in vague wavering outline the pictures of the cylinders and pipes, coiling and sprouting from each other. Following the direction of its muzzle, she saw that it must be picking up part of the hot-water system, beyond the concrete beam. So Jorgensen had told the truth about one thing, anyway. But that did not confirm the rest of his story. He was out of her reach, in a different world. She could kill him — but he could safely lie to her. She waved the tube gently through the short act of its possible movement, watching the pictures wriggle and glow on the dial.

There was little reason, now, to come out of the ceilings at all; but neither could she remain there in peace. At any moment they might come to find her. She was always in danger. During the day, habit kept her still, but in the nights she came out for brief periods, to wander nervously around the building, imagining voices, footfalls, smells, changes, everywhere. Always, she was too afraid to stay out long, and always, returning, she thought of another place she should have checked, more information she might have looked for.

The ceilings began to fret her; the narrowness of them, the chill, always the cold smell of concrete. Narrow spaces had never worried her before; had always seemed safe, in fact. But there is a terrible difference between a niche you have chosen for yourself, and a corner someone else has forced you into.

One night, driven by a great anger against the day-people, who could not even leave her to enjoy the space she had found for herself, she went back to Jorgensen's desk, longing to show him what she thought of his stupid arrogant curiosity. It would be good to threaten him, to have him afraid again. She took the chisel in her hand, ready to break his name panel, slash his chair, gouge his name in the plaster — she had thought of many pleasant ways to frighten him.

All useless, of course. She could not hurt him without betraying herself, or even attempt to harm him without betraying her own position of weakness.

The smell of paper was in the air as she approached his desk, as if conjured up by the memory of the other time she had come there. Coming closer, however, she saw that it was no hallucination — a square of paper was indeed lying there. Time, perhaps, had stopped and doubled back on itself. Maybe Jorgensen had never come and found her with his sensitive metal tube, and there were second chances after all. Yes, and maybe I did create the world as well, she thought sourly, recognizing that the paper smell was different this time. An office print-out smell it was, a memo smell.

She did not really want to read it — she no longer wanted to stay near the desk at all — but old lessons reasserted themselves (never let information go by). She shone the torch on it, and immediately the nasty word "infra-red" caught her eye — once in the text, and again at the side of a diagram at the bottom of the sheet. A true Jorgensen word, she thought, forcing herself to read slowly, from the top:

Memo No. 713, 8th Nov. To all personnel.

For some time, ministerial directives have been received on the subject of building security. At the last DM, the motion was put and carried that:
A sub-committee be formed to investigate methods of securing office space from intrusion and damage.
The sub-committee has been in operation, and recommended to the Buildings Committee on 15th July that an A-T Model Securobot be purchased for the task. Grounds for recommendation of this particular model were as follows:
1. Multi-purpose faculties (see diagram) including stair-climbing program.
2. Local manufacture, ensuring ease of servicing.
3. Cost-effective as per study carried out by the sub-committee (see attached sheet).
Accordingly, an A-T Model Securobot (new) has been purchased, and will commence operations on all general areas of the third, fourth, and fifth floors from 10th Nov. Office personnel are reminded again not to leave personal articles on or around desks after the afternoon shift, as this may impede the robot.

There was a diagram, with its ring of labels: "Audio-sensors", "Olfactory sensors (including smoke-triggering device)", "General alarm circuits", "Infra-red scanners", "Light scanners", "Stair treads", "Guaranteed 10-year power unit."

She stood looking at the diagram for a long time, thinking in a detached way what a good machine it was, and how well it covered all the skills she had herself built up over the hundreds and hundreds of hard nights. What would she not give to have eyes which would see through walls, ears to pick up pulse-beats three floors away, no need to eat?

Too late now to develop skills. The day-people had found a way to take her space from her; not by coming themselves, but by a cowardly sending of their machines to drive her out.

There was nothing to be done, of course. She stayed one night longer, but the tension of waiting for the machine was too much for her. She could have faced a person — she had done so with Jorgensen — but she had no power to threaten a robot.

Early the next morning, submerging one terror in another, she went down to the doors for the last time, and stepped out into the strange light of pre-dawn, and the restlessness of the wind.

There was a man standing hunched in a coat some way from the door, and she dared not wait for him to go away. As she passed him, hurrying to look for a place to hide from the day, he turned round, and she saw, out of the corner of her eye, the half-healed scar running diagonally across his face.

"You saw the memo," he called.

She walked on without answering.

"I wanted to warn you," he said, walking a line parallel to hers, two or three metres away.

"You told them," she said; but he shook his head. The wind was blowing eddies of dust around their feet.

"I'm a researcher," said Jorgensen, after a while. But that was like all his talk, information in a vacuum, impossible to believe one way or the other.

The light was strengthening. She saw, looking around in horror, that a great paved plain stretched on all sides of them. She and Jorgensen were the only two things moving in the vast still space.

"Soon be daylight," said Jorgensen.

Coda: The Shift Toward Fantasy
1957–1979

The items in this section represent the shift toward fantasy in current Australian science fiction. Dal Stivens' story, "The Gentle Basilisk" (1957), is included as an example of "pure" fantasy from a writer who has always moved freely between science fiction and fantasy, and whose reasons for such experimentation appear to be personal rather than a function of the "spirit of the times".

Lee Harding's disturbing urban fantasy, *Displaced Person* (1979), is most certainly a response to the *zeitgeist*, for Harding's earlier literary efforts had all been more readily identifiable as science fiction. The stories by Michael Wilding and Peter Carey should also be seen in this context, for both seek to convey an uneasy apprehension about the nature of reality, suggesting that the inner life of the imagination may have more validity than so-called public "reality".

Dal Stivens' "The Gentle Basilisk" appeared in *The Scholarly Mouse and Other Stories* (Sydney: Angus and Robertson, 1957); Michael Wilding's "The Words She Types" appeared in *The West Midland Underground* (St Lucia: University of Queensland Press, 1975); and Peter Carey's "Report on the Shadow Industry" appeared in *The Fat Man in History* (St Lucia: University of Queensland Press, 1974). The excerpt from Lee Harding's *Displaced Person* (Melbourne: Hyland House, 1979) comprises pp. 49–62.

The Gentle Basilisk

Dal Stivens

(1957)

An orphan basilisk grew up alone in an African desert. He
was innocent of his true malevolent nature and regarded himself – when he thought of himself at all – as an ordinary
kind of serpent and not very difficult from the vipers with
whom he shared the desert.

He was a gentle little serpent, aesthetically dispositioned
and given to sniffing the flowers of the hardy desert shrubs;
he was unaware that mature basilisks have breaths so
poisonous they blast shrubs and burst stones asunder.
Accordingly, his surprise was great when one day in young
manhood he smelt one of his favourite shrubs and saw it
wither under his bulging eyes.

"Astonishing!" he cried and breathed exploringly on a
neighbouring shrub. It died in seconds. "I did it, then," said
the gentle basilisk. He was so shocked he burst into tears.
He retired into a cave and stayed there for three days. On the
fourth he crawled out and wriggled determinedly across the
desert.

"I'll seek the help of the holy man who lives in the Blue
Cave," said the young basilisk, averting his head as he
approached a shrub. "He is a wise man and may well know
how to help me."

The ancient monk listened to the basilisk and shook his
head.

"There's nothing I can do," he said. "You are as God
made you. It is not for me to doubt the wisdom of the
Almighty in creating basilisks with malevolent breaths – "
here the hermit scratched his bald, scaling head – "though
sometimes I almost entertain blasphemous doubts. If you
were a human being with a soul, I could baptize you and

enjoin you to seek salvation. But it's clear you have no soul though your sentiments of not wishing to blast trees and burst boulders asunder — "

"Trees and stones," corrected the basilisk modestly.

"Trees and stones," said the holy man. "Your sentiments do your heart honour. I'm inclined to think you may have been born into a pagan state of grace — "

Here the hermit broke off in dismay at his words and crossed himself hurriedly. He resumed, "My son, be patient and accept your lot — and, pray you, continue to keep your head averted while I give you the benefit of such wisdom as the years have brought me. It is not for you to change your lot. That has been determined."

"Venerable father, I should like to accept your advice," said the young basilisk, "but I have heard it said it is possible to lift oneself by one's own shoestrings if the will is great enough — and, of course, if one wore any shoes."

"My son, it is no more possible for you to change your physical nature than it is for that gnat which I see hovering over you."

In that instant, the gnat perched on the basilisk's neck and stung him. The basilisk started violently, turned his head and wheezed painfully. The ancient withered into ashes.

The basilisk contemplated the tiny green heap with tears in his eyes. "I am sorry it happened to him for he was a good man and I meant well though I did not find his philosophy attractive. It could be argued his fate was predestined. He would not have wished it otherwise." And then added, "Boy, did you see how swiftly he went into a crisp!"

The young basilisk set off for the Yellow Cave where he knew there dwelt an alchemist.

"I should have approached him instead of that determinist," he told himself.

The alchemist listened to the young basilisk's story and burst into laughter when he heard of the fate of the hermit.

"Every dogma has its day even if it's a short one," he said. "Don't worry, my boy, we'll soon cure you. Every poison has its antidote. Just be careful to keep your head turned away."

The alchemist paced up and down the cave. "I'll soon have the answer. Anything is possible in nature. Man has merely to find the key to uncover all secrets."

He gestured. "Behold that great stack of dross lead, my boy. Any day now I'll turn it into the purest of gold." The alchemist shrugged and flung out both hands. "Why should there be any difficulty in solving your little problem, my boy?"

"None at all," said the young basilisk. "Unless — "

"Unless nothing!" said the alchemist contemptuously. "Your breath is poisonous. Find the antidote. Simple as ABC. I'll start with the premise that your breath is alkaline."

The alchemist poured a smoking liquid from a bottle into a spoon. "This is an acid and could well be the antidote. Swallow it down."

"It looks as though it might burn me," said the young basilisk doubtfully.

"Come, my boy, where's your love of experiment? Down with it. It can't hurt you. Basilisks are invulnerable — or nearly so."

"As you wish," said the young basilisk uncertainly. "But what's this 'invulnerable' business?"

"I see you are not merely timid but uneducated," said the alchemist. "Basilisks can't be poisoned. They can be slain by a knight but only if he is fortunate enough to avoid their evil breath."

"Invulnerable, just fancy that!" exclaimed the young basilisk joyfully.

"Let's waste no more time," said the alchemist and put the spoon down on the floor of the cave and stepped back. The young basilisk crawled towards it and sipped cautiously.

The acid stung his lips, tears blinded his eyes, and he tossed his head round in agony. "It burns," he protested through blistered lips. "You said it wouldn't hurt." The young basilisk threshed about for half a minute and then demanded, "Why don't you answer me, hey?"

His eyes cleared and he saw a small heap of ashes. The basilisk blinked. "I'm sorry it happened but he was unpractical and obviously brought it on himself by his cocksureness." He appraised the heap of ashes. "Golly, I crisped him to a smaller heap than the hermit!"

The young basilisk wriggled away. He had gone only a short distance when he was challenged by an armoured knight who drew down his visor and couched his lance.

"A moment, pray you, sir knight," cried the young basilisk. "I am not at all what you think I am. I am a basilisk with a gentle disposition and a genuine lover of shrubs and even boulders."

"Prepare yourself, basilisk!" said the knight sternly. "I am a plain man with no time for words."

"I beg you to believe me, sir knight. Although my breath

is poisonous, I would not harm any tree, crag, or living man. Indeed, I wish to render innocuous my malevolent breath."

"Wishes aren't achievements," said the knight shortly. "I treat things as I find them. I am a practical man. You are a basilisk. Basilisks have venomous breaths. Basilisks should be destroyed."

"But I wish no harm to any man," said the basilisk.

"That is what you say now," said the knight. "But you have the power to blast shrubs and split stones and power — as I have heard a wise man say — power corrupts. Look to yourself, basilisk!"

And shouting, "God be my guide", the knight drove the spurs into his horse and bore down on the basilisk. The serpent waited fearfully. Sweat started from between his scales. His heart beat rapidly. He panted and called piteously to the knight that it was unnecessary to slay this basilisk whatever others might be.

The knight thudded up to the little serpent, steel lance tip thrusting down, gleaming in the sun. Suddenly the lance head flickered with dancing blue flames. Blue fire raced up the shaft. The knight's suit shone red and blue-white. The horse dissolved into tumbling ashes. The incandescent suit of armour clanked into the horse's ashes.

"Golly!" cried the astonished basilisk. "It was terrific! I get more and more malevolent, it seems."

He wriggled away, meditatively slow. "It seems I cannot escape my nature no matter how I wish it." He gazed contemplatively at a large boulder. "I wonder what I could do to that?" He filled his cheeks and blew hard. The great rock split with a roar.

"Oh boy!" cried the young basilisk exultantly. "Did you see that?" He looked around him. "Let's see what I can do to that oak." He puffed hard. The oak shivered and then flew apart with a tumult of sound.

"I must be the most malevolent of all basilisks," he cried wonderingly. "What did that knight say about power? To hell with him! Now look at that mountain over there . . . and that army of knights at its foot. I wonder what I could do to them?"

The basilisk scratched his chin on a stone and then set off determinedly towards the flapping pennants.

Limbo

from

Displaced Person

Lee Harding

(1979)

Graeme Drury is an ordinary teenager growing up in suburban Victoria. He comes from a comfortable middle-class family, dresses casually but neatly, enjoys movies and records, has a NASA poster on his bedroom wall, and frequently goes out with his girlfriend Annette. He is an ordinary, normal youth.

Except that something is very wrong in his life. People seem to be ignoring him: waitresses, receptionists, tram conductors, even his parents. And to make matters worse, the world seems to be receding from him, for colours appear bleak and washed-out, and sounds and smells are faint and indistinct. Is he going mad? Is the world slipping away from him? Or is Graeme somehow becoming displaced from the world?

I wandered aimlessly through the transfigured night. Pale streetlamps shed a pallid glow. Eventually I found myself standing on the footpath outside Annette's house, staring glumly at the windows.

Well, why not?

Some feeling had drawn me there. What could I hope to find inside her house that had been denied me elsewhere? A place that was not as painfully close as my own home, and with someone to whom I felt closer than my parents, though in a different way?

My luck was in. The back door was open — it was a warm night — and the porch light was on. I heard popular music playing on the family stereo. The sound was so faint it might just as well have come from the other side of the street.

I took a deep breath and stepped boldly inside. I would have felt enormous relief to have been recognized, but I knew this was a forlorn hope.

The family were seated around the large kitchen dining table. They were busy with their meal and talking with great animation, the way some large families do.

Annette was the youngest of the three girls. Jennifer and Drusilla were twins — dark hair, slender, and very good-looking. Jenny worked as a secretary to some industrial firm. Drusilla did the same with some chemical company whose name I've forgotten. Both were very much career oriented. Annette was . . . different. A dreamer. She had always seemed poised on the edge of a far more adventurous life than her older sisters — I think it was this very quality which had attracted me to her — and she was not quite sure what to do with her life. Her father was someone very high up in governmental circles. Her mother was active in local community aid and welfare work. Nice people. Gregarious and helpful. I liked them. But Annette was the deep thinker, and also the most considerate in her relationships with other people. We were very close. She was good company and never made any demands upon our relationship. A pang of regret assailed me: Had I lost her too?

I walked slowly around the big table staring intently into each pair of eyes in turn, searching for some flicker of recognition. But their faces — even Annette's — wore the same dreadful pallor I had seen everywhere else.

Ghosts.

Or did I have it the wrong way around? Could it be that it was I — ?

The smell of cooking was missing. The bustling conversation of the family, with all its crisscrossing threads, was only a murmur on the threshold of my hearing. Moment by moment the real world — or what remained of it — was retreating.

When I had reassured myself that I had in no way trespassed upon their privacy, I proceeded to help myself to a few slices of tasteless roast beef that I carved from the platter on a nearby buffet. I grabbed some leftover baked potatoes — which I knew would be equally tasteless — and wandered out of the ghostly kitchen. I sat in the living room with my plate on my lap and got the food down. The stereo played whimsically in the background. Later, I helped myself to a cup of coffee. The coffee tasted warm, and that was all.

Later I found myself standing in Annette's room. Her bed

was unmade. Some clothes were scattered across the carpet, together with paperback books and magazines and unfinished schoolwork. I smiled. Oh, this was Annette's room, all right. No question about it . . .

I sat down on the edge of the bed and brooded. The coffee grew cold in my hands and I put it aside.

I must have lost all track of time — something I had been experiencing too frequently of late — for when I looked up suddenly I saw Annette was in the room.

It gave me quite a start. I hadn't heard her come in — how could I, with my hearing no longer reliable? I got up from the bed and was about to say something, to apologize, when I realized that it wasn't necessary. She didn't know I was there.

She shut her door and switched on the overhead light. The room seemed unnaturally dim. I glanced at her bedside clock. It was eight-thirty.

I watched her cross over to her desk, idly stopping to pick up some pieces of discarded underwear from the carpet.

I said gently, "Annette?" As if my presence, as if my affection could somehow bridge the abyss that kept us apart.

She tidied her desk.

I walked up behind her and said again, louder this time, "Annette? It's me, Graeme."

She went on with her work.

I reached out to grasp her shoulders. My hands clasped her
— and slipped
— slid away.

I could not hold her. I could not even touch her! My hands made contact only with the same viscous surface I had felt before on the banister back home.

And there was . . . a tension between us. It was almost palpable. As though an invisible barrier separated us — some sort of interface between *her* world and *mine.*

She switched on the desk lamp and sat down. She opened a book on medieval history, yawned, and with an I-must-get-this-done-tonight expression proceeded to study.

I turned away, shaking. There was an old-fashioned armchair by the window. I sat down in it, my head spinning. How much more? I asked. How much longer? Where would it all end?

I kept watching Annette. I gathered together every ounce of my will and tried to call out wordlessly across the room. *Annette, you have to hear me! I need you. I need help. I'm so lost . . .*

I kept this up until my head hurt. Then I went over to her again, hoping perhaps that mere proximity would add weight to my unspoken plea.

She had her head down, studying the printed page. I leaned my hands on the desk and hovered slightly to her left. I forged all my despair into what I imagined was a fiery psychic spear, shaped it, and hurled it into her mind . . . and her heart.

Annette — can't you hear me? Have you, too, forgotten me so soon? Help me. For God's sake — help me!

My hands were shaking and I grasped the edge of the desk firmly. I felt weak and dizzy. Any moment I expected to topple over . . .

Something happened. Annette looked up. There was a far-away look in her eyes. She held up a pencil and butted it firmly against her teeth. She frowned. A look of uneasiness crept into her eyes.

I took a step back, breathing heavily. Had I managed to get through to her, or had some other thought disturbed her concentration?

She got up from the desk and went out into the hall. I followed her. She picked up the phone and dialled a number — *my* number. There was an expression of concern on her face while she waited for the call to be answered.

And it was. She dipped her head when she talked and I couldn't make out a word of what she said. She spoke for perhaps thirty seconds and then hung up. There was a curious expression in her eyes. She gave a little shrug and went back to her room. I stared at the phone for a moment longer, then hurried after her. I slipped into her room just before she closed the door.

She went back to her desk and resumed her studies.

I collapsed in the armchair in a fit of despair. I had no way of knowing if my thoughts and feelings had actually reached her in some way and motivated her phone call; or if she had simply followed some intuition of her own.

I felt defeated. I didn't know what to do next. And I think that some kind of mental circuit breaker must have cut into my thoughts and saved me from a mounting hysteria, because the next thing I remember is waking suddenly from a deep sleep.

I sat up with a start. The room was not yet in darkness. Annette was in bed, reading by the light of a lamp on her bedside table. The time was eleven-fifteen. She wore summer-weight pyjamas and she had untied her long hair from a ponytail so that it was spread very attractively around her shoulders. Despite her dreadful pallor she looked achingly beautiful.

I could not move. I sat there watching. Abruptly she yawned, put aside the paperback novel she had been reading, reached over, and switched off the lamp. The room was plunged into darkness.

For a moment I was terrified. I had not been prepared for this sudden change in my surroundings. I tried to grasp the arms of the chair, but the upholstery felt oily under my hands and I could not get a firm grip. Again, the mysterious interface. I sat with my mouth open, heart hammering, staring into the darkness.

Slowly my eyes adjusted. I saw a faint glow creeping in through the curtains from the streetlamps outside. I could just make out Annette's features. She was lying on her left side, facing me. And although she was asleep her face wore a disturbed expression.

I could have reached out and touched her, my chair was so close. But I hesitated. The wan light gave her face a ghastly look. I turned quickly away.

I don't know how long I sat there, unmoving. I do remember that at no stage did I feel cold, and that struck me as rather odd, because at this time of the year the nights often grew cold.

I was cold *inside*, all right: That great lump of fear never left me for a moment. Eventually I fell asleep again. There wasn't much else I could do; the burden of so much thinking weighed me down.

Sometime during the night I walked in my sleep. I must have been dreaming and felt unbearably lonely. When I woke in the early hours of the morning I found myself lying beside her, on top of the bedclothes. She was still fast asleep.

I kept quite still. I wondered if I had been drawn to her during the night in search of a warmth and comfort I could not find within myself. I felt nothing underneath me. It was as though my body were supported on a cushion of air; I had no contact with the bedclothes, and there was no sensation of a bed yielding to my weight.

The interface again?

For a while I was too afraid to move, lest I disturb this strange equilibrium. Out of the corner of my eye I saw Annette stir. She sat up groggily and reached over to turn off the alarm. It must have shrilled, but I had not heard it. She slumped back on her pillow and lay there with a worried expression. She allowed herself another ten minutes to come to terms with the new day, then she got up.

She took off her pyjamas and stretched, yawning. And there was nothing prurient in the way I watched her. I had seen her naked before, but never like this. A beautiful body: small breasts, full hips, a slender waist and long legs. But now she was like a marble statue without a sheen. She stood poised on tiptoe for a moment, her languid arms stretched above her head and her image etched deep in my mind. Then she sighed, and broke the spell, and pulled on the Japanese happi coat I had given her for her birthday. It was a light-weight dressing gown with wide oriental sleeves, and it came down to midthigh. I remembered it as being bright red, with a vivid-yellow dragon motif. Now it was the colour of wood-smoke, and the motif was barely distinguishable. She tied the cord loosely around her waist and wandered sleepily out into the hall. Her face was sullen, and I wondered what bad dreams she had had, and if my presence had in any way affected them.

I managed to sit up. When I swung my legs over the side of the bed and set them down on the floor they seemed to give just a fraction under my weight.

I stood up. My legs were shaky. I took a few hesitant steps. I felt as though I were walking on some kind of trampoline. It seemed that overnight I had lost physical contact with the "outside" world. I wondered rather objectively what new developments awaited me. I felt curiously detached. Numb. I would by now have welcomed an end to my nightmare.

I made my way over to the window, getting accustomed to the slippery interface that now separated me from the "outside" world. It was rather like a sailor trying to find his "land legs" when he returned home.

I could not draw the curtains; they would not respond to my touch. I gave up and peered out through a chink along the bottom. The dreary greyworld was all I could see.

I held up my hands. They glared back at me, vibrant with life as the colour of flesh should be. The blue of my denims was a blinding affirmation of my self. This much, at least, had not changed. I took a deep breath, then called out: "Hello – is anyone there? Can anyone hear me?" And I heard my own voice ring out sharp and clear. But as for the rest . . .

The silence was complete. There was not even a ringing in my ears. The absence of any kind of sound was absolute.

I knew I was only tormenting myself by remaining so close to Annette. The more I hung around familiar faces and places, the more lonely I became, the more deeply I regretted my loss.

I waited until Annette returned from the bathroom. Her face had a freshly scrubbed look but the pallor remained. I watched her dress, conscious of the ache in my chest. "Good-bye, Annette," I said softly. There was no need to shout; she would never hear me. Now now. Not ever. I would have given anything to have reached out and held her, however briefly, before I left — but I accepted that this was impossible. The interface saw to that.

She shivered suddenly, as though someone had walked over her grave. Could that someone have been me?

I paused long enough for a lingering look into her dull eyes before I left.

I think I must have run — stumbled — half a block in blind panic before I came to my senses.

The pain of being so close and yet so far removed from Annette had sent me fleeing from her house. And it was only when I stopped to draw breath that I remembered I had not even tried to open the front door — *I had run right through it.*

Stunned, I looked back the way I had come. It was still early. Only a few people were up and about, their vague shadow shapes moving through the pervading greyness. Darker shapes of motor vehicles whispered silently by. It was too early for the morning rush. Overhead a solitary grey gull wheeled, curiously mute.

Not a sound reached me. Either I was deaf or I had been completely cut off from the "outside" world. I had been badly shaken by my experience with Annette, and I *had* bolted through her front door. I sat down — not on the foot-path but on the interface — and studied my predicament.

One: I now had no physical contact with the "outside" world. I walked on an invisible membrane which I called the interface; it kept me isolated from everything that mattered.

Two: I now had only a tenuous visual contact with my previous world. There was a multitude of individual grey shapes; some were the ghostly reminders of human beings, some were buildings, still others were inanimate objects which I had to look at closely to identify. Outlines were blurred, features almost indistinguishable.

Three: I had lost all auditory contact with the "outside" world.

Four: the interface that supported me was also a kind of prison.

Five — and this really shook me: It seemed possible that I could now move freely through what had once been solid objects in my previous world.

I tested this theory several times. I passed my hands cautiously through the stout trunk of a nearby tree; they met with no resistance. Growing bold, I deftly kicked my right foot through a fire hydrant; same result. The "outside" world lacked substance. From my viewpoint it was a ghost universe, a dreadful parody of the world I remembered.

Walking was difficult at first. I had to get accustomed to the slippery interface. But I persevered, and although I slipped many times, I never fell. I assumed that the interface also kept me correctly aligned in this nightmare world.

I wandered morosely through the greyworld, feeling more lost than I imagined any human being had ever felt before.

Limbo.

I dredged the name from somewhere in my cluttered memory. I think it must have been a literary allusion, but I couldn't remember the source. The Bible? Perhaps. The idea brought to me a vision of a region of neglect, of abandonment. A place of oblivion or a haven for lost souls, for discarded and forgotten people. Something like that. I was very confused. Discarded and forgotten by *whom*? That was what bothered me most: the great unanswered question. And the greyness seemed deeper than before.

I somehow managed to keep moving along the interface. There was really nothing else I could do. I was afraid that if I stopped for more than a moment, I would never get up again. And while I walked I wondered about the vast, silent greyworld and people who disappeared without trace, missing persons whose absence left no logical explanation. I wondered how many of them had suffered my fate. Perhaps God was a clumsy bookkeeper.

I considered Bishop Berkeley's famous conundrum about the tree in the courtyard: Was it there when there was no one to look at it? And I asked myself: Had I ceased to exist in the outside world because people had ceased to notice me?

I thought of Omar Khayyam:

'Tis but a Chequer-board of Nights and Days
Where Destiny with Men for Pieces plays;
Hither and Thither Moves, and mates, and slays,
And one by one back in the closet lays.

Was I dead?

The possibility chilled me. I had no memory of an illness or of any impending demise. I recoiled violently from the implication. Then I grew angry, and I remembered reading somewhere that when you're faced with a difficult problem and you get angry, why then you can act — you can do something about it.

I could not and would not accept the theory that I had "died" in the way that I understood the word. The events leading up to my "displacement" did not support this idea — nor did the pounding pulse in my throat; it was all the proof I needed to convince me that I was still alive and that something strange had overtaken the world.

I was still afraid, but I was determined to do something. It was not enough to stroll around and bemoan my fate. I would discover the secret of my imprisonment or die in the attempt.

All around me the ghostly rush hour had begun. I saw the blurred shapes of cars hurtling by without making a sound. Trams clanged silently down the centre of the road. Pedestrians hurried on their way to work, some seeking buses and trams, others hastily hailing passing cabs. And all this but a pantomime played out in varying shades of grey. People passed by me and around me and *through* me. I discovered that I had no more substance in their world than they had in mine. The curiously muffled sound of my own feet stumbling along the interface was the only break in this absurd continuity.

Then from somewhere nearby I heard a dog bark.

This sudden and unexpected sound transfixed me. The noise increased in vigour; it sounded like a small animal — a terrier, perhaps — lost and lonely and afraid, like myself.

Here, in Limbo?

Well, why not? I asked myself. It seemed possible that not only people but other life forms might get displaced from time to time. In which case —

I might not be alone after all. My heart raced at the possibility. But my sense of direction was unreliable. It had become disoriented by recent events. Try as I would, I could not trace the source of the sound — and it grew weaker every moment.

I made out the hazy outlines of a park on my left. Reason returned; I knew where I was. The barking brought forth no echo, but that was not surprising. It seemed likely that the animal would be somewhere in the park, so I hurried off quickly in that direction, slithering and sliding but somehow remaining upright on the slippery interface.

The soulful cry of the animal faded to a whimper. Poor creature! If we made contact then neither of us need feel alone. And if a dog had been displaced into my world then there was also the possibility that I might encounter other human beings . . .

But even as I ran through the park, blundering through the phantom shapes of bushes, trees, and benches, with no idea where the poor animal was, the air became suddenly still. As still as it had been before. Only my own hoarse breathing filled the greyworld. The barking was not repeated.

I stood quite still, straining my ears to pick up the slightest sound. I waited a long time, but I never heard that dog again.

Could I have imagined it?

No.

The sound had been real — as searing and as soulful as anything I had felt inside me since this mysterious business had begun. It had not been a renegade memory, but the first proof that I was not alone in this godforsaken place.

It was possible that I was not the first human being to have suffered the transition from the "outside" world into Limbo — and certainly not the last. But if others had experienced this before me, why had they not returned to tell their stories?

I recoiled from the possible answer. Had it been because they had never returned?

I faced a forlorn hope — but without it I did not see how I could survive in this dreary place. And then there was a matter of food: without it I would starve. Now I could not eat anything from "outside" — I would not even be able to grasp it; the interface would see to that. What then were my chances of discovering sustenance in Limbo?

I dragged my feet. They made a soft, soughing sound on the interface. I thrust my hands in my pockets again and looked downcast. Then I saw a splash of colour on the pavement.

I froze. The unexpected reappearance of colour in my monochromatic world dazzled me. Not that the object itself was unusually vivid: only a seagull, but the subtle shading of white and grey was a stunning contrast to the rest of my world. These colours *lived*.

I stooped down to investigate, my hands shaking with excitement. I could tell from its glazed eyes and lolling head that the bird was dead. I picked it up gently, feeling the last of its bodily warmth trickling through my fingers. Its yellow beak hung open and its sad eyes stared bleakly into death. There were no marks to indicate that it had been injured in any way.

Probably died of hunger.

And so might I.

A grim reminder of my position. I laid the bird gently on the edge of the side of the footpath — of the interface, that is — and straightened up, rubbing my hands on my jacket.

First the barking of an unseen dog, now a dead seagull. Limbo might not be as deserted as I had supposed, but the pathetic bundle at my feet was a warning of how my own fate might turn out if I did not find some source of food and drink. Already my mouth was parched with thirst.

I stepped around the dead seagull and resumed walking.

In time Graeme Drury encounters humans in the grey world of Limbo. He teams up with the street-wise girl, Marion, and the old tramp, Jamie, and joins in their monotonous routine of scavenging for food that has "come through" from the real world.

Then, abruptly, Jamie disappears — after complaining that he can sense " 'somethin' movin' around out there . . . movin' like a wind without a voice". Soon after, Marion disappears, and then Graeme himself starts to sense the gathering darkness . . .

The Words She Types

Michael Wilding

(1975)

Advertised it looked an interesting job: Writer requires intelligent typist. It sounded more interesting than routine copy-typing; and the "intelligent" held out the bait of some involvement. Amongst dreams had hung one of success as a great writer. Other dreams: but that one had hung there. So she answered.

The appointment required an old apartment block with heavy doors at the entrance, old, varnished wood, that swung to with a heavy oiled smoothness and closed off time at the street.

"What I expect is not difficult," the writer said; "accuracy, precision, neatness. And if you succeed in them, perhaps a little more, a little discretion. The initiative to correct, without constant recourse to me, slight carelessnesses of spelling, grammatical solecisms. But let us go along stage by stage and see how we find each other."

And within the heavy doors, the high-ceilinged still apartment, footfalls deadened on the soft carpet, walls sealed with wooden bookshelves carrying their store of the centuries, the windows double glazed against the sounds and temperatures of the street. And a small table for the tray of coffee or fruit juice or lemon tea to be placed, soundlessly. She missed only music, would have liked the room resonant to rich cadences against the deep polished wood and leather bindings.

She would come to her desk and at the right of the typewriter would be the sheets he had put for her. And as she re-typed those sheets she would place them at the left of the typewriter and as soon as she had completed a piece she would collate the sheets and the carbons and leave them in manila folders for him to collect from the drawers at the left of the desk.

The earliest days were easy, copying, from typescript. No problems, no uncertainties, no ambiguities. Occasionally he had jammed the keys or jumped a space or missed off the closing quotation mark; but often he had pencilled in the corrections himself. Later, though, perhaps as he became more sure of her, he omitted to make the corrections. And his typing became less punctilious. Words were sometimes misspelt, whether through ignorance or the exigencies of typing it was not for her to ask. He would sometimes use abbreviations, not spelling out a character's name in full but giving only the initial letter. And when he began to give her manuscript sheets to type from the abbreviations increased, the effort of writing out the obvious in longhand too much for him, unnecessary.

And she always managed. It was her pride always to manage, to transliterate from his degenerating scrawl that day by day yearned towards the undifferentiated horizontal, to expand the abbreviations, to fill out the lacunae with their "he said" or "she replied". Her intelligence at last being fulfilled she did not complain of the scrappier sheets that over time were presented to her. Her electric typewriter hummed quietly as ever, nothing retarded her rhythmic pressure on the keys.

He would write instructions in the margin of the drafts. Indications of where to fill out, where to add in, how to expand, interpret. And she would fulfil these instructions, incorporating them into the draft he had roughed out and presenting one whole and finished fabric. And when he offered sheets only of instruction, she knew his manner well enough to develop the sketched out plan as he required.

Was it a shock one morning to find blank sheets on the right of the typewriter? Yet her ready fingers took paper and carbons from their drawer and without hesitation touched the keys. Her eyes read over the characters as they appeared before her.

She read of a girl who saw advertised what looked an interesting job: Writer requires intelligent typist. It sounded more interesting than routine copy-typing: and the "intelligent" held out the bait of some involvement. Amongst dreams had hung one of success as a great writer. Other dreams: but that one had hung there. So she answered.

Without prompting her fingers touch the keys and tell the story. The girl cannot tell, as she writes this story of herself, if it is indeed of herself. Always the words she has typed have been the words he has presented, suggested, required. But are the words she types now any different from the other words she had typed? The girl cannot tell the truth of her situation, because for her to write is to give expression to his stories. Is this but another story she is typing for him, and the truth of her story irrecoverably lost? He has given her no notes from which to tell. And if it is not his story it is even more his story. For if she is telling the story of her story, it was he who established the story. The words she uses will be the words he has set up in setting up her story, even if they are coincidentally her own words.

She sees only what the keys stamp out on the blank paper before her. If it is her truth no one will know. He will collect the typescript in its manila folder from the drawer on the left, and will publish it whether the words were the words he required or were her words. Readers will read and register amusement or boredom or fascination or disdain, and her truth, if it is her truth, read as fiction will never after be available as truth, whether or not it ever was.

Report on the Shadow Industry

Peter Carey

(1974)

1.

My friend S. went to live in America ten years ago and I still have the letter he wrote me when he first arrived, wherein he describes the shadow factories that were springing up on the west coast and the effects they were having on that society. "You see people in dark glasses wandering around the supermarkets at 2 am. There are great boxes all along the aisles, some as expensive as fifty dollars but most of them only five. There's always Muzak. It gives me the shits more than the shadows. The people don't look at one another. They come to browse through the boxes of shadows although the packets give no indication of what's inside. It really depresses me to think of people going out at two in the morning because they need to try their luck with a shadow. Last week I was in a supermarket near Topanga and I saw an old negro tear the end off a shadow box. He was arrested almost immediately."

A strange letter ten years ago but it accurately describes scenes that have since become common in this country. Yesterday I drove in from the airport past shadow factory after shadow factory, large faceless buildings gleaming in the sun, their secrets guarded by ex-policemen with alsatian dogs.

The shadow factories have huge chimneys that reach far into the sky, chimneys which billow forth smoke of different, brilliant colours. It is said by some of my more cynical friends that the smoke has nothing to do with any manufacturing process and is merely a trick, fake evidence that technological miracles are being performed within the factories. The popular belief is that the smoke sometimes contains the most powerful shadows of all, those that are too large and powerful to be packaged. It is a common sight to see old women standing for hours outside the factories, staring into the smoke.

There are a few who say the smoke is dangerous because of carcinogenic chemicals used in the manufacture of shadows. Others argue that the shadow is a natural product and by its very nature chemically pure. They point to the advantages of the smoke: the beautifully coloured patterns in the clouds which serve as a reminder of the happiness to be obtained from a fully realized shadow. There may be some merit in this last argument, for on cloudy days the skies above our city are a wondrous sight, full of blues and vermilions and brilliant greens which pick out strange patterns and shapes in the clouds.

Others say that the clouds now contain the dreadful beauty of the apocalypse.

2.

The shadows are packaged in large, lavish boxes which are printed with abstract designs in many colours. The Bureau of Statistics reveals that the average householder spends 25 per cent of his income on these expensive goods and that this percentage increases as the income decreases.

There are those who say that the shadows are bad for people, promising an impossible happiness that can never be realized and thus detracting from the very real beauties of nature and life. But there are others who argue that the shadows have always been with us in one form or another and that the packaged shadow is necessary for mental health in an advanced technological society. There is, however, research to indicate that the high suicide rate in advanced countries is connected with the popularity of shadows and that there is a direct statistical correlation between shadow sales and suicide rates. This has been explained by those who hold that the shadows are merely mirrors to the soul and that the man who stares into a shadow box sees only himself, and what beauty he finds there is his own beauty and what despair he experiences is born of the poverty of his spirit.

3.

I visited my mother at Christmas. She lives alone with her dogs in a poor part of town. Knowing her weakness for shadows I brought her several of the more expensive varieties which she retired to examine in the privacy of the shadow room.

She stayed in the room for such a long time that I became worried and knocked on the door. She came out almost immediately. When I saw her face I knew the shadows had not been good ones.

"I'm sorry," I said, but she kissed me quickly and began to tell me about a neighbour who had won the lottery.

I myself know, only too well, the disappointments of shadow boxes for I also have a weakness in that direction. For me it is something of a guilty secret, something that would not be approved of by my clever friends.

I saw J. in the street. She teaches at the university.

"Ah-hah," she said knowingly, tapping the bulky parcel I had hidden under my coat. I know she will make capital of this discovery, a little piece of gossip to use at the dinner parties she is so fond of. Yet I suspect that she too has a weakness for shadows. She confessed as much to me some years ago during that strange misunderstanding she still likes to call "Our Affair". It was she who hinted at the feeling of emptiness, that awful despair that comes when one has failed to grasp the shadow.

4.

My own father left home because of something he had seen in a box of shadows. It wasn't an expensive box, either, quite the opposite — a little surprise my mother had bought with the money left over from her housekeeping. He opened it after dinner one Friday night and he was gone before I came down to breakfast on the Saturday. He left a note which my mother only showed me very recently. My father was not good with words and had trouble communicating what he had seen: "Words Cannot Express It What I feel Because of The Things I Saw In The Box Of Shadows You Bought Me."

5.

My own feelings about the shadows are ambivalent, to say the least. For here I have manufactured one more: elusive, unsatisfactory, hinting at greater beauties and more profound mysteries that exist somewhere before the beginning and somewhere after the end.

Select Bibliography

WORKS BY INDIVIDUAL AUTHORS

Anonymous. *Account of a Race of Human Beings with Tails.* Melbourne: A. T. Mason, 188–.

Antill, Keith. *Moon in the Ground.* Melbourne: Norstrilia Press, 1979.

Aulich, Chris. *It.* Sydney: Wild and Woolley, 1977.

Bailey, John. *The Moon Baby.* Sydney: Angus and Robertson, 1978.

Baxter, John. *The God Killers.* Sydney: Horwitz, 1965.

———.*The Hermes Fall.* St Albans, Herts, UK: Granada-Panther, 1978.

Boothby, Guy. *Pharos the Egyptian.* London: Ward Lock, 1889.

Braddon, Russell. *The Year of the Angry Rabbit.* London: Heinemann, 1964.

Broderick, Damien. *A Man Returned.* Sydney: Horwitz, 1965.

———.*The Dreaming Dragons.* Melbourne: Norstrilia Press, 1980.

Carey, Peter. *The Fat Man in History.* St Lucia: University of Queensland Press, 1974.

———.*War Crimes.* St Lucia: University of Queensland Press, 1979.

Chandler, A. Bertram. *Alternate Orbits.* New York: Ace Books, 1971.

———.*Beyond the Galactic Rim.* New York: Ace Books, 1963.

———.*Contraband from Otherspace.* New York: Ace Books, 1967.

————.*Empress of Outer Space*. New York: Ace Books, 1965.

————.*False Fatherland*. Sydney: Horwitz, 1968. Also published as *Spartan Planet*. London: Dell Books, 1968.

————.*Into the Alternate Universe*. New York: Ace Books, 1964.

————.*Rendezvous on a Lost World*. New York: Ace Books, 1961.

————.*Space Mercenaries*. New York: Ace Books, 1965.

————.*The Big Black Mark*. New York: D.A.W. Books, 1975.

————.*The Bitter Pill*. Melbourne: Wren, 1974.

————.*The Broken Cycle*. London: Hale, 1975.

————.*The Dark Dimensions*. New York: Ace Books, 1971.

————.*The Gateway to Never*. New York: Ace Books, 1972.

————.*The Hard Way Up*. New York: Ace Books, 1972.

————.*The Inheritors*. New York: Ace Books, 1972.

————.*The Rim Gods*. New York: Avalon Books, 1969.

————.*The Rim of Space*. New York: Avalon Books, 1971.

————.*The Road to the Rim*. New York: Ace Books, 1967.

————.*The Way Back*. London: Hale, 1975.

Cleary, Jon. *A Flight of Chariots*. London: Collins, 1963.

Collins, Dale. *Race the Sun*. London: Constable, 1936.

Cook, Kenneth. *Play Little Victims*. Sydney: Pergamon, 1978.

Cox, Erle. *Fool's Harvest*. Melbourne: Robertson and Mullens, 1939.

————.*Out of the Silence*. 1925. Melbourne: Robertson and Mullens, 1947. Rptd Westport, Connecticut: Hyperion, 1976, and Sydney: Angus and Robertson, 1981.

Dudgeon, Robert Ellis. *Colymbia*. London: Trubner, 1873.

Eldershaw, M. Barnard. *Tomorrow and Tomorrow*. Melbourne: Georgian House, 1947.

Elliott, Sumner Locke. *Going*. Melbourne: Macmillan, 1975.

Foster, D. M., and Lyall, D. K. *The Empathy Experiment*. Sydney: Wild and Woolley, 1977.

Fraser, Joseph. *Melbourne and Mars: My Mysterious Life on Two Planets*. Melbourne: Pater and Knapton, 1889.

Free, Colin. *The Soft Kill*. New York: Berkley, 1973.

Galier, W. H. *A Visit to Blestland*. Melbourne: George Robertson and Co., 1896.

Hamilton, M. Lynn (Hamilton Lewis). *The Hidden Kingdom*. Melbourne: N. Wentworth-Evans, 1932.

Harding, Lee. *A World of Shadows*. London: Hale, 1975.

————.*Displaced Person*. Melbourne: Hyland House, 1979.

————.*Future Sanctuary*. New York: Laser, 1976.

————. *The Web of Time.* Melbourne: Cassell Australia, 1980.

————. *The Weeping Sky.* Melbourne: Cassell Australia, 1977.

Hay, John. *The Invasion.* Sydney: Hodder and Stoughton, 1968.

Hume, Fergus. *The Expedition of Captain Flick.* London: Macmillan, 1896.

Iggulden, John M. *Breakthrough.* London: Panther Books, 1960.

Ireland, David. *A Woman of the Future.* New York: George Braziller, 1979.

Johnston, Harold. *The Electric Gun: A Tale of Love and Socialism.* Sydney: Websdale, Shoosmith Ltd., 1911.

Kirmess, C. H. *The Australian Crisis.* Melbourne: Lothian, 1909.

Lake, David J. *The Fourth Hemisphere.* Melbourne: Void Publications, 1980.

————. *The Gods of Xuma, or, Barsoom Revisited.* New York: D.A.W. Books, 1978.

————. *The Man Who Loved Morlocks.* Melbourne: Hyland House, 1981.

————. *The Right Hand of Dextra.* New York: D.A.W. Books, 1977.

————. *Walkers on the Sky.* New York: D.A.W. Books, 1976; and London: Collins Fontana, 1978; the latter edition is preferred by the author.

Little, William. *A Visit to Topos, and How the Science of Heredity is Practised There.* Ballarat: Berry, Anderson and Co., 1897.

Mackay, Kenneth. *The Yellow Wave: A Romance of the Asiatic Invasion of Australia.* London: R. Bentley, 1895.

Mather, Arthur. *The Pawn.* Melbourne: Wren, 1975.

McGiver, G. *Neuroomia: A New Continent.* Melbourne: George Robertson and Co., 1894.

Molesworth, Vol. *Blinded They Fly.* Sydney: Futurian Press, 1951.

————. *Let There Be Monsters.* Sydney: Futurian Press, 1952.

————. *Monster at Large.* Sydney: Currawong, 1950.

Moore-Bentley, Mary Ann (Mrs H. H. Ling). *A Woman of Mars; or, Australia's Enfranchised Woman.* Sydney: Edwards, Dunlop and Co., 1901.

Murphy, G. Read. *Beyond the Ice: Being a Story of the Newly Discovered Region Round the North Pole.* London: Sampson Low, Marston and Co., [1894].

Pengreep, William (W. T. Pearson). *The Temple of Sähr.* Melbourne: Lothian, 1932.

Potter, Robert. *The Germ Growers*. Melbourne: Melville, Mullens, 1892.

Pullar, A. J. *Celestalia: A Fantasy A.D. 1975*. Sydney: Canberra Press, 1933.

Rata (Thomas Roydhouse). *The Coloured Conquest*. Sydney: NSW Bookstall Co., 1904.

Rome, David (David Boutland). *Squat*. Sydney: Horwitz, 1965.

Rosa, S. A. *The Coming Terror: A Romance of the Twentieth Century*. Sydney: The Author, 1894.

Rowe, John. *The Warlords*. Sydney: Angus and Robertson, 1978.

Scott, G. Firth. *The Last Lemurian: A Westralian Romance*. London: James Bowden, 1898.

Shute, Nevil. *In the Wet*. London: Heinemann, 1953.

——.*On the Beach*. London: Heinemann, 1957.

Simpson, Helen. *The Woman on the Beast*. London: Heinemann, 1933.

Southall, Ivan. *Meet Simon Black*. Sydney: Angus & Robertson, 1950.

——.*Simon Black and the Spacemen*. Sydney: Angus & Robertson, 1955; reissued as *Simon Black on Venus*, Sydney: Angus & Robertson, 1974.

——.*Simon Black at Sea*. Sydney: Angus & Robertson, 1961.

——.*Simon Black in Peril*. Sydney: Angus & Robertson, 1951.

——.*Simon Black in Space*. Sydney: Angus & Robertson, 1952.

——.*Simon Black Takes Over*. Sydney: Angus & Robertson, 1959.

Spaull, George. *Where the Stars are Born*. Sydney: William Brooks and Co., 1942.

Spotswood, Christopher. *The Voyage of Will Rogers to the South Pole*. Launceston: Examiner's Office, 1888.

Stivens, Dal. *The Scholarly Mouse and Other Stories*. Sydney: Angus & Robertson, 1957.

——.*The Unicorn and Other Tales*. Sydney: Wild and Woolley, 1976.

Stone, Graham, and Williams, Royce. *Zero Equals Nothing*. Sydney: Futurian Press, 1951.

Turner, George. *Beloved Son*. London: Faber and Faber, 1978.

——.*Vaneglory*. London: Faber and Faber, 1981.

Vogel, Sir Julius, KCMG. *Anno Domini 2000; or, Woman's Destiny*. London: Hutchinson, 1889.

Walsh, James Morgan (as "H. Haverstock Hill"). *The Secret of the Crater*. London: Hurst, 1930.

————. *Vandals of the Void*. London: John Hamilton, 1931. Rptd Westport, Connecticut: Hyperion, 1976.

Whiteford, Wynne. *Breathing Space Only*. Melbourne: Void Publications, 1980.

Wilder, Cherry. *The Luck of Brin's Five*. Sydney: Angus & Robertson, 1979.

Wilding, Michael. *The West Midland Underground*. St Lucia: University of Queensland Press, 1975.

Wodhams, Jack. *Looking for Blücher*. Melbourne: Void Publications, 1980.

ANTHOLOGIES

Baxter, John, ed. *The First Pacific Book of Australian Science Fiction*. Sydney: Angus & Robertson, 1968.

————. *The Second Pacific Book of Australian Science Fiction*. Sydney: Angus & Robertson, 1971.

Broderick, Damien, ed. *The Zeitgeist Machine*. Sydney: Angus & Robertson, 1977.

Collins, Paul, ed. *Alien Worlds*. Melbourne: Void Publications, 1979.

————. *Envisaged Worlds*. Melbourne: Void Publications, 1978.

————. *Other Worlds*. Melbourne: Void Publications, 1978.

————. *Distant Worlds*. Melbourne: Void Publications, 1981.

Gerrand, Rob, ed. *Transmutations*. Melbourne: Outback Press in association with Norstrilia Press, 1979.

Harding, Lee, ed. *Beyond Tomorrow*. Melbourne: Wren, 1976.

————. *Rooms of Paradise*. Melbourne: Quartet Australia, 1978.

————. *The Altered I*. Melbourne: Norstrilia Press, 1976.

Turner, George, ed. *The View from the Edge*. Melbourne: Norstrilia Press, 1977.

BIBLIOGRAPHICAL SOURCES

Bleiler, Everett F. *The Checklist of Fantastic Literature*. Chicago: Shasta, 1948.

Clarke, I. F. *Tale of the Future*. London: Library Association, 1978.

Larnach, S. L. *Material Towards a Checklist of Australian Fantasy to 1938*. Sydney: Futurian Press, 1950.

Stone, Graham. *Australian Science Fiction Index 1925-1967*. Canberra: Australian Science Fiction Association, 1968.

CURRENT CRITICAL MAGAZINES

Science Fiction: A Review of Speculative Literature. Ed. V. Ikin. Department of English, University of Western Australia, Nedlands, W.A. 6009.

SF Commentary. Ed. B. Gillespie. GPO Box 5195AA, Melbourne, Vic. 3001.

The Cygnus Chronicler. Ed. N. J. Angove. PO Box 770, Canberra City, ACT 2601.